continued . . .

D0068628

"Fans will learn new and interesting tidbits about familiar characters and meet some fascinating new ones, making this addition to Bartlett's vampire series an entertaining read."

—*RT Book Reviews*

Real Vampires Hate Their Thighs

"Laugh-out-loud fun . . . The story that sets up several interesting prospects for future Glory adventures. *Real Vampires Hate Their Thighs* has a reserved spot on my keeper shelf!"

—*Fresh Fiction*

"The chemistry between Glory and Jerry is explosive. But when you add in the secondary characters, the result is nonstop laughter! Gerry Bartlett brings Glory to life and deals with the problems we all face."   —*The Romance Readers Connection*

Real Vampires Don't Diet

"An engaging urban fantasy filled with action and amusing chick-lit asides. Glory is terrific."   —*Midwest Book Review*

"Another must-have. In her trademark witty voice, Gerry Bartlett adds another chapter to her highly entertaining series . . . *Real Vampires Don't Diet* is honestly a tasty treat that's sure to please even the most discerning palates."

—*Romance Reviews Today*

Real Vampires Get Lucky

"Gerry Bartlett delivers another winner . . . Ms. Bartlett's gift for humor, the bawdier the better, is evident throughout . . . Fans rejoice—this one's a keeper!"   —*Fresh Fiction*

"Fun, fast-moving and introduces some wonderful new characters, along with having plenty of familiar faces."

—*RT Book Reviews*

Real Vampires Live Large

"Fans of lighthearted paranormal romps will enjoy Gerry Bartlett's fun tale starring a heroine who has never forgiven Blade for biting her when she was bloated."

—*Midwest Book Review*

"Glory gives girl power a whole new meaning, especially in the undead way. What a fun read!" —*All About Romance*

Real Vampires Have Curves

"A sharp, sassy, sexy read. Gerry Bartlett creates a vampire to die for in this sizzling new series."

—Kimberly Raye, *USA Today* bestselling author of *The Braddock Boys: Colton*

"Hot and hilarious. Glory is Everywoman with fangs."

—Nina Bangs, *USA Today* bestselling author of *Wicked Edge*

"Full-figured vampire Glory bursts from the page in this lively, fun and engaging spin on the vampire mythology."

—Julie Kenner, *USA Today* bestselling author of *Turned*

"Fans of paranormal chick lit will want to take a bite out of Gerry Bartlett's amusing tale. Glory is terrific."

—*The Best Reviews*

"A sexy, smart and lively contemporary paranormal romance . . . The plot is engaging, the characters are stimulating (not to mention, so is the sex) and the writing is sharp. Glory St. Clair is . . . a breath of fresh air." —*Romance Reader at Heart*

"If you love Betsy from MaryJanice Davidson's Undead series or Sookie from Charlaine Harris's [Sookie Stackhouse novels], you're gonna love *Real Vampires Have Curves*."

—*A Romance Review*

Real Vampires Know Hips Happen

GERRY BARTLETT

BERKLEY BOOKS, NEW YORK

THE BERKLEY PUBLISHING GROUP
Published by the Penguin Group
Penguin Group (USA) Inc.
375 Hudson Street, New York, New York 10014, USA

USA / Canada / UK / Ireland / Australia / New Zealand / India / South Africa / China

Penguin Books Ltd., Registered Offices: 80 Strand, London WC2R 0RL, England
For more information about the Penguin Group, visit penguin.com.

This book is an original publication of The Berkley Publishing Group.

REAL VAMPIRES KNOW HIPS HAPPEN

BERKLEY® is a registered trademark of Penguin Group (USA) Inc.
The "B" design is a trademark of Penguin Group (USA) Inc.

Berkley trade paperback ISBN: 978-0-425-25821-7

An application to register this book for cataloging has been submitted to the Library of Congress.

PUBLISHING HISTORY
Berkley trade paperback edition / March 2013

PRINTED IN THE UNITED STATES OF AMERICA

10 9 8 7 6 5 4 3 2 1

Cover art by Chris Long / CWC International.
Cover design by George Long.
Interior text design by Kristin del Rosario.

ALWAYS LEARNING

PEARSON

To Danielle Garrett, my superfan.
I don't know what I did to deserve your loyalty,
but thank you.

Acknowledgments

Keeping the Real Vampires series alive is a team effort. First I have to thank *my* team, my street team, which does such a great job of grabbing strangers in bookstores and libraries and telling them about the series. Then there's the enthusiastic bunch on the Real Vampires Fan Group, headed by Danielle Garrett, who's ably assisted by Gemma Stirnichuk. This is where I turn for help with details for my stories, even title ideas. You guys rock!

As always, I want to thank the Berkley team. Senior editor Kate Seaver keeps saying, "Yes," and Glory St. Clair lives on. My excellent copy editor finds my mistakes (Where is Edinburgh anyway?), and the art department gives me a pretty package. I know how lucky I am.

I'm also lucky to have wonderful agent Kimberly Whalen, who has had faith in me from the beginning and keeps me employed.

Last but not least there are my intrepid critique partners, Nina Bangs and Donna Maloy. They go through every book's growing pains with me. If you like the finished product, thank them. If you don't? Blame them. Kidding. Sort of. Really. Hmm. Maybe it's time to wrap this up. Writing is supposed to be a lonely business, but I've never found that to be true. I can call on these two gals and brainstorm whenever I hit a wall. They help push me over it. And they listen to me whine. What more could I ask for? Thanks, ladies.

One

I couldn't get out of the car. Ridiculous. I was a badass vampire. I knew this place, had been here a hundred times or more. Sure, not all of them had been good times but at least I'd had Jerry by my side. Now Castle Campbell in all its ruined beauty was just yards away and I felt the determination that had carried me across an ocean and several countries drain right out of me.

I had to smile though when I noticed the laird had let the National Trust open the place to tourists at five pounds a pop. Not that the family of vampires cared what happened during the day in the stone fortress above their heads. The family would sleep like the dead in the luxurious quarters they'd built centuries ago belowground. It was dark now and the tourists were long gone, the tea and gift shop in the tower closed.

"Get out of the freaking car." I hit the plastic steering wheel. Talking to myself. Trying to screw up my courage. Because I wasn't supposed to be here. Jerry had asked for time. To think about our relationship. And had I given it to him? Of course not. Glory St. Clair worked on her own timetable. And right now I needed, desperately, to see my man and explain some things. But actually sitting here, staring at the castle where his mother had treated me like a whore her son had dragged home centuries ago, had brought me crashing back to reality.

Maybe Jerry would be better off without me. I was a freak. Not who or what he'd thought he'd fallen for all those years ago. He deserved better. For once, his mother and I agreed. I sagged against the car window. What had I been *thinking*?

A knock on the glass next to me made me jump. My vamp instincts sucked if I could be surprised like that. I rolled down the window. El cheapo rental car didn't even have power windows.

"Aren't you coming in?" Jeremy Blade, Jeremiah Campbell III, my sire, whatever you wanted to call him, smiled at me.

"Do you want me to?"

His answer was to jerk open the door and haul me into his arms. "How can you ask that? Do you have any idea how much I've missed you?" He buried his face in my neck and just inhaled. In vamp terms that was the equivalent of the "Hallelujah" chorus.

"I was supposed to give you some thinking time." I murmured this against the soft wool of his plaid, carelessly thrown over a cotton shirt. I inhaled him too, soaking in the dear, achingly familiar scent of male and Jerry that I craved with everything in me.

"I shouldn't have taken off like that. You needed me." He leaned back and looked into my eyes. "God, but I'm sorry." He kissed me then, making sure I knew just how much he cared. Tears pricked my eyelids but I wasn't about to let them fall and ruin this moment. My gamble had paid off. And things would only get better once Jerry knew the truth about how we'd met and fallen in love.

I smiled as he pulled back. "I have so much to tell you."

"No kidding. Like how you managed to cross the Atlantic." He glanced at my rental car and dismissed it as unworthy. "I would have sent a plane for you, Gloriana."

"The details about my trip can wait. I have big news for you, Jer." I held on to him, so glad to finally be with him because the trip had been harrowing and not the lighthearted adventure I'd paint for him when I got around to sharing. I'm always on a budget and the death sleep makes travel complicated. Enough said.

"Come inside, lass. Mara had just arrived when the servants spotted you on the security cameras. She claims to have big news too." Jerry tugged me toward the heavy wooden and iron door to the family quarters hidden behind clever landscaping.

"Mara." Not my favorite person. She'd always wanted Jerry for herself.

"You can be nice to her for five minutes. Then we can be alone." Jerry gave me such a brilliant smile, I had to stop him in the doorway and kiss him again.

"Are you sure we can't slip away into the pasture for a real reunion instead? I remember a time or two . . ."

My lover laughed. "Or twenty. Not yet. Da is inside and eager to greet you. He always did love you, you know. My mother is in Paris so you can relax on that score. And we'll make sure Mara is sent on her way quickly." Jerry slid one hand around my waist and the other up to investigate my plunging neckline. "Very quickly."

"See that you do." I sighed as he kissed me again, lingering over it as his hands explored me. I'd stopped in the village of Dollar down below the castle and booked a room so I could freshen up before I'd come here. I wore a low-cut sweater in his favorite blue with a skirt that showed off my legs and distracted from my hips. I pulled back and glanced around. "Where are these security cameras? Are we giving some worker a thrill?"

Jerry nodded toward a dark corner of the doorway. "Afraid so. Da's outfitted the entire area with cameras, sensors. He's big on security and you know how the clan is about the feud with the MacDonalds."

"Don't start." I held up my hand. "Let's get this deal with Mara over with. Then we can be alone."

"I'm with you there." He pulled me into the large living area where his father sat talking with Mara, the widow of Jerry's best friend.

"Well, now, it *was* Gloriana. Welcome to the castle, lass. Mara, look who's here." The laird, Angus Jeremiah Campbell II, got up to hug me then led me to the couch to face Mara. We exchanged wintery smiles. As usual, she was dressed expensively to show off her slim figure. She had the dark red hair, pale skin and altogether perfect looks of a true Scottish lass. I was the epitome of blond, blue-eyed Englishwoman. Or I'd always thought of myself that way. It had marked me an outsider when I'd first arrived, on Jerry's arm.

After Jerry and I squeezed together on the love seat, Angus asked me questions about my trip and I answered in a general way. Apparently Jerry hadn't told his father about the problems between us that had sent him home this time. I sure wasn't going to bring them up now, and the warm reassurance of Jerry's hand on mine helped me know I didn't need to be in a hurry to do so.

"Well, Mara. Jerry says you have big news." I was eager to move things along.

"I do." She smiled shyly and glanced at Jerry then held out her left hand. The huge diamond on her ring finger should have given us all a clue. "I'm getting married."

"Wow. Just wow. Who's the lucky guy?" I leaned back, happy when Jerry stayed seated next to me, his hard thigh snug against mine.

"Davy McLeod. You know him, Jeremiah. He says you two used to race horses together at Newmarket." Mara stared down at her ring and actually looked happy.

"Sure. Davy's a good man." Jerry played with my fingers. I had a feeling he was thinking that I'd never accepted a ring from him. But then we now had a clue why not, didn't we?

"A fine clan, the McLeods. Allies in times of war. Not like those backstabbing MacDonalds." The laird got up and kissed Mara's cheek. "Well done, lass. Well done. I wish you happy."

"And you, Jeremiah. Do you wish me happy?" Mara stood and the gentleman in him got Jerry to his feet instantly.

"Of course. If you want this and love the man, have at it." Jerry put his hands on her shoulders. "But if you need money or feel pressured for any other reason . . . Well, you are my daughter's mother. I will always make sure you are cared for."

"How thoughtful." Mara stared up at him and for a moment I saw the bitter twist to her mouth that told the true story. She'd always wanted Jerry for herself. But she realized now that she couldn't make him love her and had apparently decided to cut her losses. This McLeod obviously had the bucks and was a decent guy if the laird approved of him. Knowing Mara, she'd already run him through his paces in the sack as well. I kept my mouth shut. I knew anything I had to say would be unwelcome at this point.

"You know you and I . . ." Jerry glanced back at me then shook his head. He leaned down to kiss Mara's cheek. "Be happy."

"Of course. Will you walk me to the door? Help me with my cloak?" She smiled and smoothed her designer skirt.

"Certainly." Jerry proffered his arm in the courtly manner of centuries past.

I couldn't sit still. Something about this whole show seemed off to me. Mara was being docile, almost robotic. Where was the fiery woman who would have at least made a cutting remark to me? Instead she'd treated me like I was invisible. Which was an improvement but so not like her. She should have been gloating, bragging about the rich, handsome husband she'd captured. Even waved that rock under my nose. I was steps behind the pair as they reached the door to the outside.

"I shifted here and will shift away again. I'll be all right. Davy's waiting for me in the village." Mara let Jerry help her with her long cloak. The Kilpatrick plaid, of course. Once she married, she'd start wearing the McLeod colors. Everyone in this country wore their plaids like a badge. Jerry had on his kilt and looked a treat. Even the laird was lounging in his plaid in front of his big-screen TV which he'd just turned on. *CSI* was starting. The man loved blood any way he could find it.

"Be careful." Jerry settled Mara's long cape over her shoulders and fastened it at her neck.

"Always." Suddenly a knife appeared in her hand. "Too late for you." She plunged it into his chest.

"Jerry, my God! Angus! Help!" I lunged toward her as Mara lifted the knife again. Jerry grabbed her arm but she'd obviously wounded him seriously with the first blow. He slumped, dragging her down to the floor with him where he seemed down for the count.

I jumped on Mara and wrestled the knife out of her hands, tossing it away with a clatter. Then I pulled her off of him and shoved her hard, knocking her head against the stone floor. She struggled like a madwoman, scratching and hitting at me.

"Stop it! What the hell are you doing?" I slapped her face and her eyes widened, like she was coming out of a daze.

"What? Get off of me!" She twisted her hands, trying to get free. Then she turned her head and saw Jerry lying in a pool of his own blood. "Jeremiah? Who did this to you? Gloriana! Did you hurt him?"

"No, you stupid bitch. *You* stabbed him. How can you deny it?" I climbed off of her and thrust her into Angus's arms then dropped to my knees next to Jerry. "Jerry, can you hear me?"

When he didn't answer, I got frantic, searching him for other injuries. There was only the one knife wound though, and, for a vampire, it was relatively minor. It had already stopped bleeding. I pressed my hand to his heart and felt the slow steady thump. Of course he was alive, but why wasn't he stirring? My own heart lodged in my throat as the hall filled with men and noise.

"What happened here?" Angus held on to Mara. "Lass, what's this about?"

She sobbed and leaned against him. "I don't know. I don't know. There was a knife. I only remember the knife. Someone gave me a knife. Outside the gates."

"Witchcraft. You were spelled." Angus gestured at the men who'd gathered when he'd sounded the alarm. Obviously the security cameras had caught the whole attack. A few shouted questions and hard looks at Mara confirmed my story. "Outside, search the grounds. Who gave you the knife? What did this person look like?"

"I don't know." Mara shook her head. "A woman. Old, I think, not sure. Face covered. Stayed in the shadows. I, I couldn't help myself." She collapsed on the floor next to Jerry. "What have I done?"

"Well, you haven't killed him. Lucky for you or I'd use that knife to rip your heart out of your skinny body." I cradled Jerry's head in my lap. "Come on, Jerry, please wake up." Why had he lost consciousness?

Yes, he'd bled a lot and would need to feed, but I'd be more than happy to take care of that. Jerry was strong and healthy. This kind of stab wound shouldn't even have dropped him. I heard Mara blubbering and wanted to slap her silent. Witchcraft? Not sure I was buying it, but something was off about this whole attack.

"Careful with that knife. It may have poison on it." That was the only explanation I could come up with for Jerry's condition. The servant who'd been about to pick up the weapon jumped away from it.

"Poison." Angus dragged Mara to her feet. "Are you sure you don't remember who gave it to you?" He shook her, not too gently either. "Speak up, girl. You just stabbed my son. No lies now. Why did you try to kill Jeremiah?"

"I don't know, Laird. I feel like . . ." She rubbed her forehead. "I need Davy. Can you call him for me? I only remember a woman, all in black. Outside the castle. She gave me the knife and told me what to do. I didn't want to do it. But I couldn't seem to help myself. Like you said. I was bewitched, under a spell." She stared up at Angus with her bright green eyes, almost feverish now. "He's not going to die, is he?"

"He'd better not." I couldn't look at her as I ran my hand over Jerry's strong jaw and the slight roughness of his beard, there no matter how often he shaved. To my relief he moaned and his eyes fluttered open. He stared up at me for a moment then glanced around the hallway before focusing on me again.

"Jerry, are you all right? How do you feel?" I leaned closer, willing him to say something.

"Like I took a knife in my gut. But if you're offering to feed me back to health, lass, then I reckon I'll be up and about in no time." He grinned and slid a hand to the back of my head to draw my neck down to his mouth where his fangs descended.

"Here? On this cold stone floor? Let's get you cleaned up and moved to your bed." I tried to pry his fingers off of me but he wasn't ready to let go. "Come on, Jer. This is ridiculous. I'll feed you. But not here." I glanced at his father and Mara, who both watched us.

"Tell her, Da. The lass seems reluctant. But you paid her well, didn't you? I need to feed. Let's get on with it so I can go after the bastard who stuck me. Did you see who did it?" Jerry jerked me close again.

"Wait!" I put my hands on his chest and shoved. "Look at me." I bit my lip, terribly afraid that I knew what was wrong. "Jeremiah Campbell, just who do you think I am?"

"Your name? No notion. But you're comely enough and your blood smells like fine wine, damned if it doesn't." He sniffed the air but his smile faltered when he pressed a hand to his chest. "Bloody hell but that hurts. Let's get on with it. Quit playing coy and do your duty." He struggled as he tried to sit up, then looked at his father. "Da, was it a Mac-Donald? Tell William to saddle Thunder and we'll ride out as soon as I've healed. We'll teach them to attack us inside our own home."

"Easy, lad. We'll get whoever is responsible. Lass, let him drink." Angus nodded at me.

I took a breath to keep from crying. God, please, please say I had it wrong. A comely lass bought and paid for? Jerry pulled me close until his fangs pierced my neck. He drew deep and I closed my eyes, slipping my hands up to cling to his silky hair. I sat on the cold stone floor in his father's castle, the man drinking my blood holding me as if we were strangers. Jerry, my sire, the love of my life, didn't know me. What was I going to do?

Two

I felt his scalp but couldn't find any lumps that would explain away his memory loss. Obviously Jerry hadn't bumped his head when he fell or, if he had, he'd already healed. He eased away from my jugular and licked the punctures.

"Delicious. Wait for me and I'll be happy to enjoy a bit of sport with you later, lass. But right now I've got MacDonalds to hunt." He grinned and winked, then bodily lifted me off, patting my butt as he did so.

It didn't take mind reading to see that he thought of me as nothing more than a stranger, bought and paid for to please him any way he wanted. I jumped to my feet and glanced at his father.

"Jeremiah, there's to be no riding out for you, Son. Not tonight. I've got plenty of men looking for whoever sent Mara in here with that tainted knife." The laird gave Jerry a hand up until the men stood toe-to-toe. Jerry wasn't happy with his father's order.

"But, Da, I'm fine now, fit as can be. The lass's blood healed my wound and I'm ready to ride. Bring the horses

around and we'll be off." Jerry grabbed his father's arm. "I
heard enough to understand that it's the witch the MacDonalds hired to curse us who must be behind this."

I'd heard enough myself. "Mara, what exactly do you remember? Was the name MacDonald ever mentioned?" I was
heartily sick of her. She'd fallen sniveling in a heap to the
stone floor and I jerked her to her feet. "Pull yourself together. Obviously no one here is holding you accountable.
Though why, I can't imagine." I gave Jerry and his father a
sharp look.

"Mara is a family friend. Has been for years. Why should
we doubt her word? And who are you to lay hands on her?
Or stick your nose into our business?" Jerry pushed between
Mara and me. "I don't even know your name. Speak, woman.
How do we know it's not your work, this tainted knife and
witch outside our gates?"

I opened and shut my mouth, for once speechless. Any
hope I had that I'd misread him vanished. He really didn't
know me. Oh, God, no. I wanted to kiss him until he felt
our connection. Press my body against his and show him
how we fit. But he looked at me without a single glimmer
of recognition and my bravado leaked out until I wanted to
sink to the floor and soak his kilt with my tears. Who had
done this and why?

"Son, this woman isn't a stranger to me. And definitely
not to you. The knife was poisoned. It's messed with your
mind." The laird dropped a heavy hand on Jerry's shoulder
and I saw him squeeze hard. "You aren't remembering things
aright. What year do you think this is?"

"Year? What kind of a question is that, Da?" Jerry faced
his father. "It's the year of our Lord, fifteen hundred and
ninety-six, of course."

"No, my boy. It isn't." Angus staggered, suddenly looking
older than the thirty or so he'd been when he'd been turned
vampire. "Jeremiah, lad, we've had centuries pass since those
days. You met this woman in London a few years after that

year and made her vampire. You don't remember?" Angus eased Jerry back into the living room. "Sit. Rest. I can see this is puzzling you."

"Puzzling me?" Jerry jerked away from his father's grasp. "Stop it! What kind of sick game is this? Centuries? No, I don't believe you." He did collapse onto the love seat though and run his hand through his hair, a familiar gesture that brought a lump to my throat. I must have made a sound of distress because he stared at me.

"And you claim I made this woman? Turned her? I don't create other vampires. You know that, Da. Unless she was in danger of losing her life." He glared when I sat beside him again. Like we'd sat, oh, it seemed like days but had actually been less than half an hour ago. "Are you taking her word for this?"

"Angus met me long ago, Jerry. When you brought me here, to the castle. To meet your family." I suddenly couldn't breathe and had to stop to collect myself. His face blurred but I wasn't going to cry, not until I finished this. "You made me vampire for love. We, we were in love, Jeremiah. You've loved me for more than four hundred years." I brushed away the tears that had finally fallen despite my best intentions. Damn. I hated the suspicious look he still gave me.

"Impossible. I can't imagine clinging to one woman for so long." He looked down to where my skirt had ridden up to expose my knees. "Though when you dress like a doxy, I can see the advantages in forming an alliance with one such as you." Suspicion was replaced by something I wanted to slap off his face. "A hot couple, were we?" He slid a hand up my leg.

I hissed and grabbed his wrist, ready to add to his injuries. I didn't care if he was stuck in the sixteenth century, I was not going to be treated like a cheap whore. We were going to get this straight right now.

"Gloriana, calm down. Give the lad some time to get his head straight. Perhaps you should fetch him a fresh shirt.

You know where his bedroom is." The laird settled into his chair and picked up a cordless phone.

"I'm not leaving this room. Get a servant to fetch it." I glared at Jerry when he stood to strip off his bloody shirt.

"So we share a bed." He grinned. "And in my father's house." He dropped the shirt on the floor. I could see his wound now, a jagged cut that was already a bright pink and healing. But it was his chest and strong shoulders that made me lick my lips. We'd been apart so long. Months. I itched to touch him, my anger vanishing as I remembered he'd been poisoned. This was witchcraft at its worst.

"Keep looking at me like that and we'll both go get that shirt and take a fine long time doing it." Jerry moved closer and pulled me up. He stared down into my eyes, searching, as if hoping he'd find something there he recognized. Then he shook his head. "Damn, but I can't recall . . ."

"Never mind, Jeremiah. Here's Bertie with your shirt. Get dressed and rest. I want to get to the bottom of this attack." His father nodded to one of his men who'd escorted a dazed Mara into the room.

Jerry drew on the shirt and sat again, rubbing his forehead. I resisted the urge to sit beside him this time and walked around to hold on to the back of the love seat. The attack. Yes, we needed answers.

"Mara, call your fiancé and get him over here. Let's see if he knows anything about this." Angus held out the phone.

"He wouldn't, he's not involved—" She took the phone with shaking hands. "But I do want him here. He can take me home."

"When we're satisfied your story is true." Angus frowned as he studied his son. "Witches, poisoned knives. Now Jeremiah's brain is amuddle. There's much to explain and I don't like your riddle, miss."

"It's not . . ." She flushed, then punched in a number. "Davy, can you come to Castle Campbell? I, I had a spot of trouble here and I need you." Her voice broke and she handed the phone back to Angus.

"Yes, McLeod, she's upset." Angus listened for a minute. "Just come here and we'll let her tell you all about it. See you in a bit."

"Davy McLeod? I thought you married MacTavish, Mara. Where is he? And what the devil were you talking into?" Jerry leaned forward, totally focused on Mara. Even the apparent novelty of the telephone had held his fascinated gaze longer than I had.

"I did marry Mac. But, Jeremiah, that was centuries ago. He's, um, gone." Mara looked away, refusing to meet Jerry's intense stare. "Some things are best forgotten."

"Gone? What the hell does that mean?" Jerry jumped to his feet. "I'll not forget my best friend."

"Mac was killed by a vampire hunter, Jerry. It was horrible. We all mourned him." I laid my hand on his back but he shrugged it away. "His death did force Mara to finally admit that her child Lily is yours, not sired by MacTavish."

"What's this?" Jerry rubbed his forehead. "What is the lass raving about, Mara? Lily? I remember you had a child before you were turned. But—"

"Can we get into this later? Obviously you've been poisoned and it's affected your reason." Mara's eyes were wide and she had her hands clasped in front of her. She looked appropriately pitiful and Jerry was usually putty in her hands. I waited for him to fold.

"My reason is fine. Spit it out, woman. If I have a child, I'll know it now or I'll shake the truth out of you." Jerry moved before either Angus or I could react. He jerked Mara to her feet. "Do I have a child? Did you keep her from me?"

"Yes! I passed her off as Mac's as long as he was alive. He doted on her. He was a good father." Mara's hair flew around her head when Jerry gave her a good shake. I couldn't believe he was acting out his anger. The Jerry I knew never would have laid a hand on her.

"You don't think I would have made a good father?" His teeth were gritted, his fangs down. I swear he was ready to rip her throat open.

"No, I don't! Or at least not back then. You didn't love me. You tumbled me in your father's hayloft and then went on your merry way to take advantage of the next besotted girl. I was nothing to you. Why should I give you a child after that? Mac adored me. He would do whatever I wanted, give me the world. You hied off to London soon after you got your fangs and then brought home this twopenny whore, embarrassing your parents and—" Mara gasped when he threw her back into her chair.

"I have never wasted my blunt on whores, woman. And I don't tolerate liars. I'm beginning to think this knife attack may have been your idea. That there was no witch. Where did you get the poison that jumbled my mind and where can we find the cure?" Jerry glared down at her.

"Step away from her, Campbell." A man that I assumed was Davy McLeod strode into the room and grabbed Jerry by the shoulders. He practically threw him at me and I was happy to catch him. Jerry was out of my arms in a blink, though, obviously eager for a fight.

"Careful, McLeod. I'm in a temper and beating you to a bloody pulp would go a long way toward satisfying my urge for action," Jerry snarled, his fists up and a wicked gleam in his eyes.

"What the hell's going on here? Mara, love?" Davy ignored the taunt and scooped Mara up to hold her in his arms.

"It was awful, Davy. I, I attacked Jeremiah. But it wasn't my fault. I was under a witch's spell. You've got to believe me." She looked up at him with tears running down her cheeks. Damn, how could she look so beautiful while crying?

"Of course I believe you. Why would you need to lie about something like that?" Davy gave Jerry a hard look. "Touch her again, Campbell, and I'll end you."

"You could try." Jerry was obviously still eager for a fight.

"That's enough. I hear my men returning. Let's see what they found outside." Angus stepped between them and we all turned toward the door. Several burly men in Campbell plaid crowded into the room. They brought with them the smell of damp wool and cold air.

"No sign of a witch or a MacDonald, Laird. I've sent some men into the village to search further," the obvious head of the group reported. He nodded at Jerry. "Glad to see you on your feet, Jeremiah."

"Aye, I'm on my feet, but seems I've lost my mind, Fergus. What year is it?" Jerry turned his back on Mara and her fiancé.

"Twenty thirteen. Did the lass's blood not cure you?" Fergus nodded to me. "Welcome, Gloriana. It's been too long."

"Fergus. I hope Maeve is well." I recognized Jerry's cousin and remembered his wife as a friend here. Another Campbell. Would this friendly greeting help my lover realize I did have a place in his life?

"She's tip-top. Started a business online. I'll have to give you her card. Makes some mighty fine jewelry. Celtic. You'd like it, I think. Maybe could sell a bit in your shop." He turned when Jerry punched his shoulder. "What?" He rubbed the spot. "I'm sorry I didn't find the witch but that's a bit harsh, don't you think?"

"Stop yer blatherin'. Twenty thirteen? You mean two thousand and thirteen, man? The year is two thousand and thirteen?" Jerry swayed and the laird and Fergus both jumped to catch him. He threw off their hands and pulled himself together with a shake of his head.

"Lad, sit. Gloriana, give him your wrist again. He's light-headed. Or maybe I should call for some synthetic." Angus shoved everyone aside until he had Jerry in his leather recliner, then forcibly pushed the seat back. "Now, listen to me, boy. You were stuck with a potion that's given you amnesia of a sort. Take it easy. Let us care for you."

"Da, I can't believe I've lost over four hundred years of my life." Jerry gazed up at his father. "Nothing looks right except you, Fergus and those two." He gestured toward where

Mara was trying to tug Davy out of the room. "Stay. I want to hear about my daughter. You owe me that, I think."

She cleared her throat. "Yes, I suppose I do. She's beautiful, Jeremiah. But willful. As long as Mac was alive, I didn't worry too much about her because she ever wanted him proud of her. But she's led a dangerous lifestyle since then, kept bad company. You were helping control her in Austin. She'd moved in with you."

"Austin?" Jerry closed his eyes and rubbed his temples. "Where the hell is that?"

"It's where we live, Jer. In Texas." I realized he had lost the years that even included the formation of the States. "Um, in the New World."

"What the hell was I doing in that wilderness?" He opened his eyes and stared at me. "We lived together there? Were we married?"

"No. We didn't even live in the same house. The New World's not a wilderness now. It's a prosperous country and we lived in a large city there." I moved close to him. If he wanted to drink my blood again, I was all for it.

"So we never married. Yet you claim we were together for four hundred years?" He ignored my outstretched hand. "You were my mistress?"

"I suppose you could call me that." I frowned, not liking that term at all. "If you need blood, take mine again. Maybe it will help you remember things."

"It didn't before." He jumped and looked down at his sporran, the man purse he wore over his kilt. "What the hell? There's something in my pouch." He clapped a hand over it. "Did you stuff a beastie in there, Mara? Is this another trick?"

I grinned and flipped open the flap. I knew what was happening. "It's your cell phone, Jerry, set to vibrate." Sure enough, his cell was lit up. I punched a button and held it to my ear.

"Hello. This is Gloriana, for Jeremy Blade."

"I'm looking for Blade. This is Adams, his manager in Miami. We've got an emergency and I need a quick decision."

I glanced at Jerry. He was frowning at me and the phone at my ear, clearly a mystery to him. "Look, I'm sorry, Adams, but Blade has been in an accident. He's not in any shape to talk to you about business. You'll have to take care of things yourself. Can you handle it?"

"You sure he can't come to the phone? Talk to me for just a minute?" The man was clearly horrified.

"Positive. Make the right decision and I'm sure he'll reward you. What do you think?"

"If you're sure he's not available. Seriously, he's *always* available." Adams obviously doubted me but had no choice but to take my word.

"Not this time. He hires only the best, so make the decision yourself." I skipped out of reach when Jerry tried to take the phone then ended the call.

"What the hell are you talking into?" Jerry grabbed the phone out of my hands to study it.

"It's a cell phone." I wanted to cry as he turned it over in his hands, obviously at a loss to know how to even turn it on. I pulled mine out of my skirt pocket. "Here's mine. You gave me the cover for it."

"Now that's just ridiculous." He shook his head over the pink crystal case. "What does it do?" He put his black phone to his ear and frowned. "You were talking to someone. Who?"

I had to clear my throat to speak. "Your manager in Florida, that's another state in the New World. You have businesses all over the United States, that's what the New World is called now. You go by the name Jeremy Blade over there. I'm sure you can trust him to take care of things until you can handle them yourself again." I smiled when Jerry grumbled about black magic, shook the phone then put it to his ear again.

"Son, don't worry about business or these newfangled gadgets." Angus took the phone out of Jerry's hand. "Relax, drink some blood. Get your strength back and I'm sure your mind will come back along with it." He gave me a searching look. "Gloriana, perhaps you could give him some time with Mara. To ask about his daughter."

"Oh, sure." I realized Angus had a glass of synthetic in his hand which he gave Jerry. I was getting the bum's rush. "You want me to get a room in the village? Or I can sleep in my car again."

"Now, don't get your feathers ruffled, lass. Just give them a little time." Angus eased me to the door. "You have luggage? I'll have a lad bring it in. You are welcome to stay here as long as you wish. You can even sleep with Jeremiah if he'll let you. Give Fergus your car keys."

"It's a rental. I'd like to return it if I'm staying awhile. To Edinburgh. But I guess . . ." I didn't know how to proceed. Jerry didn't know me. Angus was sending mixed signals. He was offering hospitality but the attempt on Jerry's life had arrived with me. I could read that suspicion in his mind. "Well, we'll play this by ear. Give me my own room. Right now, I'd like to look around the grounds myself." I glanced back. As long as Davy McLeod was riding herd on Mara, there was no danger she was going to make a play for Jerry, not if she wanted to keep that rock on her finger.

Davy was a handsome man, tall and blond with a keen intelligence in his bright blue eyes that dared anyone to do his fiancée wrong. I had liked him on sight. Mara didn't deserve him and he sure didn't deserve a woman like her, but men could be fools when in love. I glanced back at Jerry, my heart turning over. So could women.

"Fine. Do that. Will you be wanting one of the lads to accompany you? For your safety?" The laird really was concerned about me. I could see that. And he'd obviously seen how worried I was about Jerry.

"No, I'll be fine." He didn't know that I had developed some superpowers lately. Not that I'd tested them against a witch. It wasn't something I wanted to try either. If the men hadn't found her, I probably wouldn't either. I just needed fresh air and time to think not surrounded by people who considered me an outsider. Plus seeing Jerry so confused was breaking my heart. I'd like a chance to shed the tears in private that were clogging my throat.

"If you're not back in an hour, I'm sending a search party." Angus kissed my cheek. "I'm glad you're here. I'm worried about the boy. He does love you and has been moping about. He wouldn't tell me what was wrong, but I gleaned enough to know it was trouble between you two. Your coming here was just what he needed. He does have his pride, all the Campbells do."

"Just one of the reasons why I love him. And you." I hugged him then followed Fergus to the car. I pointed out which bags to bring inside then walked along one of the rough paths toward a stream that ran down a hillside. Fog had rolled in and it was getting harder to see, but I just wanted some space away from Angus's security cameras. I sniffed the air, trying to pick up some hint of whether another paranormal creature had been here recently. I got plaid and vampire but nothing else.

I was on a wooden bridge that crossed the shallow stream when I suddenly realized I wasn't alone.

"Who's there?" I clutched the handrail.

"The person you were looking for, Gloriana." The voice was husky and definitely feminine.

"The witch?" I could make out a dark, cloaked figure walking toward me at the edge of the path. Her footsteps made hollow sounds when she stepped onto the wooden bridge. "The one who gave Mara MacTavish the poisoned knife?"

"Poison? I guess you could call it that. The knife was dipped in something more powerful than a mere poison. I'm not a witch. Those creatures are so beneath me. Literally." Her laughter was a trill that contrasted sharply with her hoarse speech. "You should be thanking me, Gloriana. Now you have a chance to start over. A new beginning. No messy man baggage."

She knew my name. So this was personal. Had Lucifer sent someone new to torment me? We'd had some serious issues recently. "Jeremiah Campbell is not baggage. He, he is the love of my life." I cleared my throat. "Why do you care what happens to me? Who sent you? If you've come from hell, then you can crawl right back down where you came from. I'm still not interested in anything your boss has to offer."

"Hell? You insult me. I have no truck with demons." A wisp of power pushed me against the railing as she threw back her cloak. I still couldn't make out her face, though. "As to why I'm here . . . ? Well, I'll get to that in a minute. And calling Campbell 'the love of your life'?" The trill of laughter again. "How melodramatic, Gloriana. I swear you should have stayed on the stage."

"Listen, you bitch! I don't know who you are, but this isn't funny." I tried to strike out at her but couldn't move my arms. Power. She was loaded with it. "I have loved Jerry for hundreds of years. And he has loved me. Not that it's any of your business."

"What amazing devotion. From him. And foolish waste on your part. There are so many men. In the sea."

"Who are you? A Siren? One of the Siren sisters? How do you know so much about me?" I'd met the Sirens and found out I had been cast out of their ranks and made human just before I'd met Jerry in London all those years ago. If he hadn't turned me vampire, I'd have died a mortal's death back then.

"No. Nothing so simple." She threw back her cowl and moved closer. Now I could see her golden hair and eyes the color of the sea. "I am your mother, Gloriana."

"What?" I drew back, not a little scared by her. Her blue gaze was too intense, wild and terrifying. Her pale skin glowed with an unearthly light. And there were those pulses of power that reminded me of other beings I'd met recently and not fared well with.

"Unearthly. Yes, I am that. I'm reading your thoughts, of course. I am from Olympus." She smiled when I flinched.

"Oh, yes. It's a frightening thought, I know. We are very powerful there as you saw when you encountered the Storm God. That man is so crude. He told you that Sirens are a goddess's by-blows. Bastard children. Accidents. I cannot like his phrasing but he is right. That is indeed how it comes about. For some of them anyway."

"You are a goddess? And I'm one of your *mistakes?*" I put my hand to my stomach, sure I was going to be sick.

"Oh, my dear. What can I say? I get these urges, you see. To explore Earth's, shall we call them, bounties. Human men can be quite amusing." That laugh again. I wanted to shove stakes into my own ears to keep from hearing it again. "And they have something the toga-wearing gods upstairs lack. A certain, um, innocence. Thinking they can win my heart." Her smile was tinged with sadness.

I just stared at her. What could I say? If the woman had a heart, it was not apparent to me.

"Now you know why you enjoy men so, Gloriana. It is your legacy from me and has nothing to do with being a Siren once." She gave an elegant shrug. "Obviously you ended up there because one of my forays had unexpected consequences."

"Consequences." I sounded bitter but who could blame me? "Ever hear of condoms? The pill? Get a clue. What is your name anyway? I won't call you Mother."

"It's that or nothing. I won't share my name with you. It's for your own protection." Now *she* sounded bitter. "Zeus has no tolerance for bastard children in his realm. So those of us who make a mistake"—she smiled with a twist of her perfect mouth—"well, we either terminate it or play 'least in sight' until we give birth. Which I did when I carried you. I wanted just once to see what lying with a perfectly charming earthling wrought."

"Nice. So I was an experiment. And my father? Did you just pick some random guy who took your fancy, sleep with him, then abandon him? Or did you do the Siren thing and end him?" I couldn't believe I was having this conversation.

I'd had parents. Not the simple folks I'd imagined but a goddess from Olympus and some poor sap she'd used as a sperm donor. It made my brain hurt to imagine it.

"Really, Gloriana, you must quit judging me. I visited him in his dreams. He had many wonderful nights with me. He was left with fond memories. But, as a mortal, he's long gone." She smiled wistfully. "Of natural causes."

"Gee, how kind of you." My knees gave out and I sat down hard on the wooden bridge. To hell with my cute skirt. Jerry didn't know me anyway. "So you dumped me into the Siren system and left me there. Whoopee. Why are you here now and what did you do to Jerry?" I looked up, teary in spite of a vow to be strong around this bitch. "Fix this. Fix *him*."

"I'm here to help you discover your full potential." My mother, which was the only way I could refer to her, sank down gracefully across from me. She wore the Olympus uniform: white toga with some kind of gold and diamond pin on the shoulder. She had a perfect figure. I bet she hated mine.

"I was doing fine without you. You have no business meddling in my life, and certainly no right to fool with Jerry's. What's with the poison on the knife?"

"Gloriana, listen to me. I was captivated by your beauty the moment you were put in my arms. I couldn't just drop you back to Earth into some mortal family's care. So I gave you immortality the only way I could. Perhaps not the best life, but—"

"Not the best? Seducing men and then killing them for their treasure? It was horrible. I had no stomach for it. What kind of mother does that to her child?" I turned away to stare down at the water flowing over the stones below. This sickened me. That a woman could doom her child to that kind of existence . . . Her hand landed on my chin, light as air yet hot as a brand.

"A mother who can't bear to see her daughter die." Her words whispered into my mind.

"Seems to me you forgot me for, oh, centuries." I jerked away from her creepy touch. "Now fix this. Jerry hasn't done anything to you. Take that spell off him and give him back his memories."

"He made you vampire. You drink blood, have fangs." She shuddered. "It is unseemly."

"After the Storm God dumped me out of the Siren club, Jerry gave me back my immortality. I would think that would please you. Since you're all over this motherhood thing now. I would be six feet under if not for him." I scrambled to my feet. "Damn it. This is nuts. Why are you showing up now?"

"Circe came to me. She saw our resemblance and reminded me that you exist. Then she told me what Achelous did to you and I can see for myself, Gloriana, how he ruined your body. He will pay for that, the bastard." Thunder clapped and shook the bridge. I wondered if that was her warning to him or his taunt that she could try.

The damp fog surrounded us and just added to my sense that this was all a horrible nightmare. That my brain was as muddled as Jerry's right now.

"Circe needs to mind her own damned business." I shivered. Even my underwear felt damp from the fog and the cold, wet boards under me.

"No, she did me a great favor which puts me in her debt." My mother sighed. "You don't know what Olympus is like, Gloriana, the politics, the power plays. It is little wonder that I neglected you. I have been . . . busy since I gave you away. I forgot . . ." She jumped to her feet and turned to stare down at the water. "It was not right of me to abandon you. I should have taken my chances with Zeus."

"Well you didn't. So forget bonding with me now." I got up too and glanced at her. "You owe Circe two debts. Because she sent Blade in my path and here I am today, still alive. So you owe *him*. Fix his memory problem."

"No." She turned back to me. "You don't need to be with a man like that, a bloodsucker. I can take you back to Olym-

pus now that you are a woman. Rid you of those dreadful
fangs, return your perfect body." She tried to grab my hands.
"Give you everything."

I darted out of reach. "I like my dreadful fangs. Love my
blood-sucking boyfriend. And I'd never want to live in a place
with creeps like the Storm God. No way in hell or Olympus."
I wanted to slap her, throw her off the bridge, something. But
I knew better. A goddess from Olympus. I could feel her
power like electricity in the air, shoving at me, but stopping
short of actually hurting me. Restraint. Guess that was her
version of motherly love.

I knew the bits and pieces of power I had paled in comparison with what she'd have in her arsenal. Make her lose
her temper and she'd probably "forget" again that I was her
daughter and blast me until I was little more than a stain on
the wooden planks beneath my feet. Her daughter. I backed
away, disgusted and horrified at the thought.

"You can't change where you came from, Gloriana. But I
can change what you are now. Make your body glorious,
your teeth perfect, put a banquet before you that you could
actually savor—every bite. If you want your beloved's mind
whole again, come with me. I can fix him with a snap of my
fingers. Is that what you want? It would certainly please
me." She was close to me again, eyes sharp, watching me
like a bird of prey hovering over its next meal. "But you'd
never see him again."

"Never see him again?" I wanted him to remember, but
to remember *me*, our love. What good would it do to have
this woman restore his memories just to have me abandon
him? He'd mourn me. I'd seen how he still loved me. It
would be cruel, almost as cruel as leaving him stuck in the
sixteenth century. And me? I'd have my heart ripped out.

"I can't bear to see you live as a monster. If you want him
as he was, you'll leave him and come with me now. Otherwise, there is very little hope that he can get his memories
back." She smiled slowly. "Of course you could leave him as
he is and try to make him love you again. You *are* my daugh-

ter. I'm sure you are more than capable of seducing him if that is what you wish."

"This is about more than lust, woman." I wouldn't call her Mother. Never. This cold and heartless creature? "I want him to remember the last four hundred years. He'll be in shock once he leaves the castle and sees all the inventions, the changes . . ." I pressed my hands to my stomach. "God, I can't imagine how he'll feel. It will drive him mad."

"Amazing. You really do love him. I blame it on your time as a human." She looked skyward. "Another sin Achelous will answer for. Those of us who call Olympus home don't waste our energies on such trivial emotions." She sighed. "If you truly want this man, then he must prove he's worthy."

"Of course he's worthy. He's strong, loving and brave. And he's been true to me all these years."

"A paragon, it seems." Her smile was cold and knowing. "I'll believe it when I see it."

"What do you mean?" I didn't like our proximity. She held me close enough with her power that I could smell her, a strange perfume of lavender and musk that made my nose twitch. Lavender. I had always loved it, used it as a body wash. I was tossing it as soon as I got home.

"I mean, Gloriana, that I will test this man of yours. To see for myself if he deserves my daughter."

"Test? What kind of test?" I finally managed to get away from her. "Please don't hurt him. Haven't you done enough? The man can't remember—"

"I'll decide when Jeremiah Campbell has had enough. And, if you want me to spare him, you will call me Mother." She loomed over me, her power making my hair crackle and lift as if a strong wind had caught it. "Do you understand?"

"I understand that you want him to fail, *Mother*." I glared at her, dredging up courage despite my roiling stomach. "He is far worthier of me than I am of him."

"We will see, Daughter, we will see." She toyed with my hair, freezing me in place when I would have jerked away from her. "So very headstrong. No wonder Circe recognized you. You are the very image of me in my younger years." She laughed softly, no merry trill this time. "I will be watching. If you change your mind, call for your mother and I will come. And if that man disappoints you, I will be glad to make him suffer, never doubt it."

"Make him suffer? Haven't you already started?" I watched her fade from sight. "Damn you! Stay away. If you won't help him, just stay the hell away from both of us."

I turned and ran down the path toward the castle again. But before I got too close I stopped to compose myself. I could never let the Campbells know that it had been my fault Jerry had lost his memory. Oh, God, what would she do to him next?

Three

I sank down on a wooden bench not far from the castle, desperate to process what had just happened. I had a mother and not just any mother, a freaking goddess from Olympus. Lucky me. I pulled my sparkly pink phone from my pocket. Thank God. A signal. I hit speed dial.

"*Amica*, I'm glad you called. Did you make it to the castle? Was Jeremiah happy to see you? Oh, and I am in the most fun shop here in Paris. I'm buying you a little gift. Wait till you see."

The sound of Flo's voice, so full of life and normalcy, took me right over the edge. I couldn't speak, just sobbed, right into the phone.

"*Mio Dio!* What's wrong? Glory, speak to me!" I heard rustling in the background. "Ricardo, take these bags to the car. I'm going into the dressing room."

I took a breath of the cold air, glad that all trace of my mother's scent was gone, and managed to choke out a few words. "Flo. Sorry. Rough night."

"Obviously. So I'm glad you called me." I heard a door slam. "Now I'm in a dressing room. No one will bother us.

I have spent a fortune here. So talk to me. I must know everything. What happened to you? Why are you crying?"

"I got here. Jerry *was* happy to see me. Until he had an accident." My voice wobbled. Accident my left foot. The bitch who claimed to be my mother had done this. Was I going to take her word for that? The mother thing. Right now I couldn't think past wanting to send her screaming back to Olympus with her butt on fire. Instead I'd wimped out. At least I hadn't jumped to her command. And I'd sure never join her in Olympus.

"Is he all right? He isn't, um, dead, is he?" Flo's voice shook too. She did love me and what hurt me, hurt her. I couldn't have a better friend.

"No, but it's almost as bad. He's lost his memory! He doesn't know me." I gripped the phone until those pretty crystals made my hand bleed. I'd learned since I'd admired the cover at the phone boutique that sparkly didn't mean practical.

"How is that possible? *Assurdo.* Vampires remember everything. It's a curse. Why, Ricardo remembers every stupid little thing I say to him. And I . . . Well, you don't want to know how many centuries worth of nonsense I have crammed into my head." Flo opened the door. "I must ask Ricardo about this."

"Yes, ask him. I need answers. How to help Jerry. He was stabbed with a poisoned knife. It made him lose the last four hundred years." I looked around, making sure no one was within earshot. Why hadn't I done that sooner? *Get a grip, Glory.* I lowered my voice. "I have reason to believe it came from Olympus."

"No! Will they never leave you alone?" Flo broke into a spate of Italian. "Here's Ricardo. Hang on while I tell him this."

I sat with my head down, praying her brilliant husband would figure out what to do. It wasn't long before I heard his voice on the phone.

"Gloriana, how do you know this came from Olympus?" His voice was gentle and my eyes filled again.

"I, I ran into someone who told me that's what happened, Richard. Is there anything we can do? Jerry's forgotten everything that's happened after the late fifteen hundreds, since right before he met me." I was proud that I got that out without breaking down. Forget crying. I was furious, hating my mother who didn't care what this did to her child. Didn't she want me to be happy? Not unless it was *her* definition of happiness. On Olympus it was all about power plays and who had the biggest, um, weapon.

"Let me do some research. Florence wants to talk to you again. I'll call if I come up with something helpful. Take care, Gloriana."

"Glory! Do you want us to come there? We will if you need us by your side. This is *inferno per voi!*" Flo was talking a mile a minute.

I'd picked up enough Italian to know what *inferno* meant. "Yeah, hell. But stay there, enjoy Paris. Unless Richard finds a cure, there's nothing you can do and I'm not sure Angus would welcome a visit from my friends right now."

"We are Jeremiah's friends too, *sì?*" Flo sounded indignant.

"Of course you are. But things are crazy here. Just wait and I'll let you know if I need you." I sighed heavily. I should get back, see if Jerry had remembered anything. Hopefully Mara was gone.

"We're planning to go back to Austin in two weeks, Glory. If you need a ride then, just let us know. Meet us here and we will take you in our plane. There is room. For Jeremiah too if you can persuade him to come with you. *Mio Dio*, how you must be going crazy over this. If my Ricardo didn't know me?" I heard her take a shaky breath.

"I *am* going nuts and it's hard, so damned hard." I bit my lip to keep from sobbing. "Good to know I could have that ride. I might need it." Now I was the one taking a shaky breath. "Thanks, Flo. For listening. Now I've got to go. Who knows? Maybe Jerry will have come to his senses by now." I got up and brushed down my skirt. I had put it on with such high hopes mere hours ago.

"Always, I am always here for you, *mi amica*. Call me anytime. Good luck, eh?" Flo ended the call.

I tucked the phone back in my pocket and headed down the path. I needed more than luck. I needed a miracle. At home I had resources, friends who'd become more like family. Here I was an outsider already looked on with suspicion. On previous visits I'd had Jerry beside me as a buffer, always my champion. Now he just figured me for a blood donor and maybe a bed partner. Was it worth the humiliation to offer to share his bed? Hoping that the sex would stir some memories?

I looked back toward the bridge, but it was lost in the mist. If that woman, aka my mother, was right, it would take a lot more than that to break through Jerry's mental fog. I reached the door to the family quarters but it opened before I could turn the knob. Security cameras at work.

"You were gone quite a while." Jerry frowned at me. "I heard you talking to someone."

"I called a friend. And how do you know I was talking? Did you have me followed?" Damn. Had someone seen me on the bridge with my mother?

"No. But Da did send someone out a few minutes ago when it seemed you might have gotten lost in the fog." He reached for my arm and pulled me inside. "He's convinced me that we know each other, you and I. Come tell me more about this place called Austin and our lives there. Why did I come home without you?"

Oh, great. Was I supposed to tell him he'd still been licking his wounds because I'd been unfaithful? Not going to happen. Not when he needed to process one piece of info at a time. First, our relationship. Which was complicated enough.

"We had a bit of a falling out. A misunderstanding. Which is why I'm here. To clear things up. I found out some things that should make you feel better about our relation-ship." I looked around the living room. Angus had disap-peared. I guess to give Jerry and me some private time. Great. I owed him.

"I still don't understand how I could be with the same woman for hundreds of years and not marry her. It's a sin, Gloriana, living like that. I should have made an honest woman of you long ago." Jerry looked really earnest as he took a seat beside me on the couch.

I hid a smile. Sinning had never concerned the Jeremiah Campbell I'd met in London all those years ago. He really had regressed into someone I wasn't sure I knew at all. But I had to like him. He was so obviously worried about how he'd treated me.

"It was me, Jerry. I wouldn't marry you. You did offer." I put my hand over his.

"Not want my name?" He jerked his hand away. "Why not?" He stared down at my exposed legs. I kept forgetting the short skirt was screaming "slut" in his sixteenth-century brain.

"I didn't understand it at the time, but it had something to do with my background. I was reluctant to commit to one man." Uh-oh. I saw a look on his face that could only be described as distaste.

"Stop it. I wasn't a . . . a whore." I hurried on. "Times have changed dramatically since those that you remember, Jer. People no longer have to marry to be a happy couple or to live together publicly and be accepted in society."

"You can't be serious. What does the Church think of this?" He eased back so that he was as far away from me as possible on the three-seater couch.

"Doesn't approve, of course. Some things never change." Oh, great. That made him frown even more fiercely. "Come on, Jerry, you were never a churchgoer, not since I've known you." I sat back. I wasn't making headway, far from it. Obvi-ously, rebuilding our relationship wasn't going to be easy, and I was tired. Dawn was pulling at me.

"No, you're right. I never let a disapproving priest stop me from my pleasures. Mara reminded me of that. A child. That was a surprise. Have you met her?"

"Lily? Of course. She's beautiful and looks a lot like you, truth be told. But she has her mother's nature. She and Mara don't get along." I was suddenly exhausted and had a feeling the fog had done a number on my hair. I was ready to escape to my bedroom.

Jerry just stared at me and I could almost see him trying to find me in the dark recesses of his memory. He finally shook his head. "Are you all right?" He reached out and brushed a wild curl back from my cheek. "You gave me a good bit of your blood tonight. Perhaps you should rest."

"Yes, I need to. I'm worn out, physically and mentally." I grabbed his hand. "I know you are too." I was going for it. Maybe a new memory would stir the old ones. "Would you like for me to come to bed with you? If . . . if we lie together, maybe it will help. I hope—"

"I won't deny I'm tempted. There is something about you . . ." He looked into my eyes, searching for our connection again. I knew it the instant he came up empty. But he kept eyeing me. The heat of his gaze as he took in my deliberately low-cut top, the short skirt and the length of my legs, scandalous to an ancient male, gave me hope that he'd at least give lust a chance. "No. I won't use you that way."

"Will you at least kiss me? What could one kiss hurt? Maybe it will stir some memories for you. The past is there somewhere. I know your daughter. Your father has vouched for me, Jer. We have been together intimately more times than I can count." I took hold of the back of his neck, gently pulling him closer. It had been a gamble, offering myself to him, and he'd just had confirmed that once a slut, always a slut. But I could see that a kiss might be in his wheelhouse.

"Why not?" He gave in, leaning forward.

I closed my eyes when his lips met mine. I tasted the man I loved, the Jerry who'd met me at the car with joy in his eyes, so eager to be with me again. I teased open his lips with my tongue and deepened the kiss when he didn't at first. Running my fingertip along his ear, I sank into the kiss. It was dear and familiar and yet strangely new. Then over too soon when he pushed back and stared at me.

"I don't know you." He jumped up and stalked to the door to the outside. Before I could even call his name, he was gone, slamming it behind him.

I held my hand to my trembling lips. He didn't know me. Well, by damn, before the two weeks were done, he certainly would or I'd catch a plane back home without him.

Wait a minute. This was exactly what my mother hoped I'd do. Give up. Maybe move on to someone she considered worthy. A fangless wonder handpicked by her if I wouldn't shoot up to Olympus and start bonding over mother-daughter nut cracking. I shuddered to imagine it. I sucked up my flagging courage and headed out the door.

I found Jerry staring at the ruins of his once formidable castle.

"What happened to my home?" He stalked over to shove aside a fallen block of stone that most men wouldn't have been able to slide even an inch.

"Your family decided centuries ago to quit wasting money on upkeep when they spent all their time belowground or in Edinburgh at the town house." They had palatial digs in the big city, near other Scottish nobility, though, as vampires, they'd lost a lot of their power in politics. Still, they had friends in high places.

"But this." Jerry strode over to read the sign about the tours. "The National Trust? What the devil is that? Da lets strangers roam the grounds during the day?" He kicked another stone out of his way. "There's even a bloody tea room."

"Well, yes. I think that's a nice feature. Should bring in a good income." I moved closer. I hated to see him so upset. Of course it had been a shock to see the home he'd last remembered as a prosperous holding reduced to little more than rubble. Only one tower remained standing and that's where the tea room and souvenir shop were located. "The

National Trust is run by the Scottish government. Volunteers probably take care of the actual tours and such. I'm sure your family gets a tax break and maybe some kind of stipend for allowing visitors."

"Da lets strangers poke about in our home? By God, I never thought I'd see the day." Jerry paced around the perimeter of the castle, cursing and picking up loose stones. He stopped at the scaffolding erected against one side. "At least they're doing some repairs, I see."

"Yes, they can't let it fall down any further. It's a common thing. The taxes are really high. Many noble families do it, Jer. There's no shame in it." I kept up with Jerry as he headed for the stables. Horses. Of course he'd want to check on those. He'd be sorely disappointed. Most of the area was now a garage housing the various 4x4s used in the pastures along with the cars and Jeeps the family drove when in the country.

"Slow down, will you?" I wanted to prepare him.

"Why?" He stopped so fast I ran into him. "What is it? More bad news? This new century isn't to my liking, I'll tell you that."

"I'm sorry, Jerry. But you really do like the progress when you're, um—" I caught myself before I said "in your right mind." He narrowed his eyes. "Yourself."

"Spit it out. What's next?"

"Well, horses aren't such a big deal now. I'm not sure Angus even keeps any." I plucked at Jerry's plaid now thrown over his shoulder against the chill in the air. I wished for a sweater but wasn't about to go back for one. "I'm sorry. I know how you love to ride."

"No horses? How do you get around?" He glanced back at the castle. No cars were parked close enough for him to see in the mist, now obscuring everything.

"Cars, trucks, four-wheelers. Vehicles with engines, Jer. You'll see when we get there. Keep going. I don't know if we'll find horses. Maybe we will." I crossed my fingers.

Jerry charged down the path, so fast I had to run to keep

up with him. He stopped dead when he came to the garage/ stables. They were in much better repair than the castle and clearly hadn't held a horse in more than a decade. The driveway was paved and a sleek Jaguar sat in front of one of the six doors. It was Jerry's. I remembered him talking about the big engine. Lots of horsepower. But not the kind he was looking for.

He took a deep breath, obviously trying to catch a scent of horses. I knew he wasn't finding any. "Bloody hell." He stalked over to the Jaguar and stared down at it. "This is it, then? The thing I use to get around in? How do we tend the sheep?"

"You haven't tended sheep in centuries. As son of the laird I'm sure you remember that much." I had to hide a smile.

"Of course." He frowned. "We used dogs and villagers. But to get to the high pastures . . ."

"The men who take care of the woolly beasts use those." I pointed at a group of four-wheelers and a couple of bicycles leaning against a wall in an open doorway.

Jerry rubbed his forehead. "I have a headache. I'm going back to the house."

"I'm sorry, Jer. This is a lot to take in." I wanted to comfort him but kept my distance. I let him walk away and fingered the phone in my pocket. I needed to talk to someone else, someone who might know what to do. There was only one other person who might have the knowledge to help a vamp with amnesia and I had a feeling calling him would put me in trouble with the Campbells. If they found out about it. I looked around to make sure I was truly alone, then pulled out the phone and hit speed dial.

"Ian, I have a problem."

"Hello to you, Gloriana." He sounded as superior and amused at my stupidity as always. Ian MacDonald was a genius, a doctor, and something of a psychiatrist. If anyone knew how to help Jerry, it would be Ian. Of course he was also a vampire and Jer's sworn enemy. I'd have to make it worth his while or pique his interest to get him to help Jerry.

"I'm in Scotland, at Castle Campbell."

"Lucky you. No wonder you have a problem. Your lord and master not glad to see you?" He chuckled. Bastard.

"He was thrilled to see me. Until he had an accident."

"Fatal, I hope." Ian cleared his throat. "One of my kin finally take decent aim? Is the feud on again, and I need to watch my back?"

"No, it wasn't a MacDonald." I looked around again. Was that a security camera? No, I was being paranoid. "But he was knifed and it was coated in some kind of chemical. After the attack, Jerry woke up with amnesia."

"No kidding. Brilliant." Ian loved a good puzzle. I had him hooked. "Details, Gloriana. What does he remember? What *doesn't* he remember?"

"He knows his name."

"Too bad." Ian chuckled. "Keep going."

Tears clogged my throat but I fought them back down as I told him the essentials.

"Someone's been very clever. I'd like to meet them." He had that tone in his voice, the one that meant his brain was going a mile a minute and he was trying to figure this out. Good.

"Of course you would. A product like this could make you big bucks." Ian was a businessman first, scientist second.

"Of course it would. So you want my help? How? An antidote? Did you save the knife so I could analyze the potion?"

I wanted to slap my forehead. The knife. Where was it? Had Angus taken it? Of course he had. Surely he hadn't cleaned it, but someone in his efficient staff might have. I needed to find out, get it from him and ship it straight to Ian.

"Do you think you could do that? Figure out an antidote?"

"I don't know. I'd have to get a look at it first." Ian was sounding impatient. "Of course you've tried jogging his memory yourself, haven't you?"

"Yes! Everything but dance naked in front of him. That's next." My face burned when Ian laughed. But, damn it, I was desperate.

"Therapy might help but I'm sure as hell not coming there. I vowed never to return to my homeland. That clanfeud crap is in my rearview mirror. I wasted too many centuries on it." Ian sounded resolved.

"Well, now who needs therapy? A MacDonald having issues with his roots?" I smiled. Good to know the man had a vulnerability. Maybe Jerry could use that when they went head to head again.

"You'd have to bring Campbell back here. Hypnotherapy might be the thing to bring him back. Sounds like retrograde, posttraumatic amnesia. That is, if the amnesia hangs on after the drug wears off."

"Could it? Wear off?" My heart jumped and wobbled. Hope. About time.

"I have no idea, Gloriana. But it's a possibility. Pump him full of blood. Maybe that will help flush it out of his system."

"And what about hypnotizing him? You know he'd never willingly put himself under your power." I started walking back toward the castle. More blood. I could handle that.

"I'll leave the persuasion to you and your 'physical' reminders. If he still can't remember after the drug has left his system, then it's because he's got a mental block. I'd say he'll need some drastic measures to come back to his senses." Ian chuckled. "Though a Campbell doesn't have much sense to begin with."

"Drastic measures?"

"A good knock in the head, perhaps. Shock therapy." Ian chuckled. "Bring him back here and I'd be happy to try some things."

"I'm not stupid, Ian. Jerry's amnesia wasn't the result of a hit on the head. And you're not getting anywhere near him with one of your 'drastic measures.'" Egotistical man. Too bad Ian was just brilliant enough to be useful. If only he'd really forget the feud between his clan and the Campbells. I wasn't buying his "rearview mirror" comment.

"True enough. It was worth a shot. Keep me posted, Gloriana. I'm fascinated."

"Of course you are. A Campbell in trouble. I just made your night, didn't I?" This call might have been a mistake. But if anyone could figure out an antidote to my mother's potion, it was Ian, damn him. "Jerry's right not to trust you, Ian. I'd never have called a MacDonald in the first place if there were anyone else to turn to. I'll let you know what I find out." I ended the call and looked up to see Angus marching up from the family quarters. Uh-oh.

"You were talking to a MacDonald?" Angus stared at me. "Tell me, Gloriana. What exactly are you up to? Did you arrange the attack on my son?"

"No! Why would I do that? I love him." I reared back, horrified. Well, obviously security cameras had caught more than I'd realized.

Angus jerked me inside, his hold on my arm tight. "Then tell me, lass, why you were talking to a MacDonald on the telephone about my family business."

"Ian MacDonald lives in Austin. I know him, so does Jerry. He's a scientist, doctor, psychiatrist. I thought he might be able to help Jerry get his memory back." I stared down to where Angus was bruising my arm. He didn't let go, pulling me all the way to the living room.

"You claim my son has been consorting with a MacDonald in Texas? I don't believe you." He shook my arm then finally released me. "Sit. Explain yourself."

"Consorting isn't the right word. Jerry hates Ian, doesn't trust him. I get why. You people feud forever, no matter what."

"Are you trying to tell me how to run my family?" Angus had his fangs down and I was starting to get scared. I was seriously outnumbered. Two of his clansmen had come to stand in the doorway. Jerry was nowhere to be seen.

"No, of course not. But Jerry and I disagree about Ian.

Ian does have certain useful skills. As vampires, we can help each other. If he can analyze the drug on that knife, maybe Ian can come up with an antidote."

"You're daft. You think I'd let my son take any potion that a MacDonald gave him, claiming it would cure him?" Angus slammed a fist on the arm of his recliner. "This isn't the first time you've had truck with this man. You were in league with him in California, taking some diet drug he gave you. Weren't you? I would think you'd have learned from that. It gave you nasty side effects."

Okay, Angus had me there. I'd been invited to the Grammy awards and wanted to look great on the red carpet alongside rock star Israel Caine. So when Ian had claimed his drug could make me lose the extra pounds I'd carried literally forever, I'd gone for it. The side effects had been horrendous, but for one perfect night I'd looked gorgeous and almost thin. Worth it. Now Angus was staring at me like I was Judas.

"I know you have issues with the MacDonalds. But I'm desperate. Who else can we get to fix this thing? Do you know a vampire doctor or scientist? Do you?" I jumped to my feet, sick to death of feeling helpless. I kept flashing on the look of Jerry's face when he'd seen his home in ruins, realized his beloved horses had been dead for centuries. Maybe I should go up to Woo Woo World with my mother and let her restore his memories. He'd get over me and have a fine life. And I . . .

Angus had his head down, his hands clasped on his knees. "I have been trying to give you the benefit of the doubt, Gloriana. I know you love him. I can think of no reason for you to hurt him. And yet he came home without you, seemed hurt by you. You want to explain what went on that sent him here in such pain?" He looked up, meeting my eyes and probing my thoughts. No way was he getting in.

"That's between us, Angus. I do love him and I only want the best for him. You want me to leave?" I stood. "I will say this. Ian suggested that the drug might be flushed out of Jerry's system. Give him lots of blood. If he still has amnesia, then it's because he doesn't *want* to remember the last four centuries."

"I can't get past two things: The attack on my son came the same night as you did, and you are communicating with a MacDonald." Angus stood as well, staring down at me. "You block your thoughts. I take that as a sign of something to hide. What do you have to hide, Gloriana?"

"Things that are none of your business, Angus. I'll be going now." I turned toward the door. "Would one of you get my suitcases?"

"No." Jerry suddenly stood in front of the door. "I may not know you, but I realize I should. Your blood. It's what I need right now. If you are still willing."

I looked back at Angus. "Your father doesn't want me here."

"Da, let her stay." Jerry took my hand and held it to his nose. "I sense we have a connection. It, it helps me."

"Damn it, Son. She's been talking to the MacDonalds." Angus strode to where we stood. "I am afraid to trust her now."

"But you remember us together, Angus." I looked up at Jerry, almost afraid to move for fear of breaking this tenuous start of a new bond. He still had my hand and I gripped it tightly. "Did I ever hurt Jerry? Ever show anything but love for him?"

"Nay, lass. You did not." Angus shook his head. "Stay then, but I'll be watching you. I *have* found a doctor of our own. He will be here tomorrow night. Now dawn is upon us. Go to bed, the lot of you. No harm will come to you while you are in your death sleep. I have guards aplenty to insure that."

I sighed and released Jerry's hand. That had been close. I followed Jerry to the bedrooms, where we stopped at his door.

"I'll not take advantage of you, I told you that. I hope I'm not being foolish, trusting you. Why did you talk to a Mac-Donald?" Jerry stared down at me.

"Because he's a doctor and I thought he could help you. No other reason. But if Angus has another answer, then I'm happy to let his doctor have at it. You've taught me to mistrust MacDonalds too. And I've witnessed some of his treachery myself."

"All right then." Jerry stared down at me, another of those searching looks. I swayed toward him and couldn't resist putting a hand on his chest.

"You said you wanted to drink from me. Now?"

"No, I've changed my mind. You're pale and obviously need to recover from the last time I took your blood." He touched my cheek. "But I would like to try another kiss. Just to see if this potion is wearing off. I heard what you said to Da. I'll drink another bottle of that fake blood before I rest." He brushed my wild hair back from my face. The damned Scottish mist had done a number on it.

"Good. Dilute the poison as much as you can." I ran my hands up to his shoulders and breathed him in again. How could he not remember this? For me it was so perfect, our connection. Oh, if only a kiss would break the spell. He was my own very masculine Sleeping Beauty. It would be wonderful if I'd pull away and he'd suddenly remember . . . everything. I slid my arms around his neck and feathered a kiss over his strong jaw.

"Jerry. Jeremiah." I sighed. "I'm glad you want to kiss me again. We always enjoyed kissing each other. I have your taste memorized. It is my favorite flavor in the world, second only to drinking from your vein." I settled my mouth on his. His arms pulled me close and, for a few exquisite moments, this felt like old times, the familiar awakening before things moved into the bedroom. There, our special bond would leave us both more fulfilled than we could ever be with anyone else. Then he eased back, lifting my arms from him and setting me away.

"You are a talented woman. I could enjoy kissing you

longer but I must rest. Thank you, Gloriana." He smiled, as he would to a stranger, and disappeared into his room, closing the door firmly in my face.

I walked slowly down the hall to the bedroom one of the guards had pointed out earlier. My suitcases were on the floor but I had little enthusiasm for unpacking. I stripped out of my clothes and crawled naked between the sheets. I wished for about the millionth time that vampires could dream. I'd dream of a long and lusty night in Jerry's arms. I'd go for it even if he thought he was making it with a woman he'd just met. Instead, the sun must have peeked over the horizon because I fell hopelessly into my death sleep.

Four

"The doctor should be here anytime now." Angus looked at his watch for the third time in as many minutes. "Gloriana, why don't you take your rental car to Edinburgh and turn it in? You did say you were anxious to stop paying on it, didn't you?"

"Yes, I did. But maybe I should keep it. I don't know how long I'll be staying." I looked from Angus to Jerry. If just one of them would show some sign of wanting me here, it would make me feel better. But ever since I'd walked out of the bedroom at sunset, I had been waiting for that sign. No luck.

"Who is this doctor? Do I know him?" Jerry paced the living room, his agitation growing worse by the hour. He'd badgered Angus about the horses until his father had arranged to hire one for him. It would arrive soon too, borrowed from a neighboring stable and hauled in by trailer. So far Jerry had resisted going for a ride in a "machine."

"He's a vampire, related to the O'Connors. He's highly respected, trained at the college in Edinburgh, but has been all over the world. Including America for the past century."

Angus nodded at me. "I actually know his sire. We were lucky he was nearby, visiting relatives."

"Lucky?" Jerry collapsed on the sofa. "I don't like it, Da. All these coincidences. This woman arrives and right away I'm stabbed with some potion that takes my mind with it. And by Mara! An old and trusted friend." Jerry narrowed his gaze on me. "Are you in league with this O'Connor who'll be arriving shortly?"

"I've never met him." I threw up my hands. "This *woman?*" I felt wounded but wouldn't let him see my pain. "Damn it, Jerry, I came here to straighten things out between us. So that we could try again. Make a fresh start."

"What went wrong between us? Why do we need a fresh start after all these years?" Jerry stood, facing me. "I obviously left you in that place where we lived together and came home alone. What set me off, Gloriana? Was I with another woman? Or were you with another man?"

I gnawed my lower lip. Angus stared at me too. I figured I might as well get this over with. "You were faithful to me Jerry. Always." I tried and failed at a smile. "But I, I wasn't so good at the relationship. I had an affair. It was a terrible mistake. But I found out there was a reason I have these urges that, that make me stray."

"Urges." The look of distaste on Angus's face made me want to run right out of the castle. "No wonder you left her, Son. Good riddance, I say. Campbells have pride. There's no reason I can think of to justify taking back a woman who has been unfaithful."

"Just listen to me." I could see that both men were ready to toss me out of the castle on my well-cushioned fanny. "I don't think I could help myself. I just discovered that I used to be a Siren, Angus. Before Jerry found me in London." I blurted it out and got the incredulous looks I'd expected.

"A Siren? Are ye daft?" Angus stomped his foot. "What nonsense. Don't believe her, Jeremiah. They aren't of this world and certainly not the likes of this piece of work standing here before us." He grabbed Jerry's arm and jerked him well away from me.

"Stop, Da. Let her speak. A Siren? And how is that possible?" Jerry stumbled to the sofa, his face pale.

I'd never seen him weak before and it broke my heart. What had my mother's potion done to him? What was it still doing to him? I started to move closer but the look on his father's face stopped me cold. Angus had murder in his eyes, his fangs were down, and I knew how he felt. Oh, boy, did I know. If I had my so-called mother here now, I'd tear open her throat and watch her bleed out, enjoy her painful death. I stepped back, giving Jerry his space. Angus still watched me, obviously ready to jump me if I so much as touched his son.

"Okay, here's the truth."

"Truth. I should hope so." At least Angus's fangs had disappeared and he sat in his recliner.

"It seems that before I met you, the Storm God, who is in charge of Sirens, was unhappy with me. He tossed me out of his, um, harem and punished me by making me human." Angus made a noise of disbelief but Jerry leaned forward, listening.

"Go on. Are you saying you were human when I met you?" He rubbed his forehead. Headache again. I twisted my hands together to keep from reaching for him.

"Yes! Achelous figured I'd die a natural death on my own. When you saw me onstage and fell in . . . in love with me, you had no idea what I'd been and I didn't remember my past. Achy wiped away my memories and planted false ones." I realized how ridiculous this story sounded but rushed on. "Anyway, being made vampire gave me back my immortality. Which Achelous didn't know about until recently." I wiped my damp palms on my skirt. It was another short one. Yes, Jerry had noticed. I eased a little closer.

"That doesn't explain why you never married me, Gloriana. If you say you love me, why wouldn't you?" He glared at me and I was pretty sure not all of the pain in those dark eyes was from his aching head. "And why did you betray me with another man?"

"It's the Siren in me!" I glanced back at Angus, who still looked ready to intervene if I made a move he considered aggressive. I kept my distance from Jerry even though I wanted desperately to sit beside him, to touch him. "I think somewhere inside me I still have whatever it is that makes a Siren go from man to man. It must be what kept me from committing to you all those years."

"Are you buying this cock-and-bull story, son?" Angus stood. "If you *were* a Siren, Gloriana, and I'm still not buying it, then you used my boy to gain a protector. It's their way."

"Wait a minute. I still can't believe Sirens are real." Jerry stared at me like he was waiting for me to sprout a fish tail.

"They *are* real. You even knew one in Austin. Aggie. She's a friend, sort of anyway. They're selfish creatures, man magnets. One reason you came home was because you were afraid I had used you, just as Angus said. That, if I was a Siren, you'd been manipulated all these years. A true Siren can pull any man to her and he can't resist her call." I sank down on my knees in front of him, ready to beg him to believe me if it came to that.

"Did you? Manipulate me?" Jerry stared down at me.

"No. Never. I found out that it's only a Siren's song that can pull men helplessly to her. That's why I went to a hell of a lot of trouble, actually suffered, if you must know, to get over here, Jer. To tell you this in person." I put my hand on his knee. "Listen. This is the truth. I swear it." My voice cracked. The trip had been a nightmare, and then to get here and have this happen . . .

"If you sang me to you all those centuries ago . . ." He tried to lift my hand off of him in disgust but I grabbed his arm, my tears drying up in a hurry.

"I didn't! The Storm God stole my song when he made me human. I know you can't remember now, but when you met me I couldn't sing at all. Believe me, I tried. It would have helped me make a living when Achelous left me to fend for myself. But I have no singing voice. We even joked about it." He glared down at my hand but I wasn't about to let him go. "Please, please believe me." I heard Angus snort but didn't spare him a glance. This was too important. I held on and stared into Jerry's dark eyes.

"Prove it. Sing something. Right now." He flung my hand.

I couldn't believe this was the man I'd known so intimately for so long. The man who'd held me, protected me, insisted I take on a bodyguard for centuries! But this Jerry just stared at me, waiting for "proof."

"Fine. 'Loch Lomond.' It used to be one of your favorites." I sat back on the floor, took a breath and started in. "You take the high road and I'll take the low road—"

"Stop." Jerry held up his hands. "Either you really can't sing or you're making fools of us now."

"No, now I remember. The girl always did sing like someone had just stepped on a bagpipe. We forbid her to join in when we sang around a fire." Angus leaned forward, hands on his sturdy knees. "You've got my attention, lass. Go on with your tale."

I got up and collapsed in relief on the love seat across from Jerry. "You see, without my song I couldn't cast a spell on you. You could have left me anytime. But you didn't." I looked my fill while he seemed deep in thought. He wore a soft knit shirt today and jeans. Modern clothes. I guess he'd decided to test them out, to see if they brought back some memories. If only it were that simple. But he still had a stranger's eyes when he finally looked at me again.

"But you say we were together for centuries. I thought Sirens didn't bother with relationships, they only wanted to get a man close enough to kill." He didn't shrug away from me when I moved over to sit next to him on the couch.

"That's true. It's the reason Achelous got rid of me. I didn't have the stomach for the killing." I heard Angus clear his throat. When I glanced at him, he nodded with a glimmer of recognition in his eyes, remembering my reluctance to hurt anything.

"Anyway, the Storm God knew how important her song is to a Siren. It's her identity. So he took mine away when he turned me human, the rat bastard. I could never put you under my spell, Jerry, even if I'd wanted to get you that way. I was just ordinary Gloriana when you met me and f-fell in love." No, not crying. He'd finally remember me, he had to. "And you stayed in love with me for four centuries. Through good times and bad." I twisted my hands in my lap when all I wanted to do was touch him again, feel his skin against mine. But his incredulous face, his hard eyes kept me from making that move.

"In love? Sounds like an obsession. I loved you even when you had sex with other men? You just admitted you couldn't be content with just one man because of the 'Siren' in you." He jerked to his feet so suddenly the couch rocked. "By God, woman, was I not enough for you?"

If I hadn't known better, I'd have thought he was struggling not to hit me. But my Jerry never touched a woman in anger. This Jerry, this stranger with a face that could have been carved from the stones of the castle itself, paced the floor, smacking his fist into his palm. I glanced at Angus and wished I hadn't. He'd lost all sympathy for me, sending me a mental message to get the hell out of his home. I shook my head.

Jerry stopped in front of me, clearly waiting for an answer. I hated myself for hurting him. Why *hadn't* he been enough? Sure, I'd had my reasons for taking breaks. His controlling attitude for one. But now was not the time to trot out those issues. I was desperate to make a connection with him.

"I loved you, Jerry. I did. I'm flawed, I guess. But now that I know what was wrong with me, the Siren part of me, I'm determined to change. To fix this." I got up, desperate to get close again, but a pounding on the door stopped me.

"That's got to be the doctor." Angus got up. "And just in time. Quit pressuring him, Gloriana. And I think it best if Jeremiah decides for himself if he wants to forgive a woman who betrayed him." Angus brushed past me, his frown making it obvious he'd just as soon I hit the road.

"He's right. I have to decide for myself." Jerry shook his head. "I have too much to think about right now. Too many things to get used to. A bloody Siren." He stared up at the ceiling, obviously overwhelmed by what he'd just heard. "Shit. If I didn't think you were somehow the key to getting my mind back, I'd toss you out on your ass right now. Instead . . ." He pushed his fingers into his hair in a familiar gesture that made my heart turn over. "Well, hell, I don't get it, but I need to understand it."

"You want me to stay?" I stepped back as a tall handsome man stalked into the room as if he owned it. He was blond, blue-eyed and wore a suit that cost more than the rental car I'd driven to the castle, his tie a clan plaid. He swept me with a glance and then dismissed me before fixing his bright gaze on Jerry. Jerry nodded at me before focusing on the new arrival.

"Thank you, Laird. Jeremiah Campbell?" He held out his hand and Jerry shook it. "Sir, I'm Bartholomew O'Connor, your doctor if you'll permit it. Call me Bart. Let's go to your bedroom and I'll have a look at you without everyone gawking, shall we? Your father told me a bit about what happened." He held up a hand when Angus started to protest. "This is between Jeremiah and me. Am I correct, Jeremiah?"

"Yes, you are, Bart. And call me Jerry." He glanced at me. "It seems to be what my friends call me these days."

"Excellent. Show me the way." Bart stopped next to the door to collect a large black bag then followed Jerry out of the room.

"Well, that was high-handed." Angus muttered, picking up the remote and turning on the television set.

"Yes, but the right way to handle Jerry." I sighed and sat on the sofa, prepared for a wait. "The doctor seemed confident and competent. If the cost of his suit is any indication."

"He's top drawer. Cost the earth too. But I don't mind paying the freight if he brings my boy back to me." Angus settled back, a car race on the tube. "I'll give him that knife to analyze. That was a good idea. Maybe he can come up with an antidote. Not giving a MacDonald any part of this, I hope you know."

"I get it, Angus. I told you, I would only go to Ian as a last resort."

"Then we're agreed. Not that you'll have any say-so in Jeremiah's treatment, come to that." Angus looked at me, one eyebrow raised.

"Jerry has asked me to stay."

"It's his call. I do remember that the boy loved you. I hope it wasn't due to some trickery on your part. Herself will be arriving here before dawn. If you have something to hide, she'll ferret it out." Angus nodded, happy to let his wife take care of me. I could only dread it.

"Herself. You mean Jerry's mother?" My stomach did a double backflip.

"None other. I called her of course, called everyone in the family. She's hell on wheels when one of her babes is in trouble. Of course she left Paris as soon as the sun set. Doesn't take that long to get here from there, flying." He punched a button on the remote and started his usual channel surfing.

"Great. Just great." I picked up the bottle of synthetic I'd opened for breakfast and took a big swallow. I'd need my strength if I was going to face Jerry's mother. To say she hated me was an understatement. She'd tried to kill me early in our relationship. Only Jerry's interference and my own cleverness had saved me. Since then we'd declared an uneasy truce. Now she'd have even more reason to want me out of her son's life. I sighed and took another drink. Maybe it was time for me to let him go. I could almost hear my mother cackling with glee at that thought.

The door into the castle opened again and a whirlwind of activity got Angus and me to our feet. Before I knew what had hit me I was wrapped in an embrace and a cloud of expensive perfume.

"Glory, I got here as soon as I could. Did I beat Ma?"

I pulled back and looked over the woman who rushed from me to the laird. Caitlin Campbell, one of Jerry's sisters, had always been my ally. I found myself grinning as she started in on her father.

"You haven't been bullying Glory, have you, Da?"

"Now, Caitie, I have to protect your brother. She no more than arrives than he's set upon and stabbed. What do you think about that?" Angus frowned and settled back into his chair, the TV on mute.

"I say it's pure bad luck. She didn't stab him, did she?" Cait glanced at me. "Not that my brother can't be provoking."

"Of course not. We'd had a fine reunion. Jer was glad to see me." I couldn't quit smiling. I did love Jerry's sister. She was tall, with generous curves, and never failed to speak her mind. In fact, she was a lot like my best bud Flo except twice the size and Scottish.

"Da said Mara actually wielded the knife. But then she's set to marry a McLeod. Can't figure out the connection there." Cait turned and started directing the "lads" as she called them as to where to put a large amount of very expensive luggage.

"There *is* no connection, Caitie. Mara was spelled. By a witch. She didn't know what she was doing when she attacked your brother." Angus still looked at me suspiciously. "Of course it happened just minutes after Gloriana got here."

"Leave it alone, Da. Glory would never hurt Jeremiah. Not like that. Give the girl credit for more finesse." Cait sat beside me on the love seat. "Update. What's going on now? Has he remembered you yet?"

"No, not a glimmer. And I had to confess what had caused him to come home without me. It was pretty ugly stuff." I sighed then gave her the short version.

"A Siren. How cool is that?" Cait looked me over. "Powers come with that?"

"A few. I'll show you later." We all looked toward the hall when the doctor and Jerry emerged. The doctor looked grim until he spotted Caitlin. He instantly became all charm. Did I mention Jerry's sister had her brother's dark good looks? Add those to her generous curves and Cait was something of a man magnet herself.

"I'm going to have to run some tests. Jerry and I are headed to my clinic in the city, Laird." He nodded toward the love seat where Cait and I were crammed thigh to thigh. "Bart O'Connor."

Cait jumped to her feet, dragging me with her. "I'm Jerry's sister Caitlin and this is Gloriana St. Clair, his girlfriend, the one he can't remember after, oh, four centuries. Any idea what's up with that, Doc?"

"It's a very unusual case. Selective amnesia, I guess you could call it. That's why I want the tests. A brain scan for one." Bart moved closer. "I'm wondering why we haven't met before, Caitlin. Get into the city often?"

"No. I live in London now. Divorced my first husband a century and a half ago and have been bouncing around Europe ever since." Cait put her arm through mine. "Glory taught me the wisdom of avoiding long-term entanglements."

"Quit spouting your feminist nonsense and listen to the doctor." Angus moved in between Cait and Bart. "Now what do you think? Is there a cure?"

"Da, leave him alone. The man just got my case." Jerry looked pale and I could tell he needed to feed.

"Would you like to drink from me, Jer?" I scooted to his side. "I won't mind. You are obviously weak and I hope taking some of my blood will help you remember."

"Not necessarily a bad idea." Bart finally gave me his full attention. "You two really were an item for centuries?" He sounded skeptical.

"Yes. Jerry loves me and I love him. I'll do whatever it takes to help him remember that fact." I held out my wrist, waving it under Jerry's nose.

"No, I don't want your blood. Not now. After what I heard a few minutes ago, you really think I want to be that close to you?" He shoved my arm away. "Bring me some of that fake blood. It's tolerable and I won't be any more beholden to you, Gloriana, than I already am."

"Beholden?" I stepped back, bumping into Caitlin. "Damn it, Jerry, I'd give my blood, my life, if it would help you get your memory back." I turned and stared blindly at the TV, the cars whizzing past in a blur that was caused more by my tears than their speed as a yellow flag waved in the corner of the screen.

"Jeremiah, don't be an ass. Glory loves you. Let her prove it." Cait poked her brother in the chest before putting an arm around my shoulders. "You don't seriously think she was behind your stabbing, do you?"

"I don't know what the hell to think." He took a bottle of synthetic from a servant and drank. "I'm glad you're here, Caitie, but I'm disappointed that you'd take this woman's side over your own brother's."

"This woman is my friend. You loved her. Still love her when you aren't daft." Cait turned me to face him. "I believe her when she says she didn't have anything to do with your stabbing. When you get your mind back, you're going to have to grovel to get her to forgive you."

Jerry just drank the rest of his AB positive and set the empty on a tray with a clatter. "We'll see. I'm taking it one night at a time. Now let's get out of here, Bart. Don't suppose you brought a horse."

"No, of course not. We'll go in my Porsche. I like fast cars." He glanced at Caitlin. "And expensive things. I promise you'll be comfortable."

"In one of those machines? Doubt it." Jerry trudged to the door, his shoulders slumped. "Bloody hell, you'd better help me get my mind back with this."

"I'll do my best." Bart winked at Cait. "Ladies, perhaps we'll see you in the city."

"You bet your stethoscope you will." Cait grabbed her designer bag. "Glory, are you still packed?"

"Yes, I didn't bother to get out more than my toothbrush last night."

"Then let's go. You follow me in that rented junker I saw parked outside and turn it in. I'll drive Jerry's Jag. We'll stay at the town house." She grinned at her father, who grumbled about high-handed women. "We need to be close to the action, Da. In case Jerry's memory needs a nudge. You know Glory is the one to remind him, don't you?"

"I suppose. But you know how your brother is about his cars. Take care with your driving." He shook his head as Caitlin kissed him on the cheek. "And don't be so quick to take sides. Gloriana is not only claiming to be a Siren, she's been acting like one. Make her tell you the whole tale, then see if you want to be her champion."

"I will. Relax, Da. I'll keep you posted about Jeremiah's condition. Tell Ma hello for me." She started ordering the long-suffering servants to bring out her luggage. "See you in town, Bart. Might even beat you there. I like fast cars too." She smiled at the doctor.

I ended up having to deal with my own luggage since the servants weren't so keen on helping me. Obviously they'd been listening to the conversation in the living room and I was being eyed with suspicion. By the time I was on the road, agreeing just to meet Cait in Edinburgh later as she sped away in that gleaming Jaguar, I was pretty sure that I was well out of that castle. No one there wanted me to stay and a vampire sure doesn't like to fall into her death sleep surrounded by people she can't trust.

"I can't believe you hit that post." I frowned in dismay at Jerry's beloved Jaguar and the dent in its back bumper.

"The parking is impossible along here. I had to make a space. He'll never notice that little ding." Cait climbed out of the car and reached back for her purse.

"From now on, I'm driving." I looked up and down the

narrow brick street lined with expensive town houses. Bart's offices were along there somewhere. But you'd never know it unless you looked closely at the brass plaques next to the shiny lacquered doors.

"You think you can do better? Have at it. But, remember, you will be on what you Yanks call the wrong side of the street." Cait tossed me the keys.

"I'll take my chances. Now which one is his office?" I started walking down the brick sidewalk.

"The green door. I looked it up on Google maps. See? There's his name." Cait started up the steps that led to the door. "*You* look a little green. What's up?"

"There's something I haven't told you, Cait. In a way, this *is* all my fault. The attack on Jerry." There, I'd said it and I felt better already. That is until Cait threw me up against the iron railing next to the steps. I felt the metal cutting into my back and the heat of Cait's temper flaming from her eyes.

"Explain." She jerked me down the steps and up the street before I had a chance to gasp out a word. Soon we were in a dark alley with only a stray cat and a garbage bin for company.

"It . . . it's my mother." I wrenched her fingers away from my throat.

"You have a mother? Since when?" Her mouth dropped open and she stepped back.

"I just found out. She's a goddess, from Olympus. You don't want to mess with her."

"She's right, Caitlin." There was a shimmering white light and the goddess herself materialized next to us. Great, just what I needed. A visit from Mommie Dearest.

"Are you kidding me?" Cait pressed back against the wall. "This is your long-lost mother?"

"So she claims anyway. I haven't seen a DNA test to prove it."

"You dare doubt me, Daughter?" Thunder shook the stones under our feet and lightning lit up the sky. "You want a blood sample? No problem. Have that doctor of yours test it and compare." She produced a silver knife and drew a line in her palm then wiped her hand across my white silk blouse.

"Thanks a heap." I stared down at the stain. "Couldn't you have used a hanky?"

"I thought this was important to you." My mother's smile was frightening.

"You're the one who made my brother lose his mind?" Caitlin was shaking beside me but her fangs were down. Uh-oh, the Campbell temper was alive and well in her.

"Yes, I am." Mom actually smiled like she was proud of herself.

"You bitch!" Cait threw herself at the goddess, hands extended like she was going to tear out some hair, maybe claw that smile off Mom's pretty face.

"Cait, no!" I needn't have bothered. Cait bounced off what must have been a force field and landed on the bricks. Sparks flew and she looked dazed.

"What the hell?" She shook her head and I recognized the way her hair was standing on end. She'd obviously taken a good hard hit with a lightning bolt. Yep, her designer shoes would never be the same. The signature red soles were blackened.

"Get out of here, vampire, before I give you a shot of amnesia like I gave your brother."

"Wait." Cait got to her feet. The woman didn't seem to know fear. She brushed off her skirt and frowned down at her shoes. I could tell she really wanted to try another attack but thought better of it. "Okay, so you claim to be Glory's mom, are even offering up a DNA sample to prove it. Fine. But she loves my brother. Why'd you do that to him? Screw with his mind? Is that any way to treat her boyfriend?" Cait looked from me to Mom.

"I don't owe you an explanation. Run along before I decide to fry you like bacon. Now I need to speak to my daughter alone." She made a shooing motion.

"Geez, and I thought my mother was a tough broad."

Cait gave me a pitying look then took off as fast as her scorched pumps could carry her. She stopped at the street entrance. "I'll meet you in Bart's office, Glory."

"Keep this our secret, Cait. Please?" I had probably blown it by sharing my involvement in Jerry's problem.

"For now." Thunder clapped and lightning sizzled close enough to make her hair rise and swirl around her head. I saw her swallow then give my mother a middle finger salute. I closed my eyes, waiting for my friend to go up in smoke. Just in time I heard her say, "Okay! Whatever you say." I opened my eyes just as she ran around the corner and out of sight.

Five

I faced off with my mother. "Well, you've got my attention. What do you want? Is there anything I can do to get you to restore Jerry's memory?" I kept my back against the rough stone wall. The glimmering, strangely mesmerizing vision that claimed to be my mother solidified in front of me and she actually smiled. It was a terrifying sight.

"So happy you asked, Daughter." She had put herself in modern street clothes for this visit, a designer dress that made the most of her perfect figure. Was she planning to stick around, mix with mortals? I shook my head at the thought.

"Don't keep me in suspense. What is it? Some hoops for me to jump through? I will do anything to get Jerry's mind back where it belongs." I couldn't keep from cringing when she moved even closer and snapped her fingers. To my relief it was only to materialize a designer handbag which she opened to pull out a lipstick. She grabbed my chin and had the nerve to hold it steady while she ran the tube over my lips.

"Good to know." She closed the lipstick. "There, that's better. You were looking pale. Always put your best face forward, Gloriana. There's no excuse for going out in public looking less than your best."

"You're giving me beauty tips?" I stifled the urge to wipe the stuff off. "Come on, I'm in pain here. Jerry, the love of my life, is lost in a mental fog. What are we going to do about it?"

"We. Love that word. First you are going to agree to a few terms." She pulled out a compact and dabbed powder on her nose. She started to hand it to me then sighed. "Vampire. No reflection. It is just not to be borne."

"Bear it. I'm staying this way. Whatever deal you have spinning in your mind, that part's off the table. I'm not coming to live in Olympus. I can't imagine anything worse. You forget. I've met the Storm God."

"I admit the man is a dead bore with his blustering and chauvinist attitude." She made a face. "But he's the exception. There are some really delightful males to be enjoyed there. And that's part of the 'deal,' as you so crudely put it, that I will have you make with me."

"What do you mean? I have a guy. Jerry. I'm doing this so I can try to win him back." I glanced at the opening to the alley. Every once in a while someone would walk past, but it was night and this row of doctors' offices wasn't exactly a tourist mecca, or even open for business now except for a certain vampire's suite. If anyone noticed two women talking here, I couldn't imagine what they would think.

"Relax, Gloriana, no one will see us. I've put a vanishing spell around us. We're invisible to everyone, even your friend Caitlin, should she return."

"Fine. Good trick. Now tell me what you've got up your sleeve." I had to admire those sleeves. Vintage Dior. The outfit would sell for big bucks in my shop at home. Would I ever see Austin again? I wondered. Having a mother from Olympus was bound to complicate my life forever.

Her eyes gleamed. Of course she loved reading that in my mind. "Gloriana, cooperate and we can have a wonderful mother-daughter relationship."

"Now you're scaring me. What do I have to do to get Jerry cured, Mother? Spit it out." I'd thrown in the "m" word to please her but I put my hands on my hips. I was through playing games.

"You have to give other men a chance to woo you, my dear. I want you to date some eligible males I'll send from my home. I believe you have been, how you would say, settling." She smiled and put her hand on my shoulder. "You can do so much better than a rough Highlander."

"You want me to go on some blind dates?" I tried to shrug off the hand that suddenly gripped me hard. Impossible. "Seriously?"

"Yes, I am very serious. Give up this nonsense about staying on the earthly plane. You can find an acceptable mate and come live with me. There are fantastic opportunities for an intelligent woman with ambition on Olympus. If you are half the daughter I think you can become, we will rule there together before we are done. You can't imagine the power we would wield." Her smile this time was so fierce I shuddered.

"Mother, please, reconsider. I know how O-town works after dealing with the Storm God. It's all about politics. Are you sure there's not a spy listening right now? You don't want to make Zeus mad at you. And talk of a takeover . . ."

"Hush. You're right. I knew you were smart." She stroked my hair and it was all I could do not to shudder. "Enough talk. I will begin sending you likely candidates for a mate immediately. You must promise to have an open mind. Give each of them a chance to court you. Choose one to be your consort and we will go from there."

"And if none of them please me? I don't see you hooked up with a daddy dearest, do I?" I sighed when she finally released me. The wall held me up but I was close to sliding down it, a heap on the wet bricks, my legs rubber at the thought of anyone from Olympus "courting" me.

"I've never met a soul mate, as you call your Jeremiah. I have made a formal alliance of course. But no love match. So

much of what we do in Olympus is for political purposes."
She stepped back, her forehead wrinkling.

"Sounds like a swell place." I could almost feel sorry for
her. Too bad she'd started our relationship so cruelly.

"All I'm asking is that you try, Gloriana. For the sake of
my plan." She wasn't looking for sympathy, just my coop-
eration.

"And if I don't click with any of these guys? Will you
still fix Jerry's memories?" I pushed away from the wall.
Time to toughen up and negotiate. "No promises. But I *will*
keep an open mind. Who knows? Maybe I'll fall for one of
your god-lings. But I need some guarantees from you before
I start this date-a-thon."

"You aren't calling the shots here, Gloriana. I am." She
slung her leather bag over her shoulder. "Know this. If you
play along, give the men a fair hearing, then I'll consider
your request to 'fix' your lover. I don't offer guarantees.
Sometimes these things aren't as simple as they seem."

"What do you mean? Isn't your spell the only thing
keeping Jerry from remembering me?" I stepped toward her
but she began fading out. "Mother! What the hell?"

She examined her pearl pink fingernails. "All will be re-
vealed in good time, Gloriana. Cooperate. That's your best
play here."

"Send them on then. Let's get this over with." I looked
her over. "Can you fix me up with an outfit like that? You
ruined my blouse. What good is being a goddess if you can't
show off a trick or two?"

She smiled and waved her hand. "Certainly. Thought
you'd never ask."

I looked down and now wore a fabulous designer wrap
dress in a blue silk that matched my eyes. My shoes were
another great brand and my coat had a faux fur collar that
felt soft next to my chin. Even my purse had morphed into
a designer clutch. I hoped she'd tucked my cell and passport
inside. A wad of English money wouldn't hurt my feelings
either.

"Thanks, Mom." I gushed a little before I remembered that I hated her. Damn my weakness for great clothes. "But this doesn't make up for what you've done. I'll never forgive you for hurting Jerry."

"Of course you will. Or I'll have to alter *your* memories." Her smile gave me chills. "Now, don't forget the blouse." She pointed to the bloodstained satin resting on top of the garbage bin. "Test it for DNA, I dare you. You will see that we are a match. You're mine, Gloriana. The Siren thing was necessary and I'm sorry for it. If I'd had any idea that Achelous was such an ass, I never would have put you under his power."

As an apology, I figured that was as good as I was going to get. But I couldn't bring myself to hug her, something she clearly wanted.

"I need to get to the doctor's office. You'll let me know when to expect the first of . . . How many guys do I have to meet?"

"Five, I think. That's a fair number. If none of them suit, then I'll do what I can to restore your Jeremiah's memory." And with a wave, she vanished.

What she can? I didn't like that. It meant she might not be able to fix him completely. With that worry nagging at me, I headed to the end of the alley and toward Bart's office.

I walked into chaos. Jerry held a chair over his head, obviously ready to smack his doctor with it. Caitlin was trying to talk him out of it without much success.

"Jerry? What's going on here?" He didn't spare me a glance, his eyes fixed on the hypodermic needle Bart held.

"He wants to stick me with that. Says it will make me feel better. The last time I was stuck with something, I lost my fuckin' mind."

"Relax, man. I don't want to make you lose anything. You're overwrought. This is a tranquilizer. I was hoping it would help you relax enough to let me hypnotize you. Then we might get to some of those memories you've lost." Bart laid the needle on the metal cart next to him. "See? I'm putting this away. Obviously not your thing. We'll try something else."

Jerry still wasn't giving up on the chair-in-Bart's-face plan, though I could see his arms quivering with the effort to hold it over his head. Where had his strength gone? And so quickly? It hadn't even been a week since the attack and he'd been feeding steadily. A vampire *healed*, damn it.

"Come now, Jeremiah." Cait reached up and snagged a chair leg. "See reason. Bart here's a doctor. A family friend, Da says. We have to trust him."

"Maybe you do, I don't." But Jerry gave her the chair then collapsed on it once she'd set it on the floor. "Shit, I'm weak. What the hell's wrong with me?"

Cait started to open her mouth, glanced at me, then closed it again.

"Maybe the poison is still in your system. What do you think, Bart?" I glanced at the doctor.

"I'd know more if he'd let me take a blood sample. But, as you can see, he's not going to let me stick a needle in him. Are you now, Jerry?" Bart waved toward the laden cart that had all sorts of medical equipment on it. "The MRI was an epic fail too. One look at the machine and he was all 'Hell, no' and would have no part of it."

"Jerry, how can Bart treat you if you won't cooperate?" I slid close to him, but knew he wouldn't welcome my touch.

"You want a blood sample?" Jerry jumped up and stalked over to the cart. There he picked up a scalpel and, like my mother, ran it across his palm. "Here. Help yourself." He held out his bleeding hand.

My nostrils flared and my fangs descended. I looked around the room to see Bart and Cait with the same reaction. It's a knee-jerk vampire thing.

"Jerry! That's not the way we do things now." I covered my mouth with my hand.

"If Bart wants my blood for his test, that's the way I'm

doing it. What do you say, Doc?" He shook his hand in Bart's face, drops of blood scattering on the table. That got Bart moving.

"Stop it! You're contaminating my sterile equipment. Hold still." He grabbed a swab, then some glass squares, obviously readying some samples for a microscope. Whatever.

I swayed toward Jerry, taking a trip down memory lane to the many times we'd exchanged blood. He'd loved to have me drink from him as he drove into me during sex. It had made our orgasms more than earthshaking. Oh, God. Would we ever feel that close again? When I came to my senses, Bart was wrapping Jerry's hand in gauze though I was sure the wound had probably already stopped bleeding on its own. Jerry looked pale as he sat down again.

"Why is he so weak, Bart? Hasn't he been feeding properly?" I edged closer.

"It's the poison, Gloriana." Jerry frowned at me. "What do you expect?"

"She's right to be concerned. You say you've had plenty of blood, most of it synthetic, since you were attacked, but look at you, barely able to stand. Healing sleep should have set you to rights by now." Bart shook his head and picked up the samples. "I want to get on this immediately. Analyze what's still in your system. I have the knife the laird gave me too."

"Good." Jerry leaned back in the chair. "You're right. I'm not recovering like I should and I need answers."

"Can I go with you? To your lab?" Cait was on his heels as Bart headed for a staircase. "I did a stint at the medical college here. It was one of my interests for a while. Till I decided it was more fun to play doctor than to be one."

"I'll keep that in mind." Bart grinned. "And I could use the help. Follow me. The lab is upstairs." He turned around, suddenly all business. "Jerry, you need real blood. Quit being a hard-ass and drink from Gloriana. I know she's offered and she *is* part of the past you can't remember. It really might be a key to unlocking your memory."

Jerry stared at me for a moment. "Doctor's orders?"

"Yes. Now go into my lounge and get comfortable. The tests will take a while." He gestured for Cait to precede him. "The playroom, er, lab is up the stairs, first door on your left."

"Jerry, do what he says. What if this is all you need to get your memories back? Don't let the stubborn Campbell pride screw you over, brother dear. And, don't worry, I'm not messing around." She gave Bart a firm look. "No playing until we figure out how to fix my brother's problem." With that, Cait ran up the stairs, stopping once to take off her ruined shoes. I heard Bart ask her what had happened to them. Cait tossed off a silly explanation that involved stomping out a trash fire in the alley.

"I guess I should give it a try." Jerry sounded like he had been sentenced to the hangman's noose.

"Gee, don't get all mushy now." I took off my coat, laying it next to my bloodstained blouse on a chair, before I strolled into what Bart had called his lounge. It was an elegant waiting room for his clientele. A vampire doctor. I assumed he took care of paranormal patients, like Ian MacDonald did in Austin. We were immortal but that didn't mean we couldn't have the occasional medical problem.

It was Ian who'd figured out I'd once been a Siren. He was also constantly working on special vampire drugs. I wondered if Bart was also into creating drugs. There was a lot I didn't know about Bartholomew O'Connor. I hoped the laird had checked him out thoroughly. Just because I'd liked Bart on sight didn't mean I should trust him. Hard experience had taught me my instincts weren't always reliable.

"Mushy?" Jerry looked puzzled as he followed me and settled on one end of a long moss green velvet sofa.

"It means 'romantic.' Fat chance of your being that. With me anyway." I sat on the opposite end of the couch then crossed my legs, letting my skirt slide open to show off my sheer black tights. I leaned back into the corner, pretending to be relaxed. Let him ask. Yeah. I was going to play this cool. He wanted my blood, well, he could beg for it.

I pushed forward a little, just to make sure he noticed my cleavage as my dress began to come unwrapped. Of course he noticed and licked his lips. He might be weak, but his male hormones were obviously still healthy.

"You talk strangely. Is that how Americans speak?" He was far from relaxed, his eyes darting from my cleavage to where the skirt kept inching up my legs to the wide-screen television set in the corner of the room. Ha! The cleavage was winning the eye candy contest.

"Not necessarily. It's how modern people talk. When you remember everything, you'll not think my speech strange at all." I bent over to straighten a throw pillow propped against the cushion between us. His eyebrows rose when the edge of my black lace bra slid into view.

"And do modern women all dress like strumpets?" He leaned forward himself, snagging my hand and pulling me closer.

"Excuse me? I'm not a whore, nor dressed like one. Modern, decent women only wish they owned a designer dress like this one." I slapped at his hand. "If you hope to taste my blood tonight, you'll watch your tongue." I jerked my hand free and shoved at him, hard. "I can't wait till you get your memory back. You'll be horrified that you treated me so." Oh, shit, here came the tears. "You love me, Jerry. You respect me. You, you would kill the man who didn't." I turned my face away so he wouldn't see how much he'd hurt me.

"Even after you slept with this other man?" He let some of his own hurt harden his voice.

"I can't keep apologizing!" I whirled around. It was the truth. "It's over. He knows it. I left him behind to come to you. What else can I do to prove you are the only man I want and need?"

"Come here." His voice had gone low, more of a growl than a whisper.

"Just like that." I sighed. "Really? I'm supposed to just shrug off your insults and crawl over to offer my vein?"

"If you mean what you say." He held out his hand. "You must have dressed like that to please me. To seduce me." He moved with vampire speed, suddenly wrapping his arm around my waist. "It's working. I'm still a man, even with a brain empty of thoughts that make any sense to me right now. I know lust when I feel it and you are a woman who stirs me." He pulled me across his lap. Oh, yeah, I'd stirred him all right.

"Jerry, this isn't going any further than my feeding you. I hope you know that." I laid my hand on his chest. He was so cool, much too cool to be healthy, vampire or not.

"You offered to come to my bed. Before." He leaned down to nuzzle my neck, his fangs scraping across my jugular.

"I know. That was probably the strumpet in me, wanting to be with you." I ran my fingers up to his thick hair and jerked a warning when he slid a thumb across my nipple. "I've had second thoughts. That wouldn't be right if you truly don't remember me, us. I'm not going to let you use me like a cheap hooker. That's what we call whores these days. If you're interested in updating your vocabulary."

"Forget words. Kiss me again. I like your kisses. Very much." He took my mouth, making *me* remember that I liked his kisses way more than I should if I was a stranger to him.

But it was that connection that I loved, that taste, that sweet, sweet meeting of our lips and tongues that pressed me against him, craving more. I finally pulled back, though. I was here to give him blood. Period. Until he got his memories back, I had to resist his pull.

"Drink from me, Jeremiah. Heal. This is strictly business between us. You think I'm a strumpet? Perhaps I should ask you to pay for it."

He gave me a considering look. "No, you offered, I accept. Even confused as I am, I have a feeling that if I put money between us, you'd run out of here leaving me thirsty."

I fought a smile. About time he got a clue. I didn't say a word, just pulled his mouth to my neck and felt the pierce of his fangs. He drew deep, taking me. No, taking my *blood*. But it still brought me close to a shuddering orgasm. Silly me. To feel so much when this meant nothing to him. But I couldn't help it. His smell surrounded me. I ran my hands over his strong shoulders and remembered all the times this had meant everything to him and to me. Jeremiah Campbell. My friend and lover. I closed my eyes and drifted.

He held my bottom firmly, stroking it almost idly as he drank. It was so familiar that I let myself hope . . . No, he'd hold any woman who allowed him to drink from her vein just this way. I sighed, my arms around him, my cheek against his, rough with an early evening beard. My love. If only this were real. If only he would finish, look up and remember . . .

"It's the damnedest thing." Bart strode into the room, stopping quickly when he realized Jerry and I sat on opposite ends of the sofa, not speaking. "What happened?"

"Nothing. Or nothing much." I nodded toward Jerry. "Tell him."

"I drank her blood. It gave me strength but no memories. She's mad at me because I said some things I guess I shouldn't have." Jerry shrugged. "Finish what you were going to say. Caitie?" His sister had come into the room and stood next to Bart. "What did you two see in my blood?"

"Nothing. That is, it's clear. Whatever poison entered your bloodstream is gone. We checked the knife and the substance that was on it has disappeared. Your blood is now just simple Campbell blood, similar to mine. I gave Bart a sample for comparison." Cait sighed and sat beside Jerry. "There's really no sign of a contaminant, poison or anything left in your blood to account for your memory loss, Jer. I'm so sorry."

"What does this mean?" Jerry looked from Cait to Bart, then to me.

"That you've got a traumatic form of amnesia." Bart pulled up a chair and sat across from Jerry. "Sorry, but that's like a mental block."

"Block? What the hell?" Jerry shook his head.

"You suffered a trauma." Bart glanced at me and I wondered if Cait had told him about my mother. Blocks. Yep. Vamps happily blocked their thoughts when they didn't want anyone to know what they were thinking. But to block memories? Well, we constantly erased mortals' memories to keep our existence a secret. Obviously my mum had done a number on Jerry. But could she undo the damage? *Would* she?

"You're speaking nonsense. What is a trauma?" Jerry jumped up and began to pace the room. "How did I get it?"

"It's an event, a bad thing that happened to you. You returned to the family home because something bad happened in America, right?" Bart was up now, keeping pace with Jerry as they walked the perimeter of the large room.

"So Gloriana says. But she claims it was a lover's quarrel. I'm a warrior. A bad thing to me is losing a battle. My horse being shot out from under me. I'd think those things would be a trauma to me, not crying about my unfaithful girlfriend."

Bart shot me a hard look. "You're probably right."

I refused to hang my head or pull a scarlet letter out of my new designer bag. Instead I cleared my throat. "Well, Jerry, you did take the news I gave you pretty hard. But the memory loss . . ." I shook my head. "Beats me why it's hanging around."

"Men don't usually think that way, Jerry. A woman lets us down? We move on. But being stabbed by a family friend would certainly be traumatic. The fact that what you've blocked out is only your time with Gloriana . . ." Bart glanced at me. "Well, it's suspicious."

"Thanks a heap. I'm sorry, but I didn't do this." I glared at Cait when I saw her start to say something. "Jerry, you need to let Bart hypnotize you. Maybe that will unlock your memories."

"He explained that craziness. But I won't be stuck with his needle." Jerry had a mulish look. "Maybe I don't need to remember those years. I rode in Bart's blasted machine here. I suppose I'll get used to these times. Eventually." He rubbed his forehead again. "If there just weren't so many holes in my head." He tried to laugh. "Shit. You know what I mean. Like how the castle got in such bad shape. This America you keep talking about. It's too blasted much!"

"You're right. It is too much to just forget. And there's no need for needles. I can hypnotize you after you've had some glasses of fine Scots' whiskey. That should relax you enough for me to get you under."

"Under? What will I be under?" Jerry looked around the room. "This all sounds like more witchcraft." He held out his hand to his sister. "Caitie, what do you think of this hypno-thing."

Cait rushed to take his hand. "It's worth a try. It won't hurt you. It can be very relaxing. I've done it myself." She smiled at Bart. "I had a fling with an associate of Freud's in Paris. I'll try almost anything once."

"Good to know." Bart walked to a crystal decanter and glasses sitting on a sideboard against the wall. "I know most vampires don't drink alcohol, but I've done experiments. This won't hurt you. It's smooth and should go down easily. Gloriana?"

"What the hell? My night can't get any worse." I sat in a chair after it became clear that Bart was going to persuade Jerry to lie back on the sofa. I held the glass of whiskey, sniffing it and wondering if I could really drink. My friend Israel Caine was a recovering alcoholic. I sure wasn't going to share Bart's discovery with him. I thought about mentioning that Ian had brought up some of the same theories and cures Bart had, but figured throwing in the name Mac-Donald now would put Jerry off the whole thing.

Jerry tossed back his first glass with a sigh then held out the empty for a refill. Before long he was stretched out, his boots off so he didn't soil the fine velvet.

I sipped the drink. It burned going down but I enjoyed the idea of getting falling down drunk. Not yet. Not when there was a chance Jerry might wake up and know me. Really know me.

"What do I have to do?" Jerry had his head propped up against the throw pillow as he sipped the drink. He smiled. "Fine Scots whiskey. Damned if this isn't a treat. Don't know when I drank last. Guess I just thought I should stick to blood after I was turned."

"We all did. But my family is in the distillery business. I was determined to see if we could still at least check the product." Bart smiled as he filled Jerry's glass again. "To my surprise, as long as we aim for high quality and moderation, this won't hurt us. Of course you are not back to normal so I'll watch you carefully in case your reaction isn't right."

"Bart! Maybe you shouldn't have started this now." Cait looked alarmed.

"Relax, Caitie. I feel fine. Better than fine." Jerry had a lopsided grin. "I'm relaxed for the first time since Mara attacked me, truth be told. Now what?" He held out his empty glass once more.

"I think you've had enough." Bart took the glass and set it aside. "Now you're going to watch me, Jerry. Follow my directions. I will tell you to do some simple things, look at my watch, count, stuff like that. It will help you relax and open your mind. Hopefully you'll remember the past years. Ready?"

Jerry wiggled his toes in dark socks then nodded. "Go ahead. I want to remember. This empty feeling is making me crazed. This woman." He stared at me. "Gloriana. She seems to be someone I know." He held up a hand when I started to protest. "I know. I know. You *are* someone I know." He looked back at Bart. "Anyway I kissed her. Just now. Held her. Drank her blood. Sweet. Tasted, hmm, really good. And, for a minute, I thought . . . But I couldn't hold on to it." He rubbed his forehead. "Hurts when I try."

"Okay. That's progress." Bart pulled out an old-fashioned

gold pocket watch. "Stare at this as it swings back and forth, back and forth. Don't take your eyes off of it. Watch how slowly it swings. Back and forth. Back and forth. Your eyes are getting heavy. You're getting sleepy. Start counting for me, Jeremiah. Back from twenty. Are you ready?"

Jerry nodded, his eyes starting to close until he blinked them open.

"Here we go. Twenty, nineteen, eighteen . . ." Bart continued until Jerry's voice trailed off at twelve.

"All right. Now you are totally relaxed. Take me back to the last thing you remember before you were stabbed. Describe the scene."

"I was riding Thunder. He was restless. Had a hard time keeping him under control. I finally let him have a good run." Jerry kept talking about his horse. A fence that was down and some sheep missing. At one point he got excited. A MacDonald had crossed his path and they'd exchanged words. He was sure the man had taken the sheep but he didn't have proof. He rode back to the castle, where he and Da planned a raid to get the sheep back.

"Do you remember going to London, Jeremiah?" Bart glanced at me. "Remember meeting a woman with blond hair?"

"London? What business would I have there?" Jerry frowned. "My brother Thomas and I are headed up to Edinburgh to see a play after we take care of the MacDonalds. Plenty of women and sport there. London is too far away."

Cait made a sound and I noticed she was crying.

"What is it?" I hadn't heard anything that upset me so far except that I wasn't in Jerry's mind.

"Thomas. He's our brother who was killed on that raid to the MacDonalds' holding. After that Jerry hied off to London. He never admitted it, but he took Tommy's death hard, blamed himself for it. We never did prove that those sheep came from our lands."

"Can you go forward, Jeremiah? Do you remember living in America?" Bart reached over and squeezed Cait's hand.

"America? Who?" Jerry's hands began to shake and he pressed them to his temples. "The pain! Make it stop!"

"Never mind. I'm going to count to three. When I clap my hands, you will wake up, refreshed, and the pain will be gone. All you'll remember is that you had a nap and a fine drink." Bart counted then clapped his hands.

Jerry opened his eyes. "Well, that helped me feel better. Did I remember anything?" He frowned at his sister. "Caitie, why are you upset?"

"You didn't remember, Jerry. I just wished this had worked, that's all." She wiped at her cheeks. "I guess we'll have to give you more time."

"Yes, we've been rushing this." Bart helped Cait stand up. Jerry was already on his feet.

"Time? While I'm going mad?" He stomped into his boots, then sat to get them on properly. "Surely there's something we can do."

"Drugs. But you don't like needles. And there's only one doctor I know of who has done serious work on posttraumatic amnesia with vampires." Bart put his arm around Cait. "You're not going to like who it is."

"Why not?" She looked up at him. "Spit it out. Who is it, Bart?"

"Ever hear of Ian MacDonald?"

Six

The ride back to the Campbell town house wasn't exactly a fun time for all. After refusing to have anything to do with a MacDonald, doctor or not, Jerry was trying to be the stoic warrior. Cait had strapped him into the seat belt which he'd endured with only a few choice words for the way she'd made it too tight, then she'd announced she was going to catch a ride later with Bart after she discussed Jerry's case with him. That left me in the driver's seat. You can imagine what Jer thought about that.

"Are you sure you know how to run this machine?" he finally asked after I'd bumped the post for the fourth time.

How the hell had Cait gotten this car into the tiny parking space? I wasn't all that current on shifting gears either and the car kept groaning objections and dying.

"I've got this, give me a minute." I tapped the car in front of us and its alarm went off. Fantastic. I backed up quickly, made a hard turn then managed to get us out of there before an angry car owner came out to check on his Bentley. Yes, this was an expensive neighborhood. As far as I could tell, I hadn't done more than dust his bumper.

"There. We're on our way." I made a grinding shift into

second and hit the gas. "You all right?" A glance showed me he really wasn't. If his brain had been in this century, he would have been livid about how I made his Jag suffer through my gear shifting.

"What happened to all the horses?" He held on to the strap that dangled by the window, his other hand braced on the dashboard when I made a turn.

"People still enjoy horses. As a hobby." I stopped for a red light, the car died, and started rolling downhill. Edinburgh is all hills. Not exactly where I'd have chosen to relearn standard transmissions. Damn. I put both feet on the brake while I waited for the light to change before I started the engine again. "There are still race courses and events where people show off their horsemanship. But horses aren't used for transportation anymore." Green light. I got us going again, barely. It took a minute or two and the car behind me blasted his horn when I almost rolled back into his front bumper.

"What's that noise?" Jerry grimaced, his head obviously still hurting.

"An ass who wants me to go faster." I sped up. "You're still having headaches. Maybe that means you're trying to remember."

"Of course I'm trying to remember!" he shouted, his hand inadvertently bumping the gear shift during one of my wide corner turns. "Damn it, Gloriana. Slow this monster down."

"Sorry." I pulled over and stopped to study his pale face. He'd looked almost ruddy right after he'd fed. Now he was fading again. So soon. "Really sorry. I know this is hell. I can't even imagine it. Well, I sort of have a clue. A guy I knew once made me forget we were ever together. Seems he just erased a year of my life." I shook my head. "But that's not nearly the same."

"Another man? How many have there been when we were supposed to be in love for centuries?" He leaned back against the glass. "Fill in some of the blanks in my memory, Gloriana. This relationship we had. How was it?"

"We took breaks from time to time, Jerry. You would see other women. I would see other men." I looked out at the dark street, remembering. It beat me if I could understand now why I'd been so dead set on my independence. Surely we could have worked out a compromise without going our separate ways.

"That doesn't sound like love to me. What happened to being faithful? Vows?" He bumped his knees against the dash. "I have to get out of this thing. How far are we from the town house? This area looks familiar. It must not have changed that much since . . . You know."

"No, it hasn't changed in centuries. The Campbell town house is just up that hill." And the hill wasn't doing me any favors again. My legs ached with the effort to keep from coasting back when I needed to go forward. "Go ahead. Get out. And this 'thing' is your luxury vehicle that costs more than my shop makes in profit in a year." The car died again and I pulled up the emergency brake. I opened his seat belt and he reacted like he'd been released from a straightjacket.

"There. Now you can walk. I'll drive and meet you there. You'll recognize the place. The old stone buildings are historic, preserved exactly as they were back in the day." I knew I had to give him some space but hated to see him distance himself again. He fumbled with the door latch and succeeded in making the window go up and down a few times before finally managing to open the door.

"They were built to last. I guess Da put more effort into keeping the town house in shape than he did the castle since we're staying there." It wasn't a question. Jerry climbed out, slammed the car door and strode away.

I started the car again, tried not to strip the gears and drove on up the hill, keeping an eye on Jerry in my rearview mirror. When I pulled up in front of the door, a servant came out to greet me and put the car in the garage. I just stood there, waiting.

"A letter came for you, Ms. St. Clair." The servant handed me a thick envelope then got in and drove the car around to the back.

I turned the envelope over and saw a strange seal impressed into red wax. It was right out of an ancient playbook. Olympus? I broke the seal and pulled out an engraved invitation.

"The pleasure of your company is requested at nine o'clock tomorrow night. A car has been arranged to collect you. Semi-formal attire."

I couldn't believe it. My mother certainly worked fast. Couldn't her guy have at least given his name? I really, really wanted to decline this "invitation." Ha. It was more like a command performance. There was no place to RSVP. If I was a no-show, I was sure there would be consequences. To Jerry. Who would stab him this time? Or would she go straight for the lightning bolts?

He walked up just then, his face tight with pain.

"At least it looks the same. But I'm sure it will be filled with all manner of things that I don't understand." He followed me inside. "Bart tried to explain some of them on the ride to Edinburgh. Televisions. Telephones. Airplanes. No wonder my head aches. There is too much to try to understand."

"You're right. You should probably just go to bed. Rest."

"I feel like less than a man, Gloriana." He stopped with his hand on the newel post. "Bloody hell. I *am* less than one if I would tell a woman such a thing."

"No, it's all right. I'm glad you can share your feelings with me." I slipped my hands around his waist and looked up at him. "You're all man. My man. I just wish you could remember that. You've been my rock. Everything to me. You've saved me from so many horrible things, Jerry." I kissed his lips, thrilled when he just took it, didn't shrug away.

"You have always been a warrior. It's why we had to take breaks from time to time. I . . . I just didn't have it in me to be a meek woman who let a man take charge." I leaned my head against his chest. "I felt like I'd lose myself if I let you always take care of me."

"That's nonsense. I don't think I'd like a weak woman. Hate sniveling creatures afraid of their own shadows. I remember that much." He actually brushed his hand over my hair. "I'm glad to hear that I wasn't worthless. Not a brute either, I hope. Though lately I've been so bloody angry. Not sure I can keep my temper in check once I lose it. It's a bad feeling."

"You'd never lay a hand on me." I leaned back and made sure he knew I meant this, from my heart. "You were protective, possessive but not obsessive. It's taken me a long time to realize the difference. It's one of the reasons I came crawling across an ocean to see you."

"Crawling across an ocean? You really do talk strangely, woman." He smiled and leaned his cheek against my hair. "I am so damned tired of not knowing. Not knowing who I am. Where the hell I am. Who we are to each other."

"It's okay, Jerry. Start over. Pretend we just met." I stepped back and put out my hand. "I'm Gloriana St. Clair. I run a vintage clothing shop in Austin, Texas, in America. I love shopping and hate doing the books, though I can balance my checkbook."

"Jeremiah Campbell, lately from Castle Campbell in the Highlands of Scotland. I can sit a horse and, when the bagpipes call me, can dance with a sword if given enough whiskey."

"Really? I've never seen you dance, Jer."

"I guess you've never seen me drink enough whiskey then, lass." He grinned and picked up my hand. "Now I'll take one of your kisses before I go to bed. I know I've still got an hour or more before dawn but this damned head won't quit aching."

"I understand." I moved in and put my arms around his

neck, happier than I'd been since he'd greeted me at my car when I'd first arrived. A fresh start. If I could just win his heart again . . . I'd done it once. Who was to say I couldn't do it again? I slid a fingertip around one of his ears and up into his thick curls. "A kiss. I think I can spare one."

He leaned down and met my lips with his, pulling me in until I felt his body hard against me. My undead heart pounded and I wanted to pull up his shirt so I could feel his skin, dip my hand inside his jeans to tease his stomach and lower, where I felt him stir. No, we were going to get to know each other and it should be slowly. He tasted of the whiskey he'd had earlier and I quite liked it. I hummed my pleasure and tightened my grip on his hair.

He pulled back, his cheeks flushed for the first time in hours. "Gloriana. I wish I could remember. Please believe that."

"I know you're trying." I ran my hand over his rough cheek, my stomach turning with the knowledge that, even with the poison out of his system, he still couldn't or wouldn't recall me. "Relax and let this happen in its own time. I believe in us and that we are meant to be."

He leaned down and kissed me again. This time I felt his urgency, like he was trying to push a memory out of his muddled brain. Finally he gave up and put me from him. "Good night, Gloriana."

I stood there at the bottom of the stairs, my hand on my swollen lips. "Good night, Jeremiah." Close. It had felt close that time. Or was I inventing something that only existed in *my* mind?

"The servants said you got a package. From an expensive boutique." Caitlin set it on the coffee table in front of me. "What's up, Glory? Why haven't you opened it?"

I'd been avoiding Jerry's sister since sunset. She'd probably have a million questions about my "mother." I'd left my stained blouse at Bart's with a note, asking him to test it for a match to my DNA. Using one of the doctor's scalpels, I'd smeared my own blood on the other side of the blouse. Bart could toss the blouse when he was done with it. Hopefully the doctor wouldn't ask questions about the test. Yeah, right.

"It's probably a gift from my mother. I really don't want to be obligated. But, then again, maybe she owes me. I didn't exactly have a happy childhood. Not that I can remember it. Seems amnesia is an Olympus favorite." I ripped open the package and pulled out a gorgeous red dress, the kind I'd always dreamed of having. I couldn't believe it even came in my size. But a quick check in the neckline assured me it did. The red silk was soft and cut to show off my curves without hugging them too tightly. The note inside was brief: "Wear this tonight." No need to sign it. Of course my mother had sent it. So what? I wasn't about to turn down something so expensive or so beautiful.

"Wow. Tonight? What's happening tonight?" Of course Cait had read the note over my shoulder.

"I have to go out. Family obligation. To get my mother off my back. You didn't tell anyone about her, did you, Cait?" I shut the box.

"Tell anyone about who?" Jerry stood in the doorway, Bart by his side.

"Tell them, Glory." Cait grabbed my hand. "I don't feel right keeping this from either one of them. And Bart showed me the blouse you left there. I helped him run the DNA tests. They were a match. The bitch is your mother, there's no denying it."

"Mother? Gloriana, what is this about? Have I forgotten you have a mother still around?" Jerry walked over to sit in a chair across from me. "What is DNA?"

"You didn't forget her. This is a new development. Not a good one either. As for DNA, it's something in our blood. Bart could probably explain it in scientific terms but I doubt we'd understand a word of it." I smiled at the doctor. "Anyway, nowadays we can do a blood test to prove if someone is related to us or not. This woman appeared recently and has been claiming to be my mother. Last night she gave me a blood sample. I asked Bart to run the test to check out her story." I glanced at Bart.

"She's your mother all right. Or a very close relative. No doubt about it. The markers were all there." He smiled. "Cait's a witness. Must say the blood is interesting. Not like any I've examined before. I'm glad to have a sample. Bet her powers are off the charts."

"No kidding. She's the one who fried my favorite pair of shoes." Cait shook her head. "You really don't want to run into her in a dark alley. Right, Glory?"

"She's a certified bitch." I glanced upward. I was taking a chance, talking smack about her; she could be tuned in right now. Hopefully not. Maybe she was still trying to co-erce one of the Olympus single guys into showing up to-night for this blind date. Why would any of them be willing? With a vampire? Even with my goddess connec-tions I wasn't exactly in their league. Look at the dress she'd sent me, four sizes bigger than what she wore, no doubt about it.

"Tell them the worst, Glory. It might help Bart with Jerry's cure." Cait got up to stand beside the doctor. I could see that they were developing a relationship. Their body language screamed hot chemistry.

I glared at her. There was no way spilling beans about my mother's reason for poisoning Jerry would help anyone, and it was bound to ruin my tenuous start with my man.

"Spit it out, Gloriana. What is the worst?" Jerry leaned forward. "Is your mother involved in this somehow?"

Jerry might have memory issues, but he was still sharp when it came to making connections.

"Um, I had no idea who she was, if I even had a mother, until after you were stabbed, Jer. Then she showed up on the castle grounds to let me know she had played the witch and spelled Mara."

"Really?" He leaned back. "I wondered . . . I know you

think I gave Mara a pass on that stabbing, but I had my doubts. She did wield the knife."

I stared at him. He had actually sounded like modern Jerry for a minute there. Maybe things were coming back to him.

"My, uh, mother was the one who put something on the knife to make you lose your memory. She was punishing you for making me vampire. Apparently a daughter who drinks blood is disgusting in her world. She wanted you to forget me and move on."

"It worked." Jerry's fists clenched and unclenched. He was getting upset and I didn't blame him. With me? Again, understandable.

"But I don't know, now that the poison is out of your system, why your memory hasn't come back. I can't get an answer from her about it either." I glanced at Bart. The doctor was riveted. "Believe me, I've begged her to fix you, Jer. But she's not in any hurry to make you whole. In fact . . ." I was almost afraid to put this theory out there, but it was in line with what Bart had said. "My mother's having me jump through some hoops, dangling the hope that she can make things right. But I don't know. I got the feeling that since Bart's tests proved your blood is clean now, that maybe she's bluffing. That you *could* remember, if you *would* remember."

"What the hell does that mean?" Jerry was on his feet, his face like stone. He was furious. "You think I don't want my mind back?"

"No, I get it. It's involuntary. You can't help yourself." I stood and walked around the coffee table. The box on it reminded me. If my mother did have the means to cure Jerry, I had a date to go on. "And I'm doing everything I can to get my mother to fix you. She claims she's got another trick up her sleeve. Maybe I'm wrong but I'm beginning to doubt it. Bart suggested . . ." I looked to the doctor for support.

"She's right, Jerry. All the signs point to posttraumatic amnesia. There are a few things that can break you out of it, like the hypnotism we already tried. But time might be all you need. Unless Glory's mother has a magic potion of some sort." Bart stepped close to Jerry and offered a smile. "I'm not ready to give up on you and do we really want to rely on some wacked out nut job to come up with a cure?"

I nodded. He'd described my mother to a tee. I hope she'd heard him in Olympus. Maybe it would bring her to her senses. What she'd done was crazy, no getting around it.

"Thanks, Bart. But time? Screw that. I can't spend years like this." He shoved Bart aside and stormed from the room.

"I'll go after him. He shouldn't be alone right now." Cait glanced at me apologetically. "You had to tell them, Glory. You get it, don't you?"

"Yes, you're right. It all needed to come out. Especially since I have to get ready to leave in about half an hour." I picked up the box. If there was the slightest chance my mother could really help Jerry, I'd date Zeus's dog and kiss him on the lips.

"Tell me about your mother. Maybe *we* can figure out how to cure Jerry if I can understand where she's coming from." Bart blocked my exit from the room.

I filled him in on the whole Olympus thing while he took notes.

"What kinds of things have you seen her do?" Bart had a page full of notes.

"Well, she's big on lightning strikes and thunder. That's popular on Olympus. She fried Cait's shoes. She can freeze you in place so you can't move a muscle, but then I can do that too. It's a cool trick. Very handy when you're in a tough spot. She can read through paranormal blocks. You know, read your mind when you think everyone's locked out? I inherited that one too." I smiled. "So watch it around me." His eyes narrowed. "Don't worry, I only intrude in an emergency."

"Interesting. I'll be thinking about this. Can you shoot lightning too?" He wrote something down.

"I wish. There have been many times when I'd like to have fried a few people, her especially, though I know she'd have been way out of my league. The woman has mad skills." I sighed. "Good luck, Bart. I've got to go. If you talk to Ian MacDonald, to consult on this case, let's keep this about my mother between you and me. As you've noticed, the Campbells are really uptight about the Macs. Too much historically bad blood, and to Jerry history was like yesterday."

"I get it." Bart grinned. "But Ian is a great source for ideas. I gather you've had dealings with him."

"More than I'd like. He's not to be trusted. And that's learned on my own, no prejudice involved. He's played some dirty tricks on me and I'd be skeptical about whatever he suggests to do with Jerry." I sighed. The clock was ticking. "Now I've got to go get ready. I have to make this date, and a dress like this one demands serious makeup and effort on my part. Plus I have no doubt my mother will be eavesdropping to make sure I play fair."

"Sorry about that." He patted my shoulder. "Must have been quite a shock, finding out who she was."

"In more ways than one. Imagine sticking your finger into a power outlet while your feet are in water." I sighed. "But it's what I've got, so I'll deal." I paused in the doorway. "Be nice to Cait, she's a good friend."

"No worries there. I know a woman who deserves better when I meet one." He suddenly sniffed the air. "And here she comes. See you later. Maybe."

I headed up the stairs, brushing past Cait who barely noticed, her eyes locked on Bart. I was glad for her. She'd had some seriously messed up relationships in her past and Bart looked to be a good guy. Finally.

"Where are you going?" Jerry caught me as I was about to get into the limo.

"Out." I had almost made a clean getaway. Now he was eyeing me in the dress that was almost the right size but a little skimpy in the bodice. Yes, I'd gotten it zipped but the neckline was probably not intended to expose quite so much bosom. Jerry certainly noticed the landscape.

"Looking like that? Are you meeting someone?" He dragged his eyes away from my cleavage to where a uniformed driver held the back door open for me. The limo was a vintage Rolls-Royce. Nice.

"Yes. It's business. I won't be late." I slipped into the backseat, careful of my skirt, which was ballerina length. I loved the way the chiffon flowed around me. I didn't love the way Jerry grabbed the door before the driver could close it.

"Business? What kind of business? You say you own a little shop in this new world. Yet you look like a woman on her way to a seduction. Are you meeting a man, Gloriana? Was all that talk about our starting over just so much blather?"

"Please just let me go, Jer. I can't deal with this right now. I'm not out to seduce anyone. Trust me on that." I blocked my thoughts but could read Jerry's clearly. He *didn't* trust me and wasn't sure what to think. My dress was too bold for a lady to wear in public. At least to a man who still hadn't figured out what was acceptable in this new time.

"Deal with what? You think I'm jealous? Should I be? Can't I ask a simple question and get a simple answer? Obviously not. Off with you then." He backed away, slamming the car door himself before the driver could do it. I saw him cross his arms over his chest and just stand there as the man climbed into the front and drove us away.

I didn't care where we were going and didn't pay attention to the direction we went as I relived that very frustrating conversation. Of course Jerry thought the worst. I would have jumped to the same conclusions if I'd seen him drive off looking his best and he'd refused to tell me where he was headed. And I did look my best. My mother knew her stuff and I felt pretty darn good from head to toe in my expensive outfit that had included lacy underwear, even shoes. I wished I could have worn it for Jerry and been able to plan an evening with him. Dressed for a seduction? If only.

All too soon we pulled up in front of an elegant town house in a classy part of town. It might even have been near Bart's offices. I really should have noticed where we'd gone. What if I wanted to leave early? Could I even find my way back to Jerry's? Probably not. Stupid on my part but it was too late for regrets. I let the chauffeur help me out of the car and entered the stately home where a servant took my clutch purse and escorted me to a sitting room. A fire blazed in a massive marble fireplace and I would have admired the beautiful antiques in other circumstances. As it was, my nerves had me pacing while I waited for what came next.

It didn't take long. The man who stood in the doorway seemed to just appear. At least he wore earthly clothes, very expensive ones, instead of a toga. His tuxedo was custom tailored to show off a buff body. He was tall and tanned, like maybe he surfed. That crazy thought made me want to laugh. A god from Olympus on a surfboard? Okay, now I was losing it. But his blond hair looked sun bleached and his light eyes glowed with the golden warmth of the sun itself. Actually, he was beautiful. Huh? I didn't throw that word around when it came to men, and preferred the battle-scarred toughness Jerry had.

But I found myself drawn to his side when the man smiled, his perfect white teeth gleaming. It took me a moment to realize this was all probably an illusion. But it was a dazzling show.

"Gloriana, what a pleasure to meet you." He took my hand in his. The warmth of his skin surged into me, even down to my toes, which were stuffed into new designer sandals—thanks, Mom.

"Hello. May I ask your name?" I couldn't keep from smiling. His charm was contagious and I couldn't stop myself from moving even closer, to feel more of his warmth.

"Apollo." He winked, like he expected me to gasp or something. Instead I wracked my brain. I should have read up on Greek mythology before I came but I did realize this was one of the biggies.

"Apollo? Aren't you the god of the . . . ?"

"Sun." Proud grin. "Your mother assured me you'd be hungry for a glimpse of my brilliance." No bashful boy here, obviously.

Now I got it. He was daylight, that elusive sunshine I never got to feel on my skin. No wonder I was drawn to him. My mother was nothing if not a clever bitch. "Since the sun isn't something I get to see on a daily basis and hasn't been for over four hundred years, I'd have to say you're a novelty." I couldn't seem to let go of his hand. Or look away. He was shining, glowing.

I had that tingling goose-bumpy feeling I got when watching a sunrise. Which I'd been lucky enough to do briefly not too long ago with the help of one of Ian MacDonald's drugs. But that was such a rare and costly deal that I doubted it would ever happen again.

"Not just a novelty, Gloriana." He pulled me into his arms and I have to admit I didn't resist, still under the whole sunlight spell. "Close your eyes and let me take you on a little journey. Give you a taste of what your life would be like if you came back with me to Olympus."

Nothing like going straight for the pitch. Was there a timer going somewhere? Whatever happened to dating, the getting-to-know-you stage? Maybe the gods and goddesses had their own playbooks. If Mr. Perfection here was willing to take me on, my mother must have offered him some sweet deal. Even dressed in the prettiest gown I'd ever owned I felt like a troll compared to his masculine gorgeousness.

"Uh." I couldn't manage to complete that brilliant thought because my eyes drifted closed and we were off, riding in a chariot of all things, across a blue, blue sky. My mythology was coming back to me and I had a feeling I knew where this was going. Sure enough, green fields, snow-topped mountains then crowded cities raced by below us. It was magical. Because all the while the heat of that glowing orb, the sun, caressed our faces and our bodies from above. I now wore a skimpy flowing sundress and my hair blew behind me in the warm breeze. He held me firmly around my waist and I felt completely safe as we careened across the sky.

I lifted my face to the sun, thrilled to actually know the heat of midday again. My breath hitched when I imagined a life where dawn wasn't the enemy. Apollo pressed closer and I knew that he would hold me by his side forever, day after day, as we made this brilliant sun-drenched journey, seeing places I'd never even imagined existed.

A turquoise ocean gleamed under us and we swooped down to land on a tiny island. While he rested his horses, we splashed in a cove. Then he led me to a feast laid out on an elegant tablecloth. I could eat! I devoured exotic fruits whose flavors burst inside my mouth. When the juices ran down my chin, Apollo laughed and kissed it clean, calling me delicious.

Then he carried me to pristine white sand where he made slow and elegant love to me. I sighed in his arms, more thrilled by the heat of the sun on my naked body than the weight of him as he touched me and whispered Greek love words in my ear. He consumed me, giving me physical pleasure until I cried out his name. But he couldn't touch my heart. That stayed cold despite the heat all around me.

When the sun started slipping toward the horizon, we ran to the chariot, hurrying to reach our home on Olympus. We were almost panicked but made it safely before night fell. Apollo hated the night and wasn't allowed to ride after sunset or something dire would happen to us both.

I gasped and pulled away, back to reality with a thud. "No! I would never see the night again?"

"I am a man who lives only for the daylight, Gloriana. Being with me means you would never have to endure the night again—the darkness, the strange creatures who stir then and prey on the weak. I don't know how you tolerated them." He brushed a warm hand down my cheek then teased my lips closed with a fingertip when I might have opened them, showing my fangs. I knew he would hate them. For a moment I was tempted to lean into his touch, savor that warmth, say yes to a life of sunshine with a man who hadn't once mentioned my imperfections. No.

"I don't just tolerate the darkness and those creatures. I'm one of them, Apollo. To me the night is beautiful. It's where I belong." I tried to push away but he wasn't ready to give up yet. Whatever prize my mother offered, it must have been a doozy. "You can't want me. I'm in love with someone else."

"You'll forget him. Your mother says he has already forgotten you." He trailed a fingertip along my collarbone, tracing the edge of my dress where it dipped between my breasts. "Come with me, Gloriana. You'll soon be unable to call him to mind yourself, once you have experienced the glories of Olympus. I can guarantee it. We have everything there a woman could want. *I* have everything a woman could want." His eyes darkened and he gave me a look I recognized. Oh. So Apollo liked a full-figured woman. Good to know.

"I'm sure you are wonderful. But you can't make me forget the man I love without Olympus trickery. Are you that desperate to please my mother?" I gasped when his eyes flashed golden sparks. Oops. He didn't like that "d" word.

"I please only myself." His voice was hard and his hands tightened on my shoulders until I winced. "However"—he seemed to remember that there was something he had to gain here because like a switch had been flipped, he was suddenly all smiles and warm golden light again—"I have been known to please my lovers until they are never again satisfied with anyone else." He slid his hands down to grasp my hands.

"Apollo." I tried to pull away.

"Relax, Gloriana. Think this through. Surely you could never regret leaving the darkness that man you claim to love made you a slave to so long ago. I can give you the sun." Apollo's smile was a brilliant flare of pure light. "Riding by my side will make you the envy of every other woman and many men in Olympus. I don't make this offer lightly."

I finally managed to put some distance between us. It was obvious to me that his endless journeys had made Apollo forget how to share his heart with a woman. He didn't seem to care what *I* wanted but was determined to pull me into his world, to make me into what he needed me to be. An accessory. And a means to an end. Whatever he and my mother had going, he wanted to win here.

"I'm honored by your offer. Truly. I don't know what kind of favors or rewards my mother promised you if you could get me to come with you, but this isn't going to happen. As much as I'd like to see some daylight, thanks, but no thanks." I ran out of the room and grabbed my purse from a table in the hall.

Outside, I looked up at the night sky. A three-quarter moon gleamed overhead surrounded by glittering stars. I had learned to love the night and couldn't imagine a life without its beauty. My mother had played the wrong card tonight. I turned when I heard footsteps approach down the brick sidewalk.

"You turned down Apollo?" My mother clearly wasn't happy. Lightning lit up the sky and thunder shook the bricks under my feet.

"He wasn't my type. Too self-involved." I started walking. I didn't have a clue if it was toward Jerry's or not. I just wanted to get away from my mother.

"He's highly placed, very highly placed. I thought you'd jump at the chance to see the sun after centuries—"

"You thought?" I whirled to face her. "What do you know about me? You figured a vampire would be keen to see the sun. Any vampire. But I'm not just any vampire. I'm your so-called daughter. It would be nice if you'd try to understand what I really want. That's Jeremiah Campbell. Not some self-important god from on high. Get it?"

"*You* need to get it, Gloriana. Being a vampire was a tragic accident for you." She laid her hand on my arm and I felt the power surge down to my fingertips. It was like being hooked up to a Taser. If she burned out the soles of my pretty new shoes, I was going to be pissed. She must have read my mind because she let me go.

"Thank you. I admit you have excellent taste. Love the dress, the shoes, even the underwear. Do not love the man. Now will you give up on this and give Jerry back his memory?" I reached out this time, touching her lightly on her shoulder. As usual she looked perfect, this time in a blue designer evening gown that matched her eyes. Where was she going? To a fancy dress ball? No matter, she looked beautiful and I wished I had her tiny waist and flair for wearing clothes.

"Compliments are nice but have no sway with me, Gloriana. You want a tiny waist? On Olympus I will make it so." She gave me an assessing stare, waiting.

"Not worth it, Mother. Even Apollo didn't mind my generous figure. Maybe the guys get bored up there with all the females the same size." I smirked, loving the idea.

My mother shook her head. "I suppose it's possible. I'm sorry Apollo didn't suit. I was sure . . . No matter. I have four more tries. Brace yourself. There are more arrows in my quiver and I will loose the next one tomorrow night." Mother smiled and covered my hand with hers. "If nothing else, you will get a nice wardrobe out of this. And I saw that you were tempted with the Sun God. I was glad to see that you have an open mind."

Now, that left me speechless. Had I been? Tempted? Maybe for a minute. Not by the man, of course. But offering daylight had been major. I didn't like to think that I could have been so easily led off course. I loved Jerry. I wanted him well. And to stay here with him. End of story.

My mother smiled and sent a lightning bolt sizzling down to raise my hair and make it fly around my head. "No, your story is not ended, Gloriana. Not even close. The best is yet to come. Apollo was my opening salvo. You will love man number two. Just wait and see." And with that she disappeared.

Seven

"**We're** going back to the castle, Glory." Cait kept glancing at Jerry, who paced restlessly next to the front door. "My brother wants to get on a horse again and we can't do it here. You're welcome to come with us or stay here."

"What do *you* want me to do, Jerry?" I had received another invitation, hand delivered just a few moments ago. My mother wasn't wasting time. I was expected to meet her second candidate in a few hours.

"I don't know. Right now I need fresh air, to get away from all these blasted machines and Caitie's doctor friend." He glared at his sister.

"Bart's coming with us, Jeremiah. He should be pulling up any minute. He needs to keep working with you. If Glory's mother isn't going to cooperate, then hypnotism is still your best hope for regaining some memories. I don't want to hear another word about it." Cait looked from him to me. "Do you want Gloriana with you or not?"

"If she's willing, she can come. Though in a way this is her fault." He shook his head and finally looked at me directly. Maybe he could tell I was trying not to sway him but was desperately hoping he'd let me stay close.

"Jeremiah Campbell. That's not fair and you know it!" Cait stepped to my side.

"Blame it on my blasted headache." Jerry walked up to me and grabbed my hand. "I'm sorry, Gloriana. Don't you think I realize this is your mother's doing? Caitie and I know all about interfering mothers. Our own mother has spent her life doing everything she can to make our lives a misery. Right, Caitie?"

"And you don't remember most of it." His sister kissed Jerry's cheek. "I'm sorry you are still hurting."

"'Tis no worse than a blow on the head with a rock. It'll pass." He still held my hand, almost absentmindedly.

"Will you let me come back to the castle then?" I had to clear my throat to get the words out.

He released my hand then jerked the front door open. "Do what you wish, Gloriana. I'll be outside. I feel strong enough to fly home and I know the way. Bart can make himself useful, fly with me in case I weaken." He scowled. "Damn but I'm sick of not knowing my own strength." With that he slammed the heavy door.

"Oh, Cait, I hate to see him this way." I sank down on the living room couch. It was comfortable, not like the stiff formal pieces they'd had back when Jerry had first brought me here. I'm sure he'd been shocked to see the new decorations in the old home. One shock after another. I didn't blame him for being out of sorts.

"We all hate it. If you come with us, you'll have to face my mother's wrath. She won't cut you any slack in this. Once she finds out you were indirectly responsible, all hell will break loose." Cait sat beside me. "I can't protect you. Mag scares me shitless."

I sighed. "I know how you feel. My own mother is terrifying. But we do seem to stand up to them. As much as we can. You divorced the MacLaran boy and I know that just about gave Mag seizures."

Cait giggled. "Yes, indeed. But between his tightfistedness and his philandering, Mum finally saw things my way.

She won't speak to any of that clan to this day." She leaned back against the sofa cushions. "I can't believe Jerry's going to fly home. I hope he makes it." She turned when the front door creaked open. "Bart! Did my brother tell you his mad plan?"

"Yes. Did he feed properly this evening?" The doctor glanced at me.

"Not from me." I'd offered of course but he'd turned me down with a scowl. "He drank two bottles of synthetic. He's very moody." Yes, I'd call it that. Between his constant headaches and his frustrations with his memory loss, who could blame him?

"That should be enough. I'll be beside him, but keep your cell phone on, Cait. Drive my car and we'll be above you. I'll call if we have to land somewhere and need a pickup." He handed her his car keys. "You coming, Glory?"

"Not tonight. I have an, um, appointment." I stared down at my hands. "But I'd like to come tomorrow night." There was no chance I'd get Jerry to remember me if I didn't stay close. My mother could damn well follow me if she wanted these "dates" to go on.

"Good. Because I'm still convinced you are the one trigger that could bring him back to this time." Bart nodded. "Come now, Cait. Tomorrow night, Glory." He shut the door.

"Drive Jerry's car down then." Cait patted my shoulder. "I'll do what I can to defuse the situation at home. I hope Mum doesn't find out about your own part in the poisoning. I'll try to get to Jerry and make him swear to keep it a secret."

"Thanks, Caitie." I leaned forward to hug her. "I'm not sure I could take Mag's temper right now, she's cold enough to me at the best of times. I don't need her piling on the guilt."

"I've got your back, Glory. And screw the guilt. If I took responsibility for everything my mother did 'for my own good,' I'd have walked into the sun long ago." Cait knew I'd heard some hair-raising stories about Mag's interference over the years. She was right and I hugged her again for the encouraging words.

"Thanks. You're making me feel better."

"Good. Now I've got to hit the road." She smiled. "How was your date last night?"

I'd told her about my mother's conditions. Hey, I had to confide in someone, and Flo wasn't here.

"Interesting. Apollo showed up. The Sun God? Imagine living in daylight forever." I fanned my cheeks. "And I have to admit he was beautiful but with an edge."

"Sounds like just your type." Cait grinned. "Mine too. Were you tempted?"

"Not even. He had an ego the size of the sun too. And he can't be out at night." I followed her to the door. "I realized I'm a night creature after all this time. I really can't imagine giving it up." I grinned. "Though I'll say again, he was great to look at."

"No surprise there. Olympus wouldn't produce anything less than perfection, I'm sure. Be careful, though. If the gods are all as powerful as your mother, you sure don't want to make any of them mad."

"Don't I know it." I shivered, thinking about how furious Apollo had gotten when I'd turned him down. What had he wanted from my mother that he'd been willing to hook up with a mere vampire? I couldn't stop thinking about it.

"Another one tonight?" Cait picked up her suitcase from by the door. She'd given the servants the night off. Jerry had been in such a sour mood, she hadn't wanted them subjected to it.

"Yep. Can't wait to see who she drags down to hook me up with next. I'm getting on the Internet as soon as you leave to study these guys. Seems there are quite a few gods and they each have a specialty. I want to be better prepared than I was last night. Ignorance is *not* bliss." And I knew from my own past that knowledge could be power. I was desperate to figure out just how my mother fit into this whole Olympus scheme. Who was she?

"Hmm." Cait glanced up. "Wonder what your mother thinks would ring your bell."

I didn't have to wonder long. After the gang left, I hurried up to my room, where yet another fabulous dress waited for me. This one was white and cut toga style. Maybe tonight's guy was a traditionalist. The one-shoulder design made a bra impossible so the overall effect was pretty interesting. I'm well-endowed and perky. When Jerry is himself, he's pretty fond of the "girls." He'd have loved me in this.

I wasn't so crazy about looking like an escapee from Olympus.

Quick research made me wonder if there was a god any better than Apollo up there. Mom had started with her best shot in my opinion. But it would be interesting to see her next attempt. I was almost in a good mood as I headed downstairs. This date would be a piece of cake. I'd found out something on the Internet that was a deal breaker as far as future dates were concerned. Jerry was as good as fixed.

The same limo and driver picked me up and this time I paid close attention to where we were going. It had taken me too long to find my way back last night. I'd finally had to resort to flying overhead and trying to spot Jer's neighborhood. It was not something I wanted to make a habit of. While shifting into a bird or bat wasn't supposed to mess with your clothes, I always thought they were a little worse for wear after the whole thing. Sorry, but these dresses my mother sent me were just too fine to risk even a wrinkle and God forbid I lose one of my designer shoes.

We arrived at the same town house so maybe Mom had rented it for the duration. I walked in and the same servant took my purse and wrap. Mom had sent along a satin cape lined with gold this time. Even though I didn't feel the cold, it was a nice accessory on a chilly night. Once again, a fire blazed in the fireplace. This time the man waited for me. He played a small instrument, an odd-shaped guitar. The name came to me in a flash. It was a lute. Okay, that was definitely an Olympus thing. I couldn't deny the music was hauntingly beautiful. He looked up and smiled, obviously reading my mind, and set it aside.

"Good evening, Gloriana. I see you wore traditional dress. You look enchanting." He stepped forward and took my hand, kissing the back of it.

Another beautiful man, this one with dark hair that fell onto his forehead. His sapphire eyes gleamed as he studied me. He was in the traditional toga himself, a short one to show off his muscled legs. Yum.

"Good evening. You know my name. May I ask yours?" I eased my hand from his grasp. He was normal temperature. Well, for a human. Still warmer than a vampire. Were they human on Olympus? Of course not. But he was doing a good imitation. He smelled wonderful, like old money. What? Where had that come from?

He laughed. "How delightful. My name is Hermes. And besides music, money is one of my favorite things. Though actually I prefer gold." He walked over to a small table and opened a lacquered box. A rope of gold glimmered inside and he lifted it out and admired it for a moment. "This would look exquisite on you. Here." He slipped it over my head and adjusted it until it nestled between my breasts. "Lovely. You were made to wear gold. It matches your hair. I like your earrings. Eighteen carat?"

"Yes." I'd checked them out when I'd found them tucked in my gift box tonight. Mom was being very generous. You knew I wasn't going to toss her presents in her face, didn't you? This necklace wasn't going back either if I could help it. It felt like several ounces of treasure.

"I see you appreciate value. I like that in a woman." He grinned and picked up his lute again. "Your mother tells me you also appreciate music. Shall I play for you?"

"I'd like that." What in the hell had my mother done? Was she snooping into my past? Yes, I'd had a fling with rock star Israel Caine. And his music was one of the things

I'd loved about him. Still loved. Would always love about him. But our affair was over. I could love his music and realize I was meant to be with Jerry. That had been a tough decision but the right one. I sat on the silk sofa in front of the fire while Hermes tuned his instrument. I doubted he'd break out into a rock song. I prepared to be bored.

Uh-oh. I was not bored. He sang in a deep and seductive voice of love. A love that could last forever. Oh, Jerry. A love that would span the test of time. I swayed to his perfect strumming, closing my eyes as his voice wound a spell around my heart and thoughts of Jerry drifted away. I knew this was magic and tried to fight it. But he was so talented and I've always been a sucker for a great song. I still have an Israel Caine shrine in my living room, though it's tinier than it used to be. It made Jerry insanely jealous. Or used to. Now? He probably . . .

Forget history. I lay back on that silk sofa and just imagined listening to that exquisite music every day. Even when the lute went silent, the song played in my head.

"Gloriana, look at me. We are meant to be together. Your mother tells me you run your own business." Hermes sat beside me, his hip hard against mine. "You have no idea how sexy I find a woman who enjoys commercial endeavors. We could do such great things in Olympus." He toyed with the gold chain, his fingers brushing the curve of my breasts before he let it drop. "I can see us cornering the jewel market. How would you like to be the premier jewelry distributor to all the gods and goddesses on the mountain? Believe me, the men and women there are insatiable when it comes to adornment."

I took a moment to imagine bathing in jewels, becoming the spokesmodel for fabulous accessories. Diamonds, rubies, emeralds. Wait a minute. I wasn't really into such things. Or hadn't been. Of course that was because I'd made my peace with owning CZ studs and passing them off as diamonds long ago.

"You wear fakes?" Hermes shook his head. "Poor Gloriana. You should never have been brought so low, the daughter of such an exalted figure. Your mother must weep each night over your plight."

Now he'd made a serious misstep. My mother weep over me? Ha! She'd forgotten me for centuries. Then she'd chosen a harsh way of showing an interest. Had she come to me and asked for a sit-down? Showered me with presents and then begged me to forgive her? Hell no. She'd poisoned my lover and threatened to keep him locked in a past that didn't include me.

I shoved him aside then jumped up, seriously pissed. "Sorry, Hermes, but the last thing I want to do is make my mother proud. The bitch has done nothing but hurt me. Your music is beautiful and you give great gifts." I should toss the necklace in his face. Or not.

"That little trinket is just the beginning, Gloriana." His smile never wavered he was so confident that his bribery was the way to my heart.

"Did you forget to mention something, Hermes?" I played with the gold between my breasts and saw him lick his lips. "I did a little Internet search before I came tonight. Aren't you . . . married?"

"Of course. What has that to do with us?" He pulled me into his arms. "It's a political alliance. You poor thing, stuck here on Earth where it is so provincial." He stroked my hair, paralyzing me when I tried to break away. "We are free to love where we wish on Olympus, dear girl. My wife has her own lovers. I have mine."

"I'm not interested in being a member of your harem." I turned my face, his kiss landing on my cheek.

"This hard-to-get ploy is wearing thin, Gloriana." His voice hardened and he grabbed my chin. "Kiss me and let's get on with it."

"This isn't a ploy." His arm was like an iron band around me and I realized he was determined to seal this deal even if he had to use force. I swallowed and let my fangs show, hoping they'd disgust him and make him change his mind.

If anything, his hand on my chin pinched harder and his eyes narrowed.

"Vampire. No wonder your mother is so desperate to bring you home."

"This is my home. Earth. Not some mountain where powerful entities marry their relatives and seem to have no morals." My voice shook and I was relieved when he let me step back. I had a feeling the fangs had done that for me.

"I told you. Our marriages are political alliances. Certainly nothing a mundane like you would understand." He looked me up and down. "You would be transformed in Olympus, Gloriana. Beautiful, your teeth perfect. I can't understand this determination to cling to a lifestyle that is so limiting."

"No, I suppose a god would never understand where a mere creature like me is coming from." I headed for the door. "Nothing you can say will make me want to live in Olympus. I'm satisfied with my little shop. I've been making a living and that's enough for me. Thanks a heap." I threw him a kiss then froze. His glare meant I'd crossed a line.

"I offer you everything, give you something very valuable and all I get is a 'Thanks a heap'?" He stomped over to where I stood. I couldn't move or, trust me, I would have been so out of there. I'd recently discovered I could dematerialize. But that was a no go around these Olympus characters.

I didn't like the way he was looking me over. If he thought he'd bought and paid for something with his necklace, he could think again. Too bad I couldn't move my arms and legs. But my mouth still worked.

"Take your stupid necklace back. I don't know where you got the idea that I could be seduced by jewelry, but I'm not that easy." I lifted my chin. Nice that I had control of my head at least.

"Hermes, get away from my daughter." Her voice fell like chips of ice into the room. "Gloriana, you will keep the necklace. As payment for putting up with bad manners."

"If you've been listening, you know your daughter has

very harsh thoughts about you. Do you really want to defend her?" Hermes put his hands on his hips. I noticed for the first time all the rings he wore. Amazing that he could play the lute so well; the weight of those gold rings must have made it difficult.

"She has her reasons for hating me right now. We will work through them. But you are treating her like a common whore and I won't have it." She stomped her foot and Hermes's lyre burst into flames.

"You will regret that." He snapped his fingers and my necklace vanished.

"And you will regret that." My mother flung lightning at him, making the hem of his toga smolder.

"You have just made a powerful enemy. Both of you." He turned on his heel then disappeared, leaving a trail of smoke behind him.

"Spoiled brat." My mother frowned after him then turned to me. "I'm sorry about that, Gloriana. I'll buy you another necklace."

"Forget the necklace!" I'd had it with her dates and manipulations. Obviously this candidate of hers had been hard for her to control. Maybe this was the time to put a stop to her plan. "Surely you can see that I'm not right for your gods. And they are married! I'm not interested in the weird love affairs going on up there. Forget this, Mother, and let me be happy with the man of my own choosing." I put a hand on her arm. "Jerry isn't so bad once you get to know him. Look past his fangs to the strong man who took care of me for over four hundred years. I wouldn't be here today if it wasn't for him."

"How you constantly defend him!" She shrugged off my hand. "I swear he has brainwashed you. Is it this way with all vampires and their makers? Is it?"

"No. I don't know." I thought about it. "No, of course not. Many vampires go their separate ways and never see their sires again. Jerry and I stay connected because we love each other."

"And yet you recently had a tryst with a singer, that Israel Caine fellow." She made a very unladylike sound. "Another vampire."

"Yes. I was lonely after Jerry left, and Ray is a dear friend. We agreed it won't happen again." I sat down. If I was going to hear a rehash of all my mistakes, this was going to take a while.

"And you had an affair with your former bodyguard. A"—she shuddered—"shape-shifter, one Rafael Valdez. That was the reason Jeremiah Campbell left Texas for his ancestral home in the first place."

"Yes, Mother." I stared down at my shoes. Tonight's were a beautiful gold leather sandal with a rhinestone buckle. "Rafe and I are the best of friends. I've known him for years. But he knows we're done as far as being lovers goes. I chose Jerry."

"Interesting." She tapped her perfect chin. Tonight she wore a burgundy silk pantsuit with a pink satin and lace camisole underneath. The entire outfit was surprisingly sexy and I wondered if she was meeting a lover of her own later. "So when or if your Jeremiah suddenly remembers everything, he'll have a lot of your transgressions to get past, won't he, Gloriana?"

"Yes. But he told me, before your stunt with Mara and the knife, that he'd decided to forgive me." I got up, tired of looking up at her or down at my shoes, no matter how pretty. "Of course he doesn't know about Ray. At least how far it went."

She smiled. "Are you sure you want him to remember everything, Gloriana? It might be in your best interests to start fresh."

"You've been listening to my conversations, haven't you?" Now I was mad. "Stop it. Right now. I don't need you butting into my business. It's bad enough I have this dating thing to deal with without the thought that you're listening in to every word I say."

"But I have so much to catch up on. Can you blame me?"

She touched one of the gold loops dangling from my ears. "I need to know your tastes, your desires. To help me find the perfect man for you, of course. And I will find him. Every misstep brings me closer to the right choice. And, seriously, Gloriana, think about this. Living with a man who has 'forgiven' you can be hell on earth. Do you really want to be your Jeremiah's charity case?" With that she vanished, just like Hermes had done.

"Thanks a heap, Mother." I grabbed my wrap and my purse and walked outside. At least she'd left the limo for me this time. Old Hermes had certainly screwed up, dissing me. I had the feeling there were going to be a few lightning bolts tossed around Olympus later. The thought had me smiling as we tooled through the quiet streets back toward the Campbell town house.

But her last words had wiped the smile off my face. I couldn't deny I'd worried about that very thing. That Jerry would never forget how I'd betrayed him. That he'd never trust me again. And, if he found out I'd been with Ray . . . ? I'd have to start with a clean slate and confess everything if we were ever to have a life together. I couldn't live in fear that my latest indiscretion would come out. But could I do it? Confessing that I'd slept with Ray might just be the final nail in the coffin for my relationship with Jerry.

I glanced at my watch and calculated the time before sunrise and how long it would take me to drive to Campbell Castle. It was almost a relief to realize I would have to wait until the next night to leave Edinburgh. Maybe I was a coward, but facing Jerry and his harridan of a mother was more than I could take right now.

I finally mastered the stick shift on Jerry's Jag and actually enjoyed the drive to the castle. Still, it made me remember how much he'd appreciated taking the winding roads in the hills around Austin in his powerful sports car back in Texas.

Tears pricked my eyelids and I had to slow down once to get myself under control. He *had* to get his memories back. No way could he stay stuck back in the sixteenth century, afraid of the machines he'd loved so much.

I parked and grabbed my suitcase, sure that the excellent security had spotted me long before I got to the door. Of course it swung open before I could ring the bell. Jerry's mother stood in the doorway, her stare telling me all I needed to know. She'd read minds, done something to figure out that this was all my fault. I was number one on her shit list.

"Gloriana. Do come in." She called for a servant and my bag was collected. Mag's smile was brittle as she led the way into the living room. "Jeremiah is out riding. The doctor is with him. You should have heard Bartholomew's complaints. You'd think a true Scot could still sit a horse." She nodded toward Angus. "It's a good thing my husband was wise enough to send for two of the beasts."

"Yes, of course. I think Jerry should have someone with him at all times. He continues to have spells when he's weak." I didn't want to sit yet. Not sure of the dynamics here. No sign of Cait. I'd have given anything for her friendly face. Angus was on his feet, his chivalry too ingrained to let him stay seated when a woman entered the room. Now he settled back into his recliner. The TV was on as usual, a muted soccer game.

"Never thought I'd see the day when the lad had to have a keeper with him." Angus picked up a goblet of blood and took a deep swallow. "He *is* still weak, Gloriana. And we know now 'tis your doing." He set the glass down with a crack. "What says your bitch of a mum? Is she willing to reverse the spell?"

"I-I— What have you heard?" I sank down on a chair. Mag moved to stand in front of me.

"No one betrayed your trust, girl. Our Caitie would die before she let a confidence slip. But I could always read her." Mag threw back her long dark hair and put her hands on the armrests, effectively trapping me there. "She's mortified that I found out your secret. That your own mother poisoned our son." Mag's eyes blazed and her fangs were down.

"Then you know that I would never hurt Jeremiah! She did it without my knowledge. An interfering mother. Can you relate to that, Mag?" I concentrated and managed to dematerialize, popping up on the other side of the room.

Mag and Angus gasped, Jerry's mom crossing herself as she whirled around to face me again. "Witchcraft! How did you hide this so well all these years?"

"It's not witchcraft! My mother is from Olympus. I inherited some of her powers but I didn't realize it until recently." I put out my hands. "You don't know what else I can do. Trust me, you don't want to test me."

Mag's eyes narrowed. "Threatening me now?" She advanced to within a foot of me. "Think about this, Gloriana. I believe you hope to get Jeremiah back into your bed." She glanced at Angus. "God knows I have no wish to see this happen, but if it will help him gain his memory back, we are willing to have you here, to work with you."

"Aye, we will. But stop this nonsense. Threats." Angus was on his feet now, advancing to stand next to Mag. He put his hand on his wife's shoulder. "If your mother did this, then we need to know how to appease her. How to get her to take this spell off of our son. What can we do, Gloriana? Or what can *you* do to get Jeremiah back to himself?"

I took a steadying breath. Sorry, but the dematerializing thing was new and took a lot out of me. It was always a surprise that I could actually pull it off.

"First, quit threatening *me*." I stomped around Mag and sat again. As usual I felt like a poor relation compared to Jerry's mother in her designer originals in a tiny size. My own outfit had been stuffed in my suitcase way too long. My black pants could have used a wash and my sweater was pilling under the arms. I was all in black. I guess I'd been thinking I could hide if I needed to. Blend into the night. Stupid. I was a strong woman with powers. No hiding for me. I threw back my own hair, which had at least been washed and was cooperating for once.

"We're upset, Gloriana." Angus practically pushed Mag onto the sofa and sat beside her. "Bear with us. Any idea what we can do to appease your mother?"

"I'm working on it. But she can hear everything. Don't disrespect her or she'll never lift this spell she's got him under." I looked significantly at the ceiling.

Mag crossed herself again and reached for a Bible on the table next to her.

"She's not from hell, even if sometimes she does things that make her seem that way. She's a mother like you, Mag, trying to do the best for her child." I sighed when I saw Mag fire up again.

"And Jeremiah's not good enough for you? Is that what she's saying?" She started to get up but Angus held her back with a beefy hand on her knee.

"Now, darlin', what do you think Gloriana's got to say about her mum's opinion? Has Jeremiah ever had any say over yours?" He shook his head. "So what do we do now, my dear? Is there anything Mag and I can do to help this situation?"

I felt the air stir and had a very bad feeling that I knew what was coming. My good hair started rising and, sure enough, a figure appeared in front of Angus's recliner. She smiled and then settled into the leather seat.

"How delightful of you to offer, Laird." My mother crossed her legs and leaned forward. "Wouldn't it be perfect if we could work together to get our children back where they belong?"

I closed my eyes and wished I had Mag's Bible. I wasn't sure if I'd use it for fervent prayer or to throw it at the woman who'd claimed she'd given birth to me. This could not end well.

Eight

🦇

"If you are going to work together, Mother"—I managed a smile—"perhaps you'd better introduce yourself." I waited. At last I'd get a name out of her.

"Call me Olympia for now. I'm traveling incognito." She gave me a cold smile like, "Nice try." "I know you are Magdalena and Angus Campbell, Laird and Lady Campbell." She rose and held out her hand. "Forgive me for just dropping in like this, uninvited. Obviously I've been listening for a while, but I'm concerned about my daughter."

"*Forgive* you?" Angus was on his feet, Mag by his side. "You are torturing our son. Fix him, woman. Right now. Then take your blasted daughter and get the hell out of my house!"

"Oh, my. Not exactly the cordial welcome I'd hoped for." Mother glanced at me. "And this is the family you wish to join, Daughter?" She raised her hand and I knew what was coming.

I lunged, grabbing her hand before she could follow through. "Don't you dare throw lightning in here!"

"What?" Mag hauled Angus around to the back of the couch, closer to the door.

"She tosses lightning bolts when she's mad. It'll sting like a bitch and could burn this place down."

My mother shrugged me off. "She's right. I'm usually greeted with more respect."

"You poisoned our son. Surely you understand if we are less than cordial." Mag glanced at me. "Did you ask your mother to take away Jeremiah's memories, Gloriana? So he'd forget that you betrayed him?"

My mother hissed and pointed a red-painted fingernail at Mag, freezing her where she stood, mouth agape. "You dare! I'll have you know my daughter has wept over your son's memory loss, begged me to restore him. She doesn't care if he tosses her aside for her sluttish ways as long as he comes back to this century."

I stared at her. Didn't care for the "sluttish" comment but the rest of that speech had been pretty nice, actually maternal.

"Gloriana and I are working on a cure for your son. Be patient. There is hope that his memories will come back." She flicked her wrist and Mag came alive again only to cross herself and mutter about witches while she clutched Angus.

If I didn't resent the fact that it was obvious my mother was still determined to go on with her ridiculous dating game, I might have been cheered by the sight of Mag Campbell scared of someone.

Jerry and Bart chose that moment to barrel into the room smelling of horse and cold air. I wanted to rush to Jerry and kiss his smile, obviously put there by a ride on a fast horse through familiar land. But my mother's hand on my arm stopped me even before Jerry's smile vanished at the sight of his parents holding on to the back of the sofa like it was a battle shield.

"What's going on here? Gloriana, who is this?" He stepped farther into the room.

"My mother, Jerry. Olympia." I grimaced at the fake name, pretty sure Zeus wouldn't approve.

Before any of us could stop him Jerry strode forward

until he was within a foot of her. "So you're the one who spelled Mara into stabbing me. Proud of yourself?"

My mother looked him up and down, slowly. "I did what I thought necessary. You look fit enough now. Enjoy your ride?"

His fists clenched and I prepared to throw myself between them. He'd never survive if he laid a finger on my mother.

"What are you doing here?" He looked at me. "Did you bring her here?"

"No! I'd never . . ." I put a hand on his arm. "I'm trying to get her to restore your memories. Trust me."

"Aye, I trust *you*." He locked eyes with my mother again. "I don't believe you can repair the harm you've done. I think you are a manipulative bitch who thought she could control her daughter but miscalculated." He pulled me to him. "I may not remember our past, but the Gloriana I have gotten to know this past week is stubborn and doesn't give up easily."

"You are right about that. I see a lot of myself in her. We are willful women." My mother smiled her cold and scary smile. "You have stones, I'll give you that, Jeremiah Campbell. I begin to see what Gloriana admires in you. But you turned her vampire. I find that repugnant."

"If he hadn't turned me, I would have been dust these four hundred years or more! You should be on your knees, thanking him for that, not punishing him, Mother." I held on to him, so happy I wanted to dance around the room. *He'd defended me!*

"But you are not dust and I have given you my terms, Gloriana." She swept her eyes around the room. "I see no friendly faces here. A car will come for you tomorrow night. You know what you must do." And with that, she vanished.

"A goddess from Olympus in the flesh, so to speak." Bart finally spoke from the doorway. "I didn't know whether to grab one of the swords from the wall here or run like hell."

"Neither would have done you any good if my mother had decided you displeased her, Bart. Your best move was what you did. Stand still and hope she didn't notice you." I worried when Jerry stepped away from me and sank into a chair. "Jerry, are you all right?"

"Tired." He looked up at me with a weary smile. "Come here. Tell me about how we met, why I made you vampire. It wasn't something I usually do. I know that much about myself. Da turned each of us in the family when we told him we were ready." He smiled at his father. "But I never made a habit of turning others vampire as far as I remember." His smile vanished. "Did I?" He looked at his parents.

"No, son. It's not something we encourage." Angus helped Mag settle on the couch. They both were obviously still shaken. My mother had that effect on people. You'd think that might get me some sympathy but Mag still glared at me. Right. I couldn't blame her for that. I'd brought the wrath of Olympus down on their son.

I sank down on the floor and leaned against Jerry's knee. Guilty or not, I loved telling this story. I was just sorry I had this audience. His mother in particular hated to be reminded that I'd been an actress, though I really hadn't been much more than a walk-on milkmaid in one of Shakespeare's plays at the Globe. It had been illegal to even put women on the stage back then, but it had made the mostly male audience go wild. I'd been a desperate widow and had finally sunk low enough to hope to gain a protector by walking across the stage in a low-cut costume. It had worked when Jerry spotted me and fell for me right away.

I told the story with embellishments that made it seem dramatic and exciting. I left out the grinding poverty and my desperation. I ignored his parents and the doctor who'd dug out his ever-present notebook. Instead, I looked into Jerry's eyes and reminded him of how we'd fallen in love. And how I'd begged him to make me his forever. I crawled up into his lap when I got to the part where he'd given in to my urgings.

"It was meant to be, Jerry. We didn't know then that I'd been a Siren, cast out by the Storm God and left in human form to die a mortal's natural death. Achelous had even killed my young husband, leaving me to fend for myself. I was supposed to die back then." I felt his arms go around me and leaned against him. "Call it fate or the workings of a God who knew wrongs that needed righting, but you gave me my immortality back."

"Strange. That I should see you back then and have to have you. In a large city like London. I so easily could have missed your performance. Not gone to the theater when you were on the stage." He rested his cheek on my hair. "I think you're right. Someone fated us to be together, Gloriana. And we'll not let this temporary madness keep us apart."

"I've tried to make my mother realize that she should be grateful to you." I traced his hard jaw with my fingertip. "But she won't see reason. All she knows is that I'm a vampire and she can't abide them."

"So seeing us together is her worst nightmare?" He kissed my finger then sucked it into his mouth, nipping it with a brush of his fang.

"Yes." I shivered at the sensation of his warm mouth touching me. I heard Mag complain to Angus that I was sinking my claws into their son again. It was enough to make me laugh out loud.

"Good." Jerry grinned and stood with me in his arms. I gasped. Even under the influence of my mother's hateful magic, he was still so strong. He ignored his mother's muttering and his doctor's scribbling. His father raised an eyebrow but actually smiled when Jerry strode past them all and headed toward the bedrooms. He stopped at his door and I leaned down to open it.

"You don't have to do this, lass." His voice was low near my ear.

"I couldn't want anything more." I pulled his head down to give him an openmouthed kiss. It went on and on until I felt his arms quiver. I wrenched my lips free. "Put me down."

"Damned weakness." He set me on my feet then shut the door.

"Then I'll feed you first." I tugged him toward his king-size bed. "Have to admit, though, you smell more than a bit like horse."

"I'll shower first then. Will you join me?" His grin was wicked. "I'm not so weak that I couldn't enjoy a romp in one of those miracles of modern technology."

"I'd love that." I pulled my sweater off over my head, laughing at the look on his face when he saw my black lace bra. "What? Don't you recognize another piece of modern technology when you see it?"

"Are you sure this isn't some kind of torture device?" He traced the edges of the lace cups then snapped the elastic straps. "How do you get free of this thing?"

"Here." I opened the front clasp and released my breasts, tossing the bra to the floor.

He frowned at the red marks made by the underwire. "Does this hurt?" He rubbed at the pressure points before being distracted by my nipples. "Why do you put yourself through that? Your breasts are perfect."

"Thanks." I moaned when he bent his head to suck one of my nipples into his mouth. "I can't remember why I wear one. It's called a bra. Umm. That feels good."

He opened my pants without any trouble, smiling at my skimpy lace panties. "Now this is more like it. Very pretty. But again, unnecessary." He slid them down my legs and tossed them aside. I'd left my shoes by the door. He breathed against my tummy, his hands skimming along my buttocks as he was obviously relearning the shape of my body. "You are perfect."

"Oh, Jerry." I blinked back tears, dropping down to my knees to kiss him silent. How I loved this man. Before too long I had him naked as well and in the shower. His hard body felt so right against my own. We were made to be together. Why was it so difficult for me to remember that when other men tempted me? I prayed that this would help him remember it as well.

He started at my neck, kissing and licking his way from

front to back and front again. His hands slicked with soap, he pushed me against the tile and lovingly massaged my breasts then rinsed them. I pulled his head down to them again, needing his mouth there. His lips tugged and brought an answering yearning deep inside me. I almost screamed my pleasure when I felt his fangs scrape across my breasts. He licked away a droplet of blood and looked up at me, his eyes dark with hunger.

"Drink from me, Jeremiah. Take what you need."

"I need this." He eased a finger inside me as he pressed his lips to my jugular, the warm water beating down on his shoulders so that the spray barely touched me. He added a second finger, coaxing a sigh from me with his rhythmic invasion.

The smooth heat of his cock pressed against my thigh, close, so close to where I wanted it. I grasped it in my hand, matching my movements to his own. Guiding it between my thighs, I lifted one leg to wrap around his waist so that I could bring him inside.

"Now, please. Take me now." I lifted my other leg, feeling the sharp sting of his fangs at my neck the same moment he entered me. He filled me, completed me and we stayed joined at neck and thighs. One. Then he began to move and so did I. We pounded against each other, desperate to get close enough, satisfied enough, deep enough. I felt him taking in my life force, drinking it and becoming stronger. And still I wanted more of him. I dug my nails into his back and held on. I locked my legs around him and pressed harder, trying to meld our bodies together for all time. If only I could just fuse my memories into his mind. Give him all those years back . . .

He finally gasped and released my vein, his eyes fluttering open to look into mine. His hands on my ass held me firmly as he shifted me to the bench seat at the back of the large shower stall. Then he pulled away and sank down to his knees, taking me with his mouth until I fell back, so limp with satisfaction that I was sure I was going to slide to the tile floor and down the drain.

With a grin he stood, pulling me up to take me again, the friction of his insatiable cock undoing me once more. I sobbed, so wild for him I forgot that I meant to control myself. I bit into his neck, swallowing some of his own sweet blood, filling my mouth and taking it as I always had.

"Gloriana." His whisper brought me to my senses.

What was I doing? He'd been weak. I couldn't take from him. But he held my head when I tried to withdraw, kept me there to drink awhile longer. Finally, I stopped. Just laid my head against his shoulder and listened to his beating heart. Strong. And satisfied. We both were. And the water was getting cold. His hand slid down to my back and my feet finally touched the floor.

"Wow. Just . . . wow." I stepped back and wobbled a little bit. "Some reunion."

"I'd say so." He grabbed a towel and carefully wrapped it around my wet hair, then handed me another one. He put a third around his waist. "You're amazing. No wonder we were lovers for centuries."

I was afraid to ask but did anyway. "Did you remember anything?"

"I don't know. Some of what we did seemed somehow . . . familiar." He ran a small towel over his hair then tossed it aside to turn away. "But then how many women have I fucked? Could it be that it's like riding a horse? Some things just come back to you." He stalked out of the bathroom, drying his back with yet another snowy towel. I got the feeling he was pissed off. No memories. Swell.

"Don't worry about it, Jer. Like Bart told you, give it time." I dried off my body and decided to hell with my hair. I fashioned a turban then walked into the bedroom naked. If Jerry had it in him to go another round, I was all for it. One look at his face told me it wasn't happening.

"You're beautiful. I'm lucky you are willing to stick with

me through this, but who would want a man who is scared to get into an automobile? Jumps when a telephone rings? I'm not right in the head, Gloriana. And I know you didn't do this to me. I also know there are men in this Texas you say we came from who want you. It might be best if you went back there and let one of them have you."

"Jerry. Jeremiah." I rushed to his side where he now sat on the edge of the bed. "How can you say that? I love you. This is a temporary setback. And my own mother did this to you because of me. Do you really think I would leave you now?"

"I don't need your damned pity!" He came up fast, pushing me back with one hand. "You are not responsible for what your mother did. I know that. Go. Maybe that will give your mother a reason to put me back to rights. Ever think about that?"

"So you don't love me? Don't want me?" I heard my voice tremble but refused to cry. This wasn't my guy talking. "What about what just happened between us?"

He looked me over, assessing me. No sign of the warm lover now. I wanted to pick up my discarded clothes from the floor and hold them in front of me. "You are a desirable woman, Gloriana. And available. I'm a man with needs. Do you really think I'd turn down what you offered?" He lay back on his bed. "Thanks for the blood donation. Go back to Texas. You say you have a life there. It's for the best. Now leave. I'm still tired."

I felt like he'd slapped me. "I don't believe you, Jerry. I think this is your pride talking. You are not less than a man just because you have a memory loss." I sucked in a breath, desperate not to break down before I had my say. "Even if you never fill in the blanks in your life, you are more of a man than many I have known. I won't give up on you. On us. And this isn't about pity." I stared at him, willing him to look at me, say something. He didn't do either. "Do you think what just happened in that shower was meaningless to me?"

He didn't say anything. I hoped that meant he was at a loss for words. Smart move. I kicked my clothes aside and grabbed his shoulder. He finally looked at me.

"It meant everything to me. To be back in your arms again. We made love, Jerry. Or at least that's what it felt like to me. And I think somewhere inside you had to know it wasn't a meaningless fuck, didn't you?" I pleaded with my eyes. Oh, God, if only he'd felt something . . .

"Jesus, I . . ." He touched my face. "No, it wasn't meaningless. You made me happy, Gloriana. And I feel like—" He shook his head. "I don't know. Maybe we aren't strangers."

I leaned down and kissed him, taking a good long time with it, so happy I wanted to cry all over him. It was a start. I stood and saw his eyes follow the movement. Oh, yes, I was still naked.

"It's settled then. If I go back to Texas, then you're coming with me."

"You're mad." He turned his head away. "You really don't want to be stuck with me, Gloriana. Not when I'm like this and no hope of getting better."

"Yes, I do." I crawled onto the bed, grabbed his chin and made him look at me again. "I don't think riding around on a horse like you're still in the sixteenth century, Jerry, living in the same castle you lived in back then, is helping you get your memory back. I think—" I rested my hands on his bare shoulders. "I think going to Texas, where you had a new life, new friends, and have to face the present, will be the best medicine. Are you brave enough to try that, my Scottish warrior?"

"Brave? When lifting a sword might well sap my strength? You really would be better off without me, Gloriana." He started to glower, but I could see he had noticed my bare breasts, inches away from his chest.

I snuggled up against him. "We aren't big on swords nowadays. Modern weapons don't weigh very much." I put my arms around him and pressed my breasts to his chest. His towel twitched. Good. "We're starting over, Jer. If you never remember a bloody thing, it's okay by me. To hell with my mother. I don't trust her to help fix you anyway." I kissed his damp shoulder.

"No, I'd not trust a goddess from Olympus. Bart says they are dangerous. He has spent hours studying her blood and investigating her on a machine he has. It has some kind of net that catches information. But without her name, he says he can only get some vague idea of what she might be able to do."

"She's capable of plenty. None of it good." I sighed against his warm skin. Now he smelled clean and male. I had hope that we could do this together. Somehow patch a future out of new memories and maybe some old ones as time went by.

Jerry smiled. "You have some of her blood too. The blood of a goddess. Maybe that's why it's so delicious." He ran his hand down my back and along the curve of my butt. "It definitely makes me feel stronger."

"Then you must get it more often." I reached down and jerked away his towel. "Are you feeling stronger right now?" I glanced down to where he seemed to have found renewed vigor. "Strong enough to make me scream so loud that your father has to turn up the volume on the TV and your mother starts cursing me for a conniving slut?"

"How can I resist when you make it sound like so much fun?" He rolled me under him and kissed me hard, then soft, then hard again. Finally, he leaned back and got serious. "Are you sure, Gloriana, that you won't take this chance to run away far and fast? I won't give it to you again."

"Shut up and kiss me. We've talked enough, don't you think?" I pulled him down and got on with the lovemaking. Run? Wait till Jerry saw what was waiting for him in Texas. Two men who had known me intimately. He might not remember what had happened but it was bound to come out. And I didn't doubt that the new Jerry was still the jealous type. Who could blame him? Now it was up to me to get my mother to back off.

• • •

Another beautiful dress arrived the next night but I resisted the urge to wear it. I did try it on, though, then set it aside. Jerry was out riding again. We'd talked about going to Texas and I'd called Flo. She was arranging for their plane to land in Edinburgh where we could board and go with them back home to Austin. They'd be here in a few days. When Jerry's mother heard our plans, she hit the roof.

"So you've managed to pull him back to you with a romp between the sheets. Once a slut, always a slut." Mag caught me in the hallway when I tried to find a laundry room. Her servants hadn't been very helpful and I was afraid I was going to have to go into the village to do a load of wash at a Laundromat.

"I wouldn't let Jerry hear you talk like that. He's happy with me tonight. You don't want him leaving here with ill feelings, do you?" I stopped a passing servant. "Master Jeremiah asked me to have you wash these things. Now will you take care of it?" The man looked at Mag. She finally nodded and he took the pillowcase full of clothes.

"Must you take him back to Texas?" She actually looked distressed. "He's not well. Anyone can see it. And your witch of a mother is sure to follow you both there. Do you trust her not to hurt him again?"

It was a good point. I *didn't* trust her. But I couldn't stay here either. Mag hated me, Angus barely tolerated me and every night that Jerry could ride around like the old days seemed to make him regress into Highland-warrior mode even worse than he'd been when he'd first been stabbed. We had to leave. Luckily Bart had business in America and had agreed to meet us there in a week to continue working with Jerry.

"I'm going to try to convince her that this is a lost cause. That, even if Jerry was out of the picture, I'll never do what she wants." I followed Mag into the living room. Angus had gone riding with Jerry, and Bart and Cait were in the village on a date. For once the TV was off. We settled into two chairs, facing each other.

"What does the witch want, Gloriana?" Mag leaned forward.

I hesitated. This was not something I wanted to share, because you can bet Mag would have me on the first broomstick to Olympus if she could manage it.

"A mother-daughter relationship. Can you believe it? Like I could forgive her after what she did to Jerry." I sat back. That was all I was telling her.

"Well, you're right there. It was unforgivable." For once Jer's mum and I were in complete agreement. A vampire, one of their guards, entered the room.

"Sorry, my lady, but there's a man at the door. He's here to collect Miss Gloriana. He's got a limo stuck up the road. Can't get it close to the drive." He nodded at me. "Nice ride."

"That's my cue. I'm supposed to meet my mother in the village. I'm going to try to get this straightened out. Wish me luck." I got up and followed the man outside. I could see the lights of the limo in the distance. The winding road wasn't meant for long cars and the driver had given up trying to make it all the way up the narrow lane. I'd worn jeans and a sweater, not that divine black sheath with the pearls my mother had sent earlier. As soon as I got into the car and he started backing out of the lane, I heard him get on his cell phone.

"You'd better see her before she gets to the meet, Your Highness."

Your Highness? Oh, please. But I figured he was giving my mother a heads-up about my clothing. Fine. That meant I'd be seeing her, not some god full of himself and ready to make me an offer I'd be happy to refuse. We were soon on the road and zooming along toward a village not too far from the one nearest the castle. Guess Mom had decided to avoid the locals. Soon we pulled up in front of a quaint inn in a village known for its whiskey distillery. I could just picture her sampling the local brew.

As soon as the driver let me out, I headed for the door. It opened and my mother stood there, glowering. She fairly shot off sparks with outrage.

"Come upstairs to my room. Now." She grabbed my arm, electricity sending a sharp tingle through me at the contact.

"Ow!" I tried to get free but she wasn't letting go.

"You dare show up looking like that! What are you up to?" She practically threw me into a bedroom that looked like a throwback to the Middle Ages. It had beamed ceilings, a four-poster bed and a fireplace with a plaster front. I liked it. I bet she hated it.

"I'm tired of these dates when I'm sure you have no intention of doing a thing to make Jerry remember squat." I sat in a chair in front of the fire and crossed my legs. I'd even dug out my only pair of sneakers, red Ked high-tops. She gave them a look of complete horror.

"I told you I would try to bring his memories back."

"Try!" I leaped to my feet. "Seriously? I'm supposed to put up with your nonsense on the basis of a *try*?" I poked her chest, stopping for a nanosecond to admire her lacy blouse. Very vintage and expensive. No, I was furious. "Jerry is suffering and you don't give a damn. I won't have it!" I actually stomped my foot.

"You won't have it? Excuse me? Do you really think you have the power to call the shots here?" She closed her eyes. "Right now your lover is riding on the hills near his castle. His father is beside him. They are having a fine time. The laird is reminiscing, trying to help his son remember some of the good times he can't recall." She opened her sky blue eyes and glared at me.

"Leave them alone, Mother." My stomach lurched. I had a feeling I knew what was coming. Her cold smile chilled me.

"One snap of my fingers, Gloriana, and I can send both horses tumbling down the rocky slope, their riders with them. I'll make sure the fall breaks every bone in their bodies, the men, not the horses. I love a good mount." She smiled like I'd appreciate that fine distinction. I just stared at her. "Oh, they won't die. They are vampires after all. But they will have such pain! Do you want that for your lover, Gloriana?"

"Sadistic witch!" I staggered back to the chair and sat. "How can you say you want to be my mother? Have a relationship with me and then do things like that to the man I love?"

"He is wrong for you!" She paced in front of me. "You are being foolish. I will present you with the right man and you will see how insane loving a vampire is. Life on Olympus will give you everything—perfect body, mind, spirit. You'll have the finest jewels, clothes, lovers. Whatever you desire will be at your fingertips. Why won't you listen to me?"

"Because I'm not a child, Mother." I sighed. "I'm a woman who has had over four hundred years to discover what and who she wants. Trust me, it's not perfection. That seems pretty hollow right now." I looked her over. Yes, she was pretty damned perfect on the surface, but she had so many evil ways, I couldn't begin to count them. "You came too late to the Glory party. You persist in this persecution of Jerry and I'll never be the loving daughter you hope for."

"What can I do to make you listen to me?" She sagged into the chair across from me. "He is not worth your devotion."

"That is not your call." I stood. "Are you going to hurt him?"

"I'm thinking about it." She ran a bloodred nail across gleaming teeth that would never need a whitening strip.

"Do it and we're done. I will never speak to you again."

"I can take you to Olympus anyway, you know. Bind you with my powers and just carry you away." She waved her hand and paralyzed me, reminding me of how easy it was for her. Then she flicked her wrist and released me.

"Is that really how you want this to play out? Make me your prisoner? Have me resent you every day for eternity?" I knelt in front of her and touched her knee. "If you leave Jerry alone, I promise I'll try to be the daughter you want. But here, on Earth. We can start to build a relationship."

"But you'll be a vampire." She shuddered but covered my hand. "Gloriana, I don't want that for you."

"I'd say you lost the right to run my life the minute you left me in the Storm God's harem." I sighed but didn't move. "But, you see, I'm willing to forget that and get to know you, be a daughter to you, if you do this for me. Now, can you give Jerry his memory back?"

"I don't know." She winced when I stood and glared at her.

"I don't believe you."

"Really. This isn't the first time I've used that potion. Usually, the victim suffers for a while but the results are fairly temporary. After a few days, maybe less, the person starts remembering things. No one has been more surprised than I've been when your man still didn't remember you this long after the attack. I'd hoped I would have persuaded you to leave before his memory came back, of course." She looked into the fire, her shoulders slumped. "I had no idea that you would be so stubborn."

I shook my head. "You'd better figure something out, Mother. Because if you can't give me some hope, we're done."

She jumped to her feet, all business now. "No, don't say that. I'll work on it. Consult with a few of the experts on Olympus. I got that potion from a sorcerer." She watched me pace the room. "I'll check on it. But I've still got a situation tonight. You need to change clothes, though you do look very pretty in that blue sweater. Olympus likes a more formal look, it shows respect. There's a very interesting man waiting for you. He isn't someone you want to cross."

"You are kidding me. You still want me to go on one of your dates? I thought we had settled this." I stopped in front of her.

"You don't understand, Gloriana. I had already set this up. Deals were made, promises must be kept." She bit her bottom lip and actually looked worried. "I have certain powers and these gods want what I can give them. If I just cancel at the last minute, I have to pay anyway. It will make me look weak if you don't show up." She grabbed my shoulders. "Weakness is very bad in Olympus. The others seize on it and soon you are living in a hovel with no one speaking to you but a Cyclops looking for a cheap thrill."

"Well, that would be terrible." I grinned. "But no more than you deserve."

"Stop it. I'm serious." She waved her hand and I was wearing that exquisite black dress complete with pearls and Louboutin heels. I looked killer, I had to admit. "Now play along. Pretend you are tempted. Maybe you will be. This man is more your type, similar to your Jeremiah, actually." Her smile was brilliant, like she hoped I'd fall for this god and skip off to Olympus and a happily ever after.

"Dream on. I will meet this guy and try not to run screaming from the room for at least five minutes. That's all I'm promising. You promise to work on that cure." I stared into her eyes. "Are we clear?"

"Of course. The limo will take you to your assignation." She pulled out a lipstick and slicked it over my lips. "He will love you. This one is crazy about feisty women. And, don't worry. I'm sure I can find someone somewhere who will know what to do about poor Jeremiah." She dropped the lipstick back into her purse. "Of course this is the first time the potion was used on a vampire. Maybe that is the problem. Hmm. I'm going to have to check on that." Then she disappeared.

Which left me to go downstairs to face yet another date with destiny. And I still didn't know my mother's name. Maybe I could wring it out of Mr. Wonderful Number Three. That put a smile on my face. It was good to have a purpose and I did love that little black dress. But pearls? I glanced up at the night sky as I walked to the limo. The least my mother owed me was a diamond drop. I laughed when I felt a tingle around my neck. Sure enough, I now wore a one-carat beauty on a platinum chain. Bull's-eye. Now if she could fix Jerry, we'd be all good.

I heard the rumble of thunder, and lightning struck a

nearby tree, a reminder that I didn't run this show. Of course not, that would be too easy. And now I had to face a god who liked feisty women? The limo raced toward the distillery nearby. Interesting. A date in a whiskey-making establishment. What if the god got drunk and out of control? With that unsettling thought I rifled through my stylish new purse, relieved to see my cell phone. But would it do any good? Who do you call when a god crosses the line?

Thunder boomed again. Oh. She'd certainly handled Hermes when he'd tried to push me around. Well, hopefully I wouldn't have to worry about that with this god. One look and he'd probably take off. Feisty, yes. Fangs, no. I could only hope anyway. But what did my mother have that these gods wanted? I needed to know. I scrolled through my contacts in my phone and saw that she'd added her own number. Olympus 19. So I texted her.

"What is your name?"

No answer. Which told me a lot. That meant if I looked her up on the Internet I'd find her and her area of expertise. The driver had called her "Your Highness." Which meant she was pretty big in the hierarchy. One of Zeus's daughters?

Thunder boomed again. I had a feeling I was getting close. I put the phone away as the limo slowed. Showtime. This was the last date and I had a feeling it was going to be a challenge. A man my mother thought was like Jerry? Had to be the God of War, whose name I couldn't remember at the moment. As I stepped out of the car, my stomach clenched. Playing house with a Highland warrior was one thing, but turning down the God of War? For the first time, I was afraid.

Nine

I knew the minute I saw him that this guy was going to be a challenge. For one thing, he wore a helmet, short body armor and carried a shield. On a date? I had to admit he was cute with his short curly beard and mustache but I could feel his power from the doorway. I was going to have to be very careful. He'd laid his spear on the table in front of him. But I had no doubt he'd pick it up if he thought I'd brought surly friends or if I acted the least bit like the angry vampire I wanted to be.

We were in the large hall in the distillery that I guess was used when they hosted dinners that featured some of their whiskeys. Someone had laid out a feast on the long banquet table. What part of my being a vampire didn't he get? Or maybe he'd decided to torture me. It was working, the delicious smells making my mouth water.

I managed a smile. "Nice plume." It was bright red and looked positively jaunty waving in the air when he nodded.

"Are you mocking me?" His eyes narrowed.

Oops. No sense of humor. "No, seriously. Love red and I'll bet it makes it easy for the troops to spot you in the middle of a battle." I was babbling but he had a dangerous glint in his eyes. "I'm Gloriana."

"Of course." He marched around the table like he was about to inspect the troops. I backed up a little, intimidated. "Please, join me. You're right of course. It's important for a leader to be easily seen when he's leading men into combat." He held out a chair to the right of the seat that looked a lot like a throne at the head of the table. "Will you have a whiskey? I've been assured that it's some of Scotland's finest."

"Umm. Sure. Thank you." I was glad Bart had told us a little wouldn't hurt. I was desperate for a numbing agent. How was I going to let this guy down easily? He gave me a sharp look. Damned mind reader.

"You aren't interested in coming to Olympus?" He set the shield aside but kept on his gleaming silver helmet. Beautiful but ridiculous to wear to a dinner party. He nodded and slipped it off, ruffling his light brown hair until the curls looked like they'd been professionally styled. "Is that better?"

"It's rude to read my mind, but, yes, it makes you look less, um, intimidating. You could lose the body armor too. I promise, I won't attack you." I smiled again and picked up the glass he'd set in front of me. The amber liquid smelled delicious and I took a cautious sip. It was potent but went down smoothly. Jerry would have called it a treat.

"No, I'm sure you won't." He slid the armor off over his head. "That would be very foolish of you." He leaned the metal against the wall. "I know you have powers, my dear, but nothing compared to what I bring to the table." He sat and stared at me like he was thinking about a demonstration. What? Knocking me against the wall? He smiled and picked up his whiskey.

"Hey, I come in peace." I took another sip of the whiskey, aggravated when my teeth clattered against the glass. "I'm sorry if my mother led you to believe I was interested in a, uh, relationship. But I'm not an Olympus kind of girl. I'm perfectly happy with my life here on Earth."

"But you haven't had a chance to see what we enjoy there. It can be paradise compared to your simple life." He leaned against the table, his hip close to my left arm. He wore a short tunic that showed off his muscular thighs, a strong warrior even without all the trappings.

"What's your name? I did a little research so I know there are several gods up there who specialize in, um, war." I sipped again, very aware of his proximity. He smelled masculine, with an odd blend of some ancient musk that made me want to explore where it came from. Uh-oh. Powers. He'd gone from intimidation to seduction in a heartbeat. I could see it in his dark eyes. I leaned back in my chair to put some distance between us.

"There may be others who dabble in war craft, but they bow to me as their leader. I am Mars." He popped himself on the chest with a fist, so hard it had to have hurt. He didn't even wince. "I'm Roman. Not Greek like so many on Olympus. And I am the one who invented any strategy worth using and most weapons worth having. Some claim I shouldn't be there. Your mother, though . . . Never mind. Tonight is about us." He leaned down until his face was inches from mine. "Would you like to see my . . . spear?"

"No! I mean I'm sure it's a fine weapon." I pointed to the steel resting on the table even though I knew he had another weapon on his mind. My face felt hot and it wasn't from the whiskey. No subtlety here. And if he and my mother had been lovers, how creepy was that?

"You have no idea. Men from the earthly plane can't compare to a god and his gifts." He brushed my hair back behind my shoulders then gestured at the food in front of me. "What do you think of the feast on the table?"

"Feast?" My voice squeaked. The subject change left me reeling. I dragged my eyes from his—they were a deep brown, the color of dark chocolate—and glanced at the roasted pig with the apple in its mouth, the bowls of steaming vegetables and piles of fresh fruits. The smells had been hitting me since I'd walked into the room; now I let myself inhale, my stomach growling.

"I had the staff here prepare this for us. What do you think?" He pulled a grape off a bunch and popped it into his mouth.

"Are you mocking *me* now? Didn't my mother tell you I'm vampire? I can't eat food. I only drink"—I let him see my fangs—"blood."

"I know. Your mother felt it wise to disclose the facts to me. On Olympus you soon learn not to make me angry. I have a nasty temper when crossed." He tore off a hunk of meat. Then he held it dripping near my lips, his palm cupped beneath it to keep from soiling my dress. "Taste, Gloriana. I have the power to keep you well. You can eat to your heart's content tonight and none of this will harm you. You could dine this sumptuously every night if you returned to the mountain with me."

"You're kidding me." The bite was so . . . close.

"I don't kid." He popped the meat into my mouth.

Oh, wow. Moist, tender and delicious. I actually moaned when I finally swallowed.

"This isn't going to get me to change my mind." I felt I had to say it, even while I was reaching for a roll and butter.

"Gloriana, just relax and enjoy. I swear you won't become ill from this. Trust my magic." He slid back into his chair and filled a plate with any number of delicacies then placed it in front of me with a smile.

Trust. Not easy when I'd had bad reactions from eating before. But as I sipped fine whiskey, devoured roasted pork, cheesy potatoes and an array of ripe fruit that I'd never tasted before, I never felt a twinge. I admit it was a little bit of Heaven. Finally I reluctantly blotted my lips with a napkin, set down my knife and fork and pushed back from the table, so full I was afraid my zipper wouldn't hold.

"All right. I'll admit you have some pretty amazing magic." I smiled while keeping my distance. He hadn't eaten, just watched me pig out with an interest that was beginning to unnerve me.

"You have barely seen any of my magic." He touched my hand. "I've enjoyed watching you eat with such enthusiasm. In Olympus such banquets are commonplace. Boring."

"Not to me." I eased my hand away to gesture at the table. "This was a miracle, Mars. Thank you. I have just enjoyed the first truly delicious and satisfying meal I've had in hundreds of years." It was no more than the truth. I'd gotten to eat fairly recently thanks to a drug I'd tested. Too bad it had had nasty side effects. I'd also wasted the opportunity on a pretty sad excuse for a meal cooked by someone who should have been banned from a kitchen.

My stomach gurgled and I was suddenly afraid Mars had lied. Luckily the only thing I suffered was embarrassment when I tried to swallow a burp. Mars just laughed when I quickly covered my mouth with my napkin.

"I love to see a woman who appreciates her food. It was my pleasure." He held up his glass, which had never seemed to grow empty. But then neither had mine though I'd drunk steadily. In fact, the room was swaying a little. "A toast. To firsts."

"Firsts?" I let him clink glasses with mine but waited for an explanation.

"Your first meal with me. The first time I've sat like this with a woman and not lifted her skirt before dessert." His grin was wicked. "You do want dessert, don't you?" He nodded and a servant entered with a chocolate cake that I could smell from across the room.

"Now you're just torturing me. I was sure I couldn't eat another bite." I rubbed my stomach. For chocolate, I'd make room. He cut a big slice of cake, chocolate through and through, and handed me a plate. Before I could pick up a fork, he broke off a piece and brought it to my lips.

"Open for me, Gloriana." His voice had dropped to a husky demand.

"Mars." I didn't like the look in his eyes but couldn't help myself. My lips closed over the delicate cake and frosting. Before I could stop myself I'd licked his fingers clean. Bad, Glory.

"One kiss. Just to see how a vampire tastes. Humor me." He leaned in and I saw a touch of chocolate on his lower lip. It was enough for me.

"One. Then I must go." I met his lips with mine, more intent on getting to that chocolate than on the kissing part. But he was a wily creature. He slipped his hand to the back of my head and moved his mouth over mine. He wasn't just a god who was an expert on violence. Obviously he had a passionate nature as well. He toyed with me, explored my fangs and seemed to like the novelty as his tongue roamed through my mouth.

I was too far gone with the whiskey to do more than hold his shoulders, trying to keep some space between us. Before I knew it I'd jammed my fingers into his soft curls. His beard was soft too and tickled my face but in a pleasantly sensual way that encouraged me to keep this going.

"No!" I shoved him away, suddenly finding my sense when he slid his hand down to cup my breast. "I am not going to Olympus. No matter what you offer."

"Really?" He stood and his shield, which had never been far from his hand, suddenly leaped into it. Magic. His spear moved too and he gripped it with his other hand. "This coy act isn't as cute as you think it is. I find it irritating." He gestured with his shield and suddenly everything on the table crashed to the floor. I jumped up and backed away. Obviously Mars had a temper.

"It's not an act. I'm happy here on Earth. I have a vampire lover who I will not betray." *Again.* "My mother must have misrepresented the situation." I thought about dematerializing but one gesture from Mars and every power I had deserted me. Damned Olympus magic.

"I can take care of that vampire lover. It will be my pleasure." He gestured with his spear. "Your mother claims he was once a warrior. Though I'm sure he will be no match for me, I could enjoy a moment or two of sport with him before I take his head." His grin reminded me of someone who thought drowning kittens would be a good afternoon's entertainment.

"You won't touch him." I picked up an apple which had rolled across the floor and threw it at him. In a display of finesse, he caught it on the end of his spear. Show off.

"I will if I want to." Now he sounded like a petulant little boy.

"Really? Is that all you have to occupy your time? Take women who don't want you and kill vampires, who my mother assures me are well beneath your notice?" I lobbed a golden squash that had been used as part of the centerpiece at his head. This he slashed in two, dead center. I swallowed at his perfect coordination and the sharpness of his blade.

"It's true I usually consider them little more than earthly roadkill." He laughed, cracking himself up. "Get it? Dead, undead?"

"You think mocking what I am is scoring you points?" I really wanted to snatch his helmet off the table and break his plume.

"Watch it, woman." He set the helmet firmly back on his head with a scowl. Then he slashed his spear through the chair that stood between us. Sparks flew, the chair fell apart, and I realized he had more than a sharp blade in that spear.

I dashed to the other side of the room. "Don't you have real work to do, Mars? Right now in several parts of the world there are real wars going on. Bloody, hellacious ones. I'm sure you can find some interesting action there." I saw him stalking me, kicking scattered fruit and dishes out of his way. He could paralyze me no doubt, like my mother could, but he probably didn't consider that sporting.

"I told your mother I'd try to get you to Olympus. I find that an interesting challenge." He leaped on top of the table.

"Admit it, Gloriana. You enjoyed that kiss. You were tempted by the feast."

I had nowhere to run. He dropped down to within a foot of me, his eyes ablaze with the need to win. I recognized it; hadn't I seen it in Jerry's eyes when he'd fought in the past? I dared reach out to touch Mars's chest. He was hard and warm, breathing rapidly and excited by my resistance. My fingers were shaking because I knew just how helpless I was to fight him.

"Are you the kind of warrior who carries away women as the spoils of war? Is pillaging and rape part of your scene?"

"You dare!" The blast of power from him knocked me flat on my back. I lay there for a moment, stunned. "I have never raped a woman in my life."

"Well, that's the only way you're going to get me back to Olympus as your, um, consort." I shook my head to clear it. Whoa. Whatever he'd unleashed in his temper fit had hit me like a body blow.

"To hell with you then." He turned on his heel, throwing out his arms and sending the contents of the room into a swirl of destruction that left everything in bits and pieces. I held my hands over my head to keep from getting hit.

"Mars, please. I'm sorry, but I told my mother I wasn't interested. It's not you, it's me."

"Zeus's toenail, woman, I can't believe you just said that." He whipped around, his spear close to my chest.

"It's the truth. You want to be mad at someone, be mad at my mother. I . . . I like you. You're charming when you're not throwing a temper tantrum." I got slowly to my feet, being careful of that really sharp blade. "And you gave me a wonderful gift." I glanced at the total disaster of the room. "A meal I'll never forget."

"You are very like your mother, Gloriana. Most women after what I just did would be a sniveling heap on the floor." He lowered his spear. "Damned if I don't think I like you. Your warrior is a lucky man."

"Uh, thank you."

He smiled. "I only wore my old battle gear tonight to impress you. I can tell you like it." He stepped closer, back to flirtation.

I held up my hand in a classic stop gesture. "Mars, I can't go to Olympus. But my mother told me she has to follow through on whatever she promised you no matter what I decide tonight. Is that true?" I smiled to take the sting out of that, relieved when he seemed to take what I said calmly.

"Yes, it is. And she won't tell anyone you turned me down." He nodded. "I have some secrets of hers that I can use as leverage too."

"There you go." Olympus politics sounded even worse than American. "Seems like it'll be a win for you." I held out my hand. "Can we part as friends? I'd like to think that if I got in a spot of trouble, I could call on a powerful god like you for help. I figure we're probably related in some way, if my research about Olympus is true. Seems like just about everyone comes from Zeus up there." And wasn't that an ick factor? I was afraid Mother had tried to fix me up with some really close relatives.

"Oh, yes, we're definitely related." He leaned his spear against the wall and took my hand. "I'd like that, Gloriana. To help you. Your mother will hate it."

"There you go. Anything my mother hates, I love. We're on the same page." I gasped when he brought my hand to his lips and kissed it. "Or are we?"

"Just a courtesy, my dear." He laughed. "I got your message. But if you ever change your mind or need me, just call my name. I will hear you."

"What about my mother? She won't tell me her name. Will you?" But he'd already disappeared. Damn. I turned on my heel and walked out of the room, only stopping long enough to pick up an unbroken bottle of that fine whiskey. I had a feeling Jerry would enjoy it and maybe it would help him remember something. It had certainly relaxed me and put me in the mood to jump all over him as soon as I got back. I was feeling optimistic for the first time since he'd been stabbed. No more blind dates and my mother was supposed to be cooperating. If Mars had the magic to make me eat, then surely she could find someone with the mojo to help Jerry get his memory back.

My stomach gurgled again and I waited to see if my meal was going to reappear. No, false alarm, though I did feel like I could burp "The Star-Spangled Banner," a trick my pal Rafe Valdez had taught me. I know, nothing to brag about.

I thought about that dense chocolate cake with the creamy frosting. Heaven on a fork. I had to admit Olympus did have its charms. Thunder boomed but I ignored it. Sorry, Mom, but I wasn't about to give up Jerry for fine dining. And wasn't that a revelation.

Two nights had passed without a word from my mother or much progress with Jerry's memory. Bart had tried hypnosis with Jerry again but they'd had no luck. We were leaving for Edinburgh to catch the plane the next night. Mag and Angus were unhappy about it but saw the wisdom in taking Jerry back to his more recent haunts. Plus, he could finally meet his daughter.

"I've got a surprise for you, Gloriana." Jerry had seemed to regain his strength as he drank from me each night. Now he dragged me through the living room and outside into the cold night air.

"Oh?" I didn't like surprises. History had shown me that they were usually nasty ones. A breakup. Unwelcome guests. I could go on. But Jerry's eyes were bright with excitement so I hoped that this was a good one.

"Da and I have arranged a party for tonight. A going away bonfire and pipers are coming. Most of the clan that still lives around here are coming too." He picked up the bottle of whiskey I had brought back from my date. I'd explained it away, claiming my mother had given it to me as a bribe, trying to get back into my good graces. "I'll take this with me."

I held his hand, enjoying his firm grasp and happy smile. "Bagpipes!" I'd learned to appreciate their music long ago.

"Yes. Did you ever learn the dances here?" He swept his eyes down my outfit. I'd bought a short skirt made from the Campbell plaid in the village. I'd paired it with a low-cut black sweater and black boots. "You look ready for a jig or two."

"Thanks, I wore it for you. Plaid isn't my first choice. Makes my butt look big." Now I'd done it. He turned me to check that big butt out. Of course he looked fantastic in his kilt and knee socks. Oh, but the man had great legs.

"Nonsense." He gave my bum a friendly pat which turned into a squeeze. "I'm growing very fond of this ass. Besides, the Campbell plaid looks good on anyone." He put his arm around my waist and pulled me close. "Are you going to dance with me?"

"You bet. I love to dance. You don't remember but I supported myself for a while as a dancer. A few years ago. Before I moved to Austin. And when I was here last, the girls taught me some of the dances." I grinned up at him. The air was crisp and smelled of wood smoke. This was beginning to feel like old times. "Lead the way."

He held up the whiskey bottle. "If I drink enough, I'll even get out the swords."

"Oh, would you?" I kissed his cheek. "I'd love to see you sword dance. Ancient warrior style."

"It's the only way I remember, lass." His smile slipped. "Come on." He pulled me toward a clearing where we could see people milling around a large fire. Just then the pipes started. It was a merry song and a cheer went up.

"Look!" I pointed as Angus bowed to Mag, and Laird and Lady Campbell took a spot near the fire to begin a lively jig. It was fun to see them cut loose. The crowd clapped and cheered as they whirled and turned, clasping hands and then dancing around each other. Finally, the song ended and everyone hooted and stomped their feet. Angus bowed, Mag curtsied then several other couples took their places as the music started again.

"What fun!" The voice came from the darkness. "It's high time the Campbells entertained again."

Jerry turned to face the couple walking from the car park next to the garage. "Mara and Davy! Well met!" He shook hands with Mara's fiancé and kissed Mara's cheek. "I'm leaving for America tomorrow so Da and I thought we should have some kind of send-off."

"Leaving?" Mara's face fell. "Are you all right? Have you got your memory back?"

"No." Jerry glanced at the merriment around the bonfire. "I realize staying here is like living in the past. Gloriana has urged me to go where I have lived the last few years. It's a good idea. We hope it will help me remember some of what I've lost." He rested his arm on my shoulders.

"Gloriana's idea, of course. Honestly, do you have to drag him away from his family so soon? But then I'm sure Mag and Angus won't be sorry to see the last of you, Gloriana, will they? Too bad you've persuaded Jeremiah to go with you." Mara had that pinched look around her mouth she got whenever she talked to me.

"My parents realize I need to meet our daughter. Lily, you said her name was." Jerry tightened his arm around me.

"Yes, and she's still in Austin. I got a text from her just yesterday. She's wondering why she didn't get her allowance from you this month. Apparently you've been supporting her, Jeremiah." Mara frowned. "It's ridiculous of course. She should be making her own way by now."

"Like you did?" That popped out before I could stop myself. But the truth was Mara had married money and had never worked a day in her life.

"Gloriana, not all of us are willing to stoop as low as you

did to earn our keep." Mara's smile was cold. "After all, you will do anything to be independent, won't you?"

"What does that mean?" Jerry gave us both searching looks.

"It means that I'm not afraid of hard work, Jerry, even if it's acting on the stage. That I don't take money from you and that I live on what I earn." I kept my arm around his waist. "I'm not ashamed of it. I guess I could have a talk with Lily, help her figure out a way to earn her own living without depending on her father or some other man." I gave Mara a meaningful look.

"My daughter doesn't need advice from such as you." Mara's nostrils flared. Not a pretty look for a change.

"Does she need to work? I hope I can afford to support my own child." Jerry growled. "Can't I?" He ran a hand through his hair. "Hell, I have no idea what condition my finances are in."

"You are quite wealthy, Jeremiah." Of course Mara had looked into *that* situation. "And, as her father, you can do as you please. The generous allowance you give her has helped her get rid of some undesirable friends who were paying her way so she could live an unsavory lifestyle. The allowance and inviting her to live with you was a wise decision."

I had heard enough from the shrew. "Yes, you can afford it, Jerry, but Lily isn't a child at over four hundred years old. It would be nice if she had a sense of responsibility."

Davy McLeod cleared his throat. "That's awfully good music going to waste while we discuss such thorny topics. Can't we dance now, my love, and put this off for another time?"

"Of course, darling." Mara sneered at me. "Trust Gloriana to turn a pleasant evening into a disagreeable wrangle. Jeremiah, Lily will love you. Does love you. Your generosity literally saved her life. I'm sure you will figure out your relationship with her. Now let's dance." She pulled Davy toward the bonfire.

"Sorry. Did I cause that?" I looked at Jerry's pensive expression.

"No, Mara was trying to pick a fight. That was obvious even to my muddled brain. Now it seems Lily might be a problem when I had hoped she'd be a joy. Shit. I've had a lot on my empty mind lately, Gloriana. Money, family, even trying to figure out if I can go up in a flying machine tomorrow night without acting the fool." He pulled me against him. "So I thought I'd try to forget all that for a while with a bit of fun. Are you with me?" His smile was a good effort, but strained.

"Of course. Put all those worries on the back burner. It does no good to strain to remember things and might even make it worse." I leaned up and kissed him. "I have to warn you, though. It's been dozens of years since we've come here together. Be patient with my dancing. I may be rusty."

He just pulled me closer and kissed me again. I had a feeling he was gathering strength. Then he stepped back, bowed like a courtier of old and urged me closer to the crowd. Once there, he found a spot among the dancers and made sure I could follow the steps. Soon we were laughing and leaping around with the best of them.

Bart and Caitie joined the dancers and proved to be quite a couple, showing off their skills. Bart wore the O'Connor plaid, which got him some looks, but Cait made sure he got a warm welcome. He wasn't the only one in a different plaid; Davy and Mara's stood out too. Neighbors wore their own clan plaids and some had come in their modern clothes. Still, everyone seemed to have a good time, enjoying the old-fashioned entertainment which included a local singing group.

Several hours went by and the whiskey Jerry had brought plus many other bottles were passed around. Then the laird called for quiet and swords were brought out.

"Now this is the way they danced in ancient times." Jerry tossed aside his empty bottle, his eyes bright. "The swords are wicked sharp. One misstep and I'll ruin my boots." He laughed then set two swords on the ground to make a cross. Several other men did the same. The pipers were tuning up, waiting for a signal. They began to play as soon as the men raised their arms, their feet on the ground between the swords.

It was a delicate dance with fancy footwork that still looked entirely masculine. Of course these were warriors who leaped over their swords, gleaming in the light from the fire. I could imagine this as it must have been hundreds of years ago. Jerry proved to be a master of the dance, his feet never once brushing the steel as he skipped lightly around the swords. He turned and twirled, bent and straightened. It was mesmerizing.

Suddenly he froze. He turned, swept up both swords, one in each hand, and stared into the darkness just outside the light from the fire. The pipes stopped with an eerie whine.

"Come closer, you coward. I can smell ye."

"Can you really? I swear I bathed before I came." The voice was amused but the man who stepped into the circle of light looked entirely serious. "Really, Jeremiah, are you still holding a grudge?"

"Damn you, MacDonald, why wouldn't I be? You killed my brother."

I gasped, my heart in my throat. So this was one of Ian's clan, obviously wearing his plaid. The man looked like Ian with the same blond hair and harsh features that spoke of a Viking raid long ago. He didn't carry a sword of his own but then why would he? He wasn't like Jerry, still thinking with a sixteenth-century mind.

"I had heard rumors that you were off your head. I guess they're true. Your brother has been dead for centuries, man. Let it go."

Jerry tossed one of the swords toward the MacDonald who caught it effortlessly. "Let it go, Douglas? Would you let your own brother's death be forgiven and forgotten so easily?"

"What's this?" Douglas gave the sword a few slashes as if he were testing the steel. "Are you seriously thinking of a sword fight? What are you? A throwback?"

"Aye. It seems I am. Come on. Or did you leave your guts in your other sporran?" Jerry stepped closer and flicked his sword toward the man purse Douglas wore, cutting off one of the foxtails that hung from it.

"Now you've pissed me off. This is my best one, you thug." He brushed his hand down the front of the fancy sporran closed with a large silver clasp that featured a snarling creature.

"You're stalling." Jerry wore plain leather embossed with the Campbell crest.

"I have guts aplenty but no taste for ancient sports." He threw down the sword and the crowd gasped when it clattered to the ground. "You want to keep up a stupid feud? I have no interest in it. Neither has my brother Ian. When you get to Texas, you will find that he is no longer going to bother you or your"—he bowed toward me—"loved ones."

"Why did you come here?" Angus stepped forward. "You were not invited."

"I heard you were having a clan gathering and thought this might be a good time to propose a truce. I am laird of Clan MacDonald now and have brought members of my own clan with me." He raised his hand and a dozen burly men dressed in the MacDonald plaid appeared out of the darkness. "We mean you no harm or we could have already ambushed you. Do you believe that?"

Angus nodded. "I believe you have a goodly number of men here and managed to sneak up on us. 'Tis reason enough for me to ban whiskey here from now on." He stepped closer to Jerry. "Feuds are a waste of time, I agree with that. And your brother was avenged long ago, you just don't remember it, Son." He rested his hand on Jerry's sword arm.

"That he was, Laird." Douglas's face hardened. "I remember it well. We have both lost brothers, Jeremiah. Yet I am still willing to put our differences aside. Because the world seems smaller than it used to be. We both have holdings elsewhere, and looking over our shoulders in case an enemy lurks there is a waste of energy and manpower."

"That it is." Angus gestured but Jerry wasn't about to give up his sword yet. "I would have you swear a blood oath, MacDonald, as the head of your clan, that this is a true and honorable end to any and all hostilities between us. This will be witnessed by all those here from both sides, tonight. Are you willing, Douglas MacDonald?"

"Da, no!" Jerry wrenched away from his father. Before he could get close to Douglas, six men in the MacDonald plaid stood in front of their leader with guns drawn. More than one also held a stake.

"Touch me and you'll be dead before you can lift that sword." Douglas glanced at the laird. "I'm willing to take the oath but you'll have to make sure your son here understands that this treaty between us is binding upon him as well. Both here and in Texas if he goes back there. My brother is as weary of this endless hostility as I am."

I wondered about that. It hadn't been that long ago that Ian had played one of his dirty tricks just to get Jerry's goat. Would he really forget their feud now?

More than twenty Campbell men now flanked Jerry, and every sword that had been on the ground had found a hand. The other men held dirks, those wickedly sharp knives the Scots favored.

"Tell your men to stand down, MacDonald." Angus pulled Jerry to his side and gestured to some of his own men to back off when the MacDonald men put away their weapons at a nod from their leader. "My son knows that my word is law in our clan." One of the Campbells took Jerry's sword though he was cursed for it. My heart broke to see Jerry humiliated like that. But he knew the rules and had always abided by them.

This was the right thing to do. It was a miracle a MacDonald had been the one to propose the truce. Modern Jerry would have still hated it, but would have understood the necessity of letting an ancient feud go.

"I'm glad I won't be here to see this." Jerry again wrenched away from his father. "You know you can't trust him. As soon as your back is turned—"

"You'll abide by my decision." Angus clearly would tolerate no argument.

"Aye." Jerry nodded, his face like stone.

"Then spill my blood. For the oath." Angus gestured and a man handed Jerry a dirk. I knew Jerry had one tucked into his belt. It was a miracle he hadn't thrown it the minute Douglas had come into view. "Careful now. I don't fancy losing a finger."

Jerry muttered a curse but made a neat slice on his father's palm.

Douglas did the same with his own dirk. Then the two men stepped forward and clasped bloody hands.

"Peace!" Angus roared then said something in Gaelic. Jerry stayed silent.

"Peace!" Douglas and the rest of the crowd echoed. Then the two leaders spit on the ground and the pipers began to play a lively tune. Whiskey reappeared and everyone started talking.

Jerry stood pale and brooding near his father. Enough. I walked over to him and pulled him aside.

"Let's get out of here," I said quietly. He nodded and we started walking toward the castle.

"Miss Gloriana?" Douglas was there, too close to ignore.

"How do you know who I am?" That really bothered me. This man shouldn't have known my name or recognized me.

"My brother and I communicate. He sent me a picture of you when I told him who was staying at the Campbell castle." Douglas smiled like it was perfectly all right to have spies in his enemy's camp.

"This MacDonald in Texas has a picture of you, Gloriana? Why?" Jerry pulled me to his side, clearly ready to get away from Douglas and this whole party gone wrong.

"He's a doctor, remember? Bart mentioned him. I was sick recently. I used his services. He took a picture then, I guess." Of course he had, probably with a security camera. Did Douglas know my entire long and complicated history with Ian? It was certainly nothing I wanted to get into now with Jerry. "We're leaving for home tomorrow. I hope you mean this feud is really over because I think Ian might be able to help Jerry regain his memory."

"Ah, yes. Amnesia. Most unusual in a vampire." Douglas tried for a sympathetic expression but failed. "My brother will certainly be fascinated by it. He is always curious about the unexplainable." The implication was clear: Jerry was a freak and if he stayed that way, Douglas wouldn't be sorry to hear it.

Jerry stiffened beside me. "Feud or no feud, I will never trust a MacDonald and certainly not to be my doctor." He pulled me toward the castle. "Come, Gloriana. I think I've had all of this company I can tolerate."

"Good night, Gloriana, Jeremiah." Douglas smiled. "Believe it. This feud is done. I have better things to do with my time than worry about petty squabbles between Highland chiefs."

"I'll bet you do." Jerry stopped and looked him up and down. "If I remember aright, you were fond of sneaking up on the backside of sheep. Ever get a woman to stand still for you, Douglas?"

His answer was a wooden stake pressed against Jerry's heart in the blink of an eye.

"Stop it!" I grabbed Douglas's arm.

"Maybe the people around here feel sorry for you, asshole, because you've lost your memory, but I won't put up with that kind of insult from anybody." Douglas pressed hard enough to make a spot of blood appear on Jerry's white shirt. I tried to pull him away but he wasn't budging. Jerry just smiled, apparently not worried about death pressing against his heart. "You ever speak to me like that again and I'll send you to hell, feud or no feud. Understand?"

"Stop it, I said. One yell and you'll have a horde of Campbells staking *you*, Douglas. Back the hell off."

"Hush, Gloriana. This is between the MacDonald and me." Jerry grinned and grabbed the stake, his arm shaking as he shoved it away. "Sorry if I touched on a sensitive subject there, Dougie. Put away the stick or shove it up your ass, whichever you prefer. My father has sworn peace or you'd already be dead at my hand for killing my brother." Jerry raised an eyebrow when Douglas cursed and tried again. They ended up wrestling for it, the MacDonald finally stepping back out of reach when he realized he couldn't win.

"Four hundred years ago you came back and killed my own brother in retaliation for your loss. Convenient that you forget that. Darren, his name was. You fought hand to hand but he was no match for you." Douglas slipped his stake into a holster. "I thought long and hard before I offered this truce. Because those wounds never heal. But, as I told your pa, I'll not waste another second watching my back for the likes of you." With a kind of dignity I wouldn't have expected, Douglas backed away.

"We are done, Campbell." He turned on his heel, striding away just as others noticed our group and some of the Campbell men started toward us.

Jerry stared after him. "So I killed Darren MacDonald." He shook his head. "How can I not remember something that important?"

"I don't know, Jerry, but you're bleeding." As soon as we were inside I tore open his shirt. He had a slice in his chest from that damned stake.

"It's nothing. I was lucky he didn't take me down. I still don't have my strength back, Gloriana. It took everything in me to fight him off. Damn it." Then Jerry looked me over. "Well not everything. I've been thinking about you all night, lass, watching you bounce around in the dance."

"Now, Jerry, you said you were weak." I smiled as he pulled me to his bedroom.

"Then feed me first, there's a good lass. Tell me, do you

have one of those torture things on your breasts? The black one? I'd like to see if I could get it off of you myself this time. Got to learn these things, you know."

And that quickly, his mood turned again. He was cheerful as he led me to his bedroom, his humiliation obviously soothed by what he considered his revenge for his brother's death. I hated his taunt to Douglas. It wasn't like my Jerry, the man who knew when to cry peace and when to keep his mouth shut. This angry man . . . I had to blame it on his frustration with the memory loss. Of course it had affected his personality.

But it hadn't bothered his lovemaking. Once we shut the door to his bedroom, he slid his hand up under my skirt to discover that, afraid I might show the crowd too much skin, I'd worn my black granny panties under my mini. Then he puzzled over the front clasp of my bra, crowing when he managed it. Maybe it was the whiskey, but, after drinking from me, he was untiring as he took me that night, over and over again. I had no complaints. So why was I still worried?

Ten

We arrived at the Edinburgh airport just as the small private plane taxied to a stop on the tarmac. Jerry's eyes were wild. He'd been watching the airplanes coming down since we'd arrived at the area where we'd been told to meet our friends. The noise was bad enough, but when a large jet roared overhead and then headed up into the clouds at a sharp angle right above us, I thought Jerry was going to dive under the car. Only the warrior in him kept him leaning against the hood, pretending this was business as usual. I touched his shoulder and could feel the tension vibrating through him.

"Relax, Jer. Planes have been flying people places for a hundred years. You'll enjoy it. Much better than taking wing yourself across the Atlantic." I slid my arm around his waist. "I honestly don't think you have the strength for that right now."

"Are you sure? Da said that's how I got home before." Jerry squeezed my shoulders. "I'd much prefer—"

"No argument." Bart had driven us here. "You will let them take you in the plane. I think a long shift would be too much for you. If you want to get your memory back, you need to conserve your strength."

"So this must be part of that shock therapy you talked about." Jerry managed a smile.

A joke? I hugged him then heard a squeal. Flo was coming down the stairs from the side of the plane.

"Gloriana! Jeremiah! You look wonderful!" She rushed toward us, arms outstretched. I met her halfway and hugged her tight, fighting tears. It was so good to see her again. I was dying to tell her everything—all about my witch of a mother, my dates, Jerry's condition. Later. She moved past me and hugged Jerry then leaned back. He looked awkward in her embrace and it didn't take her long to figure things out.

"*Mio Dio*, you don't know me?" Tears filled her dark eyes. "Don't worry. We will fix." She sniffed and gestured like she was checking it on her to do list. "Now. Who is this handsome man?" She turned to Bart.

"Bartholomew O'Connor, Jerry's doctor." He held out his hand.

"And I'm Jerry's sister Caitlin." Caitie had been chatting with one of the flight attendants who serviced the private planes but she had hurried over as soon as Flo appeared. Now she put a proprietary arm on Bart's. Interesting.

"Yes, please meet everyone." I ran to pull Richard forward to introduce him too. "This is Flo's husband, Richard Mainwaring. Jerry, do you remember him?"

Jerry smiled suddenly. "I think I do. Did we meet in Europe? Maybe it was Rome. Aren't you the renegade priest?" He looked at Flo. "Guess not anymore."

"No, I gave up the Church. At least as a priest." Richard slapped Jerry on the back. "That was centuries ago. You'd just been turned and were taking a grand tour, of sorts." He smiled as I introduced him to Bart and Caitie. "I hope to talk to you, Doctor. I've been doing some research of my own on Jerry's condition."

"Excellent. Your reputation precedes you and I could use

the help. I have some cases to wrap up here and should be in Texas by the end of the week. But here's my card. You can call me, or we could set up a video chat." He passed the card over then slid his arm around Cait. "I'm hoping to persuade Jeremiah's sister to come with me to Austin. She's never seen the Wild West."

"Is it? Wild?" Jerry looked around the group. "Gloriana assured me it would be civilized. A big city."

"He's pulling your leg, Jer." I flushed when Jerry actually looked down at his legs clad in jeans for the trip. "It's an expression. Means he's joking." I glanced at Flo and saw her getting teary again. "Does the plane need to refuel or anything or are we ready to go?"

"The pilot says we'll be here about thirty minutes before we can take off again. There's paperwork." Richard grinned. "If you'll excuse me, I'll use some of my vampire mojo to clear the way there."

"What does he mean?" Jerry looked at Flo.

"Oh, he does this all the time. He'll mesmerize the authorities to overlook things like passports and all the little things they want to see when we land and take off. No matter. Come and get on board. CiCi, Freddy and Derek are inside. They are anxious to see you both. Best that they stay out of sight, though. These paper pushers—" Flo glanced at the airport security. "They don't need to get excited about all the people we are taking in and out of the country." She made a face. "Such a fuss we had in Paris until Ricardo got involved."

"You tried to smuggle out one of their treasures, my love." Richard was back. "Now let's go."

"Flo? What did you do?" I left Jerry and Richard to deal with our luggage. I saw them talking like old friends, which made me happy.

"It was nothing. A little trinket that belonged to Marie Antoinette. Some claimed it belonged to a museum. I say it belongs around my neck." She pulled a chain from between her breasts. She wore a to-die-for silk blouse in a deep green. The emerald on the end of the platinum chain was carved with a profile that did seem to resemble the beheaded queen.

"It's beautiful!" And had to be worth a fortune.

"Yes, and wasn't my Ricardo sweet to buy it for me? We got it from some shifters in the cutest little shop. But then they disappeared with our cash when the *polizia* showed up." She shrugged, typical Flo. "I don't care if they stole it. I won't give it back. It's mine now. The French, they are out of luck. Ricardo, he took care of everything." She tucked it out of sight again.

"Hmm. I hope so." We stepped inside the luxurious cabin of their rented jet and greeted our friends CiCi, Countess Cecilia Von Repsdorf, and her son Freddy along with his partner Derek. Then we had to reintroduce Jerry to them. Unfortunately he stared at them like they were strangers. This got CiCi upset and didn't make Jerry too happy either.

When the hatch was closed and locked, Jerry's mouth tightened and his eyes were wide. We all took our seats, Jerry beside me. I helped him with his seat belt, then held his hand. The whine of the engines starting made his grasp tighten.

"It will be all right, Jer. Once we're airborne, you won't even realize we're flying. We'll fall into our death sleep when it's dawn and wake up just before we land. Great timing." I smiled across the aisle at Flo.

"It's true. We always arrange our long flights this way. The pilot is an old friend of Ricardo's. He's a shifter and we trust him completely." She smiled at her husband and picked up his hand. "Once the seat belt sign goes off, you can get up and walk around." She frowned. "The pilot knows we can't be hurt when he takes off, but he insists everyone stay buckled in while he gets the plane off the ground. Says we will make the plane unstable or something. Pah!" She threw up her hands. "Stupid rule. So unnecessary."

"Florence doesn't like seat belts. Says they wrinkle her

clothes." Richard smiled at her indulgently. "Are you all right, Jeremiah?"

Jerry nodded but I knew it for a lie. Flo and Richard whispered together.

"I remember my first time in an airplane." Flo threw up her hands again. "*Madre di Dio!* I was ready to smash a window and leap off the thing." She smiled at Jerry. "But I found that I loved it once we got off the ground. That was in the early days when airplanes were little more than sticks glued together. You remember those days, don't you, Ricardo? Glory?"

"She's right, Jerry. This is a five star modern jet." Which was now absolutely roaring. We had to raise our voices to be heard. I had both hands around Jerry's now.

"It's very comfortable. Your seat will lie back and we have movies you can watch, Internet once we're in the air." Richard frowned. "Oh, hell. You won't care about that. Glory, anything we can do?"

"I don't think so." I leaned against Jerry. He wasn't saying a word, just staring panicked around the plane while the engines got even louder and the plane started moving with a lurch. It hit a bump and I saw him reach for one of his knives. "Steady. We're not under attack."

"You sure?" He pulled out his knife anyway and laid it across his knees.

Flo noticed. "If you are thirsty, we have every kind of synthetic blood you could want. I'll bring you something as soon as we're airborne." Flo wouldn't give up. "There's a new one that tastes like a strawberry milk shake, Glory."

"Interesting." I didn't think I could drink a thing, not with Jerry looking so freaked out. I held up my hand to let her know I was through with the chitchat. She nodded, picking up a fashion magazine and popping in earbuds, satisfied that she'd done her best as our hostess. If Jerry wanted to slit his wrists then let me drain him dry, it was our business. That was my wild imagination at work. I'm sure Flo just hoped I could calm Jerry down. I glanced over. Richard didn't look too keen on this experience either, his eyes closed tightly while he gripped his armrests.

"I have to get out of here." Jerry struggled to open his seat belt with shaking hands.

"No. You can do this." I turned his head toward me. "Look at me. This is easy compared to some of the things you've faced. Battles where you've been outnumbered. Fighting vampire hunters who had technology that put them at an advantage. You have no idea how much I admire your bravery."

"I lost that when I lost my mind." He gritted his teeth. "Fuck!" He almost crushed my fingers when the plane hit another bump as it taxied toward the runway. "Sorry." He kissed my hand. "Mesmerize me, Gloriana. You know how to do it. Maybe it's the coward's way but make me think we're somewhere else. Anywhere else. Spin a fantasy for us so I'll forget I'm trapped in this metal box that, against nature, you say is going to leap above the clouds."

"Are you sure?" I hated to do that to him. It *was* the coward's way. So unlike him.

"Just *do* it, damn it." He almost crushed my fingers again.

So I looked deep into his eyes and sent him a mental picture. We were in a forest as far away from here as we could get. It was very quiet. Not even the birds were chirping, asleep for the night as we walked together, hand in hand. The air was cool, leaves crackling under our footsteps. We came to a clear pond and sat down beside it. We threw off our shoes and dipped our toes into the water. It was perfect, not too hot or too cold. We kissed, taking our time to taste each other. Then we undressed, watching as clothing dropped to the forest floor until we were naked.

He pulled me into the water, swimming to where a waterfall tumbled over rocks and into the pond. The water showered us as we laughed and chased each other, our bodies brushing from hip to thigh to chest. Finally he found a flat rock behind the falls and pulled me up to lay me down.

There he kissed every inch of my body. My eyes drifted closed. We were both well into the fantasy now.

Jerry's hands were everywhere, stroking me, finding those pleasure points he knew so well. I tasted his mouth on mine. We were all warm skin and slick heat as he entered me, his rhythm perfect as he sent me to that place where only he could take me. We rolled over, touching, kissing and pressing hard against that rock as we searched for completion. His mouth branded me his, devoured me and sent us both tumbling into the water. We kept falling, locked together, all the way to the bottom of the pond. We couldn't breathe but didn't need to.

He sank his fangs into my neck, his steady draw on me another pulse of fire inside me. I came again, just from the force of his pull as he drank. Finally we burst to the surface, the moonlight shining down on us as we climbed out to lie panting on the grass.

This was the only thing that mattered. That we were together. The world could end in a minute, a day, a week. The plane could plummet to the earth. None of that mattered. Because we were together. We'd found what we needed. Each other.

I opened my eyes and stared at Jerry. He smiled and let go of my hand.

"I think we must be up in the clouds now." He brushed my cheeks with fingers that were no longer shaking. "Is it possible?"

I reached across him and slid open the window covering. "Look." Sure enough there was nothing to see but black night sky and white clouds down below us. The plane was rock steady and the others were opening their seat belts and getting up. Flo stood next to me and held out a goblet.

"Try this. It's probably the best thing you ever tasted."

I leaned forward and kissed Jerry's lips. "Nope. This is the best thing I ever tasted. Right here." I laughed and leaned back. Life was good.

Until dawn hit everyone around me, and I was still wide

awake. I looked around and saw a familiar figure strolling down the aisle like she owned it. She gestured to me and I followed her to a pair of empty seats near the restroom.

"What the hell is going on, Mother? Why are you dropping in here? And why am I still awake? I assume this is your doing." I plopped down in the seat. Okay, staying awake past the dawn is cool. My friend Ray pays big bucks for a drug that lets him do that very thing. But in a vampire it's downright unnatural. The lights were dim and everyone else had pulled their chairs back until they were reclining. It was almost creepy the way they were laid out, still as corpses. Which is what I'd expected to be about now too.

"I thought you'd appreciate a little extra awake time." She smiled and waved her hand. My jeans and sweater morphed into a stylish pantsuit, black silk with a red and black print tank underneath.

"Stop that! I don't want to explain the wardrobe change. And I don't like surprises. I wish you'd get that." I glanced around. "Seriously. Put me back in my own clothes."

"But you look so much better now. Your friend Florence certainly knows how to dress for travel. Vintage Givenchy." She kissed her fingertips in a French gesture of appreciation. "And the countess looks divine in that new number from Chanel. Obviously she knows how to shop in Paris." She sighed. "Your friends have style and money. And look at you." She flicked her wrist and I was back in my jeans and old sweater. What could I say? It was the end of a long trip and I hadn't wanted to explain any of the clothes she'd given me to my friends.

"I'm a working girl. I do all right. Eventually I'll run across a nice Chanel of my own on consignment. Leave me alone." I tried to get up. She froze me in place.

"No, we need to have a little chat." She blinked and a glass of champagne appeared in her hand. "Want one?"

I licked my lips. I could have used a drink but didn't trust her. "No thanks. What are we discussing? Did you bring an antidote to that horrible spell Jerry is under? Can you cure him before we touch down in Texas?"

"Would that I could." She took a sip. "Mmm. Delightful. I only drink the best. Sure you won't have a glass?" She materialized a second flute and I took it in spite of better intentions. I sniffed and figured if it was good enough for her, it was okay for me. Hey, Mars had allowed me to eat, so why couldn't my mother figure out a way for me to enjoy champagne?

"Yes, you did dine with Mars." She smiled as she watched me sip. "He liked you."

"I kind of liked him." Uh-oh, her eyes lit up. "Not to run away to Olympus with but he was pretty cool. A warrior like Jerry. We came to an understanding. I could reason with him."

"Yes, he indicated as much." She frowned as she polished off her champagne and the glass disappeared. Mine she re-filled.

"He give you a hard time?" Now this was good news.

"You could say that. He wants me to back off. Let you live your mundane little life with the vampire of your choosing. Can you imagine that?" She examined her nails and they changed color, a gold to match the trim on her beige wrap dress.

"I knew I liked him. He was sensible. Pay attention, Mother. Maybe he could help you find a cure for Jerry's amnesia." The chilled champagne tasted really good, the bubbles tickling my nose, and I finally started to feel sleepy.

"I suppose we could work together. He *is* a powerful ally. You did well there." She patted my hand. "Now I brought something for you to try. A sorcerer I know thought it might jog your man's memory." She opened her purse, a tiny jeweled number that had to have cost a fortune, and handed me a vial full of a bright green liquid. "Slip this into your lover's next meal. Blood I suppose." She shuddered. "Then see if he shows signs of remembering anything. If it works,

I can get more, though the cost is high." She smoothed down her skirt. "The man is a freak and he likes me." She shuddered again. "He'll want me to, um, play his games in trade."

"Mother! Seriously? You'll have to sleep with him?" I set down my empty glass. "You'd do that for Jerry?"

"No. I'd do that for *you*." She smiled and touched my cheek. "But this man's games aren't exactly sexual ones, thank the gods. They are much more complicated." She shrugged. "I can't explain them but, trust me, they are not to my taste."

"Well, thank you. I'll let you know if it works. I have your number. I'll text the results." I held on to the vial and stood, moving into the aisle. I felt that pull of sunrise and almost fell.

"Go, lie back before your sleep overtakes you. I can only keep you awake so long though I'm working on that. I'm sure you'd like to see more daylight, wouldn't you?" She stood and grabbed me for a brief hug. "Oh, how I have waited for a chance to do that."

I shoved her away. "Tipsy on champagne or not, I haven't forgotten why Jerry is in such sad shape that he's terrified to fly. And quit with the bribes. Nothing you can do for me will get me to Olympus. Nothing."

She frowned and the plane lurched. "Careful, Gloriana. I could make this airplane drop like a rock. Do you think your lover or any of your friends would survive a fall of thousands of feet into the ocean?"

"Neither would I. Are you ready to give up on me?" I held on to a seat back as the plane lurched again. Air pocket or Olympus temper tantrum?

"Stubborn brat. I could whisk you away in time to save you of course." She tapped her chin as if thinking about it.

"All you'd gain is a daughter who would never ever forgive you. Mars is my ally now. I bet he'd help me make you pay for a trick like that." I was getting woozier, stupid dawn.

"Look at you, into Olympus politics." She smiled proudly.

"All right then. Try the potion. Let me know the results." And with that she vanished, the woman did know how to use an exit line.

I wobbled my way back to my seat, the vial stowed safely between my breasts. At least she was trying for a relationship, but if she expected me to be a grateful daughter she would have to cut the threats and ramp up the cure efforts.

I looked at Jerry and sighed. He didn't deserve this, any of it. That was my last thought before I fell into my death sleep.

I woke up with a start. Everyone else was on their feet and milling around, pulling down their carry-on luggage from overhead bins.

"Where are we?" I pushed my hair out of my eyes.

"Austin." Flo stopped next to me. "You slept past sunset, *amica*. I helped Jeremiah get out of his seat belt. He and Ricardo are outside. Both of them were eager to get out of here. My husband doesn't like to admit it, but he's not comfortable with little places. Spent too much time in a cell as a monk, I think."

"I thought he was a priest." I undid my seat belt.

"Priest, monk. Are they not the same?" Flo patted my arm. "Come. It is good to be home."

"Sure. Just a minute." I felt for the vial. It was still there. Then I grabbed my purse and dug for lipstick and a brush. I had to look horrible and didn't want Jerry to see me this way. Oh, who was I kidding? I was stalling. I dreaded everything and everyone I'd have to face in Austin. Even if Jerry didn't get his memory back, I'd have to clue him in on what he'd forgotten. One thing at a time. I'd take him home. We could probably get a taxi. I headed out.

Well, we wouldn't need a taxi. Jerry's daughter, Lily, stood next to her father, holding on to his arm and talking a mile a minute. He looked a little dazed when she pointed to his car sitting next to a hangar. I hurried to join them.

"Glory!" Lily grinned at me. "Dad was just telling me that I'd have to drive. He doesn't remember how. Can you believe it?"

I couldn't believe she was acting like this was good news. Spoiled brat. "Lily, your father has amnesia. He's going to have to relearn some things. Give him some time to adjust." I took his arm. "Jerry? I guess you know by now that this is your daughter."

"Yes. And a bonny lass she is too." He smiled down at her.

She laughed. "Knock off the accent, Dad. It's just too quaint." She quit smiling. "Oh, is that part of the amnesia? That you talk funny? I didn't mean . . ."

"Sorry." Jerry frowned. "I've been in the Highlands. At your grandda's castle. Everyone speaks that way there. But the modern talk's coming back to me. I'll try not to embarrass you."

I sighed. This was not going well. "Lily, thanks for picking us up. How did you know when we'd get here?"

"Mother texted me. She got it from someone. Count on Mother to have spies everywhere." Lily picked up a bag. "Come on. Or do you need to tell somebody you're going?"

"Yes, let me thank Flo and Richard." I touched Jerry's back. "Go on with your daughter. I'll be there in a minute." I hesitated. I didn't live with them. Maybe . . . "Or I can catch a ride with someone else and you two can go on. Call me when you want to get together." Jerry had mastered his cell phone though he had no idea how or why it worked. I'd shown him his contact list. I was first on it, of course.

"No!" Jerry grabbed my hand. "We stay together, Gloriana." His grip was firm. "Don't give me any nonsense about it. Come home with me or we'll go to your place. Whatever you prefer. Lily, you understand, don't you? Gloriana is working with me to help me get my mind back."

"My place then." I saw Lily's face fall.

She looked from me to her father. "I get it." She dropped the bag. "Glory, you take Dad's car. I'll shift for myself.

Mother explained everything. So I guess you owe him this TLC. Fix this, Glory." She stormed off toward the private plane terminal.

"What's wrong with her?" Jerry started to follow her. "What's TLC? Glory?"

"She's mad, Jer. Let her go. She's right to hate me now. Mara told her it's my fault you were hurt. I'm sure the way she spun it I practically gave the order. TLC is tender loving care. Which I'm glad to give you."

"I have to set Lily straight." He kept watching his daughter as she disappeared around the side of the large building. "Where's she going?"

"Somewhere she can shift without being seen. You can talk to her later. Give her time to calm down. I'll drive you over there and you can have a long talk. Right now let me thank Flo and Richard for the ride. Can you take care of our luggage?"

"Of course. I'm daft, not helpless." He grabbed a suitcase in each hand and stalked toward the car.

I leaned down and picked up the car keys Lily had tossed on the ground before she'd stomped off. She looked and acted like a teenager even after hundreds of years. The girl definitely needed her strong father back. After a quick conversation with Flo and Richard and promises to get together soon, I slipped into the driver's seat of Jerry's Mercedes convertible. The top was down and it was a perfect cool Texas night as I drove us toward my place on Sixth Street.

"This is a big city." Jerry had figured out the seat belt on his own and actually seemed fairly relaxed. He'd had plenty of practice riding in cars now. Compared to a jet, this was easy. Traffic got heavier as we got closer to downtown and my shop. My apartment was on a floor above it. "It's not the Highlands but there are hills. The weather is good."

"Yes, I enjoy this Texas climate. The winters are mild but the summers are terribly hot." What was this? We were talking about the weather? But it was a safe topic since the major one, the vial I could feel hard and cold next to my skin, was something to be discussed when we were alone upstairs. We arrived at our destination and I stopped in front of the shop. No parking places and the store looked busy. That was the good news. The bad news was that the window display hadn't been changed since I'd left. Hmm.

A honk behind me got me going again and I pulled around back to the alley to park next to my own car, a nifty sports model I'd acquired after a deal with the Devil's evil twin. Don't ask.

"We're here. I live upstairs. Look around. Is any of this ringing any bells?" I glanced at Jerry. He was in warrior mode, checking out the dark alley for predators. The light was burned out again. Not good. I can't tell you how many ambushes I'd endured back here. It was death alley as far as I was concerned. But parking was at a premium on Sixth Street. I had no choice.

"This looks a little run down. Are you sure it's a safe place for you to live?"

"No, but I can't afford better." I huffed, a little irritated. Not having this argument now. He didn't realize this was an old one. "Let's go." I popped the trunk. "Help me with the suitcases."

"I'll get those." The voice out of the darkness was achingly familiar.

"Rafe!" I lunged for him, hugging him tight. All the tears I hadn't shed yet came pouring out—my pain at what had happened to Jerry, my hurt that everyone had believed the worst of me, even the isolation I'd felt in Scotland. I laid my head on Rafael Valdez's broad chest and sobbed my heart out.

"Who the hell is this?" Jerry stood close, near my back, his voice edged with fury. "And why are you crying, Gloriana?"

"Rafael Valdez. You hired me to be her bodyguard. Glory and I are very good friends." He rubbed my back. "She trusts me. Don't you, Glory? So she knows she can let down her guard with me. Right, sweetheart?"

"Answer him, Gloriana. Are you his sweetheart?"

"Don't start this please." I pulled back and wiped at my wet cheeks. True to form Rafe came up with a handkerchief and I blew my nose. "I'm not going to watch you two fight. I love both of you. You don't remember him, Jerry, but Rafe has saved my life more than once. He's a dear friend. Shake hands with him."

"I'll not." Jerry pulled me back against him. "You need to cry, I have a shoulder for that."

"Relax, Blade. Glory and I aren't involved anymore. It's all good." Rafe shoved his hands in the pockets of his snug jeans.

I didn't want to notice how good he looked to me in his black N-V T-shirt. How had he known I was back here? Of course, I'd driven past his club, which was right down the street. He always had a man at the door, who'd probably spotted me in the slow moving traffic. All of his employees knew me and knew Rafe would want news of my arrival.

"Blade? And what does he mean 'anymore'? Were you lovers?" Jerry's hand went to his back. Oh, shit. Those knives. He'd loaded up with them before he'd left home.

"I can't deal with this now." Nothing like refusing to answer. "Jerry has amnesia, Rafe. He doesn't remember anything since right before he met me in London in 1604."

"That's convenient." Rafe smiled. "Who masterminded that?"

"My mother. She gives bitch a whole new meaning. I'll clue you in about that later." I stayed between the two men. It was obvious they'd decided to be enemies again. Instinct.

"You're a shifter." Jerry said it like it was the worst kind of insult. It was a pretty common vampire attitude unfortunately. Vamps hired shifters to work for them but didn't always see them as equals.

"Yes, and you were happy to hire me to protect Gloriana. I guarded her night and day for five long years. Long enough to know her very well." Rafe smiled meaningfully. "That's why we are so close."

Jerry had a knife in his hands. "How close?"

"Stop it!" I put myself in front of Rafe. "You are not fighting. Rafe was in dog form when he guarded me. You insisted on it. He slept on the foot of my bed."

Jerry laughed, a deep belly laugh that made Rafe's face darken. I threw myself on Rafe before he could launch himself across the alley at Jerry.

"Now that's brilliant. Gloriana fond of dogs, is she? Did she scratch you behind the ears? Rub your tummy? Play fetch?" Jerry wiped tears of glee from his eyes and put his knife away. "Come, Gloriana. I want to see this place of yours. We can handle our own luggage, Valdez."

"Don't you want to know why I called you Blade?" Rafe kept his hand on my shoulder when I started to reach for a suitcase.

"I suppose it's because I love my knives and am very good with them." Jerry lifted his jeans to show off yet another one strapped to his ankle. "Quit hiding behind my woman and I'll show you how I can throw one that will skewer you before you can shift your dog body out of here." He pulled a knife out of his boot, obviously ready to rumble.

"I have no need to hide behind anyone. You went by Jeremy Blade here in town." He glanced at me. "I did some research. Seems you were the one doing some hiding. Ask him, Glory, why he had to change his name."

Where had this come from? I looked at Jerry. Did he have a secret I didn't know about? As it stood, he didn't know it either. He'd shown up with the new name after one of our breaks. If he'd been hiding something, it was news to me.

"You're talking gibberish. I'm a Campbell, proud of it." Jerry gestured threateningly with his knife. "Glory knows who I am and is happy to be mine."

Rafe laughed. "Keep that up and she won't be for long. Your ancient Scot attitude doesn't play well with the lady here. She's not any man's woman." Rafe ran his hand down my arm. "Tell him, Glory."

"Don't confuse him, Rafe. Jerry's still trying to figure out this new world." I touched Rafe's cheek. "I appreciate your standing up for me. And I want to see you, to talk. But can we table this for now? I'm doing what I need to. Work with me."

"Playing nursemaid? I get it." He looked over at Jerry. "You get the pity vote this time, Blade. Enjoy it while you can. Glory knows she can always count on me." He leaned down and kissed me, a quick landing on my lips that I didn't have time to dodge. "Later, Blondie." Then he took off down the alley so fast that the knife Jerry threw stuck in a telephone pole instead of in his back.

"No!" I whirled around. "He's my friend, Jerry. If you'd killed him . . ."

"What? You'd never forgive me? Stop taking care of me?" Jerry's voice was tight as he pulled the knife out of the wood and examined the blade for damage. Apparently satisfied, he shoved it back in his boot. "I don't want your pity, Gloriana."

"You don't have it. I love you. I want to help you. To make up for what my mother did." I shut up, digging a hole for myself.

"Then I guess you do owe me. Tell your 'friend' to stay out of my sight. I don't like the way he was pawing you. It might have been all right when he was a dog, but now that he's on two feet, it needs to stop." He nodded toward the back of the building. "Now let's go."

Did he remember the door there led to my apartment? Probably not. It was the logical place to enter.

"Fine." I picked up my carry-on. He had the other suitcases.

"I'm fading. Guess I need to feed. You have a synthetic upstairs?" He was all business. Man to nursemaid. I wanted to slap him, hug him. Both.

"Yes, of course." I dug out my key. Time to decide if he should take the potion my mother had given me. Could I trust it? The last thing she'd brought from Olympus had ruined him. What would this one do? Did I dare find out?

Eleven

Upstairs, Jerry roamed my tiny two bedroom apartment while I found bottles of synthetic blood and poured them into glasses.

"This is all the room you've got?" He settled onto the couch. It was fairly new and I'd bought it secondhand. At least I'd had it steam cleaned and it was comfortable. Compared to Campbell Castle and Jerry's own large house, where Lily no doubt pouted, it was a dump.

"It's enough for me. I usually have a roommate. If the shop has a slump, it's hard for me to make the rent on both it and this place. Luckily the business is doing pretty well now, though I need to get down there soon and take a look at the books." I handed him the glass. "It's cold. I can heat it if you'd like." In Scotland they'd served everything room temperature. I kept my synthetic in the fridge, a habit left over from when I'd lived in hot Las Vegas.

He took a cautious sip. "No, this is fine."

I put a hand on his arm before he could drink more. "Wait. We need to discuss something." I pulled the vial from between my breasts.

"What's that?" Jerry reached for it and held the container to the light. "Strange color."

"Almost a neon green." He gave me a quizzical look. "Means it looks like it could glow in the dark. Anyway, my mother gave it to me. Claims some sorcerer she knows told her it might help bring your memories back." I sighed. "I'm afraid of it. You know what her last potion did."

"Am I supposed to drink it?" Jerry looked excited, obviously desperate enough to try anything.

"She suggested we put it into your next meal. That would be the synthetic I just handed you." I wanted to grab it back. "Don't drink it! I'm scared of what it might do. The last thing she tried, the memory-loss potion, was supposed to wear off. She told me that. Because you were vampire, it didn't. Now she's got this. Again, you're vampire. Who knows how you'll react?"

"But could it be much worse than not remembering what century I'm in, Gloriana? Who *you* are?" He pulled the tiny cork out of the vial.

"You know who I am now, Jer. There are just gaps—"

"Gaps? Holy hell, woman!" He jumped up, but not before he dumped the contents of the vial into his glass. "I know what I was like when I rode a horse named Thunder, a beast who's been dead for centuries. I call myself Jeremiah Campbell, not Jeremy Blade, a man who must have secrets, maybe shameful ones. I have to know what the hell I've been up to all this time." He began to drink, fast. I watched his throat move as he downed the liquid in enormous gulps. When the glass was drained, he looked it over, I guess to make sure he hadn't left anything, then flung it crashing into the wall, where it shattered.

"Fuck those gaps! I want my mind back and I'll do anything, anything, to get it." He threw open the hall door and charged out.

I heard him clattering down the stairs and decided to let him go. He was a vampire. He'd figure things out. And where would he end up? Right back here because he didn't know where else to turn. Unless his memories came back. I looked up and prayed it happened. Poor Jerry. And, man, would he hate that I thought of him that way. I couldn't imagine living with such a huge blank spot in my mind. I was so going to jump on Rafe for that "research" he'd done. He had no business investigating Jerry. But what could Jer have done to make him hide things from me?

I don't know how long I sat there, rehashing everything that had happened since that night I'd arrived in Scotland, before I heard heavy footsteps coming up the stairs again. Of course I knew it was Jerry. I had his scent memorized, that earthy Scot who had my blood inside him.

One look at his face and I knew the gap still remained. I walked into his arms and held him. But something was wrong. Different. It took me a moment to realize what it was. He felt warm, way too warm.

"Jerry?" I leaned back and checked his face.

"I'm all right. Or as right as I can be after getting lost and wandering around for an hour or more. Finally I had to ask strangers where Glory St. Clair might live. At last one took me to the shop downstairs. The girl working there knew me." He ran a hand over his flushed face. "That was damned embarrassing. I didn't have any idea who she was. She treated me like a child after she figured out what was wrong with me."

"I'm sorry, Jer." I touched his forehead. Fever. "How are you feeling?"

"Hot. It's strange. I usually don't notice the temperature and it's cool outside. But I'm all right otherwise. Just damned stupid." He sat on the couch. "Best give me another glass of your synthetic. Straight, no more of your ma's magic." He put his feet on my coffee table. I usually wouldn't tolerate that, but didn't have the heart to fuss at him when he looked so dejected. "Fat lot of good her first dose did."

"It's doing something, to raise your temperature this way." I hurried into the kitchen to get a fresh bottle and glass. I had cleaned up the mess he'd made. Luckily I didn't have nice crystal or I'd be mad about his temper tantrum. When I came back, Jerry had picked up one of the magazines on my coffee table—*GQ*, because I liked to see hot guys wearing good clothes—and was thumbing through it.

It was kind of sad, really. Before, he would have already been using the remote to channel surf for sports to watch. Obviously he didn't have a clue what the black plastic thing close to his feet did, though he and his father had watched TV together at the castle. Then I noticed wisps of smoke curling up from the pages of the magazine.

"Jerry?"

"What the hell?" He threw the magazine down to the hardwood floor and stomped out sudden flames with his boot. "Did you see that?"

"You taking up smoking again?" I handed him the glass. "I haven't seen you with a cigarette in years."

He just looked at me strangely. "No, I don't know what you're talking about. Though I wouldn't mind a fine cigar about now. Richard mentioned on the plane that we used to enjoy a smoke together. It was good to see at least one familiar face among all those strangers." He took a sip. "You decided to heat it this time. I think I like it better this way." Then he exclaimed and set the glass down on the table. "You didn't have to boil it!"

"I didn't!" I watched it bubble. "Uh, Jerry. Hold out your hands."

"What do you mean? Didn't you heat the blood?" His eyes narrowed. "Don't play with me, Gloriana. The glass was hot."

"Not until you touched it. And that magazine. It burst into flames on its own, if you didn't get out a lighter." We could both see the smoke in the air. And smell it. Or at least I knew I could.

"I thought maybe I'd brushed against a candle or something." He peered around the room as if in search of one.

"You know I don't burn those things. Masks smells of

intruders. Bad defense. You taught me that." Well, of course he didn't remember that he had. I shook my head. One more gap.

"No candles." He stood, staring at his hands like they were alien objects. "Hand me something. Anything you don't mind losing." He started toward my Israel Caine collection. Oh, no, he didn't.

"Here!" I tossed him a piece of junk mail from the pile of letters and bills on my kitchen table. My employees had been collecting it for me while I was gone.

He grabbed it. We both watched, fascinated, as it began to smolder. When it flamed, I hurried to hold a metal trash can under it so Jerry could drop it inside. A high-pitched squeal meant my smoke alarm was working.

"What in God's name?" He clamped his hands over his ears.

"Careful!" Would he burn himself? But he seemed to be okay, still holding his ears like he normally would. I ran for a stool and jerked the battery out of the alarm. Blessed silence. "That was an alarm. Lets me know if I have a fire. Usually handy. Oh, God, Jerry. This is, um, unexpected." I carried the can to the kitchen and used the sprayer in the sink to put out the fire. Now my apartment stank of burned paper. I ran over to throw open a living room window for ventilation.

"Unexpected. Yes, I'd say so." He stood next to the door frame, careful not to touch anything. "Do you think your mother planned this outcome? A bit more torture for my turning you vampire?"

"She seemed sincere when she offered the cure for you." I looked skyward. "But then what do I know? She's from Olympus. Apparently devious is her middle name. I'll text her. She is supposedly busy paying off some sorcerer for this 'cure.' I'll let her know that not only didn't it work, but now we need a cure for her cure. If she did this on purpose, then she's burned her bridges with me."

"Burned." He stared down at his hands again. "Shit! I

can't live like this. I have to find out something." He came up to me where I stood next to the sofa, his eyes on my face. "Brace yourself, lass. I must know. If I touch you, will I set you aflame as well?"

My heart broke at the look in his eyes. "I'll gladly risk it. Kiss me, Jerry. Let me see if you breathe fire." I pulled his head down, horrified that his cheeks were so hot to the touch. When our lips met, it was like a flame licked me, blistering me immediately. I gasped in spite of myself at the pain.

"God, no! Look what I've done to you." He jerked back, putting several feet between us. "This I can't stand. I've got to do something or just walk into the sun."

"No. Surely we can find a cure. We need a doctor and there's only one in town, Jerry, who works on paranormals." I didn't want to say it, but if anyone might know what to do, how to fix this, it was him.

"I can guess." He turned on his heel, putting even more distance between us. "Take me to him."

"Ian MacDonald. You're sure?"

He looked back at me, clearly resigned but not happy about it. "I'm not so hung up on an old feud that I'll die rather than try for a cure. What other choice do I have?"

"None, I guess. You certainly can't just wait around to see if this wears off." I grabbed my cell phone out of my purse. "Let me call him first. Make sure he's in town and willing to see you." Of course I had Ian on speed dial. Much as I hated him, it seemed like I'd done business with him way too many times.

"Gloriana." Ian answered right away. "Are you back or still frolicking in the Highlands? My brother said you even wore a kilt of sorts when he saw you there. Apparently it barely covered your bum." He chuckled. "Would have liked to have seen that."

"Give it a rest, Ian. I have a medical emergency for you."

"Really. What happened? Are you hurt?" Say what you will, Ian was a good doctor. I could hear him practically vibrating with interest.

"Not me. Jerry took a potion that was supposed to help him get some of his memory back. I assume, since you've talked to your brother, that you know Jerry still has amnesia. Anyway, now this 'cure' he took has turned him into a fire starter." I fought the urge to cry. "Everything he touches bursts into flames, Ian. Can . . . can you fix him?"

"That's a hell of a thing. Literally." Ian chuckled. "Forgive me but the thought of Campbell as a living torch . . . Well, it doesn't exactly hurt my feelings."

I counted to five. "Are you going to help him or not?"

"I'll try. You know how I love an interesting case. Where'd he get this potion? Got any of it left? Describe it." His voice was crisp, no-nonsense now.

"Thank you. The vial is empty now but it's still got some bright green slime clinging to the inside." I grabbed it and stowed it in my purse. "My mother, who is a goddess from Olympus, got it from a sorcerer. Or so she claims. What do you think?" I watched Jerry pace, wired. A living torch. That about summed it up. He started to straighten his shirt then stopped before he touched it, obviously worried he'd set his clothing on fire. He was probably right.

How would he handle his death sleep? I guess he'd have to strip. No, I'd have to get his clothes off of him somehow. Then he'd have to rest his hands on his own naked body before dawn hit or he'd set even the bed aflame.

This was intolerable. Would it wear off? I had a million questions. Silence on the phone. Was Ian thinking about solutions or deciding whether to blow Jerry off? I'd just dumped a lot of information on the doctor.

"Bring him out here. I know we've formally ended our feud. Jeremiah's father and my brother sealed the deal in blood of all things. Ridiculous. Anyway, are you sure Campbell's going along with that truce? Douglas said he was an asshole about the whole thing."

"Jerry is the one who suggested we see you, Ian." I swallowed. "Please, he's desperate. He can't touch anything or, or anyone. It's hell."

"Sounds like it. A Hellfire spell. Your mother was either tricked or she did this on purpose. If that is so, you have my sympathy. She sounds like a real bitch. Bring him now, Gloriana. I'm going to look up a few things, maybe call someone, and see what I can do." Ian disconnected.

"Okay, we're going." I touched Jerry's back. He'd been staring out the window. I noticed the singed hole in my blackout curtain where he'd obviously brushed it aside. It seemed that as long as I didn't touch his hands or mouth, he didn't hurt me though his body felt hot.

"It's going to take some getting used to. Going to a Mac-Donald for help," he said quietly. "I've never trusted one in my life."

"He's a doctor. It's his job." I prayed Ian would act professionally and not rub Jerry's nose in the fact that he was doing him a favor. "You'll pay him just like you would any trades-man." There, that should make Jerry feel better about it.

"Did he know anything about this curse?" Jerry faced me. Even after he'd first lost his memory, he hadn't looked this discouraged. But then I'd always been able to hold him. I could still do that.

"Lift your arms." I slid under them and hugged him, pressing my cheek to his chest. It felt like holding a steaming caldron dressed in a knit polo, but I refused to let go. "Now I want you to have faith. Ian did seem to have heard of this curse, and that's what he thinks it is too. He's working on finding a cure. There's nothing he likes more than solving a problem, so don't give up, Jer. Promise me."

"If you were wise, Gloriana, you would run like hell. The shifter is obviously more than ready to take my place." Jerry's forearm brushed against my hair. "I could see that well enough downstairs even with half a brain."

"Rafe is a dear friend but you are my love. And your brain is perfectly fine. Now let's get going. We have to fix this. I want to make love with you again and I don't particularly want to risk getting roasted and toasted doing it."

Jerry followed me to the door. "You are determined to

deal with this, no matter what. Why? If it's guilt, I won't have it. There is nothing for you to feel guilty about, Gloriana. Our parents make their own decisions and they can be wrongheaded. It was clear to me that my own mother never welcomed you to the castle."

"No, she didn't." I decided not to share the time she'd tried to kill me. "But you never let Mag's feelings about me sway you and I'll certainly not let a mother who I've known for five minutes influence me. Especially one who deals in dirty tricks."

Jerry stopped next to the car. "No one could accuse you of not being steadfast, Gloriana." He opened the passenger door, dew on the steel steaming when he touched it. I saw how careful he was as he got in to keep his hands from touching anything else. "You'll have to do up the seat belt for me."

"Sure. No problem." I couldn't meet his eyes, my own burning. Steadfast. God. I'd been anything but. When his memories returned, he'd know the truth. Valdez. And I'd have to tell him about Ray. Our ancient history he could brush off. Our partings had been mutual. But Rafe had just thrown my recent slip in Jerry's face. Luckily Jer hadn't caught just how bad a slip it had been. But he would and his forgiving nature might have disappeared after what he'd just gone through.

Damn. The best thing I could do for Jerry would be to walk away from him. My Olympus connection was ruining his life. But love, guilt, whatever my motivation, I just couldn't leave him, especially not like this. I hurried around the car, eager to drive us toward Ian's swanky digs on the outskirts of town.

First, I pulled out my cell and texted my mother: "The sorcerer's stuff was a Hellfire spell. Not a fix. DO SOME-THING." That should clue her in that the sorcerer who'd given this cure had failed. She could quit playing his games and start hunting for a real cure. Olympus was sounding worse and worse to me. I never wanted to find out what it was like firsthand, but it might turn out to be the only way to get Jerry back to where he needed to be. With that thought giving me a killer headache, I started the car.

"You really don't remember anything after the late fifteen hundreds?" Ian made notes on a tablet computer. He and Jerry had exchanged stiff greetings. Of course Jerry had recognized him—Ian looked very much like his brother and they'd known each other anyway back in the bad old days when they'd played battle of the clans.

"That's right. But this is more urgent." Jerry walked across the room, picked up a log which burst into flames. Then he tossed it into Ian's fireplace. Since it was a mild night, Ian hadn't lit a fire. Now he had a nice blaze going.

"Interesting. Let me see your hands." Ian set down the tablet and walked up to Jerry. He grabbed one of his wrists first, carefully. "Your body's extremely warm. I'd like to take your temperature." He looked over his shoulder. "Bring me my bag."

I'd mentored a genius vampire who'd worked for Ian for a while and used to assist him. Penny had quit to go to medical school and was now in California, doing her thing at night. Ian's new assistant was a beautiful vampire.

"Nice window dressing."

Ian cocked an eyebrow at me. "Melanie is a doctor, has a PhD in genetics and has done quite a bit of her own research in the medical field. Don't be fooled by the pretty package."

"Sorry, Melanie." I said that as she reentered the room carrying Ian's medical bag. I figured that with vamp hearing she'd probably overheard my remark.

"You're not the first and I'm sure won't be the last to make assumptions about me." She smiled. "Mr. Campbell's problem is going to be a challenge. I hate working with sorcerers but, Ian, I think we're going to have to call one in if it's what you say it is."

Ian pulled a thermometer out of his bag. "Open your mouth, Campbell. This goes under your tongue."

"Be careful. I tried to kiss him and it blistered my lips." I touched my mouth, all healed thanks to the synthetic I'd had just before Jerry had started his flame throwing.

"What the hell?" Jerry stared at the digital thermometer like it would poison him or puncture his tongue. Of course taking anything from a MacDonald was still hard for him.

"It's a thermal material specially formulated to withstand a dragon's breath. Mel brought an interesting clientele with her. Hopefully Campbell here isn't that hot." Ian passed it to me. "You do the honors, Gloriana. I doubt he'll take it from me anyway."

"It's a small machine, Jer. Just close your mouth over it. It'll beep and let Ian know your body temperature. It's to help him figure this out. Won't hurt a thing. I can do it first if you want me to." I put it near my own lips.

"Give it to me. I'm not afraid of such a tiny thing. Just wanted an explanation." He took it and thrust it into his mouth, frowning when it started beeping.

"I don't see any sparks coming from his hand." Ian aimed Jerry's finger at a piece of paper. "Look, Mel. See that?"

"A flame. Shooting right out of his fingertip. Wow." She picked up Ian's tablet. "Do it again. I'd like to try to get a picture of it."

I could see Jerry getting angrier by the minute as Ian manipulated his fingers like they were inanimate objects. Jer's face went from pink to bright red. When Ian pulled him closer to a table, Jerry suddenly jerked his hand away and shot flames that made the whole wooden table go up in smoke.

"Holy shit!" Melanie aimed the tablet at the ruins. "I got the entire thing." She glanced at Ian. "Oh, sorry. That was a one-of-a-kind antique, wasn't it?"

"No matter. Incredible. His temper seems to increase the fire power." He grabbed the tablet and started typing. "Hand me my phone. I'm calling Cornelius. If anyone will know how to handle this, he will."

"Cornelius?" I'd really like to know what Ian was typing.

"A powerful sorcerer." Ian scrolled through his contacts on his cell.

"You have a sorcerer's phone number?" I took the thermometer out of Jerry's mouth when it signaled it was done and handed it to Melanie.

"You never know when you'll need one." Ian walked out on his terrace, apparently deciding on privacy.

"His temp is one twelve. That's serious." Melanie looked worried as she typed into the computer. "Dangerously high. Sit down, Mr. Campbell. Would you like a drink?"

"That's a problem. The last time I tried to hold a glass, the blood boiled. And call me, uh, Jerry." Jerry looked at me. "Any suggestions?"

"You can use a straw if you have one of those glass ones. Surely he can't melt glass."

"We've got a pipette. Good idea, Gloriana. I'll get one."

"And I'll hold the glass for you." I smiled at Melanie. "Thanks for offering. Bring him some of Ian's best synthetic, B negative. That's one of Jerry's favorites."

"Good. He needs to hydrate. This fever could kill him, I think. I'll discuss it with Ian when he gets off the phone." She hurried out of the room.

Ian came back inside. "He's coming. It'll take him a little while because he has to gather some things. Where's Melanie? What was his temp?"

I told him.

"Damn. That's too high. We need to get him into a tepid bath."

"Here's his blood. I didn't heat it and I put a straw in it, like you suggested, Glory." Melanie handed me the glass. "She tell you his temperature? I'm worried."

"Yes, that would be fatal in a human. And I can't imagine a vampire's brain can endure that kind of long-term exposure to body heat either." Ian watched me hold the glass so Jerry could drink. "Never thought I'd say it, but I feel damned sorry for you, Campbell."

Jerry didn't acknowledge the sympathy. He let the straw

slide from his mouth. "A cool bath? That sounds good right now. Here? Or should Glory take me home?"

"Here. You need to wait for Cornelius. He said he has some ideas, some things to try to rid you of the spell. Said it definitely sounded like someone had cast a Hellfire spell." Ian held out his hand. "Give me the vial, Gloriana. And explain exactly who gave this to your mother and why."

I handed it to him but realized I didn't know much. "She has some enemies apparently. I have a feeling this guy played a dirty trick on her."

"He certainly did." My mother appeared, dragging a man behind her. He had a long beard and wore dark robes that looked wet. "This is the incompetent cretin who swore to me that the mixture he gave me would cure you, Jeremiah." She dropped the man on the floor in front of her. "Tell them, Waldo, what you told me."

"Please, I swear, it was supposed to work. I mixed it so carefully—"

"Lying sack of peacock poop! Do you want me to drag you through the ocean again?" She kicked him with one of her high-heeled pumps. "Look at his red face. Do you not see how it worked?" She pointed to Jerry. "Show him, Jeremiah. Burn something." She gestured around the room. "That!" She aimed at a painting on the wall above the fireplace.

"No! That's an original Van Gogh!" Ian grabbed a newspaper and held it up. "Hit this with your best shot, Campbell."

Jerry actually grinned. "But I like art. What is that supposed to be? A harvest?"

"Burn the damned newspaper," Ian said through clenched teeth.

"Not nearly as much fun." Jerry ran a fingertip over the front page and it burst into flames. Ian dropped it on the tile floor and stamped it out.

"There! What did I tell you?" My mother shot the quivering man at her feet with a lightning bolt and he yelped, his robes smoking.

"Please, perhaps I hurried the process. Madam was impatient, standing over me. I'll do another batch. Do you have unicorn tongue here, sir?" He looked around wildly.

Ian shook his head. "I assume you're Gloriana's mother? I'm Ian MacDonald." He started to hold out his hand then obviously remembered the lightning and thought better of it.

"Call me Olympia. Yes, Gloriana is mine." She smiled at me then frowned. "Still in those awful clothes? By all the gods above!" She waved her hand and I swear everyone there except me shrank back, afraid of what was coming. I knew. Sure enough, I had on a new outfit. This one, I kept. The red and black dress fit the fire motif and had the deep vee neckline I loved.

"Mother, Jerry is in serious distress. This fire thing is killing him. He has to drink this then hop into a tub of cool water. His temperature is through the roof. I hope you've brought a cure." I held the glass to his lips again. Jerry drank though he couldn't take his eyes off my mother. She was quite a sight in her sparkly red evening gown. We almost matched. It made me wonder what she and the sorcerer had been up to when she'd gotten my text. Of course the fact that she kept zapping Waldo every minute or so was enough to keep anyone eyeing her warily.

"Well, go to it. I'll work on this slug and see what we can do." She kept her high heel on the whimpering sorcerer's arm. "What do you think, Dr. MacDonald? Should we let this creature into your laboratory for another try?"

"First, I'd like to examine this vial Glory brought along. And question, um, what was his name?"

"Waldo. You know, like those books. He does like to hide. Which is the game we were playing when I got Gloriana's text. Where's Waldo? I can't tell you how much I despise such nonsense." She smiled so evilly that I'd have crossed myself if I'd been Catholic. "Son of a shrew! Beetle dung!" She gave him another lightning jolt. "Just try hiding from me after this." She nodded. "Don't worry, he will answer all your questions." She gestured to me. "Gloriana, take your man to that bath. He looks like he's about to fall down."

"Jerry, come on." Mother was right. Jerry swayed where he stood, his eyes closing. I grabbed one of his arms while Melanie took the other one. We were both careful not to touch his hands.

"I can walk." He pulled away from Melanie but stumbled. "Shit. The blood seemed to give me some strength for a moment, but I'm so on fire I can't, uh, can't focus." Jerry grabbed Ian's leather sofa to steady himself. We all exclaimed at the smell of burning cowhide.

"Careful, man!"

"Hush, Ian." I got a better grip on Jerry's waist while Melanie took hold of him again on the other side. "No nonsense now, Jerry. Let Melanie and me get you down the hall. It's like you've been poisoned. It's okay to take some help."

"I hate this weakness." Jerry finally leaned against me. "For God's sake don't let me touch you with my hands, Gloriana."

"I won't." I wanted to cry. Melanie and I got him down the hall where I stripped him carefully while she ran a large tub full of water. He had to make a fist to get his shirt over his hands but we finally managed it. Jerry gasped when we helped settle him into it. But much too soon it was steaming.

"Wait here." Melanie ran out of the room and I heard her call for help. Ian had plenty of guards around the place. He'd always had lots of security because of his expensive equipment and secret experiments. He also sold very high-end drugs to vampires. Soon she was back with a bowl of ice. She dumped it into the water where it melted immediately.

"Jerry, can you hear me? Do you feel any better?" She put her hand on his forehead. He had his eyes closed and I was afraid he'd lost consciousness. "I think the fever's come down a little bit."

"I hear you. Leave me to die in peace. So . . . hot." He leaned his head against the back of the tub, his hands on his stomach. Whenever they touched the water, it started boiling.

"Jer, can you lift your hands out of the water?" I heard footsteps and then several men came in carrying more ice to drop into the tub. I reached under Jerry's feet to pull the drain so the water level could go down some.

"Yes, that's better." He rested his hands on top of his head. "Cooler now." He sighed. "Crazy this."

"Yes, but they're working on a cure. Don't worry." Melanie looked at me. "I'll be right back."

I sank down on the floor beside the tub, my hand on Jerry's bare shoulder. Every few minutes another man would come in and pour more ice into the tub. I couldn't imagine the torture this must be for Jerry. I rubbed his bare chest, trying to comfort him. What I really wanted to do was make that damned sorcerer pay for what he'd done. If he was still there when I got back to the living room, I was going to kick him myself with the new suede pumps my mother had materialized for me. I sighed and leaned my cheek against the tub.

"Gloriana, I'm sorry." My mother stroked my hair.

"You should be." I stood and shook out my skirt. "Look at Jerry. At what you've done. This all started with that first potion on the knife you gave Mara."

"He's a fine looking man." She did look, clearly checking out naked Jerry stretched out in the tub.

"Ooo! That's not what I meant. What's wrong with you? He's mine." I shoved her out of the room.

"Relax, darling. On Olympus we don't care about family connections. Everyone is fair game when it comes to the bedroom. You mate with whoever takes your fancy." She patted my cheek. "I'd think after your stint as a Siren you'd be more open-minded."

"That's not being open-minded, that's creepy. And I don't remember a thing about my life as a Siren, the Storm God took care of that."

"Yet another vendetta I must take care of." She frowned. "Many have wronged us, Daughter. But I'm here to tell you the new sorcerer has arrived. Come. The guards will pull your man out of the tub and get him dressed. I'm sure you're eager to hear what this magician has to say."

"Yes, let's hope he can do some good because I'm telling you, Mother, I've had it with your 'tries.' You are about to lose any chance with me. Seeing Jerry suffer like this has done it. I can't take any more. Hurt me if you want to, but leave Jerry the hell alone!" I wiped away my wet cheeks. I'd never meant anything more.

"I just wanted to fix things." She actually looked surprised by my hard line.

"Good intentions aren't worth peacock poop. It's the results that count. I think you would agree with that." I marched down the hall ahead of her.

In the living room, a rather ordinary looking man was doing a tap dance all over the hapless Waldo.

"What in the name of all that's magic were you thinking? It's ocelot's tongue, not unicorn tongue." He whirled around and I saw his eyes, not ordinary at all. They were orange, vivid orange, and so bright I had to look away.

"Cornelius. Please. I looked in the book." Waldo squinted up at him. "See how I've suffered?" He held out his robe, full of charred holes obviously made by the lightning bolts my mother had been shooting at him. "Haven't I been punished enough?"

"Your vanity makes you stupid. Buy some glasses and wear them." Cornelius threw a fireball at the man, reducing his head of gray hair and long beard to frizzled black tufts which began to break off and fall to the floor in a rain of ashes. "Honestly, who hired this man?"

"I did." My mother stepped forward. "He came highly recommended."

"By who? The troll under the bridge? He couldn't spell his way out of second grade!" Cornelius pulled a wand out of his pocket. He wore an expensive gray suit, so I had no idea where he'd hidden it. He bopped Waldo on his now bald head. Waldo sobbed and begged for mercy. We all ignored him.

"No, it was one of the gods. He . . ." My mother frowned. "Well, now that I think on it, he does have a reason to hate me." She glanced at the ceiling. "Oh, but he'll have even more reason when I get back up there." I heard thunder and knew there would be quite a payback coming.

"I'll let you deal with your own issues, madam. I brought some supplies. Where's the victim?" Cornelius stared down the hallway. "Oh, here he comes. I'm just in time I'd say or his brain would start boiling. No one survives that. Not even a vampire."

I gasped. Jerry was being carried by two strong vampires. His skin practically blazed, so red from his fever I might not have known him except for his wild eyes. He wore only a pair of boxers. Apparently the men had given up trying to dress him or maybe he couldn't bear more clothes on his overheated body.

"If he dies, Waldo, I'll turn you into a dung beetle then crush you under my heel." Cornelius stood over a sobbing Waldo then finally hit him with his wand again.

"Help me," Jerry said, locking eyes on Cornelius. Then he passed out.

Twelve

They laid Jerry on the tile floor in Ian's lab, his hands on his chest. It was the only way to work on him, apparently. He was unconscious. Cornelius stood at a worktable. He muttered while stirring some things together that he'd pulled out of a purple velvet bag. He paused occasionally to drag Waldo over to point out something.

After each of his lessons, which I guess is what they were, he banged Waldo's head against Ian's workbench as if to get the information into the junior sorcerer's brain. Ian frowned, probably at the dents in his porcelain table, but he didn't say a word. He was too busy furiously taking notes on his computer.

"He looks bad, Gloriana."

"Thanks, Mother. I really needed to hear that right now." I sat on the floor beside Jerry, brushing his damp hair back from his forehead. His fever had spiked again and it was all I could do not to scream at the sorcerer to hurry. They'd pushed ice packs up against Jerry's body but those kept melting and had to be replaced constantly. Finally I heard Cornelius approaching, his silk slippers and robe swishing across the floor. I don't know when he'd changed clothes and didn't care.

"Move." He didn't ask, he commanded.

I got out of the way, jumping up to watch and pray.

Cornelius paced in a circle around Jerry, chanting and tossing some kind of grass or herbs or whatever into the air. They smelled fresh, then bitter. A mist began to form above Jerry, like storm clouds gathering, swirling into a gray mass above his prone body.

I glanced at my mother and gave her a warning look. This wasn't the time for one of her displays of power. If she started to toss thunder and lightning around, I'd never speak to her again. She shook her head and kept her hands folded in front of her, apparently just as interested in the proceedings as Melanie, who darted around for the best angle, capturing the whole thing on video camera.

"All right. Now this is important. He must drink this elixir now." Cornelius was obviously in his element. His eyes glowed, juiced sunbeams, and he raised his arms in their long sleeves toward the clouds he'd created. He began chanting something in a strange language. He gave Waldo, who'd crept closer to observe, a hard look and the incompetent sorcerer scurried back to a spot farther away. Finally Cornelius lowered the glass and faced me.

"You are this man's lover, the person closest to his heart in this room. Is that right? I believe your name is Gloriana?" Cornelius held out a glass beaker etched with symbols. Not one of Ian's I was sure. It held a few inches of a pale pink liquid.

"Yes. Gloriana. I will do whatever you need, sir." I felt like I should bow or something but just nodded, stepping forward. If this would save Jerry, I would do whatever he asked. I felt a whisper in my mind.

"Careful, Gloriana. I have reason now to know these sorcerers can't be trusted."

I turned and glared at my mother. As if I'd listen to *her* advice. "Go ahead. What do you need me to do?"

Cornelius frowned at my mother, apparently a mind reader too. "Good. You exchange blood with the victim?"

He smiled as if this was a good thing. I liked his attitude. No prejudice against vampires here. I took the time to give my mother a "How about that?" look.

"Yes, of course," I said, ignoring my mother's sniff. Had she said "Disgusting"? This time I speared her with a warning glance. I was in no mood to be messed with and she'd better not interrupt again.

"Use this to cut yourself, then allow some of your blood to fall into the glass along with this potion I have mixed. I think it more likely he will drink it if he smells your essence in it." Cornelius handed me a curved blade made of gleaming silver. It had a symbol on the handle, a crescent moon with an open eye staring from the center. Words in some strange language were engraved on the blade.

I didn't hesitate. I slashed my wrist and watched the blood flow into the glass.

My mother gasped. "That's enough. Surely." She rushed forward with a silk scarf and pressed it to my cut, snatching the glass out of my hand.

"Yes. We don't want to dilute the mixture too much." Cornelius patted my shoulder. "I know you meant well, but a few drops from your finger would have served, my dear."

"You think . . . Will this cure him?" I stood there while my mother tied the scarf around my wrist. It coordinated with my dress of course. Silly detail and so like her. I batted her away when she kept fluttering around me. I was already healing.

"We will see. Perhaps you'd like to give it to him. Speak to him. Coax him to drink." Cornelius stirred the mixture with the blade handle then handed me the glass.

My hand shook as I dropped to my knees and lifted the glass to Jerry's lips. "Jerry, please, wake up. I have something here that I hope will make you feel better." I slid one hand behind his head, holding it up so I could wave the glass under his nose. He was so hot my fingers stung even with his hair cushioning them.

"Smell. This is my blood. You know you want it." I swear his nose twitched. Or had that been my own wishful thinking?

"Let me help you." Ian knelt on Jerry's other side and slid his own hands under Jerry's head. Smart man, Ian wore thick gloves now. "Dip your finger into the beaker and slip it into his mouth. That should get him going. His fever has come down enough that it shouldn't blister you."

"I'll take that chance." I smiled in gratitude and did as Ian suggested. He was being kind. Or was it just the doctor in him anxious to see if this worked? Whichever, I dragged my finger through the mixture and pushed it into Jerry's slack mouth.

Hot. Of course his mouth was hot, but I could take it. Damn it, why didn't he respond? I did it again, rubbing the liquid along his teeth. Finally, finally I felt some movement.

"His fangs are coming down!" I glanced at Ian.

"I see them." Ian helped me hold the glass to Jerry's lips. Together we managed to pour the contents, a little at a time, into his mouth. When some dribbled out, I scooped it up and pushed it back in again. I was determined that Jerry get every single drop, even holding his mouth closed until he swallowed. When the glass was empty, Ian gently laid Jerry's head back on the floor.

"He should have a pillow." I knuckled away a tear. "Why the hell doesn't he have a pillow?"

"Here, Gloriana." My mother handed me a fluffy down pillow clad in an Egyptian cotton case, something that must have come from one of Ian's beds. Ian lifted Jerry's shoulders and together we settled Jerry on it.

"Why isn't he waking up?" I looked around and saw Cornelius, still muttering. He had an ancient leather-bound book in his hand and was paging through it. "Do something!"

"Relax, child. Give it time to work. Feel his forehead. See if the fever is coming down." Cornelius had on old-fashioned spectacles now, perched on the end of his nose. He stabbed a page in the book and moved to the workbench. He said something to Waldo and the man scurried after him.

"What's Cornelius doing, Ian? Shouldn't he be here, checking on his handiwork?" I touched Jerry's cheek. Was it my imagination or did he feel a little cooler? "Take his temperature."

"I will. And, as for Cornelius, now he's working on Campbell's memory problem. He thinks he may have a way to restore his past. I assume that's important to both of you." Ian threw off his gloves, then pulled out his thermometer. He shoved it into Jerry's mouth, then rested the back of his hand on Jerry's forehead. "Feels better, I think. And his foot jerked. I think he's coming around."

"Oh, God, I hope so." I couldn't think about Jerry's memory until I was sure Jerry survived this thing. The thermometer signaled and Ian pulled it out. "What does it say?"

"He's better." Ian grabbed Jerry's jaw. "Wake up, Campbell. Talk to him, Glory." He tapped Jerry's cheeks, harder than I thought necessary. I shoved Ian's hands aside.

"I will if you move." I leaned down and kissed Jerry softly. "Please, wake up, Jeremiah. I need you." I kissed his cheeks then his eyelids. I felt them flutter against my lips. "He's coming around!" His eyes opened and he stared up at me.

"Gloriana? What happened?" He closed his eyes again. "Head hurts."

"That's only natural after a fever like that. I have something I could give him for it, but I think we should wait to see what Cornelius comes up with." Ian touched Jerry's shoulder. "Campbell, hold up your hand."

"Leave me alone, MacDonald." Jerry turned his head toward me.

"Do it, Jerry. Ian is trying to see if the sorcerer's potion got rid of your flaming fingers." I wasn't about to test his hands myself. At least his mouth hadn't burned mine. "Jerry, will you touch something? For a test?"

He squinted up at me. "What do you want me to touch?"

"Here." Ian handed me a piece of newspaper.

"Put your hand on this, Jer. If it doesn't burst into flames, you're all good." I grabbed his arm and aimed his hand at the paper.

"I can do it, Gloriana, I'm not helpless." He sat up, groaning. Then he snatched the paper and crumpled it in his fist. We all waited while he held it in his palm. Nothing. Not a wisp of smoke.

"Genius. I certainly know who to call the next time I need a potion." My mother stood close by. "Cornelius, I need your number." She whipped out a cell phone, ready to punch it into her contact list.

"I try not to do business with anyone from Olympus, Your Highness." Cornelius bowed toward her but kept mixing. "Look what a mess Mr. Campbell is in right now. All because of your 'games.'"

"Well! I'd not call them games. With Waldo, yes. But Gloriana . . ." She lifted her chin in a gesture I'd used myself a thousand times. "I wanted my daughter with me. Is that so wrong?"

Cornelius threw a powder in the air and I smelled brimstone. Trust me, I recognized it. I'd had some bad dealings with Lucifer himself. "Next time you want something, examine your methods, Your Highness." He went back to work.

"Listen, Sorcerer." Thunder cracked and she flushed. "Are you trying to tell me . . . ?"

"Mother, he's right. With all your scheming, your plans didn't pan out. Your sorcerer screwed you over. Learn from it. Now let Cornelius work. If he can give Jerry his memory back, maybe you have a shot at a relationship with me. Otherwise . . ." I couldn't take my eyes off of Jerry, who was flexing his fingers as if checking them for damage. Knowing him, he probably wanted to toss a knife around to see if he still had his old accuracy. I glanced at Ian, happily making notes on his computer. Not a good idea. I could see a pair of guards nearby. They were never far away.

"You are being very bossy this evening, Gloriana. I don't like it." My mother sat in a chair and gave herself a new outfit, one she must have decided suited the occasion better than an evening gown. Now she wore a severe navy suit that made her look like a professional woman. Of course it also showed off her perfect figure and she hadn't bothered to wear a blouse underneath. The single button was placed so that she showed plenty of cleavage and just a hint of bare midriff. I turned my back on her, sick of her theatrics, and helped Jerry to his feet.

"How are you feeling, love?"

"Like I've been hell's gatekeeper at the fiery furnace. I had no idea a man could feel so hot and still survive. Let's go outside where it's cooler." Jerry put his arm around me and headed for the terrace doors.

"Go ahead." Ian looked up from where he and Melanie were now seemingly fascinated by the playback of the video they'd taken of the exorcism or whatever you called what Cornelius had done to Jerry. "Don't leave, though. We may soon be able to solve your bigger problem, Campbell."

"Don't worry. If there's any hope I'll get my memory back, you couldn't run me off with the entire MacDonald army." Jerry pushed open the French door, then collapsed on a chaise lounge. Ian's home had a lake view and the night was cool and clear. "God, but I don't think I've ever felt worse, not even when I took a spear in my gut during a Viking raid."

"I was scared, Jerry." I snuggled up next to him, then thought maybe he'd like to put on more than those boxers which probably belonged to Ian. "You want your clothes?"

"Not yet. Let me just cool off awhile longer. Everyone here has already seen me naked so this is an improvement, I'd say." He wrapped his arms around me and ran his hands down my back. "For a while there I thought I might not ever get to do this again."

I shuddered. "I know. Stupid Waldo. I want to go inside and kick him myself. I wonder if it was incompetence or if he was bribed to betray her."

"I saw your mother shoot him again with her lightning. She knows how to get the truth out of a fellow. Either way, Waldo will think twice before he deals with her again." Jerry chuckled.

"You think that's funny?" I stared at him. "Brain damage. I'll have to ask Ian about it."

"It's laugh or throw myself off this cliff in front of us."

I glanced at the forty-foot drop to the lake. "Okay, laugh all you want. When you get your memory back, we can have a laugh riot." I laid my head on his chest and listened to the slow but steady beat of his heart. So close. I'd been way too close to losing him. I heard someone clear his throat.

"I have consulted the books and questioned the idiot who mixed the original potion that caused your amnesia, Mr. Campbell. I think I have a solution." Cornelius held out a glass vial filled with a dark blue liquid. "There are no guarantees. I know it won't turn you into a billy goat, which is what Waldo's next cure would have done." Big sigh. "And allowing for your vampire nature, I am fairly certain it won't kill you." He almost smiled. "Now drink it down and we'll see what happens."

"Perhaps I should just live like this. No memories. A fresh start." Jerry took the vial like he was handling a poisonous snake. "I'm not sure I have much confidence in sorcery after what I just barely lived through."

"Come now. Waldo is a third-degree sorcerer. A mere trainee. Barely qualified to turn princes into toads." Cornelius glanced at me. "What do you say, Gloriana? Do you want your man to remember his past or to stay the way he is?"

What a loaded question. Of course Jerry should have his memories back. The gaps he'd railed about earlier tonight were driving him mad. Driving. He needed to remember how to do that at the very least. And I wasn't such a coward that I'd rather he stay lost in a fog than face my infidelities, was I?

"It's up to you, Jerry, but I know you want to remember everything you can. You've been furious at your lack of knowledge." I waved my hand around—at Ian's place, the computer nearby, up to where a plane streaked across the night sky. "As long as Cornelius thinks it will work, I think you should go for it. He certainly proved he knows his stuff when he cured you of the Hellfire spell." I stood and stared into the sorcerer's strange eyes. "Really, no bad consequences?"

"Unlikely. But, as I said, no guarantees either. It may do no good at all." He pushed his hands into one of his robe pockets and pulled out a round mirror trimmed in bronze vines. The handle formed into a loop that he held in one hand. "Let me see if I can predict . . ." He stared into it, his pumpkin-colored eyes losing focus. "Hmm. I see you alone, Mr. Campbell, driving a car." He blinked and smiled. "A good portent, I think."

Was it? Or had the slippery sorcerer just read my mind again? I gave him a narrowed-eyed look but Jerry sat up and swung his legs down to the deck.

"I'll take it! As it stands now, Gloriana must drive me everywhere." Jerry smiled at me. "Wish me luck?"

"Of course." I held my breath as he downed the inky liquid in a single swallow.

"Tastes like shit." He made a face. "Warm in my stomach, though." He pressed a hand to his forehead. "I have to lie down." He fell back on the chaise. "Cornelius, the world is spinning."

"That's all right, Mr. Campbell. Your brain is searching for your memories. Let it do its work. Close your eyes and try to relax." Cornelius laid his hand on my arm when I started to speak. "Leave him be, Gloriana. This should take a few minutes. I'm going to get Dr. MacDonald. He'll want to see this in action. You are not like your mother, I can see that. If you ever need me . . ." He slipped a card out of his sleeve. "My unlisted number."

Well, that was a surprise. I tucked it into my bra before I sat on a chair across from Jerry. Use a sorcerer? If Cornelius could pull off this miracle, I'd definitely add him to my contact list. Of course I hoped I'd never need him or any of his magical powers again.

I stared at Jerry hard, as if I could *will* that potion to work. His chest rose and fell, like a runner's after a hard race. Hyperventilating. His fists clenched. What was happening in his mind? Was he watching a movie in his head? Did he see his life unscroll before his eyes? Could he be reliving every single event of the last four hundred years? The good and the bad? I saw him wince, then smile. This went on and on. At one point he moaned, then gritted his teeth. What could have caused that? A chuckle, a sigh of satisfaction. I wanted to read his mind and even tried but I came up empty. I was well and truly blocked out from whatever he was going through.

I sensed someone beside me. Ian, then my mother stood there. Jerry wouldn't like such an audience. I shooed her away and she went back inside. Of course the doctor wouldn't budge.

"This is fascinating."

"And frustrating. I wish he'd wake up." I leaned forward, desperate to help Jerry through this but able to do nothing, not even to touch him, even though I tried. It was as if the sorcerer had put a shield around him. Any move toward Jerry left my head spinning, like I would pass out. I stopped trying.

"He was mad at you when he left here, wasn't he? When he headed back to the old country?" Ian sounded happy about that. Bastard.

"When I got to the castle, before he lost his memory, Jerry was glad to see me. He'd forgiven me." I refused to look at Ian.

"Good for you. Hopefully he'll remember that part. Of course he may not know everything you were up to after he left. Does he?" Ian pulled up another chair.

"There was no need to bother him with that when he had amnesia, Ian. And you'd better not get into it either." My stomach leapfrogged into my throat. Ian knew all about my affair with Ray. Ray was addicted to Ian's daylight drug and he'd made a special trip over here just so he could clue Ian in to our hookup before I'd left town.

Ian smiled, happy to have some dirt he could use against me. "Relax, Gloriana. I don't plan to exchange gossip with Blade." He leaned forward in his chair. "But if he ever asks me about your relationship with Caine, I won't lie for you."

I didn't need to hear this now. Not when Jerry was on the brink of remembering his life. Or at least I hoped he was.

"I get it. Jerry and I will work it out. Just stay out of my business." I went back to watching Jerry, who was still twitching and making faces. God, what was he going through?

"Blade had better hurry with this rewind. We've got less than an hour before dawn. If he stays out here, he's fried." Ian looked up at the sky.

"If he's not done by then, your men will have to drag him inside to a safe place for his death sleep and you know it." I did finally face Ian. "The feud is over, remember?"

"Of course. I helped save his life tonight, didn't I? Something I won't share with my brother. I don't know what Campbell said to Douglas but it was almost enough for Dougie to call off the truce. Seems this amnesia made your lover into even more of a bastard than usual." He shook his head. "Care to share, Gloriana?"

"No. Jerry wasn't himself. When he has his mind back in the present, he'll realize the truce was for the best. Both of you know it was a ridiculous waste of energy." I sighed. This was taking too long! "And thank you for what you did. Send Jerry a bill. I assured him this was a business transaction, not a favor."

"It's not that simple. I'll explain it to him when he comes to his senses." Ian ignored my suspicious look. Then I noticed the cell phone he was holding.

"Are you taking video of this? Right now?"

"It's for science, Glory. Of course I am. Look at his face. Makes you wonder what's going on inside his head, doesn't it?" He'd been surreptitious; now he held it up for a better shot. "I wish Cornelius would share his formula."

"This is an invasion of Jerry's privacy, Ian. He didn't give you permission to take all these pictures."

"He was awake when we taped him before and didn't object. I'm taking that as a tacit agreement. This is priceless. I need this film for my archives. No one will see it except fellow scientists." He stood. "Look! I think he's coming out of it. Get ready, Glory. Old Jeremiah or new Jeremy? I hope you know which one you want."

I hoped I did too. Whichever one I got, I had to be ready to deal with him.

Jerry opened his eyes and looked around. "Where the hell am I?"

Uh-oh. Was this a new onset of amnesia? Had he forgotten what had just happened?

"You're at Ian MacDonald's, Jerry. Don't you remember? You were under a spell. Ian's a doctor and arranged for a sorcerer to cure you." I was close by Jerry's side in an instant. The shield was down and I could touch him.

"Of course." He rubbed his forehead. "What a night. And, God save me, I'm lying here in Ian's underwear." He frowned at the doctor who stood behind me, taking this all in with his camera phone. "What the hell? Put that phone down. What's that for? Planning to put my picture on the Internet? Make me a laughingstock?"

"No, it's for my archives." Ian put the phone away. "Internet? What do you remember, Campbell? Did the new spell work? Are you cured?"

"Wouldn't you like to know?" Jerry smiled grimly. "Can we get the hell out of here, Gloriana?"

"No! I mean, please answer Ian, Jerry. I have to know the answer too." I put out my hand when he stood but he shrugged off the help. "What do you remember?"

"Let's see. I remember you arriving at Castle Campbell, determined to make things up with me." He pulled me to him. "I was more than ready to let bygones be bygones since

I'd missed the hell out of you." He dropped a kiss on my lips. "Then I was stabbed. By Mara of all people. I've got a bit of a blur there but seems to me you told me your mother arranged that. So I'd forget you. And it worked for a while."

"God, Jerry!" I threw my arms around him. "You remember. Cornelius!" I looked around for him but both he and Waldo had vanished. "Oh, he's gone. Anyway, a sorcerer Ian summoned found the cure. For a Hellfire curse and your memory loss." I couldn't quit smiling. "Really, you remember everything?"

He suddenly put me from him. "Indeed. What's *she* doing here?" He stalked over to where my mother stood just inside the terrace doors. "She-devil! How dare you show your face here! Where are my weapons?" Jerry looked around and picked up a heavy metal ashtray.

"Not a wise idea." My mother lifted her hand and Jerry was frozen. "Gloriana and I have arranged a truce, just as your clan and the MacDonald clan have. I'd advise you to rein in your temper, Jeremiah, before you lose more than your memory this time. I can make your manhood vanish like that vase over there." She flicked her wrist and a blue and white vase disappeared. We all gasped, even Ian. "How will Gloriana like you then?"

"Mother, release him. And stop with the threats!" I grabbed her arm, sick to my stomach at the thought of what she was capable of. "Give him time to adjust to things."

"You promised we could have a relationship, Gloriana. If he and I are both to be in your life, then he must learn to respect me." She threw back her shoulders, not wise when you only have a single button on a jacket. I didn't bother to tell her she was exposing one of her boobs. Let her embarrass herself. Or not. She still wouldn't let Jerry move, though the ashtray he'd been holding vanished.

Ian and Melanie just watched. They weren't stupid, and she was clearly not in a mood to be messed with. I sent them both a mental message that their best move right now was to stay quiet and observe like the good scientists they were.

"Mother, you didn't cure Jerry, Ian did. I'm not sure there's a reason you could give me that would allow you a place in my life." I glared at her. "Now let him go."

"Not until we work this out." She smiled at Ian. "I must say thank you, Doctor. I know how these sorcerers conduct their business. You had to promise a future favor to Cornelius for him to work that last spell. I'm sure he doesn't come cheap."

"No, he doesn't." Ian moved closer. Which showed how much he listened to me. He touched Jerry on the shoulder. "Let the poor bastard go. Hasn't he suffered enough tonight? Gloriana, I think you're going to have to let your mother see you occasionally. Can't you see that she only wants to share in her daughter's life?" He bowed to her. "Beautiful lady, I'd be more than happy to make my home available if you need a place to stay while in Austin."

My mother's eyes sparkled with interest. Great. Now she and Ian were setting up a flirtation. I wasn't going to bother to warn him anymore. He was a big boy and partied at his own risk.

"Ian, you have no idea what my mother's idea of sharing is." I really didn't need his advice. I was so over this whole scene though and knew Jerry had to be sick of standing there in Ian's underwear like a damned statue. "Mother, thaw Jerry out and disappear at the same time. I want to take him home. Now. I'll text you when we can meet again. Is that enough for you?"

"Fine." Mother smiled at Ian. "I'll be seeing you, Doctor. I can tell we might have a few things in common. An appreciation for the beautiful and rare." A priceless antique table appeared where his other one had been burned, the pieces obviously swept away by a servant earlier. "Gloriana, I expect to hear from you soon, very soon. Or I will be dropping by. And it might not be at a time convenient for you. Are we clear?"

"Yes, now go!" I suffered through one of her hugs. She vanished just as Jerry began to move.

"Where are my clothes?"

"In the bathroom." Ian smiled at Melanie. "Show him."

"No, I'll find them myself." Jerry charged down the hall. In moments we heard a roar. "Where the hell are my knives?"

Ian laughed. "Did he really think I would let him keep a weapon around me? Old Jeremiah Campbell or new Jeremy Blade, I was taking no chances."

Jerry stormed into the living room, fully dressed. "Well, are you giving them back?"

"They are in your car, Blade. That *is* what you go by these days." Ian smiled.

"And you'll send me a bill for tonight. I have no desire to owe you, MacDonald." Jerry held out his hand, surprisingly steady considering what he'd been through. "Car keys, Gloriana. I am itching to drive again. I can't believe I was so damned helpless for so long."

"You hated it." I dropped the keys in his hand.

"Just a minute." Ian stepped in front of us when we headed for the door. "You will get a bill, but that's not all you'll owe me, Blade. Sorcerers deal in favors as Gloriana's mother pointed out. Cornelius required a promise of one in order to come here. Then a second one for the restoration of your memory." Ian's smile was wolfish. "So you see you'll still owe me, Blade. When I need a favor, I'll be calling on you. Never doubt it."

I saw Jerry's jaw tighten. This was a matter of honor and, old or new, he always paid his debts. "Very well. I won't deny the amnesia was driving me mad." He nodded at Melanie. "Thank you both. Good night."

At the car he held the door for me but stopped me before I could slide into the seat.

"Gloriana." He pulled me against him and breathed into my hair.

"Yes, Jerry?" My heart pounded. What was this? The kiss-off as all those memories of my transgressions plus the fact that I had a mother who could make his life disappear added up to reason enough to let me go?

"I know I wasn't easy to live with these past weeks."

"Well, I'll not deny I won't miss the ancient warrior." I touched his dark brow with a fingertip. "Over the years, you'd turned into a modern man I admired. A clever businessman, a brilliant lover, I could go on."

"And wasn't ancient Jeremiah a brilliant lover as well?"

"I'll never tell." I couldn't stop smiling. This teasing meant all was well, didn't it? Then he got solemn.

"I will never be able to thank you enough for what you've done for me. I remember how difficult I was. How I hurt you. My only excuse is that I lashed out at the person closest to me. The woman I love." He ran a hand through his hair. "Shit. That's no excuse. Just please know how sorry I am. You deserve better." He leaned down and kissed me then. I sighed into his mouth, held on and tried to absorb him into my own skin. He was back. No matter what happened, I had all of him with me now. We would deal with what came next together.

Thirteen

"Your place or mine?" he asked as he started the car.

"Well, Lily is at yours. She wasn't too happy the last time we saw her. Remember?" I fastened my seat belt.

"Surprisingly I remember almost everything. Except for when I was shooting fire out of my hands. Did I blast it out of my eyes too or was that a nightmare?" He drove down Ian's driveway then stopped to wait for the iron gates to open. A pair of guards eyed us but waved us through.

"Nightmare. Mouth and fingers, that's all. Like some kind of unwilling superhero. FireMan. PyroBlaster. Has a certain ring to it, don't you think?" I reached over and squeezed his hand.

He laughed and shook his head. "Keep it up, Gloriana, and I just might have to pull over and make you pay for mocking me."

I smiled, loving his teasing. "If it wasn't so close to dawn, I'd beg you to." I sighed and leaned my head against his shoulder. "It's good to see you driving again, Jerry. You sure you're up to it? Not that long ago you were laid out in a tub, incoherent."

"Nice picture." He hit the accelerator and drove onto the

highway. "I'm fine. Your place. I'll face Lily tomorrow night.
She needs some tough love. That temper tantrum at the airport wasn't necessary. I do remember that. I think a job would
be good for her. If Lily will listen to you, it's a good idea for
you to talk to her. If you're willing." He glanced at me.

"I can try." I settled back in the leather seat, the cool
wind blowing my hair, my worries safely tucked away for
tomorrow too. Tonight, since Jerry was feeling so chipper, I
was going to make him very happy when I took him to bed.

"Only have a half hour until dawn." I looked up at the
dark cloudless sky. My plans for a big night were slipping
away with the ticktock of the clock.

"Let's make the most of it." He stopped at a light and
pulled me to him for a kiss. His mouth on mine sent a different kind of flame licking through me. I could tell he was
having the same reaction. He seemed desperate to get closer
to me. When he finally drew back, his eyes were dark and
shining. "God, but I didn't think I'd survive tonight.
Now . . . I need you, Gloriana."

"I need you too. I'm so glad you're back, really back,
Jerry." I ran my hand over the bulge in his jeans. "Hurry." I
glanced around. We were the only car on the road, even as
we neared downtown. I slid down his zipper and eased my
fingers inside to find him hard. His cock sprang free with a
nudge and I bent down to run my tongue across the bead of
moisture that had collected on the tip.

"God, Gloriana." He stepped on the gas. "What are you
doing?"

"Testing your recovery. Can you multitask, Jeremiah?
Drive and play at the same time?" This car had automatic
transmission and I pulled his right hand over to plunge it
into my dress's gaping neckline. Then I went back to work,
taking his cock into my mouth and rolling my tongue
around it. He pinched my nipple, his breath hitching when
I squeezed his sac.

"Temptress. You realize there are traffic cams getting all
this action."

"Hmm. Giving some poor bored sap a thrill, aren't we?"
I went back to pleasing him until he slowed to make the
turn into my alley. Then I sat up. Someone had replaced the
lightbulbs and it was almost as bright as day. I pushed my
dress back into place and zipped him closed. "I'm going to
have to check on my shop sometime."

"Not tonight." He leaped out of the car and jerked open
my car door, rushing me to the back of the building while
I fumbled in my purse. "Hurry or I'll break the bugger
down."

I laughed and held up the key. He grabbed it and made
quick work of the lock while I punched in the security code.
We ran up the stairs and I gasped when Jerry pushed against
me from behind, unzipping my dress and opening my bra
while I unlocked the apartment door with shaking hands.

As soon as we were inside he ripped off my panties,
pushed up my skirt and leaned me over the couch, taking
me from behind before I could do more than drop my purse
on the floor. My landline was ringing. No way was I going
to answer it now. Jerry pushed my dress and bra forward to
bare me to the waist as he pounded into me, his hands
clamped onto my breasts, two joysticks on his ride toward
release.

I just held on, my fingers gripping the fabric while pleasure spiraled through me. I panted his name over and over
again wanting more, more, more. I didn't mind his rough,
take-charge lovemaking. I knew I could turn the tables anytime and make Jerry mine the same way he was claiming
me now. The answering machine clicked on.

"Glory girl. I just heard you're back in town. Call me,
babe. Tell me what happened with the hardheaded Scot. If
he didn't take you back, you know where to find me. Love
ya." Ray. Israel Caine. His voice was unmistakable. And just
in case I didn't recognize it, he ended the message with a
chorus from his latest hit, a love song with an erotic message. "Oh, baby, do you remember what we did last night?
Let me do you again."

Jerry stopped moving. "Caine. What the hell was that about?" He pulled away, his hands sliding off my breasts.

"Tomorrow. We'll talk about it tomorrow." I turned, refusing to give Jerry time to think, and pushed him down to the floor before I climbed on top of him. He still wore all of his clothes, only his zipper was open. I wrestled off his shirt then bit one of his nipples before I sucked it into my mouth. He growled, definitely distracted.

"Yes, we will talk about it." He grabbed my ass and pushed into me, hard. "But right now I need to feed again, Gloriana, before this ends too quickly. Are you up to it?" He bared his fangs.

"Of course." I leaned down, meeting his thrusts eagerly. All my senses were alive as I touched his face, felt the press of his belt buckle into my stomach, my breasts bouncing against his chest. It was wonderful to know he was actually seeing me, his longtime lover, remembering everything we'd been through together and yet still wanting me. "You need me, take me."

He didn't misunderstand, just brought my throat down to his lips. "I love you, Gloriana. I hope to God you haven't made a fool of me again." Then he sank his fangs into my vein.

Made a fool of him again? I woke at sunset lying in my bed with Jerry's words ringing in my ears. He rolled over and took his time making love to me. No words. No explanations. Neither of us seemed ready to get into it. Instead we celebrated Jerry's return to mental health with the kind of slow, sweet loving that left me limp and barely able to stagger into the shower. There he washed my back, massaged shampoo into my hair and then pleasured me one more time.

Of course I realized Ray was the elephant in the room. I wanted to say something. Open the conversation. But how much should I tell Jerry? I couldn't just dump my betrayal into his lap. He'd been through so much and I really didn't want that to be the first thing he had to deal with. Ray and I had slept together right before I'd headed for Scotland. At a low point for both of us we'd offered each other comfort. It had been easy for me to rationalize that Jerry taking off for his homeland had left me free to finally give into my fantasies about Ray.

But I'd discovered that my infatuation with a rock star was just that. Something that had no real future. Ray was kind, generous and exciting. But he was simply not Jerry and Ray's history with loving 'em and leaving 'em didn't recommend him as a keeper anyway. Unfortunately Ray still had hopes that he and I could work things out between us. I needed to see him to set him straight on that. I was with Jerry as long as he wanted me to be. It was that simple.

Lucky for me, unlucky for Jerry, his phone rang and all the business problems that had been put off when he'd been out of commission began to catch up with him. I had to jump in the shower again by myself when he frowned, booted up his laptop and began to scroll through what looked like a thousand unanswered e-mails. I hoped my business was in better shape as I blew my hair dry, threw on makeup and headed downstairs wearing one of the dresses my mother had given me. As I could have predicted, the expensive wrap dress got an appreciative audience in the shop. If I ever decided to sell it, I could get big bucks.

"Glory, we heard you were back." Lacy Devereau, the were-cat who was my day manager, had hung around after her shift was over so she could meet with me. She'd been running the store while I was gone.

"Who is telling everyone that?" I led Lacy to the back room. I was dying to see the books, to see how my finances stood. I had payroll, rent, merchandise to pay for. My mind was getting an overloaded feeling when I thought of how much I had to handle.

"Jerry's daughter, Lily, has been by on a regular basis. She kept us updated since you haven't exactly touched base." Lacy smiled. "Not that we expected you to. Anyway, Lily left a few of her vintage pieces here. She wasn't too happy with our consignment policy. Actually thought she'd get the money up front, like at a pawnshop." Lacy sat on the worktable while I pulled out a stack of receipts. "Seems she was short of cash. Her daddy didn't send her a check this month. What's that about?"

"Jerry had amnesia for a while. Guess Lily didn't share that tidbit. He's upstairs right now trying to catch up on his business. Nice to know Lily was smart enough to come here. Did she bring anything good?" I started piles of shop bills versus income. It was going to be a tough month.

"You bet. And she goes for the Goth look so we've sold quite of bit of her stuff already. Corsets, vintage leather. You'll love it. If you see her, tell her to clean out her closet again." Lacy put her hand on mine. "Amnesia! Wow, that had to have been rough. Megan said Jerry was in here last night and looked confused. Is he okay now?"

"Yes, thank God. His memory is back and he's good as new." I laughed, still not sure I believed it.

"Good." Lacy pushed a ledger closer. "Hate to bug you, boss, but here are the time cards. All of the clerks really need to be paid as soon as you can manage it. I know I have rent, car note. Living expenses."

"Sure. I'm sorry. I had no idea I'd be gone so long or I would have put you on the checking account. If there's a next time, you can stick to the schedule and take care of payroll yourself." I pulled out a calculator. I'd start with Lacy's hours.

"Good idea. You can trust me, Glory. I'd never take advantage of you." She smiled and pointed. "These extra hours are because Becky quit. Graduated and took a job in Oklahoma. Can you believe it?"

"Good for her. But what's she going to do with a fashion degree in Oklahoma?" I didn't want to show her how that total was hitting me. Lacy was getting a big check. I needed to run some numbers, check my balance, before I paid my other bills.

"She's going to work for a big retailer up there. She was all excited about it." Lacy chattered on about the other clerks, a new one she wanted to hire, her family, even a boyfriend she was thinking of breaking up with. I wrote her check then started in on the rest of the payroll checks. It had to be done. Fortunately there was a large deposit to be made too. I should have left better instructions. Lacy could have made these deposits sooner.

"Great." I had no idea what she'd said. I hoped she hadn't just called her boyfriend a loser. "Here are all the checks for the clerks. I'm going to drop this cash into the night deposit. The bank lobby is open late on Thursday nights. I'll get things set up for you then and from now on you can deposit our cash daily." I handed her the envelopes for the staff then zipped the bank bag closed. "We should have done this years ago."

"Well, yeah. I didn't want to say anything but you are a bit of a micromanager, Glo." Lacy smiled and hopped down from the table. "No offense."

"No, you're right." I picked up the bag. "I had a serious wake-up call in Scotland. My priorities have shifted now. Jerry didn't know me and I had to start over with him. It made me realize that I wanted to put my relationship with him first. This business supports me but it's not the center of my existence."

Lacy hugged me. "Wow. That's major." She pulled open the door into the shop. "We handled things here for you. That's why we didn't call while you were over there."

"And I appreciated it. My mind just wasn't on this place." I glanced around the store and realized that, except for that front window display, everything looked fine—stock straight and new things out for customers to see. "The store looks great, Lacy. As soon as I balance my checkbook, I'll see if I can squeeze out a bonus for you and the rest of the staff."

Lacy flushed. "Thanks, Glo." She hugged me again, unusual in a were-cat. "If you're going to the bank now, be careful. There have been some ATM robberies lately."

"I'm a vampire, Lacy. I think I can take care of myself against some mortal thief." I held the bag against my chest. "No one is getting this money. It's all that's keeping this store afloat right now."

"Okay then. And thanks. It's good to know you appreciate us." She waved the envelopes and the night clerk, Megan, came running over.

I stopped to talk to her for a few minutes then headed for the bank down the street. It was still fairly early for Sixth Street, not yet ten o'clock. I passed Rafe's nightclub which had a line down the sidewalk. It was a Friday night and he had a popular band playing according to the poster beside the door. The shifter letting in the crowd saw me and waved. I waved back but kept walking. Of course I knew him. I knew most of the people who worked for Rafe. I should stop and talk to Rafe too. I wasn't happy with the way he'd confronted Jerry. Maybe after I dropped off this deposit.

I passed the crowd and got closer to the financial district where the bank was located. The night deposit drawer was near the ATM and both were well lit. I held the bag tightly as I approached the building. My spidey senses told me something was up. If some desperate yahoo thought he was going to take this deposit, he was in for a surprise. He'd end up with fangs in his throat. I wouldn't mind a little human blood for a change, though I wouldn't kill him of course, just take a donation.

A police car drove slowly down the street. Good. I walked faster, eager to get rid of the bag and back to the nightclub. Rafe stocked blood with alcohol and I would enjoy a drink like that. Maybe I'd call Jerry and see if he was ready for a break. That band played good dance music. Flo and Richard might come over too. I was making up a guest list when something hit me between my shoulder blades. The bag went flying across the pavement and I hit the concrete.

"What the hell?" I was up in a flash and saw a person in black running down an alley, my bag tucked in like it was a football and the perp was going for the goal line. "Oh, no, you don't."

I sprinted down the alley, sure I could catch up to a human in no time. But this person wasn't jogging along at human speed. I sniffed the air and realized I was after something paranormal. Shit. I shifted and took off overhead. I could see the dark figure cutting through a parking lot, zigzagging around rows of cars like he was trying to make a trail impossible to follow. Good luck with that. I swooped down and landed in front of him. One touch and the creep was frozen. Oh, but I loved a good skill set.

I reached out and jerked off the ski mask my thief wore. Original disguise. Not. Long dark hair tumbled out. Oh, no. I knew this robber.

"Lily!" I thawed her out.

"You are kidding me." She threw the bank bag in my face. "You have to ruin everything, don't you, Glory?"

"Excuse me?" I stuck the bag in my purse, though it hung out over the top. "What the hell do you think you're doing?"

"I needed money." She picked up her ski mask and shoved it into her waistband. "So I figured out a way to get it." She smiled. "Mortals are so easy."

"I can't believe you. Where's your conscience? Are you the one holding up all the ATMs around town?" I grabbed her arm and shook her, so mad I didn't realize just how hard I was holding her until she hit me.

"Ouch! Let me go! This is all your fault anyway. First you piss Dad off so he leaves for Scotland. Then Mother explained why Dad lost his memory. That left me high and dry. I had no cash. How was I supposed to live? Answer me that." She

wrenched away from me. I noticed she didn't answer me
about the ATM robberies. Which was an answer in itself.

"You had Jerry's house to live in, his car to drive. I'm sure
Jerry left you well stocked with synthetic." She made a face
and I had a feeling she shared her father's love of a fresh
donor. "And there's always a mortal to sip from if you're
careful. Quit being so dramatic."

"Oh, why would you understand? It wouldn't bother you
that I even had to sell my clothes. Do you know how hu-
miliating that was for me?" She snarled. "Of course not.
You're just a shopgirl. Probably wearing someone else's castoffs right now."

"There's nothing wrong with recycling vintage clothing."
I bit back an explanation that my dress was new. Shopgirl.
Nice to know that what I'd thought was a blossoming
friendship had been nothing but condescension on her part.
She'd sounded like her bitch of a mother just then. God
knows Mara and I had never been friends, never would be.
"Why didn't you ask your mother for money?" I crossed my
arms. Point for Glory.

"She's too busy impressing her new fiancé. Doesn't want
him to think she comes with baggage like a daughter to
support." Lily shoved her hands in her pockets. Skinny
jeans, probably a size zero. She had her mother's great body.
I wondered why she didn't have a boyfriend paying the
freight at the moment but I definitely wasn't about to bring
up what might be a sore subject.

"It was smart to go to my shop. Lacy said you brought in
some great things. You'll have plenty of money when you
stop in tomorrow night. I'll make sure she has a check ready
for you."

"Yeah, sure. *Now* you pay me. But it's a little too late."
Tears filled her dark eyes, so much like Jerry's. "Shit, Glory.
I couldn't even buy my own drink at N-V."

Rafe's club. Of course Lily, slim and gorgeous, probably
never had to buy her own drinks anyway. Not the time to
mention that. She was well into her pitiful act.

"Look. I'm sorry about that. I'll take responsibility for my payout policy." I sighed. "Which is about to change. But forget that. Stealing, Lily. Your father will stroke out when he hears about this."

"Will he? Seems like he's too busy worrying about his lost mind right now to give me a second thought." Lily stared into the darkness, her shoulders slumped.

I wanted to shake her again. Where was her sympathy? Selfish twit. But what did I expect? She was clearly the center of her own universe.

"Good news. Your father got his memory back last night. He was going to call you. Maybe you have a message right now. I'm sure you turned off your cell when you got ready for your big heist, didn't you?" I tapped my foot, waiting for her reaction.

"Yeah." She threw back her dark hair and pulled a cell out of her back pocket. She looked so much like her father it was a miracle Mara had been able to fool her first husband into believing Lily was his instead of Jerry's. "Okay, there's a call here. I'll listen to the message later." She lifted her stubborn chin. "Go, make your deposit. Maybe Dad found his checkbook. Is he at your place?"

"Last I knew." I waited to see if she would beg me not to tell him about her life of crime. She didn't bother, just shifted and flew off into the night sky. What a character. Mara had had four hundred years to screw up her daughter, Jerry only a year to try to give her a moral compass. Did I want to tell him about the robberies? Not now.

One more thing to keep from him. He was going to have to get used to my thoughts being permanently blocked from him. Which would make him suspicious. So far he hadn't mentioned it, but sooner or later, he'd ask why I wouldn't let him peek into my brain. We were lovers, we shouldn't have secrets. Damn.

I pulled out the bank bag and walked back to the night deposit slot. Dropping it in was a huge relief. What next? It seemed nothing was simple anymore.

"Glory? Are you all right? Billy said he saw you walk past the club with a bank bag. There have been robberies lately." Rafe walked up behind me.

A police car pulled up. "Everything okay, ma'am?" The policeman opened his door, ready to come to my aid if Rafe happened to be the ATM robber. Lucky for the cop he was a few minutes too late. Lily would have made sure he wouldn't have remembered seeing her, or she'd have had him for dinner, or both.

"Yes, Officer, I'm fine. This is a friend of mine. I already made my deposit." I smiled and held out my empty hands, my purse strap safely on my shoulder.

"Just checking. We're trying to stop the rash of robberies around here." He closed his car door.

"Hey, I appreciate it." Rafe walked over to the police car. He handed something to the cop. "On your night off, stop by my club, N-V, right down the street. That's a coupon for a free drink."

"Thanks. My wife's been after me to take her there. You get some great bands on the weekends." The cop listened to his radio, which had come to life, a disturbance near the UT campus. "Maybe some Saturday I'll actually be off and can do that."

"Take a couple more coupons. Make a party out of it." Rafe tapped the top of the car when it sped off, then strolled back to me.

"Good PR for the club. So why did you follow me? Surely you weren't really worried about me. I can handle a thief." And had. I began walking back down the street toward N-V and my shop.

"You know why. What's up with you and Blade? Is he still out of it?" Rafe took my elbow and brought me to a stop. "Talk to me. I'd rather do it here than in a noisy club where I usually have a fire to put out."

Fire. That reminded me of Jerry's ordeal the night before. I wanted to check on him, make sure he was suffering no aftereffects. But first things first.

"No, he had a setback and we went out to see Ian. Believe it or not."

"Blade asking a MacDonald for help? He must have been desperate." Rafe knew all about the feud and Jerry's distrust of Ian and anything MacDonald.

"He was. But Ian came through. He called a sorcerer and, hocus-pocus, Jerry got his memory back." I went on to explain what had happened. Rafe whistled.

"Man, that had to have been rough on you. To see Blade like that."

Tears filled my eyes. Rafe always, always thought of me first. "Yes, it was. I love him, Rafe. I'm sorry if it hurts you to hear me say that, but I've made my choice. Jerry and I are together now. I'm not going to do anything else to pull us apart."

"It's tough to fight hundreds of years of history. I get that." He slid his arms around me. "But do you remember why you had such a hard time sticking with him before? I do. He's domineering, controlling, and you're a modern woman, Glory. He's still an ancient male even without a memory problem. With secrets."

"Last night you said something about that. About his name change. What did you mean?" I fought the urge to lean into him for a moment. No. I pushed back. It wasn't fair to Rafe to keep giving myself comforting touches when I was never going to let them lead to more.

"Ask him. Now that he remembers everything, make him tell you why he had to change his name a few years back, when he came to Texas. Ever wonder why he was so happy to pull up stakes and follow you here? It wasn't just for love, Glory." Rafe smiled, like maybe he had a few cards up his sleeve yet to play.

"Don't try to break us up, Rafe. That won't guarantee I'll end up with you." I stepped back out of reach. "I'd like to be able to go to your club, have a drink with friends and be *your* friend. But if you're always going to have this agenda . . ."

"No, relax. I'm here to catch you if you fall, nothing more." He held out his hands as if to show me they were empty. "Come on, I'll buy you a drink. Call Blade and invite him over. I'm not threatened by him, no matter how loud he blusters or how many knives he throws." He grinned, his teeth very white under the streetlight.

"You won't goad him?" I wasn't sure I trusted Rafe. He had that wicked twinkle in his eyes that I loved, but that also promised mischief.

"If he behaves, I behave. Swear to God." He held his hand over his heart. "Now come on. Hey, how are Flo and Richard?" He kept up a steady conversation as we walked on to his club, past the line and into the noise. The music was loud and the place was packed. Rafe signaled the bartender and I soon had a glass of premium synthetic blood in my hand, the kind with alcohol. The mortals surrounding me probably thought I was drinking a tomato juice cocktail. Rafe grabbed my hand and pulled me toward a table marked reserved on the balcony overlooking the dance floor. It was a little quieter up there and he settled me into a chair.

"I keep a table handy." He leaned close and whispered. "For my vampire buddies when they come by." He stood and looked around the busy club then frowned. "Call your man. I've got to go down and fix a problem with the band. Told you." He took off down the stairs.

So I did call Jerry. He was happy to take a break though he had Lily with him. I invited her along. When Jerry seemed reluctant to spend an evening in a club Rafe owned, I assured him that I'd had a talk with my friend and we'd come to an agreement that Jerry would be happy with. Okay, they were on their way. That left me feeling like I needed reinforcements because I was pretty sure Lily wasn't on Team Glory. Flo answered on the first ring.

"*Amica!* I have been dying here. How is Jeremiah?"

"Cured, Flo. He remembers everything now." That reality struck me hard suddenly and I had to blink back tears. "Come see me and I'll tell you how it happened. He'll be here soon too." I sipped my drink. The DJ was playing a popular hit and everyone was dancing. I should be celebrating. I had my old Jerry back.

"Where are you? I hear music."

"At N-V. Can you come?" I smiled and shook my head at a man who stopped by my chair with a question in his eyes. Too bad. I did like to dance. But no way was I going to be on the dance floor with another man when Jerry arrived.

"We're on our way. I am so happy!" Flo hung up.

Jerry and Lily would be here soon too. Would she be wearing her all black outfit? I'm sure she'd ditched the ski mask before she'd arrived on my doorstep to see her father. I was on my second drink when I saw them coming up the stairs. Lily had obviously stopped at the shop and rescued one of her consigned pieces. It was a red satin corset that barely held her generous breasts and looked good with those skinny black jeans and high heels. Hmm. Hadn't she been wearing running shoes earlier?

I narrowed my gaze. Those were *my* new shoes my mother had given me, an expensive designer label. Lily and I obviously wore the same size. I'd damn sure get them back and they'd better not be damaged. Not right away obviously. Lily was getting major interest from the men in the room.

Of course Jerry looked more like her date than her dad. But when he kissed me on the lips and settled down next to me, a pair of twentysomething men swooped in to ask Lily to dance. Her eyes lit up and she took both of them down the stairs with her before I could say something about those shoes.

"It's good that she's dancing. She was pretty upset when she got to your place. Chewed me out good for leaving her without so much as a credit card." Jerry waved at a waitress and put in a drink order. "What brought this on?" He nodded toward the crowded dance floor.

"I needed to talk to Rafe. To make sure he knew you and I were together and that I wasn't putting up with his shit. Like that scene last night." I tapped my fingers to the beat of the music. "You know this is the only club in town that caters to us." Meaning vampires. I didn't think the mortals nearby could hear us over the band but we didn't use the "V" word in public. "I wanted to be sure we could still come here without a showdown between you two."

Jerry grinned. "And did you set him straight?" He leaned back in his chair, obviously happy with that idea.

"Yes. I told him he was my good friend but would never be anything more." I rubbed Jerry's hard thigh. "How are you feeling? Any residual problems from last night?"

"Other than accidentally setting fire to your Israel Caine collection?" He laughed when I gasped. "Kidding. I know better than to touch that, just like you may hate my smoking cigars but you would never toss out my stash of Cubans."

"Exactly." I kissed his smile. It was so good to see him back to his old self.

"I'm afraid there is a bit of fallout from our trip to Mac-Donald's." He covered my hand with his. "He's called in his favor."

"Already?" I felt that last drink do a slow churn in my stomach. "What does he want you to do?"

"I have no idea but I'm to bring you with me. I told him hell no but he was adamant. Seems he needs your Olympus connection to solve this issue he's dealing with. Of course he had to be mysterious on the phone. Typical MacDonald tactic." Jerry squeezed my hand. "Sorry, Gloriana, but we're going to have to go out there and see him again. If you're willing, of course." He picked up the drink the waitress set down in front of him and signaled that she should go ahead and bring us both another round.

"Of course, whatever you need. But my Olympus connection. Crap, Jerry, I really don't want to have to get involved with my mother again." I drained my own drink.

"Darling, how can you say that? We have such fun when we work together." Her perfume sent waves of fragrance across the table and reminded me of an overblown bouquet.

Too intense, cloying. I couldn't breathe so I didn't bother. Had she just appeared or walked up the stairs? We weren't getting stares so I guess it didn't matter.

Fun. Right. I ignored her and turned to Jerry. "When do we have to take care of this favor?"

"Tomorrow night." He glared at my mother. "Olympia, why don't you run on out there to MacDonald's house? You two seemed to hit it off. Maybe you could handle whatever he needs done and spare your daughter the hassle. Tell him you're doing it for me. I think you owe me that much."

"*Owe* you?" She lifted a perfect eyebrow.

"Mother." I leaned forward. "Jerry's been through hell. His brain almost boiled because of your interference. Yes, you certainly do owe him."

She acted like she didn't hear me. "Ian and I did hit it off. He was quite charmed, of course. Most men are when they meet me." She preened, adjusting the bodice of her stylish leopard print dress to show maximum cleavage and pulling a compact out of her black patent clutch. If she heard Jerry's snort, she didn't acknowledge it. When she started to reapply her lipstick, I'd had it.

"Are you going to do it?"

"Really, Gloriana, just because you run around town without even bothering to use a hairbrush doesn't mean I do." She snapped her compact closed. "I'll go see Ian and we'll discuss what he wants done. Then I'll see you both tomorrow night. You did promise we'd visit with each other occasionally, Gloriana. Remember?" With that she just vanished, heedless of the mortals all around us.

"What is she thinking?" I glanced around, sure someone would exclaim, say something, point. No one seemed to have noticed. Maybe she'd only been visible to us. I could hope.

"She obviously has her own rules. We are nothing to her, Gloriana. It's strange that she even wants to bother knowing you. Maybe you'll explain that to me now that I'm myself again." Jerry smiled suddenly. "Here are Florence and Richard. I'm glad they're here. I never thanked them properly for giving us a ride home on the jet. Or apologized for acting the fool about it." He stood and kissed Flo's cheek. He and Richard clapped hands, discussing Jerry's miraculous and almost fatal recovery.

I tried to perk up and get into the spirit of a celebration, even ran a hand over my hair. Trust my mother to make me feel like I looked a mess. Now I had something new to dread. Tomorrow night. Doing a favor for Ian was bad enough, but when it involved Olympus? It was too much to hope that my mother would fix things and then just go away. No, somehow I'd be up to my eyebrows, which needed a serious plucking, in disaster.

The only thing left to do tonight was to order another drink. I was already feeling a buzz. Then I glanced over the railing and saw Lily dancing with her new male friends. She stumbled then jerked off my shoes and tossed them aside. One landed in a puddle of beer. Okay, that did it. I was out of my chair and halfway down the stairs before Jerry caught up with me.

"Going to dance by yourself?" He laughed and grabbed me around the waist. "Next slow one I'll be happy to partner you." He noticed my glare in his daughter's direction. "What is it? Did Lily do something?"

I stopped and made myself calm down. Starting a war with Jerry's daughter wouldn't help anything. I turned and smiled up at him and didn't that take every bit of my acting skills?

"Lily had on my shoes. Did you tell her she could borrow them?"

He glanced over at her sandwiched between the two men who were taking turns bumping into her with their hips. "She's barefoot. Hell, I didn't notice what she wore in here. She said she needed to borrow your hairbrush and went into the bedroom. If she got into your closet, I'm sorry." He hugged me. "I know how you are about your shoes. I'll buy you a replacement pair, even better than whatever she appropriated."

We both saw one of my black pumps go skidding across the dance floor when someone kicked it. "Not the point, Jerry. I wish she'd asked." I leaned against him. "Never mind. Lily and I need to talk. And not just about the shoes. Do you care?"

"No. Go for it." He kissed my cheek. "Ah, a slow song. Come on, dance with me. And I will buy you those shoes. It's the least I can do if my daughter makes off with yours. I'll not have a thief in the family." He pulled me onto the crowded floor. "All right?"

"Sure. Thanks." I leaned my head against his chest. A thief in the family. If he only knew. Yes, I needed to talk to Lily, but I owed it to Jerry to talk to him first. Yet another thing to dread. He ran his hands down to rest on my hips. Forget dread. I needed to focus now on what was good. I was in Jerry's arms and he knew me. The music was working on me like it always did and the alcohol had lit a fire in my blood. I was getting anxious to take Jerry home. One night at a time. That was the only way I could deal with my ridiculous life.

Fourteen

The next night came all too soon. I hadn't called Ray back yet and had two more messages from him. He was high on my to-do list but first I had my mother and Ian to deal with. Jerry strapped on his knives as usual when we were getting ready to go pay back that favor he owed Ian.

"I don't have time for this. I need to deal with some business issues." He slipped a stake into a holster under his arm before he put on a dark sports coat. I hadn't seen him carry a stake before. Did it have Ian's name on it? I was afraid to ask.

"I know, neither do I. Can you sit a minute? I hate to bring this up now, when your plate is so full, but I have one more thing to add to it."

"Now what?" He wasn't exactly in the mood for another problem. Too bad. This couldn't be put off.

"Jer, I caught Lily stealing, or trying to."

"What?" He shoved a knife into his boot. "Explain yourself."

"Come into the living room. Sit and I'll bring you some synthetic. I don't think you're back to full strength yet." He looked a little wobbly to me though he shrugged off my hand.

"I'll do." He strode into the living room. "You sit and tell me about Lily."

"I was taking a deposit to the bank. My clerk had warned me there had been robberies lately at the ATMs in town. I no sooner got to the night deposit area than a masked burglar snatched my bank bag. I gave chase of course. I can't afford to lose even a dollar with the bills I have to pay. Being gone so long really set me back." I headed for the kitchen to fetch two bottles of synthetic. I remembered he had preferred his warm and nuked his for a few seconds.

"Go on, finish. Where does Lily come into this?" He stood in the doorway, snatching the bottle from me as soon as I pulled it out of the microwave. He took a deep swallow.

"Well." I headed back to the living room but he stopped me with a hand on my shoulder. "Okay, I'm getting there. Let me sit." I shrugged away and settled on the couch. I knew he wasn't going to take this well so I waited until he was seated in the chair across from me.

"I ran down the thief a few blocks away, had to shift to catch her because it became clear immediately that this was no mortal thief." I sipped my drink. Jerry just kept staring at me. "Anyway, I froze her, with that statue trick I know, and jerked off her ski mask. Imagine my horror when I realized Lily was the thief."

"Son of a bitch." He slammed his bottle down on the coffee table and jumped to his feet. "Did you get your money back?"

"Yes, of course. She had no choice. She was paralyzed. I had her dead to rights. And she knew better than to try to get me to promise not to tell you."

"I should hope so." He paced the living room and ran a hand through his hair, his go-to move when he was upset. "This is my fault. I left her here without money, no resources."

"Wait. Hold it." I was on my feet now. "The woman is four hundred years old. She is able-bodied, more than. Why can't she work for a living? I sure do. She can mesmerize any store manager up and down Sixth Street into hiring her. Stealing from hardworking people . . ." I jumped in front of him when he started a third lap of the living room. "You know as well as I do that it's dead wrong."

"Yes, of course. But she expected an allowance from me. I didn't follow through." He shook his head. "Damn your mother. This is her fault."

"I won't deny she started this. But come on, Jer. Lily showed no remorse when I caught her. She doesn't have her head on straight. Where's her moral compass?"

Jerry sat again and picked up his synthetic. "Damned if I know. I wonder if there's any hope for her."

"Of course there is. Mara and Mac raised her. Mac was a fine man."

"Yes, he was. He would have taught her the difference between right and wrong. I'm sure, though, that since he died Mara has let Lily run wild." Jerry stared down at the floor. "If I'd known . . ."

"You didn't. And Lily isn't a child. Running wild? Please. She chose to keep bad company. I'm wondering why she wasn't left some kind of trust from Mac. What do you bet Mara made sure *she* got all of Mac's fortune?"

"That's something I should look into. Mac's will, his estate. Though vampires don't usually bother with those formalities, since he had a child, I'll bet Mac did." Jerry looked up. "Good notion, Gloriana. But I've got to do something with Lily in the meantime."

"Can you pretend you don't know about the thefts? If Lily knows I told you, she'll hate me. I would like to work with her, try to show her a way to earn her own living. I am sort of an expert on the subject. If she knows I've been a snitch, I won't stand a chance."

"You're right about that. No one likes a tattletale." He stood and pulled me into his arms. "But you *had* to tell me. A parent has the right to know what his child has been up to, especially when it involves breaking the law."

"I thought so." I leaned against him.

"Yes, I'll keep it between us. And start investigating Mac's records. The MacTavish family may very well have copies of his last wishes. He could have left Mara in charge of a trust for Lily and she's kept it a secret." Jerry kissed the top of my head. "Have I told you lately how sexy I find your mind?"

"That too?" I smiled and lifted my face for a better kiss.

"Want to call and cancel?" He said it but I knew he wouldn't do it.

"Tempting. But this is something I think we'd both like to get over with." I patted his cheek.

"I can't cancel but you could stay here, go down and work in your shop. I'll make your excuses." He pulled me to him. "Seriously. This is my debt, not yours. I know you aren't eager to mix it up with your mother again."

"No, I'm not. But I can't miss this. My mother won't help anyone if she doesn't feel like it. If I don't show up, she's liable to just disappear like she did last night." I smiled up at him. "Besides, Ian asking a favor is unusual enough, but needing Olympus? This is huge. Let's go see what this is about."

"Huge is right, Gloriana. You can quit smiling about it. It's bound to be dangerous." Jerry put me from him. "If you insist on going, arm yourself." He handed me a knife. "This can slow someone down. Remember how I taught you to throw it?"

"Jerry, I can freeze people in their tracks now. Just like my mother froze you at Ian's." I wouldn't take it. I hated his knives, always had. "And I can dematerialize unless one of the gods gets involved and takes my powers away."

"Really? That's new. Your mother give you that power? Or is that from the Sirens?" He put the extra knife somewhere on his own body.

"Apparently I've had it all along I just didn't know it. It's an Olympus thing. A gift from the goddess herself. Watch." I concentrated and poofed. Then showed up again behind him. He whirled when I touched his back.

"I always knew you were an amazing woman, just not how amazing." He brushed his thumb down my face. "Don't forget to use it if we get in a tight spot. Promise you'll be careful. I don't trust MacDonald and neither should you. The only reason I'm letting you go is that I'm sure your mother won't allow anyone to hurt you."

"News flash, Jer. You're not 'letting' me go anywhere." I tempered that with a smile. "I'm going anyway, even if I have to shift to get out there." I strutted to the door. "Now I can ride in the car with you or do my bird thing. Your choice. What's it going to be?"

He watched my hips move then shook his head. "You are really full of yourself, aren't you, woman?"

"You'd better believe it." I unlocked the door and flung it open. "Get used to it, Jerry. If we're going anywhere with our relationship, it will be as partners. Glory the little woman is old news. I'm not meekly obeying your commands again."

"I can see that." He walked past me into the hall. "Can't say I mind it either. Strong women are sexy." He ran his hand down my hip. I'd worn snug jeans and a scoop-necked sweater in a deep red. "Took me a long time to figure that out and get on board, but I'm there now. Lock the door and let's go. You can drive."

"Now you're talking." I snatched the keys he tossed me out of the air and used one of them to lock the door. We grinned at each other then headed down the stairs arm in arm. It was about time Jerry gave me credit for holding my own. Because of my new skills? Who cared? The main thing was that he was treating me as an equal. I hadn't thought I could love him more, but the feeling that swelled inside me and made tears clog my throat convinced me it was possible.

When a rain shower started, I was glad the top was up on the convertible. It got worse as we neared Ian's place in the hills outside of Austin. The roads were slippery and I had to watch my driving. For once Jerry never said a word, though I thought I saw his grip on the armrest tighten a few times. How about that? He was trusting me to get him there without his usual backseat driving. When the car hydroplaned across a slick spot, he grunted and held on to the dashboard but never complained about the way I rode it out. Of course if we'd ended up in that ditch a few yards away, I'm sure it would have been a different story.

"You okay over there?" I couldn't resist asking.

"You're doing fine. You don't need me to tell you how to drive." What a liar. I knew he was itching to do that very thing. He peered out the side window at the pouring rain and finally pointed up ahead. "There's a low water crossing coming up. See it?"

"Sure. Thanks." I slowed down. Low water crossings were notorious around Austin and dangerous. The markers next to them would tell drivers how deep the water was where the road dipped. Thank God for the warning sign up ahead. Water rushed across the road and the sign indicated the usually dry ditch now held five feet of water. No way was I driving into that death trap. The current could sweep the car downstream toward the lake not far away.

"I'm pulling over. We can't cross now." I made sure we were on a high spot on the shoulder and stopped the car. The skies were still dumping so much rain it was hard to see even though the wipers were on high. I had the fleeting thought that this could be something the Storm God had whipped up. But why would he be here tonight? No, it was probably just one of Austin's freak storms. Could we wait it out? I glanced at the dashboard clock. We were already running late. Did I care? Not really. But I didn't like the idea of Ian giving Jerry a hard time about it.

"What do you think?" I turned off the motor. I hated the idea of leaving the cozy warmth of the car and shifting out into the storm.

"Do we have a choice?" Jerry pulled out his cell. "Let me check with Ian. Maybe he's called this off for tonight. These aren't ideal conditions for much of anything." He started to make a call. "No signal. Try yours."

I opened my purse. I should have already stuck my phone in my pocket anyway. When I tried to make a call, I realized I couldn't get a signal either. Decision time. The wind blew the rain almost sideways against the car, shaking it. The convertible top was holding but I didn't feel very safe where we were. Have I mentioned how much I hate storms? I shivered thinking about getting out of that car. The motor was still running and I turned the heater on.

"We'll be soaked before we can shift. My clothes . . ." I really, really hated the thought. My sweater was bound to shrink and it was one of my favorites. Vintage cashmere, high quality and a good color on me. And don't get me started about my jeans. They'd barely zipped as it was. Wet, they'd be a lost cause.

"You're right. The rain will ruin your clothes. We should shift naked." Jerry grinned. "Stow the clothes in my backpack. It's waterproof. I can carry it during the shift. I've done it successfully before." He reached for the backpack, already on board with the plan.

"You just want to see me strip." I couldn't stop my own smile. It was a good idea. I pulled my sweater off over my head and stuffed it into the pack while he took off his jacket and tossed it into the backseat.

"Wonder if we could be really, really late." Jerry reached across the console to open the front fastener of my bra.

"Not happening, Blade." I slapped his hands away when he fondled my breasts. "Check the time. We're already late."

"I'll be quick." Jerry pulled me toward him and licked the tip of my right breast.

"Stop." I grabbed his hair. Pull, no, push. How could I let go right now when I had no idea what we'd be facing at Ian's? Men. Jerry saw boobs and thought sex. Whatever came next wasn't even on his radar. "Please, Jerry. We can do this all you want later and take all the time in the world. All of this"—I gestured at my breasts—"will be here when we get back to the car."

"Spoilsport." He sat back and unbuttoned his cotton

shirt. "I'm holding you to that. Hot sex in this car. Here on the side of the road. It'll be awkward, but worth it."

I touched his chest, then ran my hand down the fine hair on his stomach. "Oh, yes, I promise you it will be totally worth the wait."

"Undress or we won't make it to Ian's at all. When we get there, we'll find a spot where we can dress and stay dry. A place without an audience, hopefully. I'll be damned if I'll let Ian see you naked." Jerry toed off his shoes and stuck them in the pack. It was already pretty full.

I wiggled out of my jeans, deciding to leave my shoes in the car. I could always hit my mother up for another pair when we got there. I left on my panties. I could go commando when we got to Ian's.

"I'm ready." I glanced at Jerry. "That rain is going to be ice cold."

"No doubt. Be brave." He grinned, obviously enjoying this. "On three. Try not to get the car soaked." He shrugged on the backpack and put his hand on the door handle. I braced myself as he counted. Then we threw open the doors and slammed them at the same time. I locked the car, tossed Jerry the keys to slip into the backpack then shifted. Soon we were hurtling up into the air as fast as we could go.

I could tell my hair was already wet, the rain pounding my wings as I flew beside Jerry up the hill toward Ian's. Thank goodness it wasn't too far away. Amazing that Jer could shift and the backpack would merge with his bird form. But then I had shifted with my purse strapped across my body many times and never lost a thing either.

Ian's house came into view below us. Jerry led the way, swooping down to land under a walkway that led from the five-car garage to the house. None of the guards were in sight but the security lights were blazing. We both shifted near the back door.

"Hurry, hand me something." I tried to wring out my wet hair. I was shivering and sluiced water off my body with both hands.

"Here's your sweater. I left the bra in the car, not enough room for it." Jerry tossed me my sweater while he stepped into his jeans. They clung to his wet legs.

"Great. Now everyone's going to see nipple." I whipped off my panties and tossed them aside then struggled to get my jeans up my own wet legs. It wasn't easy.

"Need some help?" Jerry moved closer, sliding his hand between my thighs.

"Are you kidding me? You're making a move now?" I tried to wiggle away but he had a pretty firm and intimate grip. He jerked me to him and kissed me, his fingers moving inside me.

I didn't want to feel anything. This wasn't the time or place. But there was something so dangerously exciting about leaning against Ian's back door and knowing that we were just feet from the man himself and a half dozen guards. Jerry pushed his knee between my legs to give himself more access, his other hand under my sweater so he could massage one of my breasts.

"Gloriana. The sight of you almost naked in the rain took my breath away." He ran his tongue along the edge of my jaw and down to my throat while he kept up his rhythm, the heat building inside me until I raked his bare shoulders with my fingernails.

"Jerry, please." I hiked one leg around his hips, my own hips shoving against his hand. I was close, so close. He kissed me again, pushing harder, deeper until I fell apart, screaming his name inside my head.

I leaned my cheek on his chest while the rain still poured, rushing over the roof in sheets to splash our bare feet. I let my leg collapse, sliding down his until my foot landed on the flagstone walkway. Could I even stand on my own? He kissed me one more time, lingering long enough to make me grasp his hair and press against him before he eased his fingers from me. Then he pulled up my jeans, carefully zipping them closed.

"Well, well. That was quite a show." Ian stood in the

open back door. "I do have security cameras, you know." He laughed and gestured. "If you're through pleasing your woman, Blade, I could use you in here. There's action coming. All hands on deck. Gloriana, good to see you are still a lusty woman." He turned on his heel, still laughing.

My cheeks burned. Jerry just pulled his shirt out of the pack then began to rearm himself. Of course. No room for a bra, but knives and stakes aplenty. I saw the wisdom in that. I rescued my cell phone from the pack and checked. I had service. And a new message. Ray again. I turned off the phone and stuck it in my back pocket. No way was I going to be interrupted tonight.

Jerry stopped me before I could go into the house. "I'm sorry, Gloriana. I didn't mean to embarrass you. MacDonald's an ass."

"No argument there. But I will never regret a minute with you, Jerry." I kissed his lips then walked past him. My mother would be inside. Had she seen the video? I dreaded facing her if she had. Me with a vampire. I could only imagine her reaction.

We stepped into a scene I'd never have expected. My mother obviously didn't have a clue about a security video. She was too busy with something else. She looked stunning, dressed as usual in a designer dress and heels. Tonight's ensemble was my favorite shade of green. I was tempted to compliment her but she barely acknowledged my entrance. Instead, she was focused on someone I hadn't seen in a while.

Aggie, or Aglaophonos, as she was formally called, was a Siren. Tonight she was in human form, tossing her long blond hair around while she talked to my mother. Her very presence made me think that this horrible weather was courtesy of her boss, the Storm God.

"Ladies, they're here. Aggie, darling, calm down." Ian walked over and pulled the Siren into his arms. "I told you we'd fix this and we're going to."

I could only stare. Ian had called her darling. Had his

arm around her in a loving gesture I'd never seen him make. Could it be that the cold, calculating Scot had finally fallen in love? I glanced at Jerry. He grinned like he'd just won the lottery.

"What have we here? Heard the Siren's song, have you, MacDonald?" He strode forward. "Aggie. Don't believe I've seen you since Florence and Richard's wedding."

"Don't remind me. What a mess." Aggie smiled at me. "Thanks for coming, both of you. Ian told me you had quite a trip to Scotland, Glory."

"Can we dispense with the reunion?" My mother had been ignored long enough. "Gloriana, where are your shoes?"

"I had to shift out here, Mother. The road was flooded." I raised an eyebrow. "Maybe you could take care of it for me. Something in a medium heel. Designer of course. I know you won't go cheap."

"Of course not. A name brand." She smiled and moved one of her fingers. "What do you think?"

I glanced down. "Perfect. You do have exquisite taste." The shoes were red Keds. Her idea of a joke. I just played along. "Now why are we here?"

"This Siren, who claims she is a friend of yours, wants to stay in Austin. Is even thinking of defecting." My mother smiled and looked up at the sky. "As you can see, Achelous isn't too happy about it."

More dealings with the Storm God. Was it too late for Jerry and me to shift back to our car? I never wanted to mess with that egomaniac again. He'd fried my hair, tormented Jerry, thrown around lightning until I had only to hear his name and feel a tingle of electricity run through me. Of course he'd tried to kill me more than once too. Only the fact that he was afraid of my mother's wrath had saved me the last time we'd met. I smiled at the woman who'd given birth to me. Okay, this was going to be an interesting night.

"Ian and I are in love, Glory." Aggie had her arm around Ian and I couldn't believe he didn't shrug away from it. I knew she had the power to sing any man to her as a Siren.

Obviously she'd done her thing and put him under her spell. Ian MacDonald and Aggie, a loudmouthed bitch if ever I'd met one, just didn't match up.

"Gloriana, Blade, quit looking at me that way." Ian frowned. "I'm not under some Siren's spell." Ian leaned down and kissed Aggie's lips. "She's beautiful, and has been misunderstood and held prisoner for years by that asshole she works for. It's slavery! Prostitution!"

All right, I could have gone all night without hearing the "P" word. I'd been a Siren myself once.

"Shut up, Ian. Sirens aren't prostitutes. They're victims of a master who makes them sing men to their deaths. Forget the sex. If it happens, it's because they are programmed that way. They can't help it. All of it, the song, the killing, is to enrich the coffers of Olympus. The women don't get a penny." I was hot.

"Now, Ian, Gloriana, calm down. She's right. We are cursed. It's horrible. A terrible fate. But, look, lover. They all came here to help. So I'm sure I'll be free soon. Just like Glory is." Aggie's smile was brilliant.

"They think you ensorcelled me, darling. Not so, damn it!" Ian stared at Jerry, then me. "You know me well enough to realize I'm too smart to be suckered by some Siren's song."

"Oh, yeah, you're a freaking genius." Jerry kept his arm around me, highly entertained.

"Stuff it, Campbell. I do love her. I've finally found a woman I want to be with for more than one night. Is that so hard to understand?" Ian was livid.

I bit my lip. Poor misunderstood beautiful Aggie. The only part that truly fit was the beautiful part. With her long blond hair, leaf green eyes and size-six body, she was close to perfect. She wore a deep green mini and matching top with high heels that I would have had trouble walking in. But forget beauty.

Aggie hadn't killed because she'd been ordered to, she'd enjoyed it, kept count and was thrilled when she hit a million with her body count. Ray and I had barely escaped being notches in her Gucci belt. Of course she'd been full of reasons why she'd been driven to making us her victims. Small comfort when we'd been fighting for our lives. Old grudge aside, I knew her as a vain woman who didn't know how to be a friend, plus she had a temper that made her use her powers in some pretty mean ways.

"Say something, Glory. Don't you remember the wedding shower I threw for Flo? I've tried to make up for how we met." Aggie looked at my mother. "We were in the lake here. Circe was mad at me and made me collect some vampire sacrifices. I'm sure you know Circe. She hates the night and anything to do with it, especially vampires."

"Oh, yes. I've heard her on the subject." My mother glanced at me. "It's a common prejudice on Olympus, Gloriana. Vampires are demons, to hear the gossip."

"Trust me, Mother. I've met demons. Vampires are vintage Chanel. Demons are last year's markdowns." I tried to put it in terms she could understand.

"Ah, I get it." She winked at me. "I must set Circe straight, I see."

"Whatever." Aggie had played sweetness and light as long as she could stand. "Anyway, I caught Glory and her pal Ray the first night. Glory thinks I was going to kill her."

"You aren't going to rewrite history, Aggie. It was only fast talking that got us out of there. That and Ray's singing. You always were an Israel Caine fan." I definitely wasn't an Ian MacDonald fan but he *had* helped Jerry so I felt I owed him a warning. "Ian, listen to me. You never saw Aggie the way she was then. A sea monster, cruel and disgusting. Are you sure you want to hook up with her or get Achelous on your case? I've been toe-to-toe with that guy and almost didn't come out of it alive. I can't tell you how long it took me to grow back my eyebrows."

"Gloriana, we don't need to interfere in Ian's love life." Jerry pulled me away from Ian. He'd probably noticed that the doctor was about to blow. Ian's stare would have killed me if he'd had the powers some paranormals had. Of course

Jer didn't care if Ian spent forever tied to a shrew. "Why are we here, anyway?"

"Ian asked for my help before but why should I come to his aid? I don't owe him anything." My mother had obviously endured my red Keds long enough. I suddenly had on cute red heels. "He decided to use you two as leverage to get what he wants. The favor you owe him, Jeremiah, is the connection he needed. I have come to terms with the fact that my daughter will do anything for you." My mother clearly didn't like being manipulated.

"Thank you, Mother." I was glad that she finally got that.

"Now you say that the Storm God has hurt you, Gloriana. No eyebrows! If only I had known, you wouldn't have suffered for even a moment." My mother grasped my hand. "Achelous has always been an arrogant bastard. It will be fun to bring him down a few pegs. I think I'm going to enjoy this night." She tossed her hair and looked out at the storm that still raged. "Look at his little temper tantrum. All this just because his Siren asked to be released. Ha! I can do so much better. I could make a water spout that would lift your Texas capitol building and set it in Arkansas. Would you like to see?" She turned to us, obviously eager to show off her "talents."

"No! We'll take your word for it, Mother." I had to admit she was damned scary when she was worked up. "Awesome." I made sure she knew I was impressed.

"Yes, well. He should know better than to harm my loved ones." She stomped her foot. "You wish to no longer be a Siren, Aglaophonos?" She stepped up to Aggie, her eyes gleaming. "Do you have any idea of the consequences? You will become mortal, you know. Powers, song. Gone."

"Yes, I do know. But Ian has promised to make me vampire." She cuddled up against him. "So I'll still be with him forever. And vampires have powers. I've seen them at work."

"That's illegal in Austin, Ian. Making a vampire." I felt

it my duty to at least mention it. The vampire council had strict rules against turning new vampires. Flo's brother Damian was head of the council. They'd already staked one vamp who'd broken that rule.

"You think I give a damn about rules? And it will be to save her life. They can make an exception. I know my way around petty officials." Ian seemed ready for whatever came next. I pitied him. He had no idea what he might be facing. The council was the least of his worries. First, he'd have to contend with the Storm God.

"Brace yourselves, my dears. Here comes Achelous now." My mother smiled, obviously itching for a fight. "Oh, look, he managed a tiny water spout on the lake. Huh! I could do such a one in my sleep by wiggling my pinky toe."

The air shimmered with golden light. The French doors blew open letting in wind and rain but that all stopped suddenly when the man appeared. He strode into the room, his sandaled feet thudding against the tile.

"Come here, Siren." He stretched out his hand and blue sparks flew from him to Aggie. She screamed and leaped away from Ian. Uh-oh. I knew just how she felt. No wonder her hair was standing on end.

"Don't hurt him, Sire." She threw herself down on the floor, prostrating herself at the Storm God's feet.

"I will if I want to." He wore the formal Olympus dress of toga with a crown of leaves on his golden hair. He zapped Ian with a bolt of lightning and we all saw the vampire jerk, his Italian leather loafers steaming.

"Still a bully, I see." My mother strolled up to Achelous, obviously not intimidated by the shower of sparks around him or his golden glow. "Let her go, Achy. I have a bone to pick with you."

"Oh, really?" He kicked Aggie out of the way. "Wait over there." She slid to the side. Ian rushed to help her up but Achelous gestured and Ian was turned to stone. "Vampire, you will not touch her again. Disgusting."

This made my mother glance back at me. I narrowed my gaze. She obviously didn't need a reminder of my feelings on that subject because she just turned back to him.

"Mind your tongue. My own daughter is a vampiress. You will not speak ill of her." She flashed me a smile which I returned. Progress.

"You can't be serious. You're claiming Gloriana? Announcing it upstairs?" Achelous laughed. "You will be a laughingstock."

"No one will dare. You forget who I am." My mother tossed lightning around like it was confetti and we all reeled from the pulses of electricity in the air. Since it was aimed at Achelous, he was the only one who seemed to be hurt by it. Blackened holes appeared in his toga but they disappeared with a motion of his hand.

"Calm down, my dear. It is certainly your news to share."

"Remember that." My mother's eyes blazed. "This face-to-face is long overdue. I have heard what you did to my daughter, Achelous. A girl I gave to you for safekeeping centuries ago. Did you conveniently forget where she came from?" She raised both her hands and the room shook from thunder so loud that a vase fell off the mantel. Jerry and I staggered and held on to each other. I heard more glass breaking in other parts of the house. It was a reminder that I needed to be careful not to make her mad at me.

"Oh. Yes. An oversight. I am responsible for so many young women, you see. Impossible to keep straight who each one belonged to when they were dropped off." Achelous glared at me. "You should be glad you didn't keep her. Nothing but trouble. I don't know who you mated with to create the girl, but big mistake, Hebe." He raised his own hands and the skies poured rain so hard that water rushed into the house through the open doors.

"Stop. We can play with the elements all night but that doesn't prove anything. We could also go to Zeus." My mother smiled and I had a feeling she knew who would win if that happened. Achelous frowned. It obviously wasn't him. The rain stopped suddenly.

Hebe. I finally knew my mother's name. I couldn't wait to get to a computer and look her up. So many goddesses and each with certain powers. Hebe. What? I wracked my brain but couldn't remember what she was famous for. Obviously she had a strong connection to Zeus, though. Achelous had almost cringed when she'd suggested going to the big boss.

"What do you want?" Achelous brushed his toga with his hand and the water on the floor evaporated. I guess he didn't like standing in it.

"First, you will apologize to Gloriana. Then you will make sure she has her song back." She smiled at me. "Oh, yes, I've heard you singing in the shower, darling. So sad." She turned back to him. "Bastard. To strip the girl of her beautiful voice. It's disgraceful!"

"I had to punish her. You don't know what she was like, Hebe. She refused to kill. She was an embarrassment to the sisterhood. Ask Aglaophonos there." He gestured and Aggie was at his feet again.

"I don't care about that, you stupid man. You think I'd be proud of a daughter for her *kills*?" My mother walked around Aggie's body toward me. "I am proud of her because she is beautiful and smart. Because she is not afraid to stand up to a man who tries to push her around." She faced Achy again and thrust a pink fingernail into his toga. Achelous just stared at her heaving breasts.

He grabbed her hand. "She is like her mother in that regard. Why don't we go somewhere private, Hebe? Where we can discuss these things to our"—he kissed her fingertips—"satisfaction."

For a moment she seemed interested. Then she jerked her hand away. "Men! All you think about is how to talk a woman into your bed. Don't you get enough of that sport with your harem?"

He grinned. "Never enough. And I'll not let you talk me out of Aglaophonos. She is one of my favorites. Very clever and with one of the best kill rates in the sisterhood." He glanced down at her. "Get up, child." Of course she obeyed instantly. "What is this about wanting to leave me?"

"I'm sorry, Sire. But I have fallen in love. With that man." She pointed to Ian. "I wish to be with him forever."

"Foolish child. It is infatuation. It will pass. You are used to variety. One man forever?" He laughed. "How dull that sounds. Kill him and be done with it. That will satisfy you." He stroked her hair. "Come with me and I'll remind you of why I am the only man who can truly satisfy you."

I glanced at Ian. His eyes were wild but he couldn't move. This had to be making him crazy. If he truly loved Aggie, the idea of her as this egomaniac's love slave . . . And how casually Achelous had ordered Aggie to kill Ian. Like it was no big deal. Sickening. Would Aggie do it? She didn't move, just stood there, clearly still held in some kind of thrall to her master. Her eyes were trapped by his.

"Let her go, Achelous." My mother touched Aggie's shoulder. The Siren shuddered and dropped to the floor.

"What did you do to her?" Achelous roared.

"Released her from your bondage." Mother smiled. "I am above you in rank. You owe me reparation for what you did to my daughter. I am claiming Aggie as payment. Now get out! If you complain about this to Zeus, I will tell him how you left his granddaughter in the mortal world with no protection. I'm sure Circe will back me up. We had a long chat in Olympus recently. She told me that she played a part in making sure Gloriana didn't die a mortal's death as you planned. Amazing, knowing how she feels about vampires, that she used one to save my daughter's immortal life." My mother smiled at me.

Then she whirled to stab Achelous in the chest again with her fingernail. He actually winced. "How do think your original plan will play with our king?"

Achelous's face turned red and thunder roared. My hair

lifted and the house shook again. I recognized a Storm God temper tantrum and wished I were miles away from it. I slapped my hands over my eyebrows. A blinding lightning flash lit up the room. When it was over, Achelous was gone.

"Well, that was fun." My mother smiled and walked up to me. "No apology to you but I'm not really surprised. Gods are so ridiculously proud. What did you think, Gloriana?"

"You were totally amazing." I gave her what she wanted, a brief hug. "How's Aggie?" Ian was picking her up off the floor.

"She's dazed but seems okay." He held her in his arms. "She's coming around." He pressed a finger to her neck, taking her pulse. Then he leaned in and sniffed her. "You know, she *is* a mortal now. I can't believe it. Nice blood type, the same yet different."

"Oh, yes. Once you're pulled out of the Siren program, you're mortal, defenseless." I sank down on Ian's damaged leather sofa. "I found out much, much later that I still had my powers. But she may not. Mine came from my goddess connection—thanks, Mother. Aggie, well, who knows how she got dropped into the Siren program? Mother, maybe you can find out who left her there."

"I don't know. Achelous keeps the records. I doubt we're speaking." She smiled and ran a finger down the neckline of her low-cut dress. "Though I'm not without means of persuasion."

I tried to block that picture from my mind. "When are you going to make her vampire, Ian?"

He just stood there. "I don't know. She isn't really awake yet and no wonder. That Storm God. I've never seen anything like him." He shook his head like he was coming out of a fog. "I'm taking her to the bedroom. As to the vampire thing . . . Mortal blood. I'm in no hurry." He stalked off down the hall.

"Once a bastard, always a bastard." Jerry sat down next to me. "I hope Aggie gets her immortality before she's an old lady."

"Perhaps she'd be better off without the transition." My mother sat across from me.

"Don't start. I was actually feeling happy with you for a moment there. You handled Achelous really well. Thanks for standing up for me, Hebe." I grinned. "And now I know your name. Are you going to tell me your area of expertise, or do I have to go to the Internet for answers? You can't imagine how many conflicting stories I'll get on there. You might want to give me the straight scoop."

Jerry picked up my hand. "She claims you're Zeus's granddaughter? If I had good sense, I'd be intimidated, Gloriana."

"You should be." Mother frowned at him. "Gloriana really should make a visit up there. Be introduced around. It never hurts to have important allies. Of course Achelous was right about one thing, being a vampire will be seen by many as a negative, but she *is* my daughter. It will be overlooked. If she gets in a bind here, she can call on some of the gods and goddesses for help. Mars has already agreed to come to her aid."

"Really? Now, why would he do that?" Jerry was interested.

"I'll tell you later. You're stalling, Mother. What are your powers?" I leaned against Jerry, finally realizing that it was kind of cool to be related to a genuine goddess from Olympus.

"Very well. I am known as the goddess of youth. Zeus is my father, Hera is my mother. I am also the goddess of pardons." She smiled. "That's why so many of the gods seek me out for favors. Naughty men frequently need my services." She brushed back her hair which had been blown about by Achy's temper fit. "Oh, I must be a mess!" She pulled out a compact and brush. "Dealing with temperamental males can be such a trial."

"Go back. Goddess of youth. What does that mean?" I leaned forward, itching to jerk the hairbrush out of her hand. Finally she put it away.

"It means I can make someone young again. A tired soldier. A woman who feels her beauty is fading." She smiled at me. "Would you like to look eighteen instead of twenty-two? I could make it so."

"No! I have enough problems blending with mortals as it is." I tried to picture how this worked.

Her face fell. "There is a downside to this gift, Gloriana. You have two brothers, my precious twins. Alex and Ani guard Olympus. I am very proud of them. But they are forever young boys. They will never become men." She dabbed at sudden tears with a linen hanky. "Their father, Heracles, hates me for this. We do not have a happy marriage. Fortunately he is frequently gone on his quests, as he calls them. He doesn't mind if I enjoy other men. I am told he has dozens of mistresses."

"I'm sorry, Mother." And I was. Brothers stuck before puberty? I couldn't imagine anything worse for them. And a husband who cared more about quests than his wife . . . Well, no wonder she had an edge.

"I'd like you to know them. Your brothers. They would love you. But they cannot leave their duties on Olympus. Perhaps someday you will come." She put away the hanky. "I hope you understand why I was so eager to know you. You are my only adult child. A woman who I could talk to, shop with." She smiled. "I loved you the moment I saw you."

I stood. "Then isn't it a shame you forgot about me all those years?" It was too much. A brother, a stepfather. Zeus as a grandfather. My mind was spinning. And I was in Ian's house, a place where I'd never felt comfortable. Through the open glass doors I could see his guard patrolling the grounds. I wondered briefly where Melanie was, then figured Ian must have sent her off somewhere so she wouldn't witness what had happened tonight.

"You don't understand how it works there. In Olympus time is nothing. And I am pulled this way and that constantly with the politics. My powers are important. Everyone is always wanting me for something. I have so many responsibilities." She was on her feet too. "Don't be angry, Gloriana. I wish to make it all up to you. Please, think about it. I won't pressure you. But someday, I hope you will come with me. Just for a little visit."

"Right. And time means nothing up there. A little visit could last centuries." I grabbed Jerry's hand. "Let's get out of here, Jer. The rain's stopped and I need some air."

"Gloriana!" I turned on my heel and stared at her. My mother. She looked beautiful but actually distressed at my rejection.

"Thank you for tonight. You did a good thing, saving Aggie. I don't particularly like her, but no woman should be the property of a man the way the Sirens belong to Achelous. I just hope Ian keeps his word so she doesn't regret this decision." I sighed. "Good night."

I heard her call, "Good night," but didn't look back as I tugged Jerry out of the house. We shifted, flying out the back door and to our car. The night was clear now and it didn't take any time at all.

This time Jerry drove. Neither of us mentioned that promise of hot sex in the car. The mood had definitely changed. We were both silent. Jerry must have realized I had a lot on my mind. I just stared out at the scenery going by, my thoughts chaotic. I couldn't be some goddess's accident. This was crazy. I didn't feel magical or godlike. I was plain Gloriana St. Clair and wanted to stay that way. By the time Jerry pulled into the parking lot, I felt drained.

We headed upstairs and I was thinking of crawling into a hot tub and soaking away my worries. Then I saw the man leaning against my apartment door. Israel Caine. Of course. I hadn't had enough drama yet tonight.

Fifteen

"Glory, Blade. What's up?" Ray smiled but I could tell he was on edge. Hey, so was I.

"Not a good night, Caine. Gloriana's had a bad one." Jerry unlocked the door and helped me inside. Seriously, my legs were wobbly. The reality of being around the Storm God had finally hit me in the car. Flashback I guess. I had been in that creep's harem myself for a thousand years and change. Working as a killer.

"What's wrong, babe? Anything I can do?" He followed us inside. Ray never felt like he needed an invitation.

"Aggie, the Storm God. Do you need to hear more?" I collapsed on the couch.

"That's enough. What's the bitch been up to now? You know I hate her guts." He settled next to me, ignoring Jerry, who handed me a glass of synthetic then sat across from us.

"She's at Ian's and she's mortal now. I don't think we have to worry about her for a while." I took a deep swallow. It tasted good. Jerry must have ordered in some of the premium that he liked and I couldn't afford.

"No shit? Bet that's quite a story." Ray laid a hand on my thigh. "Quit growling at me, Blade. I get that Glory has you back. You're here, aren't you?" He rubbed a circle on my leg, just above my knee. I was sure it was just to bug Jerry. "I came by to let you know I got the message. You dodged my calls. It doesn't take a neon sign to tell Israel Caine to back off." He stood. "One last hug?"

"I'm sorry, Ray. I wasn't dodging but we've been really busy since we got back. I wanted to get together with you. To talk. Tell you about my trip. We can still do that." I let him pull me to my feet. When Jerry started to say something, I stared at him until he subsided. "Tomorrow night. Meet me at N-V? I owe you that much."

"You don't owe me a damned thing, babe, but I *would* like to see you. Without the buzzkill here. If that's possible." He nodded at Jerry then pulled me into his arms. "Hmm. No bra, just the way I like it." He laughed when Jerry lunged to his feet. "Nine o'clock. See you then." And he was out the door.

"You just had to do that, didn't you? Hug him, arrange a date right in front of me. You know how I hate that guy." Jerry slammed the door and locked it.

"You're so cute when you're jealous." I patted his cheek then danced toward the bathroom suddenly reenergized. Guess having two men wanting me had done it. I tore off my sweater and tossed it behind me. "I'm going to sing in the bathtub. Try out my Siren's song. Want to see if you can resist it?" I laughed when he grabbed me from behind and swung me up into his arms.

"You know you don't need a song to bewitch me, Gloriana." He buried his face in my hair. "Skip the bath and come to bed. I'll show you what jealousy does to me. Caine had a look in his eyes I don't like. He loves you, Gloriana. But I'll be damned if I'll let him have you." He carried me to the bed and tossed me onto the mattress. Then he ripped off his shirt, buttons flying everywhere. "Deal with it. You're mine, woman. And I'll fight any man who tries to take you away from me." Then he fell on top of me, ravenous.

I can't say I minded his declaration. What I did mind was a sense of impending doom. If he didn't like the look in Ray's eyes now, what would he think when he heard the whole story? I should go ahead and tell him. Could I make it sound meaningless? A minor bump in the long road Jerry and I had traveled and hopefully would still travel together? It wouldn't be easy because I'd be lying and Jerry would see right through it. Nothing with Ray had ever been trivial or meaningless to me. And hopefully Jerry knew by now that I didn't just use people and then cast them aside.

As I pulled Jerry into me one more time, I tried to shelve my worries. It would only make this night less than I wanted it to be. But I knew all this sex was a cop-out. Sooner or later Jerry and I needed to sit down and have a conversation without touching each other.

The next night Jerry went home. To his house where Lily waited and he had plenty of business to take care of. So did I for that matter. I had put off the big talk. First, I would meet with Ray and get things settled with him. Yes, he knew we weren't going to have a future, but I wanted a face-to-face. To clear the air. I felt bad for dodging his calls.

I walked into N-V wearing that black and red dress my mother had given me. I knew I looked good. Rafe caught me before I reached the bar.

"He's waiting for you at a table upstairs. I've tried to keep the groupies away from him. It's not easy." Rafe gave me the once over. "Nice outfit. New?"

"Yes, my mother gave it to me. There are some perks to having a mother from Olympus." I grinned at him. Rafe knew my wardrobe well after five years as my bodyguard. Not that I had that many clothes. I had sold a lot of them when I'd started my vintage clothing business.

"She's got great taste. How's it going with your mother?" Rafe walked with me toward the stairs. I'd managed to call him and explain about my mother and what had happened in Scotland while Jerry had been in the shower. Rafe was still one of my best friends and a good listener.

"Better. I think she's finally figured out that I'm not going to Olympus with her. And I'm staying vampire. She isn't happy about either but it's the only way I'll agree to any kind of relationship with her." I put my hand on his arm. "She says I'm bossy. Which I realize I am. I'll try to work on that. How are you doing? Any new girlfriends?"

"I'm seeing someone. You know her." He frowned. "That's the problem. Any woman who knows my history soon figures out I'm still hung up on you."

"Who are you seeing? And you know you've got to stop being hung up on me." I realized I was being bossy again. I shook my head. "Okay, easier said than done. I get it. Who, Rafe?"

"Lacy. I've been hanging around your shop, keeping an eye on it while you were gone. The cat and I hit it off." He shook his head. "Probably was a bad idea. She wants more than casual and I'm not ready."

"Well, I have nothing to say. Except thanks for watching the shop." I kissed his cheek. "And good luck, I guess." I knew Lacy was thinking about dumping him. "Try, Rafe. She's a nice girl. Worth the effort."

"Yeah. And you're obviously sticking with Blade this time. So what's up with Caine? Why's he waiting for you?" He nodded toward the balcony.

"We're friends. I thought we needed to catch up. In a public place." I sighed. "Remember how hung up on *him* I was?"

"The Israel Caine shrine. No kidding. For a long time it was all fantasy. But then you two finally hooked up before you left here. Did you tell Blade about that?"

"Not yet. But I will." I grabbed Rafe's arm. "Don't you dare mention it."

"It's your secret, not mine. But I can tell you from experience, these things tend to leak out. Don't stall, Glory. If Blade hears it from somebody else first, he'll think it meant more to you than it obviously does if this meet is a kiss-off." Rafe rubbed my shoulder. "And that's what it looks like to me."

"Yeah, that's it. Better go. You know he saw me come in." I ran up the stairs, quite a trick in high heels.

"Glory girl, sit down." Ray jumped to his feet. He had two glasses in front of him. "Have a drink. You'll be happy to know I'm off the sauce. Have even been going to some meetings. AA. Nate insisted. We've started work on a new album and the record company wouldn't ink the deal until they knew I was sober." He settled me into a chair.

"I'm glad, Ray. Not that they were playing hardball with you, but that you wised up and sobered up." I grabbed my drink. "To your next hit record. And another Grammy."

"I'll drink to that." He took a swallow. "Blade won, I saw that."

"It wasn't a contest." I set down the glass. "But we're together. I'm sorry if that bothers you."

"Of course it bothers me. I love you, Glory. You knew that when you left here." He picked up my hand. "Shit, babe, I laid it all out for you. I don't do that for any woman."

"I know." Tears filled my eyes. "And it was wonderful. Our time together. Rafe called it. He said you were my fantasy."

"Yeah, yeah. I get it. But my reality isn't such hot stuff, is it? I drink, drug, can be an asshole when I'm under the influence, which has been most of the time you've known me. Not the steady soldier Blade is."

"And I'm not the kind of woman you're used to, Ray. I introduced you to our world. You think you love me, but mixed up in that is a whole lot of gratitude, reliance, whatever you want to call it, because I helped you figure out how to be a vampire." I leaned forward to whisper that last word, aware that Israel Caine, rock star, was always being watched when he was in a public place. The mortals at the next table had been trying to get a good angle with their cell phone cameras the whole time we'd sat here, probably video too.

"Don't sell yourself short, Glory. You're more than a mentor to me. Always have been. And the women I'd always hung out with before, used me. You never did." He drained his glass then frowned at it. "Shit. Being sober bites. I really want to get out of here. Notice the yahoos behind us? What do you bet they sell those pics to the tabloids and we are either back together or having a baby this time next week?" He grinned when I dropped his hand which I'd been holding across the table to try to make my words more palatable.

"I could take those phones and flush them down the N-V toilets. Then wipe their memories so that they had no idea Israel Caine even existed." I glared at the people and they quickly hid their phones.

"Relax, babe. You and I know it's all bull and free publicity. You look killer in that dress. Smile for the cameras and stand up like you could care less who takes your picture." He slid his arm around my waist as soon as I was on my feet. "Did I tell you I've got a new Harley? How about a ride in the hills? I gotta get a rush from somewhere." I gave him a look when his hand slid down toward my butt. "Okay, I won't try any funny stuff. Let's just have a little fun. Blow off some steam."

I glanced down at my dress. "What the hell? If I'm having your baby, the least I can do is enjoy a little more time with you first." I grinned and waved at the idiots clicking away. "Let me go change clothes and I'm game."

"That's my girl." Ray threw some bills on the table and followed me down the stairs. At the bottom he was surrounded by fans who wanted his autograph. He grinned and signed everything from cocktail napkins to full breasts clad in tight T-shirts. "Go ahead, Glory. I'll meet you in front of your place."

"Right. Ten minutes." I left, glad to see him happy. If a motorcycle ride would help us smooth things out, I could humor him. I hurried down the sidewalk and up to my apartment. In minutes I was in jeans and a shirt, a jacket over it. When I heard the deep roar of a motorcycle engine, I ran down the stairs. The bike was a thing of beauty, all chrome and shiny black. It reminded me of the one Richard, Flo's husband, rode when he was in a certain mood. Of course Ray being Ray, he hadn't bothered with a helmet so I just climbed on the back, grabbed his waist and we were off.

He seemed to revel in the power of the engine and the way it took curves. We went up and down steep hills. It reminded me of a roller coaster, something I'd never been too fond of. You'd think a vampire who could fly like a bird would be okay with a little danger but I'm not a fan. Ray laughed like a maniac when he made me squeal and clutch at his waist at a particularly crazy plunge.

Finally he pulled into a hilltop overlook and killed the engine. He slid off the seat and helped me climb down. I admit my legs were rubbery, and he hugged me, laughing again at my complaints about his crazy driving.

"Check it out. This is why I love Austin." He threw his arms wide. It was a beautiful view of the twinkling lights of the city. "It's quiet too."

"I'm glad you're happy here, Ray." He'd come to Austin to be near me. Luckily it also had a great music scene that suited him. Now that he realized we weren't going to be together I wondered if he'd soon move on.

"I'm staying." He looked at me, his bright blue eyes reflecting the moonlight. "I know you say we're done and I believe you mean that. I'm moving on with my life. Sienna's coming and we're going to make another record together."

"A duet. The last one was your Grammy winner." He and Sienna Star made beautiful music together. I thought about telling him I had my song back but figured this wasn't the time.

"Exactly. So we're trying for a repeat." He smiled, that wicked upturn I knew so well. "And not just with our music. She's a little young for me, but we've always had chemistry and hooked up before. Nothing much came of it then." He stared out at the city. "I'm going to see what happens this time if I put in a little effort."

"Good. That's good." I laid my hand on his arm. "But she's a mortal, Ray. Be careful. You've already let one mortal in on our secret. It's not good practice to reveal it to too many people."

"Nate handled it well. Which I knew he would." Ray sat down on the dry grass. You'd never know there had been a rainstorm the night before. Maybe it hadn't rained at all up here, only near Ian's house. Typical Storm God maneuver.

"I think 'well' is a slight exaggeration. Nate did freak out at first. The idea that vampires do exist threw him for a loop. Then we asked him to donate blood once too. Luckily Nate's levelheaded and is now pretty cool with our whole paranormal world." I liked Ray's manager and best friend. They'd grown up together. Ray had insisted he tell Nathan the truth right after he'd been turned. I'd been Ray's mentor and discouraged it, but Ray always did what he wanted to do, so Nate got the news.

"Yeah, I couldn't ask for a better friend." Ray looked at me. "Except for you, Glory."

"Yep. Friend." I changed the subject, telling him all about my trip, Jerry's amnesia, even my mother. I wound up with an account of Aggie and her relationship with Ian.

"You're shittin' me. I heard you say she was now a mortal but it didn't register. That little bitch gave up her Siren gig for Ian?" Ray laughed so hard he fell over. "And what do you bet Ian never does turn her vampire? Oh, God, but it would serve her right. You remember how she tortured us? Dragged you through Lake Travis until you were spitting fish and seaweed?"

"I'll never forget it." I lay back next to him and stared up at the stars. It was beautiful. I was glad to be lying here with a friend. Jerry took things so seriously, always wanting to fix everything. And you couldn't mention a MacDonald without Jerry pulling out a knife, ready to go to war. Ray knew how to laugh. He kept talking, telling another story about Ian, and we both cracked up. I rolled over and pounded the ground we got so hysterical.

"God, Glory." He put his arm over my shoulders. "Don't get so hung up on Blade that you give up this, hanging out with me, having a laugh. I'd hate to see you as uptight as he is all the time."

I smiled. "Ray, relax. Can't I have friends that I have fun with and a lover who is there for me when things get tough? Life isn't all fun and games, you know." And hadn't I had plenty of examples of that lately?

"Seems to me, the best thing would be a lover you have fun with who is also your best friend." He leaned over to kiss me. I saw it coming and rolled away.

"You promised, Ray." I frowned at him.

"You know me too well to think I don't lie like a rug when I need to." His grin teased an answering smile out of me. Then he got serious. "I'll never forget being with you, Glory. I've tried to move on. It's tough. Mortals don't cut it and other vampires . . ." He shook his head. "Ignore me. I am inching toward pathetic here. I'll put this into a song. Make people sob into their beers." He turned away to stare out at the lights of the city again.

"Ray. Part of me will always love you." I leaned against him, shoulder to shoulder, for a moment. "But I made my choice and my relationship with Jerry is none of your business. Now I think it's time we headed back to town." I stood, brushing the dirt and grass off my jeans.

He jumped up and grabbed my shoulders. "Your choice? I can't see it, Glory girl. You with Blade. He's too intense. The brooding Scot. I bet he wears a knife to bed." He stared, trying to read my mind. Not happening.

He was determined to make me hurt him. "Ray, I hate to break it to you, but Jerry doesn't wear a damned thing to bed." I touched his cheek. "I'm fine. Just be my friend. I would like that."

He took my hand and pressed it to his lips. Of course he had to scrape his tongue, then a fang against it. Unrepentant, he grinned when I tugged it free. "You say you're happy, so I'll take your word for it. But I'll always be here when you need to relax and let go. Just don't fool yourself into thinking that Blade is perfect, he's not."

"Never said he was, Ray. Now, are you taking me back to town or do I wing it?" I knew I sounded defensive, but he was hitting a nerve. There was no such thing as a perfect man. Didn't he know that? If he weren't vampire, all he'd have to do was look in a mirror to see how far from perfect *he* was. If Jerry was too serious, then Ray wasn't serious enough. The rock star had way too many issues, including those addictions he'd listed. Now he was setting himself up for another problem. Hanging out on a nightly basis with a mortal lover. How long would that last before he landed in trouble?

He started the engine with a roar then we headed back to town. He didn't try any tricks this time, though the steep hills were unavoidable. I just held on, a lot on my mind. I wasn't stupid. I loved Jerry, but that didn't mean I was blind to his faults. I just thought his virtues outweighed them. By the time I got back home, I'd decided to surprise him at his house. I needed to see him, reassure myself that I'd made the right choice. Being around the other two men I loved had shaken me up more than I wanted to admit. So I packed a small bag and jumped in my car.

Most of the lights were on when I arrived twenty minutes later. I parked in front since there were a couple of cars I didn't recognize in the driveway. I walked up the sidewalk and rang the bell. It was three o'clock in the morning but there was still loud music playing inside. It was a wonder the neighbors hadn't called the police. I wasn't surprised no one heard the doorbell. I had a key but tried the knob first. It was unlocked.

"Hello?" I saw a couple of men in the doorway to the kitchen through a haze of smoke. I knew at the first inhale that it wasn't from regular cigarettes. One of them finally heard me and turned around.

"Oh, hey. It's the girl who was with you at the club, Lily." He strolled over and hooked an arm around my neck. "Want a drag? It's good shit."

I pushed him away. "Where's Jerry?"

Lily appeared carrying a tray of cheese and crackers. She set it on the coffee table in the living room. "He's upstairs in his office. Working. What are you doing here?"

"Does he know you have company and that they've brought illegal substances into the house?" I stalked over to the stereo and turned off the music. "It's too late for that noise. You have neighbors, you know."

"Hey, we didn't bring anything illegal here. It's hers." The guy who'd taken a fancy to me passed the joint to his friend. "Not that we're complaining." He picked up a glass that I could tell had booze of some kind in it. "We're having a party. Don't go upstairs. Join us."

"No, she's no fun. Let her go." Lily pulled him to her by his shirtfront and laid an openmouthed kiss on him. "I have another girlfriend I can call, or not. Let's get this party started."

"Now you're talking." The other man pushed against Lily's backside, rocking as he grabbed her breast.

"Lily, get these guys out of here or I'm telling your father what I caught you doing the other night." I hated to see her degrade herself this way. It reminded me of how she'd acted with other friends. Like she was willing to do anything to keep these men here. Where was her self-esteem?

"Fuck off." She ignored me, grinding her hips against the man that she kissed again.

I ran upstairs, refusing to believe she wouldn't get rid of them as soon as she saw I meant what I said. When I got to the landing, I looked down. Unbelievable. She had pulled off her corset top and thrown one of the men onto the leather couch. Was she high?

Heartsick, I opened Jerry's study door. He was on the phone, his laptop open in front of him. He looked up and smiled, obviously happy to see me. That wouldn't last long. He held up a finger, like he'd be off the phone in a minute.

I sat in a chair, dropping my suitcase and purse next to my feet. I could see that he had a stack of mail he'd been going through and a file open on his laptop. It was obviously something to do with his hotel in Florida. I could tell from his side of the conversation that whatever crisis had erupted while he'd been in Scotland was still going on. Finally he hung up and swung around in his office chair to look at me.

"How'd the meeting with Caine go?"

"Okay. He's moving on. We parted as friends."

"That's good." He cocked his head. "Glad to hear the music's stopped. I thought I was going to have to go downstairs and turn it off. It's too late for that racket. The neighbors would have started to complain." He smiled. "But I was happy Lily felt comfortable inviting friends over again."

"Jerry, they were smoking pot when I got here."

"That's not good. They shouldn't have brought it into my home." He frowned but didn't get up.

"They said Lily had it when they got here." Obviously Jerry wasn't too worried about it.

"That was stupid of her. She was just complaining about how broke she was and it won't even get her high. I've tried it."

"Are you kidding me? That's your problem with it? That it's a waste of her money?" I jumped up. "It's illegal, Jerry."

"Relax, Gloriana. We're vampires. Some mortal laws mean little or nothing to us." He smiled at me indulgently. "You know how we can manipulate minds if the police are called. I've seen you do it yourself when you were stopped for speeding."

"A traffic ticket isn't the same as knowing your daughter is out doing drug deals." Who was this man? "Maybe you'll tell me now why you had the name change? You remember. Rafe mentioned it the other night. How you were so eager to come to Texas not just to be with me but because you had to give yourself a fresh start? What's up with that?" I was pissed. Forget Lily. She could screw two guys from one end of Jerry's leather sofa to the other. Of course I'd not be sitting on it ever again. Yuck.

"It doesn't concern you." He picked up his phone when it

buzzed. "Excuse me. I have to take this." He listened then started talking into the phone.

I couldn't believe it. It didn't concern me? What had happened to all that love talk? We were supposed to be partners. Lovers who shared everything. I wasn't moving a muscle until we had this out. I sat and waited. It took a while. He was typing into his computer. Going from screen to screen. He raised his voice, clearly not happy with whatever the guy in charge in Florida had done to try to fix the problem there. Finally he slammed the phone down.

"I've got to go out there. The man's incompetent."

"I'm sorry. But I'm not letting what you said go. Everything you do concerns me, Jerry. I thought we were clear on that." I managed to say it calmly even though I was shaking I was so angry. How dare he close me out when we'd been through so much?

"Gloriana, not now. My business is going through a crisis. I might lose the hotel in Miami. That's millions of dollars down the drain. You're a businesswoman. I thought you could understand." He hardly looked at me, busily going through papers and stuffing them into his laptop case.

"I understand that our relationship means more to me than a business deal. I got my priorities straight after nearly losing you in Scotland. I thought you had the same concerns I did. To keep our lines of communication open." My nails bit into my palms. How could things go to hell between us so quickly?

"Why are you taking this personally? I told you, it's business. It has nothing to do with you, us." He ran his hand through his hair. "I don't have time for this. Did you have something you wanted to say to me? About Lily?"

"Never mind. If you're going downstairs, you may see for yourself. Are you leaving tonight?" I looked at my watch. "Three hours until dawn. Not a good idea. You should wait until sunset tomorrow night."

"I'll wing it. I should get as far as Louisiana tonight." He stood and jammed his laptop into its case. "I have a safe house there in Shreveport." He stopped and put his hands on my shoulders. "If this weren't important, I wouldn't leave now. Stop pouting and wish me luck." He leaned down like he wanted to kiss me good-bye.

"Pouting?" I threw his hands off me. "I'll chalk that up to the fact that you're obviously out of your mind with stress. Good luck, Jerry. Don't let the sun get you." I turned on my heel and picked up my bag, ready to head to his bedroom. I'd sleep there tonight rather than walk through Sodom and Gomorrah.

"I give up. I'm sorry if you're pissed. We'll talk when I get back. Hopefully it will be in a few days. I'll call you." He ran out of the room and down the stairs. I didn't hear him shout so either he didn't notice what his daughter and her friends were up to or he didn't care.

I threw my bag on his bed and plucked out the silky nightgown I'd brought. Too bad it was going to waste. I tried to give Jerry the benefit of the doubt. Stress over business. I knew what that was like. But keeping secrets and then labeling them not my concern? I wasn't going to let that slide. And yet one more opportunity had passed and he still didn't know about Ray and me. At this point? I really didn't give a damn if he ever found out. It wasn't his concern either.

When I woke, I realized I wasn't alone in the king-size bed. I rolled over, ready to defend myself if Lily had dared bring her scuzzy friends up here. Instead my mother reclined on a pink satin pillow. Her ivory silk negligee was lace-trimmed and made my mouth water.

"Oh, you like? Do you want one for yourself?" Mother waved her hand. "What color?"

"Don't bother. I'm too depressed." I sank back on my pillow. I really wanted to talk to someone. Normally I'd call Flo. But here was a woman desperate to have me confide in her. Did I dare trust her with a little mother-daughter talk? Could she handle it without going off on Jerry and the whole vampire thing? I rolled to face her. One thing I knew, my mother had a wealth of experience with men.

"What's the matter, darling?" She propped her head on her hand. "Is that man making you unhappy? I did like seeing you with Israel Caine. Vampire or not, he is one handsome man." She smiled knowingly. "I can see why you had to have him at least once."

"Mother, please don't spy on me. It makes me hate you." I wondered if I should stop this right now.

"Oh, dear. I'm sorry. But how can I resist? We have so much catching up to do. The way you two laughed together." Her hand landed lightly on my shoulder. "Admit it, darling. You still love him, just a little."

"Of course I do. But it's not anything I wish to pursue. It was a fling. I know you understand flings." I glanced at her then looked away again. I couldn't take the sympathy swimming in her bright blue eyes.

"My, oh my, yes. Mars and I had a passionate weekend once. You met him." She sighed. "He is an incredible lover. So inventive. What he can do with that plume . . ."

"Please spare me the details." I faced her again. "Now see if you can give me some motherly advice."

"I would love to." She sat up straight and threw back her hair, obviously thrilled.

"Jerry doesn't want to tell me something about his past. Should I press him about it? Or let it go?" I struggled to sit up. Lying down wasn't working for me. This was important.

"Well. Let me think. Is it something that you think will irrevocably harm your relationship? Another lover? A betrayal?" She tapped her chin. "A child you don't know about? I have had those crop up from time to time. Deal breakers, Gloriana. Every time."

"Well, it couldn't be a child. We went through that with Lily. And while she's proving to be a trial, it's not really

Jerry's fault." I studied her nightwear again. "Black, I think."
She didn't misunderstand and I now wore a gorgeous set just
like hers in black with ivory lace trim.

"It was something Jerry did that made him change his
name. And want to move." I fingered the lace. Alençon.
Lovely.

"Ah. That could be one of several things. A business deal
gone wrong. A run-in with the law. A woman after his
blood." She giggled. "Literally, with a vampire, I suppose."

"Not funny, Mother."

"Did you ask him about it?" She watched me play with
the negligee. "Of course you did. What did he say?"

"He said it was none of my concern." I said it quietly.

"No! I'll bet you let him have it for that attitude." She
snatched my hand away from the piece of lace I'd managed
to tear. "Gloriana! He can't get away with that."

"I know. But then he just left town. Business." I stared
down at the ruined lace. "Look at what I did." Tears ran
down my cheeks. "And it was so beautiful." I sniffled.

"Darling. Of course I shall fix it." She waved her hand and
it was perfect again. "That bastard. He has hurt your feelings. Would you like for me to punish him?" She sounded
eager.

"No! This is between Jerry and me. When he gets back,
I'll make him tell me what he's hiding." I took the hanky
she handed me and wiped my cheeks.

"If he won't, I've found a new sorcerer, much higher level
than that fool Waldo. He has a truth serum that will make
your Jeremiah spill every secret he has ever clutched to his
brawny and quite handsome chest." She smoothed my hair
back from my face. "I've quite enjoyed our little chat. Now
I must go. My father is holding a council meeting. I owe
some pardons and must be there to dole them out. Such is
my life."

"You know you told me that Zeus disapproved of your
dallying with mortals and that's why you hid me among the
Sirens in the first place. How can you even suggest taking

me back to Olympus with you? Wouldn't Zeus be horrified at a granddaughter like me?" I wasn't considering it, but it wouldn't hurt to find out what she had in mind.

"I was young and foolish when I gave you away." She sighed and climbed out of bed. Her gown suddenly changed into the traditional toga. For her meeting, I supposed. "Zeus is a family man. He will accept anyone who has some of his blood running in her veins. Don't worry about that." She smiled brilliantly. "Are you thinking about coming?"

"No, not really. Just curious." I waved my hand. "Go, you don't want to be late. I'm sure your father has a temper."

"Yes, he does." She came to my side of the bed and leaned down to kiss my cheek. "Thank you for this little chat. You have made me very happy." Then she vanished.

Well. It hadn't been so bad for me either. If she could behave herself, I wouldn't mind having a mother. A truth serum. Now, that was a handy tool. But her sorcerers were not to be trusted if Waldo was any indication. Of course I could read minds past their blocks anyway. If I really wanted to get at the truth, I could do that to Jerry. It was simpler, but I wanted him to offer the truth, rather than trick it out of him.

I started when there was a knock on the door.

"Come in."

Lily stuck her head in. "Where's Dad?"

"Gone to Florida. He'll probably be there a week. Why? Out of money again?" I threw off the covers and got out of bed. Her eyes widened when she saw my fabulous nightgown and robe. *Yeah, Lily, eat your heart out.*

"Did you tell him about last night or the ATM thing?"

"He had to have walked right past you. I didn't have to tell him anything about last night except that you had pot downstairs. That didn't seem to bother him."

"We moved the other action to my bedroom. He didn't see a thing." She clearly wasn't the least bit embarrassed. "Two mortals, Glory. I dined quite well." She showed her fangs.

"Obviously you have no standards. If you erased their memories, who am I to say what you can or can't do? I'm not your mother." And thank God for that.

"Exactly." Her face was hard. "What about the robberies?"

"Are you still doing them?" I walked up to her, deliberately avoiding the answer she wanted. "People work hard for their money, Lily. It's not right to take it from them."

"Yeah, I get it. You work, I don't." She reached into her jeans pocket and pulled out a wad of cash. "The guys last night won't remember where they lost this either. So you see, Glory, I guess I'm just made for a life of crime."

I grabbed her and shook her until the bills fell to the floor. "What the hell is the matter with you? Why are you living this way?"

"What choice do I have?" She jerked away from me and scooped up the cash. "Tell me that. I have no skills, no job. Nothing. Dad gives me a bedroom but then when I try to have company downstairs you barge in. So I essentially have no privacy. I hate it here!"

"Stop. Go back. You have skills." I held on to her arm when she would have stormed out of the room. "You have wonderful taste. Look at this sleep set I have on. What's it made of?"

"I don't know how in the hell you afforded it, but it's fine silk, from one of the best boutiques in Paris. Your friends Florence and the countess shop there. That's Alençon lace trim and it retails, both pieces, for about fifteen hundred bucks." She touched it gently, running her finger down the lace like I had done. "Gorgeous. A lover give it to you? Not Dad, surely. I can't imagine him stepping foot in that little shop."

"No, my mother. She had the same one in ivory."

"Yes, very classic. I'd have preferred ivory myself." She sighed. "I couldn't afford a hanky from that place this century."

"Okay, what you just did is a valuable skill. At least in my shop. You know your clothes and their value. I'll hire you. I have an opening right now. I don't pay much but I can probably talk your father into setting you up in your own apartment if you have a paying job. It'll be fun. You'll be working around great clothes and the kind of young people you seem to prefer."

She started to say something.

"Yes, they're used clothes, Lily. We call them vintage. But our customers appreciate them. You'll soon learn that."

"You'd really get him to pay for an apartment?" She obviously was more interested in the privacy issue than the job offer. She could have all the orgies she wanted. I wanted to shake her again.

"If you're working. That has to be part of the deal. And I have rules in my shop, Lily. No stealing. From me or anyone. You have to be nice to the customers and to the other clerks too. Lacy liked you, she's the day manager, so that's a start."

"Yeah, she was still there when I came in a few times. She's cool. A were-cat." Lily was thinking. "Could I have a discount? If I actually found something decent enough to buy there? I'm sure my dad would still give me my allowance."

"Of course. All of my clerks get twenty-five percent off anything they purchase." I could see she was considering it. "One more thing. We don't drink from our mortal customers. If you want to sip from the mortals on Sixth Street, do it somewhere else, not at Vintage Vamp's."

"Seems reasonable." Lily smiled suddenly. "For an apartment of my own, I'd work for Lucifer himself." She stuck out her hand. "It's a deal, Glory. When do I start?"

I shook hands with her then wondered if I'd lost my mind. I'd just hired a thief to work in my shop. Good going, Glory.

Sixteen

Flo and I had a date to meet in the shop. I had trained Lily on the credit card machine and she was surprisingly quick to learn. I don't know *why* I was surprised. Her father was a businessman who was good with numbers. She'd obviously inherited his abilities in that direction. I'd had to fuss at Jerry's daughter a few times when she got on her high horse, declaring some of our stock too crappy to wear. We were a college town. Not all of our customers could afford the designer originals she considered worthy.

"*Mi amica*, it is about time we have a chance to catch up and have a little girl talk." Flo came rushing in carrying packages. I recognized the logos from some of her favorite boutiques in Paris. She'd brought me presents.

"Come to the back room. I hope that's not all for me." I never felt my own lack of money more than when I was around my best bud. She'd always been wealthy—she made no secret of the fact that she'd built her fortune through a wise collection of fabulous jewelry from grateful lovers. When she'd married Richard, it was like she'd been unleashed. He was even more ancient than she was and had a gift for investing. I couldn't imagine what the two of them were worth together now.

"Of course I can buy my BFF a few *piccolo cose*." Flo waved to my clerks as I tugged her to the back. "You will not spoil my fun by refusing a single thing."

She dropped her bags then paused. "Wait a minute. Did I just see Jeremiah's daughter out there? Was she helping a customer? Working?" She grabbed me. "What is going on, Glory?"

"I'm trying to help her." I shut the door. I wasn't going to share the ATM thing. The fewer people who knew about that the better. There had been no new robberies reported on the news so I hoped that meant Lily had actually stopped. "You know she tends to keep bad company. Jerry's out of town so I thought she could earn some pocket money here and stay out of trouble."

Flo's eyes got big. "Working as a shopgirl?" She put her hand over her mouth. "*Mio Dio*, I didn't mean . . . Of course there is nothing wrong with her working here. It's just that her mother will have *un attacco*. You know, hate it. She is so . . ." Flo put her finger under her nose and lifted it in the air.

"Yes, I'm sure Mara . . . What did you say?" I was trying not to show how Flo's reaction had bothered me.

"Will have a fit. Yes, that is what I say." Flo giggled. "I'd like to see her face when she sees this. But Lily. She agreed? Is she doing well? She is not making the customers feel bad? She is her mother's daughter after all."

"So far, she's okay. She looks young, acts young, the students relate to her." I picked up one of the sacks on the table. "I hope you didn't go overboard, Flo."

"You had a terrible time in Scotland. *Poverina*. Jeremiah didn't know you. And his mother was there. I know Magdalena wasn't kind." She knew both of Jerry's parents. Had even had a brief affair once with the laird when he and Mag had been separated.

"No, she was pretty mean. The whole trip was more or less the pits." I pulled out a gorgeous blouse in a blue that matched my eyes. It was even the right size. "It's perfect. I'm trying it on right now." I wore black pants that would go with anything. I tore my black and white sweater off over my head and carefully slipped on the blouse. The silk was light as a feather and felt wonderful against my skin.

"Perfetto." Flo hugged me, tears in her eyes. "Please accept these little gifts. It makes me so happy to see you pretty in something new." She gestured around the back room, crammed full of vintage finds that had yet to be priced and put out in the shop. "You deserve it. I hate to see you always wearing someone else's castoffs."

My hands stilled on the last button. Flo too. What was with everyone lately? I didn't mind wearing vintage. Loved the history in it and the fun of taking something worn in a previous era and pairing it with a modern piece. I didn't say anything because I knew Flo and I would never agree on this. She liked everything right off the store rack. Had closets full of clothes only worn once because then they weren't "fresh." Someday I was going to talk her into letting me have them to sell. Otherwise they were just abandoned, left to languish when someone else could bring them to life again.

"Thank you, my friend." I smiled and picked up another sack. "Your taste is wonderful. I can't believe you were thinking of me when you had all of Paris at your feet. Speaking of . . . Tell me what shoes you bought over there. The ones you have on are fabulous."

That got her off and running and we spent an enjoyable evening together, catching up. But something was missing. I loved Flo and knew she would do anything for me. We just didn't have the same feelings about certain things. It was a reality check and a reminder that my ordeal with Jerry had given me a new perspective on a lot of things.

By the time we said good-bye, I had cheered up. No big deal. I could still love her, laugh with her and plan an evening out with her and Richard once Jerry got back. Just because she thought my whole business was tacky—my word, not hers—I couldn't let that ruin our friendship.

After Flo left, Lily stuck her head into the back room where I was trying to figure out which bills to pay first. "I'm going to take my break now."

"Wait. Tell me how it's going." I gestured for her to come inside and close the door. "Any word from your father?"

"He called and told me where to find a gas card in his office." She smiled. "That's better than when he went to Scotland. At least I can fill my tank."

His tank. She was driving Jerry's Mercedes but I didn't correct her. "Did you tell him about the job?"

"Yes. I told him you thought he should get me my own apartment too. That I was working here to prove I could be responsible. He was surprised." She examined her fingernails, painted black with white skulls.

"Surprised? By the apartment thing or the job?"

"The job. He wasn't sure I'd like working in a shop." She started peeling off the black. Stick-ons, obviously. "I am so over these. Anyway, I told him I didn't mind it. I'd met some nice kids and I like Sixth Street." She grinned, showing fang. "Great dining."

"Lily, remember what I said." If I caught her taking someone down a pint in a dressing room . . :

"I take my action outside. Relax, Glory. Dad said he understood about the apartment. He'll get right on it once he gets this deal in Florida worked out. He's interviewing for new management." She was on fingernail number six. "You'd think with the job market the way it is he'd have plenty of quality people to choose from."

"Maybe you should talk to him about what he does. He owns several hotels and casinos. If you're into that scene, you could work for him. Though it would be in another city instead of here." I don't know why I hadn't thought of that sooner.

Lily dropped the last decal in the trash can. "Trying to get rid of me, Glory?"

"No, just laying out some options for you. Flo reminded me that your mother might not like the idea of you working in a shop. You do come from a wealthy family."

"Fat lot of good it's doing me." She made a face. "I want to stay in town awhile. Get to know my dad. Sorry if that's cramping your style, but that's my plan." She opened the door. "Now I have thirty minutes coming to me for a meal break. If I plan to eat, I'd better hustle." She flashed the tip of a fang. "See ya in thirty." She sauntered through the shop, waving to the other clerk before she headed out the door.

Okay, that had been interesting. She'd talked to Jerry but I hadn't. He hadn't called me and I wasn't going to make the first move. We were at an impasse. Fine by me. We needed to thrash things out face-to-face.

I heard a scratching at the back door, so faint I wondered if I'd imagined it. No, there it was again. I opened the door and saw a familiar face.

"Aggie? What are you doing here?" She didn't look right. Her hair was wild and she still wore the same outfit I'd seen her in the last time we'd met, almost a week ago, at Ian's. Now it looked a little worse for wear with stains on the sweater and the hem coming out of the skirt. She held her shoes in her hand.

"Quick, shut the door." She ran over and slammed the one into the shop. "Hide me."

"What's the matter? Who are you hiding from?" I noticed she was trembling. I helped her to the chair where she collapsed and dropped the shoes carelessly next to her. Not Aggie-like behavior since they were this season's Manolos. I could tell at one whiff that she was still mortal.

"Ian. I . . . I had to sneak out of his compound, Glory." She jumped up and ran into the bathroom, stopping to examine her face in the glass. "God! Where are my cheekbones? I look like one of those dolls they used to say came from a cabbage patch. Remember them? I always thought they were scary when I saw mortal children playing with them." She pinched her cheeks. "Do you see what he's done to me?"

"Aggie, what are you talking about? Sneak? I thought you and Ian were in love." I stood behind her while she washed her hands, using lots of soap.

"Get out of here, I have to use the toilet." She shoved me out the door. "It's hell being mortal." The door shut in my face and I heard the lock turn.

Well, well, this was interesting. I heard a flush then water running again. Finally she emerged from the bathroom. She'd obviously used the brush I kept in there because her hair, which had been in a tangled mess, was now under control. She'd washed her face too. She looked younger without makeup, almost innocent. I knew better.

"So why did you have to sneak out and how did you get here?" I sat on the table, ready to hear the whole story.

"That asshole, that lying piece of shit won't turn me vampire, Glory." Aggie grabbed my hand. "You do it. Right now. Every minute I'm mortal, I'm getting older. Look at me." She ran into the bathroom again and peered at her reflection. "Lines! Around my eyes. Do you see them?"

"That's because you're squinting. Relax, Aggie, it's only been a few days." I leaned back on both hands so she couldn't grab one again. "Did Ian say why he wouldn't keep his word?" I had a pretty good idea but I wanted to hear it from her.

"Well, first"—she dragged herself from her study of her face and sank into the chair again—"he took blood from me. Claimed I was delicious." She rubbed her throat. "I took that as a compliment. It is, isn't it? Coming from a vampire?"

"Sure. I can smell your blood from here. You're A positive. It's pretty common, but tasty." I smiled and showed fang. "I wouldn't mind drinking from you myself."

"Stop it! You will not come near me with a fang." She glared, like she was still the badass she used to be.

"Try and stop me." I laughed at the look on her face when I got up. I walked right past her to my minifridge and took out a bottle of synthetic, twisting off the cap. "Relax. I have this. Your mortal blood is safe from me. Now go on, what other reason did he give you for not going through with his promise?"

"Well . . ." She picked up a shoe and slipped it on. "He realized our love wasn't exactly true." The other shoe got a lot of her attention and she wouldn't look at me.

"What do you mean? He was certainly declaring his undying love when the Storm God was there making it rain like we should start building the ark." I set down my bottle and put my hands on her shoulders. "Look at me, Aggie. Did you sing him to you? With your Siren's song? *Make* him fall in love with you?"

"Of course I did!" She threw off my hands. "How else could I get a man like Ian to love me?" Her eyes filled with tears. "You think I don't know what you people think of me? I realize I'm not an easy person to deal with. Sirens don't need people skills, we have powers. You guys here in Austin are the first friends I've ever had besides the sisters." She started sobbing. "Now my powers are g-g-gone!"

I knew she meant the other Sirens. They called themselves a sisterhood. Basically a group of serial killers who called men to them in the sea, used their bodies for sex, then tossed them on the rocks to die. It still made me shudder to realize I'd been one of them once. I was glad the Storm God had wiped my memory of that time in my life. Aggie thought we were friends now? Pathetic.

"Why did you do it, Aggie? Why Ian?"

"He is so s-s-smart, handsome, and a w-w-wonderful lover." That last word was a wail that could have cracked glass.

"Jeez, Aggie. Have a meltdown, why don't you?" I glanced at the door to the shop and switched on the radio. Okay that wasn't very sympathetic, but she'd manipulated him. "People will hear. Pipe down."

"I can't. Look at me. I'm dying by inches. I lost the man I love and now he sees me as nothing more than a meal on heels." She grabbed a vintage tablecloth from a nearby shelf and cried into it, her shoulders shaking.

"Okay, calm down. Maybe you can go back, work on developing a real relationship with Ian. Become, I don't know, loveable." I knew it was a stretch, but she did look awful. Nose red, eyes puffy. Heartbroken.

Her head snapped up. "Are you serious? If I go back there, I know exactly what will happen. I'm nothing but a blood donor to him now. He wants me to be healthy. So I'll be able to give him plenty of that good A positive every night. Did you know he hired a chef? Just for me. You should see the food he has this guy whip up. Gourmet treats, desserts, everything fattening that I love." She stood and jerked up her sweater. "Look at me. I can't button my skirt! And it's been less than a week."

I bit my lip, trying not to laugh. Petite Aggie, size six Aggie, had a little round tummy. Oh, there was justice in the world. Ian had been stuffing her like a Thanksgiving turkey.

"Where's your resistance? You don't have to eat what's put in front of you." She'd told me once though that Sirens often had lavish banquets but never gained an ounce. Part of their magic. Obviously another perk gone along with her immortality.

"Oh, yeah? Well after Ian gets through with his mind games, I can't resist jack." She shoved her sweater back down. "He's doing it on purpose. Punishing me. There's nothing Ian hates more than being manipulated. He told me that. I played a mind game on him so now he's getting even. *Quid quo* whatever."

We both jumped when there was loud pounding on the back door. "That's him! Don't tell him I'm here. I'm hiding in the bathroom. I won't go back there, Glory. Not unless he'll turn me vampire."

Great. Like I needed to be in the middle of a domestic dispute. Aggie rushed into the bathroom and locked the door.

"Who is it?"

"Ian MacDonald. Let me in, Gloriana." He sounded furious.

"Why should I?" I loved having the upper hand with Ian for a change.

"Because if you don't, I'll send my men through your store and make a scene. How will that affect your business?"

"Oh, come on in." I threw open the door. "If you're looking for Jerry, he's out of town. He's still fine, by the way. If that's why you're here, Doctor."

"No, I don't give a shit about Campbell. Where's Aggie?" He turned toward the bathroom. "I can smell her. Get out here, woman, before I knock that door down."

"Ian, relax. You don't own her. She came here asking for sanctuary. I'm thinking about giving it to her." I let my hand hover inches from his chest. "You fancy being turned into a statue again?" I smiled at his bodyguards who stood near his back. "Tell them to wait outside. I don't think you want witnesses for this, do you?"

He nodded. "Go, wait in the alley. She's here. I can handle this." Ian glared at me. "Keep your hands off of me, Gloriana. You really don't want to defend Aggie, do you? I remember a time when you hated her as much as I do."

"She's mortal now. Helpless." I smiled. "I kind of like Aggie that way. But you've turned her into a blood slave. That goes against my principles. You can afford a good synthetic. Drink that."

"Please. What is this? Women sticking together? Or something else?" He pounded on the bathroom door. "Come out and look me in the eye, woman."

"No way in hell. You'll just use your mind control on me. I'm not stupid." She hit the door from her side. "Go away. I'm not going back."

"She tell you what she did?" Ian paced around the small room, kicking the chair out of the way. "Used her Siren song on me. Damn her! I should have known it. No woman has ever measured up, been powerful enough to truly hold my interest for long before. Then suddenly it was like I couldn't imagine my life without her. I wanted to be with her constantly. Had to have her no matter what it took. You were there. I even called in a favor from Campbell." He slammed his palm on my table and I heard the wood crack. "Under a fucking spell. The whole idea makes me insane."

"I'm sorry, Ian. Of course you hate it. She was wrong to do it. But don't you think losing her immortality and her powers is a pretty good punishment?" I stayed out of his way. I'd never seen Ian out of control like this before.

Suddenly he stopped pacing, his bright blue eyes zeroing in on me. "It helps but it's not nearly enough." He smiled and moved closer. "Now you, Gloriana. Daughter of a goddess. *You* interest me. Did you know Aggie tried to use her Siren powers, other than the song, after she became mortal? Zip, nada. Yet you have discovered you still have many of them, like the statue trick you threatened me with. I wonder why."

"I guess my mother is responsible for that." I didn't like the way his eyes were gleaming.

"Your mother the goddess. That's quite a pedigree. Fascinating." He leaned his hip against the table, too close. "Have you been to Olympus yet? Seen Zeus? I heard her say he's your grandfather." He grinned. "Think what he could do for you." Ian slid his hand up my arm. "And he's bound to love you."

I'd had a variation on this conversation with him before. If Ian thought a woman could give him something he wanted, he could pour on the charm. After seeing him in action, having suffered as a result of his manipulative scheming, I was immune.

"Go home, Ian. Without Aggie. You two are done. Drink synthetic or find yourself another blood donor, a willing one. You've had your revenge. Aggie can't squeeze into a size six now. It's killing her."

"That's something." He looked me up and down, smiling

in a way that made me want to check my buttons. "Though I have always preferred a woman with a more generous body myself."

"Ancient males tend to be that way. Which is why I prefer them. But you and me together? Not in a thousand years." I put more room between us without letting him know that he made me uncomfortable. "Now aren't you leaving?"

"Fine. I guess the fact that she's doomed to live a mortal's short life *is* a pretty good payback." He nodded. "Because I bet you aren't going to turn her either, are you, Gloriana?" He stepped over to the bathroom door. "Hear that, Aggie? Your pal Glory follows the rules. She'll never turn you vampire. You're stuck, chubby cheeks. How do you like that?"

He turned and ran a fingertip down my own chubby cheek. "I find power such a turn-on. You haven't seen the last of me, my dear. And if it takes a thousand years? Well, we both have time, don't we?" With that, he opened the alley door and signaled to his men. They shifted and flew off into the night.

The bathroom door creaked open. "Is he gone?" Aggie peered out cautiously.

"Yes. I'm sure you heard that." I shut the back door and slid the dead bolt closed.

"He said you wouldn't turn me vampire." She dropped to her knees in front of me. "Tell me he was lying, Glory. Please! You *have* to do it. You can't doom me to this horrible, powerless and ridiculously short existence."

"No, Aggie, Ian was right. I'm not turning you." I pulled her to her feet, then grabbed a top and pants, those in an eight, from the shelf. "Come on, I'll take you to my apartment, where you can clean up and change clothes." I sniffed. "You smell funny and not in a good way. *How* did you get here?"

She jerked away from me. "I was desperate. I hitchhiked. The only thing on the road out there in the boonies where

Ian lives this late at night was a chicken hauler. The truck driver had his prize rooster in the front seat next to him, so I had to ride in the back. So, yeah, I reek of chicken shit. That's my life now, Glory." She threw open the door into the shop. "Don't think I'm giving up. I've always been stubborn when I want something. I'll wear you down. You *will* turn me."

"Keep your fantasy, Ag, if it helps you get through the night." I followed her out of the shop, stopping to let my clerk know I'd be gone awhile. What was I letting myself in for? Aggie for a roommate? But where else could she go? I passed Lily, who had flushed cheeks and a satisfied smile on her face. One more problem child. Seemed like there was a saint for helpless causes. I'd have to ask Richard about that. These two women needed to set up an altar to that one.

Jerry had left a message on my landline. That told me he really didn't want to talk or he'd have called my cell. The message was short and to the point. He'd be gone another week. There was no promise of a heart-to-heart talk when he did get home. Of course he hated those anyway.

In the nights to come I realized living with a mortal was even worse than living with a shape-shifter. Valdez had loved junk food and thrived on it. Aggie was still worried about her figure and had picked up a diet book. She wanted me to buy her special foods and a treadmill. On my budget? She was lucky the book had been on a shelf in my shop.

As it was, the lettuce and celery went bad while she sneaked out to Mugs and Muffins, next door to the shop, and gorged during the day while I was in my death sleep. I wouldn't know about it except she charged it to me and I got the bill. Nasty surprise. Sorry, but when I can't have a chocolate chunk muffin and a latte with whipped cream, I sure as hell don't want to pay for it. We were due for a showdown.

"You have to figure out a way to earn some money." I picked up the remote. Who knew that *Judge Judy* ran ten times a night?

"Hey, she was about to decide whether the woman got to keep the ring. That idiot she was engaged to ran around on her. I say it's hers all the way." Aggie stuffed a carrot stick in her mouth. The fact that it was loaded with ranch dip didn't seem to bother her, it was diet food in her interpretation of the book.

"Aggie, the judge always lets the woman keep the ring. Now listen up." I sat across from her. "You are running up bills I'm having a hard time paying. Food, electricity, water." She took long showers and then soaked in a tub. A holdover from her Siren days, that craving for water. Or so she claimed.

"Hey, we can solve that with one bite." She smiled and pointed to her jugular. "When I'm a vamp, I'll go drink from those people I see walking down the street. And I'll be dead when you are. No TV going all day, lights either. Guess it would cure me of the water thing too." She sighed. "I'd miss that."

"I won't turn you. Now let's be realistic. We have to figure out if you have any marketable skills." I'd just had this conversation with Lily. I was turning into a regular guidance counselor. But no way was Aggie working in my shop. I was already sick of her. She complained constantly. Becoming mortal hadn't improved her personality.

"I think I should sue Ian for support. I could go on Judge Judy's show. Like you say, the wronged woman always wins. He made certain promises and Ian didn't follow through." Aggie sat up, excited. "That's perfect. I'm calling the show first thing tomorrow morning."

"Slow down. Are you nuts?" I wanted to beat her over the head with my red throw pillow, which now wore ranch dressing stains. "Ian is a vampire. Your problem is about being turned into a bloodsucker. No court is going to listen to that. They'll think you're cracked."

"Yeah." She sat back, dragging another carrot stick through the dip. "Wait a minute! We do have a court of sorts here. The vampire council. You said it yourself. It has rules. I could take Ian in front of them. Damian, you said, is the head of it. Right?" When the carrot stick fell, she dabbed at the front of her robe, one she'd appropriated from the shop. "He liked me. We made a connection at Flo's wedding."

"Will you get a grip?" I grabbed the dip and carrots and dumped them in the trash. "And quit eating like a pig. Too much of anything, even diet food, will make you fat. Any more of that and you'll be lucky to fit into a ten."

"Now you're being mean." She sniffled. "I'm trying, Glory. You won't buy me a membership to that health club down the block. If I could work out . . ."

"Forget it. Walk around the block. You've got all day to do it and it's free." I could see this conversation going nowhere. "Forget suing Ian. If he turned you, the vampire council would be all over him. They would never award you support."

"But what if they fined him for holding me prisoner as his—what did you call it?—blood slave." She stood. "I have Damian's number. He gives every woman his number. Casanova he calls himself. Easy to see why. Anyway, I'm running this past him. Why shouldn't Ian pay a fine? There's bound to be a rule against white slavery or whatever you want to call it." She pulled her phone from her purse. "Oh, shit. I forgot. The Storm God cut me off. No service. Can I use yours?"

"A fine would go to the council, not to you, Aggie." I dug out my phone. "But maybe you could ask for damages. Mental anguish. It's worth a shot." And I'd do anything to get her out of my apartment.

"There you go. I knew you'd help me." She smiled and found Damian in my contact list. "And of course you have his number. You two ever hook up?"

"No, but he tried." I sat back while she dialed. Yes, it had been a flattering move but a long time ago. I liked Damian.

I could see him trying his luck with Aggie. She was still beautiful when she wasn't covered with food stains. Probably wild in bed. Men would always be after her, as long as they didn't have to live with her.

I could see her chattering away, making Ian sound like a heartless bastard. It was pretty much the truth. Would the council listen to her story? Apparently so. In a few minutes she hung up, all smiles.

"He's going to arrange a hearing. You'll have to go with me, Glory. You were a witness, of course. You heard the whole thing both with the Storm God and Ian's threats at your shop. And you know how Ian is." She rubbed her hands together. "I bet the council has had other complaints about him. What do you think?"

"Possibly. He's a doctor, though, the only one paranormals have here. They'll be careful not to make him want to leave town. He did save Jerry's life." I wiped off the coffee table, gathering an empty glass, paper napkins, and a bag of chips, empty too, of course. Aggie was a slob. I was ready to testify to anything to move her out.

"Somehow I'm going to get big bucks. And there will be handsome men there. All of them vampires. If I can make a good connection, maybe one of them will turn me." She headed to the kitchen carrying the garbage I'd thrust into her hands.

"They're all members of the council, Aggie. They *made* that rule against turning mortals."

She came out with a pint of chocolate ice cream and a spoon. "Couldn't resist. Sorry you can't join me. Got to get it while I can." She winked. "Anyway, when I lay my sob story on the council? How I lost all my powers? I bet you my last pair of Manolos that they make an exception for me." She grinned and took a bite, sighing with pleasure. "Oh, yeah. I'll be rich and a vampire, Glory. Count on it."

I leaned back and wondered if my mother had any of her first potion left. Amnesia looked really good right now. Or maybe I'd stick Aggie with it and she could forget she knew me. Clearly I had the makings of a manipulative goddess. Like mother, like daughter?

I glanced at the ceiling. I never knew when my mother would tune into what was happening in my life. So I'd better watch my impulses or Hebe might decide to take these random thoughts as wishes and act on them. Damn. I couldn't even safely fantasize about murder anymore. Life was so not fair.

Seventeen

Of course Ian called me as soon as he got notice that the council wanted to see him. I ignored the call and then deleted the message that contained more bad words than good. He knew I'd show up there with Aggie. I tried to call Jerry, sure he'd be interested in this. I got voice mail. Dodging my calls or just busy? I'd drive myself crazy wondering about it so I left a message that I missed him, which was true, and hung up.

I'd been thinking about our relationship. I had secrets so why couldn't he have them? If the reason he'd hotfooted it to Texas and changed his name didn't concern me, then I should probably let it go. I'd done things I wasn't proud of in my past. When we'd taken breaks, it had been tough for me to make a living. During gold rush days I'd been a saloon girl who'd always promised more than I'd given. I had never prostituted myself but had come close. And there had been a few mistakes, especially when I'd been with mortals, that I would be ashamed to trot out into the light of day.

I decided then and there that when Jerry got back I was going to let this little rift go. No more questions. Rafe had tried to make trouble and I knew why. I wasn't going to let him break Jerry and me apart. We'd been through too much to have that happen now.

So when the night of the council meeting rolled around, I was feeling pretty optimistic. I should have known that was a bad sign. Whenever things are going well for me, that's when it all goes to shit. But if I could get Aggie out of my apartment and on her own somehow, I'd be a happy camper.

"Glory, I'm counting on you." Aggie was beside herself with nerves. It had all started when she was trying to decide what to wear to this showdown. Of course she couldn't fit into anything of mine, still too loose. Her happy dance over that made me want to pick her up and toss her out my third-story window. But the few pieces I'd brought up from the shop in a size eight were too tight. Hmm. How's that diet book working for you, Aggie?

We'd finally trucked down to the store and she'd tried on clothes until she settled on a pair of black pants in a ten and a black tunic.

"I look like I'm going to a funeral," she declared. "But that's okay. It will be Ian's if I play this right." She turned around for me to inspect her. "Are you sure you can't see that bulge at my waistline?"

"No, the tunic is your friend. Now let's go. You don't want to be late." The hearing was set for midnight.

"Aggie really is lodging a complaint against Ian?" Lily had been an interested spectator. "I wonder if he'll be represented by counsel."

"What? A lawyer?" Aggie had learned a few things from *Judge Judy*. She grabbed my arm. "I should have one. Do we know any? Who can we call, Glory?"

I could think of only one vampire who would be qualified. I'd hoped to keep him and his wife out of it, but Lily was right. Aggie needed someone to speak for her. She tended to get emotional, more so since she'd gone up another size.

"I'm calling Richard." And of course he'd tell Flo. They

didn't keep secrets from each other. Not like Jerry and I did. I ignored the catty voice inside my head and punched in the number. "Richard, you ever been a lawyer?"

"Among other things. Why? You're not in jail, are you, Gloriana?" I heard a sudden burst of rapid Italian in the background.

"No, I'm fine. Tell Flo to relax. I've got Aggie here and we're scheduled to go in front of the council in about an hour. She's lodged a complaint against Ian." I glanced around. "Can you meet us at Damian's? I'll explain it all there."

"That is freaking awesome. Richard Mainwaring is legendary." Lily slapped Aggie on the back. "You go, girl. What's the case? Sexual harassment? These guys can't get away with it."

Several customers crowded around. Lily hadn't exactly whispered.

"I've been to night court about that. Had a boss once who kept feeling me up." A woman who'd been on her way to the dressing room with a pair of leather pants leaned in. "Asshole. Just because I wear short skirts doesn't mean I'm issuing an invitation, you know?"

"You tell it, sister." A woman nodded and looked down at her own mini. "I ain't going to dress frumpy just because a man don't got no control."

There were murmurings of agreement. Aggie looked around. "Sister? Are we? Like a sisterhood?"

"That's right, honey. Girls got to stick together." A woman held up a book on feminism. It was decades old and collectible. "I still don't get equal pay. Do way more work while my boss sits on his can. Of course then he gets all the credit."

"I hear ya. Just got passed over for promotion. Again. You want to guess who got the job? That good-old-boy system is still going strong." The angry murmurs were getting louder.

I glanced at my watch. "Fifty percent off anything green for the next half hour only!" I shouted to break up the crowd. The discount got the women diving for the racks and shelves. Shouts of "Green blouse. That's mine." and "Here's a scarf. Isn't that green? Close enough." meant I might lose some money but at least we could move on out.

"We've got to go, Aggie." I pulled her toward the door when I saw she was heading for a green and white robe that I'd have to give her. She sure couldn't pay for it.

"You know I think I'd like to be a lawyer." Lily followed us to the door. "It would be megacool to preside over a court, decide who's right or wrong."

"Like Judge Judy." Aggie smiled. "Yeah, that's a great job. Lawyer first, then you move up to the bench."

"If you're interested in the law." I tried not to roll my eyes. This was the girl who had embraced a life of crime only days ago. "Tell your dad. I'm sure he'd be happy to send you to school. There's a great one, several of them in fact, here in town." I smiled, imagining her safely in night classes hitting the books.

"Maybe you'd end up on that council here. The first woman. You said they were all men, didn't you, Glory?" Aggie snatched a green bracelet off the display near the register before another woman could add it to her pile. "There. This adds some color. I don't want to be dowdy." She ripped off the tag, dropped it on the floor and clipped it onto her wrist.

I gritted my teeth then picked up that tag. I was keeping a running total of Aggie's debt. If a miracle happened and she actually squeezed some money out of Ian, I was getting paid first.

"We've got to take off. Looks like you're going to have a busy night here, Lily. Me and my big mouth. You make sure that green is green, nothing bluish green or yellow." I hustled Aggie toward the door.

"Got it, Glory." Lily actually looked happy for a change. "Good luck, Aggie. Come by and tell me afterward how it went. I want all the gory details."

"Yeah. Maybe we can celebrate." Aggie sighed. "I hope so. I realize I'm in the minority. Everybody else there will have . . ." She leaned in and whispered, ". . . fangs. Is this Richard really any good?"

"He's the best, just wait and see." I dragged her outside to where I'd pulled my car out front earlier. We needed to hurry. Knowing Richard, he would be able to argue Aggie's case well, but first we had to fill him in. I listened to Aggie complain about the seat belt wrinkling her tunic as we set off. Just like Flo. Who I bet would be there too.

Luckily Damian's place wasn't far, just a few blocks away, on a hilltop with a killer view of the state capitol building. He lived in a castle. Yep. In Austin. Trust Damian to find the only castle in the city. He was one of the few vampires I knew who didn't mind being noticed. Mortals who wondered about the man who only came out at night and gave lavish parties usually finishing with a bat flight always ended up with amnesia if they saw anything they shouldn't.

We pulled into the circular drive already crowded with cars. The house was lit up from top to bottom and there was almost a party atmosphere. I was surprised Damian didn't have a servant at the door offering the blood with a champagne kick. Instead, we were ushered into his library, a large room I'd been in before. Richard was waiting for us.

"There you are. We don't have much time. The council is set up in an upstairs room. Apparently Damian always holds his meetings there. We have a little while to confer before they're scheduled to begin." He gestured and we sat on the sofa while Richard sat across from us. "Aggie, what's this about?"

She told him the whole story. Of course she left out an important detail.

"Aggie, you have to tell Richard everything. Especially why Ian is so mad at you."

"I don't want to. Can't I plead the fifth amendment? I shouldn't have to incriminate myself." She kept tugging at her tunic like she didn't think it was covering her new lumps and bumps. I could relate. My own dress felt snug.

Richard stood, his hands behind his back as he paced in

front of her, just like he might in a courtroom. "First, Aglaophonos—"

"Call me Aggie. My real name is such a mouthful. Now that I'm mortal, I want to be called just Aggie. I need to pick a last name too. Still thinking about that."

"All right, Aggie. Here's the bottom line. You don't have any rights here. This isn't an American court of law. This is the vampire council. You can't plead the Fifth. Second, if Ian knows this information you're withholding and it helps his case, he's going to tell it anyway. Best if it came from you."

"Well, hell." She nibbled on her thumbnail, a bad habit she'd started recently. "This doesn't seem fair, just vamps deciding things. Where's the jury of my peers?"

Richard shook his head. "Correct me if I'm wrong but didn't you ask for this hearing?"

Aggie sighed. "Yes. I thought . . . Never mind. Here's what happened. I used my song to make him love me." She stared down at her lap. She went on, telling of a temper fit by Ian, her fear when he found out the truth. Big dramatic story. She wiped tears. I should have loaned her my waterproof mascara.

Then she segued into the blood slave thing, big emphasis on the forced feeding and no cheekbones. Finally she ended with a flourish. "And he said, 'At least you have blood I like. I'll keep you until I get tired of you. Then I'll just drain you dry!'" She bent her head and covered her face with both hands.

"Very affecting. Tell it just like that." Richard nodded to me. "The tears are a nice touch."

"Richard! Come on. You're supposed to be on her side." I patted her back, sure that last line was pure fabrication. Ian was more likely to toss her out on the streets to starve when he tired of her.

Aggie looked up. "You don't believe me?"

"Oh, I'm sure that's probably your version of what happened. The problem is no one up there is going to like a Siren, Aggie. And the fact that you tricked Ian isn't going to play well." He frowned. "Glory, what happened when you got involved?"

"I saw Ian before and after he was under her spell. As soon as Aggie was made mortal it became obvious the spell had worn off. He got interested in her blood. Just like we all do when a mortal is around. He'd lost that loving feeling." I gestured at Aggie. "I agree that what she did was despicable." I ignored the noise she made when I said that. "But then he held her prisoner. She had to sneak out of his place, past his guards, and hitchhike to town."

Ian nodded. "I can use that. Then I assume he came after her."

"Yes, practically knocked Glory's door down. Was going to drag me back whether I wanted to go or not." Aggie had the indignant act down pat. "Coercion!" She held up a finger.

"Why didn't he take you back? He's certainly powerful enough to overcome a mere mortal."

Aggie smiled. "Ian's afraid of Glory. She has mad skills." She patted my knee. "Like I used to have." Oh here came the waterworks again. "She gave me sanctuary. Such a wonderful friend." She threw her arms around me, soaking my good black dress with her tears.

"Dry up, Aggie." I peeled her off of me. "You chose to leave the Sirens and give up those powers. But she's right. Ian figured she owed him some donor time for deceiving him." I dug a handful of tissues out of my purse and thrust them at Aggie. She blew her nose and wiped her cheeks.

"Arrogant bastard. It's like I was an entitlement!" Finger up again. Where was she getting these words?

"Aggie, did he take your blood every night? Leave you weak? Force you to do other things? Sex, for example?" Richard had a tablet computer like Ian's and made notes.

"I wasn't weak because he practically force-fed me. Mesmerized me when I tried to go on a hunger strike. More coercion." She gestured down her body. "Made me fat against my will. It was all about my blood for him. The minute he found out I'd tricked him into loving me, he-he wouldn't touch me again. Like that."

"No rape then." Richard just kept writing. Obviously this kind of intimate detail didn't bother him.

"No. I wish . . ." She looked up. "Instead he'd look into my eyes, use that damned mind control and I'd be helpless, just sit there while he drank my blood. He'd use my wrist. I could have been a stranger." She wiped her eyes. I was going to have to steer her to the bathroom with a makeup bag before the hearing. She looked a mess.

"So what are you after here?" Richard set the tablet aside.

"I want him to suffer. He held me prisoner. He should pay for that. For my pain and suffering. I need money, Richard. He's rich. Have you seen where he lives? The cars in his garage? He can afford to throw a few million my way and never miss it." Aggie jumped up and grabbed Richard's arm. "He said many times that he'd turn me vampire. Then he didn't. That's breach of promise."

I knew she'd gotten that straight from *Judge Judy*.

"The council won't go for that. They have a rule—"

"Damn their rule!" She took a deep breath. "I heard him say that many times. He laughed at the council and their rules. Use that against him. He was really going to do it. Turn me. But then he got mad and refused. I never would have left the Sirens if I'd known I'd be stuck as a mortal." She batted her eyes at Richard. The effect wasn't what she hoped since her black mascara decorated her cheeks in splotches. "Can you imagine? I lost everything because he'd promised me my immortality back. Now I'm dying every day."

"You made the choice." Richard removed her hand from his sleeve. "I'm just telling you what you'll hear from the council. Now, Aggie, when we get up there, follow my lead. Try not to let Ian goad you. It will only make the council turn against you. Honestly? You don't have a very good case." He looked at me like "what have you gotten me into?"

"Aggie, here, take my makeup bag and hit the bathroom. There's one by the front door. You look terrible."

"Gee, thanks, Glory." She made a face but took the bag and walked off.

"I'm sorry, Richard. She set this up. I've had her living with me and I was desperate to get her out of there. Maybe with some income."

"I don't know, Gloriana. It'll be difficult. The one thing we've got going for us is that nobody here likes Ian either. Are you willing to testify?"

"Sure. If you think it will help."

He glanced out the window. "I'm not sure anything will. Just stand by. Here comes Florence. You knew she wouldn't miss this, didn't you?"

"Will they let her watch the proceedings?" Flo waved and I saw her walk around to where I knew there were glass doors into the house.

"These hearings are usually closed to spectators, but she's Damian's sister. She talked him into letting her sit in. She promised to stay quiet." Richard led the way out into the hall.

"Glory, what's going on? Richard wouldn't tell me anything. Attorney-client privilege. Pah!" Flo waved her hands. "This has got to be good. I heard him mention Aggie and Ian. You know I love gossip."

"Flo! Are you here for moral support?" Aggie grabbed Flo from behind and hugged her. She'd just washed her face, obviously going for the pale and pitiful look. "Remember how I stood up for you at your wedding? Just the best bridesmaid ever! And the wonderful bridal shower I threw for you. The water spouts, the high dives!" She leaned back, her eyes shining. "You can help me now. Testify. As a character witness."

"Your character? I remember other things you did not so nice." Flo sniffed the air. "What is this? You are mortal now. *Disastro!* Who did this to you?"

"I did it to myself. For love!" Aggie put her hand to her heart. There was nothing like watching two drama queens at work. Flo gasped and grabbed Aggie's arm. Then the former Siren proceeded to tell Flo the whole tale with appropriate gestures. All of it ended up being in rapid Italian. I really needed to download that free translator app for my phone.

"Keep your voices down. You don't want the council to hear all of this." Richard pulled them toward the staircase. "Remember what I said. Follow my lead, Aggie. Answer the questions. Don't get carried away. Tears won't sway them."

"Ricardo. We must help her. To be stuck in this dying body." Flo held on to Aggie. "My heart is breaking." She turned to her new buddy. "If you lose, there are people, rogue vampires, who will do anything for a price."

"My God, Florence. Am I going to have to send you home?" Richard stopped on the stairs.

"I don't have any money. The Storm God took everything from me. I told Glory once that there was a Siren fortune. Turns out the treasurers in Olympus won't give anyone who's fallen from grace—that's what they call it, Glory—a dime. I checked before I decided to take the plunge. Of course Ian's rich so I didn't think I'd have to worry." Aggie sighed then checked out Flo's designer pantsuit. "Now look at me, wearing an outfit scraped together from Glory's shop. God knows who wore this last."

Flo patted her hand. "I understand. It is hard. But if you want to win money, it is good to look *pietosa*." She frowned. "You look a little bigger than the last time I saw you. What size is that?"

Aggie jerked her hand away. "Never mind. Shouldn't we get up there? Richard? I'll say whatever it takes to get what's due me." She stomped up the stairs. Her only pair of Manolos looked a little worse for wear even though she'd spent an hour trying to repair a gouge in one of the heels.

I followed the rest of them up the wide staircase. I could hear Aggie and Flo whispering together about black market vampires. If Flo offered to pay . . .

Richard stepped in. "That's it. Not another word, you

two. Or I walk. Understood?" He glared at his wife. "You will not be helping her in any way, shape or form."

"Now, Ricardo. If she loses a few pounds, I could let her shop in my closet. How about that?" Flo ran her fingers along the lapels of his gray suit.

"Fine. Now not another word. Go inside and sit in the back. Aggie, you're with me. Gloriana, sit next to Florence. If I need you as a witness, I'll call you." He opened a door at the top of the stairs. "Everyone just stay calm."

Aggie nodded. "You sound like Judge Judy. So . . . official. Will I get to go first? I'm the plaintiff, right?"

Richard sighed. "God save me from reality TV." He glanced at Flo. I knew she watched it too. "Yes, Ian is the defendant. Now hush."

We walked into the large room and saw a long table at the front. Damian sat in the center, facing us. He was flanked by two other male vampires. I knew them by sight, but not well. Two rows of gold and white chairs divided by an aisle down the middle faced the table. I could see Ian and two of his surfer type bodyguards sitting in the front row on the left side. Richard ushered Aggie to the right front, pointing to the back row for Flo and me.

"Shall we get started?" Damian said as soon as Richard stood in front of him, Aggie seated next to him. "Are you here representing Miss Aglaophonos, Mr. Mainwaring?"

"I am, Your Honor."

"Perhaps I should explain that we don't take oaths here, Miss Aglaophonos. As vampires we expect to be able to read each other's minds for the truth. If a witness chooses to block his or her thoughts, we take that as an admission of guilt." Damian was as serious as I'd ever seen him. "You, a mortal, of course are no challenge to us."

"Can we dispense with the formalities, Sabatini?" Ian stood. "I came here as a courtesy to the council. I like Austin and plan to stay. Why don't you explain to me what this is all about?" He turned to Richard. "Mainwaring, what is she claiming now?"

Richard glanced at Damian, who nodded. "That you kept her prisoner and used her as a blood slave. She's asking damages for pain and suffering."

Ian laughed until he had to sit down and wipe his eyes. "Pain and suffering?" He jumped to his feet so fast his chair toppled over. For the first time I noticed four guards at the door, obviously there to protect the council. They moved down the aisle.

Ian held up his hand. "Relax. I'm fine. But let me tell you what happened."

"Your Honor, I object. This is out of order. The plaintiff should testify—"

"Relax, Rich. Your client isn't a vampire. We'll hear from MacDonald first. Go ahead, sir." Damian nodded.

"Thank you. This creature, a Siren, tricked me. I was put under a spell, a victim of her Siren's song." He pointed a finger at Aggie, his finger shaking. "It's the kind of thing we all dread. To be made a fool of. But I'm a man with a weakness for a beautiful and willing woman and she was both. I would have said and done anything to have her. I was ensorcelled." He shook his head as if ashamed. The council members stared at Aggie, probably trying to see what she had that made her so irresistible.

Aggie lowered her head into her hands and sobbed. Richard kept a firm grip on her shoulder, probably to keep her in her seat.

"But her little trick backfired. She thought I'd turn her vampire so she asked to be released from the Siren harem." He curled his lip. "Yes, gentlemen, that's what they call it. I should have paid attention to that."

"Bastard!" Aggie struggled against Richard's hold.

"Order!" Damian banged a gavel. "If you want a fair hearing, Miss Aglaophonos, you will control yourself. Counselor."

"Sorry, Your Honor." Richard pushed her down into her seat and whispered in her ear. We could still hear her furious hissing.

"She became mortal and her spell was broken. I saw her

for the manipulative bitch she was." Ian held out his hands. "Of course I wasn't going to turn her vampire. You have rules against that sort of thing. But I felt the least she owed me after such a humiliation was a few nights' feeding." He smiled, showing fang. "I'm sure any of you would have done the same."

"And what about this accusation that you held her prisoner?" This was from one of the other council members.

"Gentlemen, I have the latest in high-tech security around my home. As I'm sure all of you do. We are vulnerable during the daylight hours and I have valuable equipment and priceless art in my home as well. I brought witnesses here who can testify to the extent of that security." He gestured at his two companions. "And I have an affidavit here from the company where it was purchased." He passed papers to Damian, who barely glanced at them.

"Go on." Damian and the other two council members were riveted.

"Honestly? Aggie never could have escaped from my estate if I hadn't allowed it." He looked over at her and smiled. "I'd be happy to share the video of her 'escape' if you'd like to see it." He reached down and pulled out a laptop. "But I have to warn you, the part where she climbs over my gate is X-rated. Miss Aglaophonos doesn't wear underpants." He set the laptop in front of Damian, opened it and pushed a button. The three men leaned in and watched.

"Do you usually have guards on your gate?" Damian had to clear his throat before he got that out. One of the other men pushed a button. Obviously for a replay.

"Of course. I was tired of her complaining so I decided to see if she would take off if given the opportunity. I let her overhear me giving them the night off. She proved to be surprisingly enterprising." Ian looked back at me. "No surprise that she ran straight to another former Siren, Gloriana St. Clair."

"I think we've heard enough." Damian slammed the laptop shut when the man next to him started to replay the tape a third time. "We're going into the next room to deliberate now."

"But, Your Honor, you haven't allowed my client to speak. Or heard her side in this." Richard was on his feet.

"Do you really think that will be necessary, Counselor?" Damian stared at Aggie. "Do you deny you used your Siren's song on Dr. MacDonald?"

"No." Aggie didn't look up at him. She was probably afraid of his ability to use mind control.

"Did anyone try to stop you the night you escaped from Dr. MacDonald's home?" Damian passed the laptop back to Ian.

"No." Aggie spoke so quietly it took vampire hearing to pick up her answer.

"We'll return with our findings shortly." Damian stood.

"Wait. He promised to turn me vampire. What about that?" Aggie struggled against Richard's hold.

Damian shook his head. "He didn't do it. That's all we need to know." He led the other two men out through a side door.

"I can't believe you." Aggie glared at Ian. "You let me hitchhike in the middle of the night. I could have been killed! Worse!"

Ian smiled. "Worse than being killed? What's a fate worse than death? Oh, I suppose you mean some man might have taken advantage of you. Poor Aggie, stuck in a mortal body and no powers." He snarled. "Serves you right."

"That's enough." Richard stood between them when Aggie came out of her chair. "I don't suppose you feel like offering her a settlement. She gave up being a Siren for you. She did love you, Doctor."

"The woman doesn't know the meaning of the word." Ian turned his back on her. "She made her bed, let her lie on it and earn her living that way. Her talents always were in that direction."

"I hate you! Yes, I started our affair with my song, but I was sure you had real feelings for me, Ian. How can you be so mean?" Aggie stared at his rigid back, tears streaming down her face.

He whirled around and glared at her. "You wouldn't know a real feeling if it bit you on your ass, which is a bigger target now, isn't it?"

"Ack!" Aggie tried to claw her way past Richard. "You made me fat. This is all your fault!"

"Better shut up, Aggie. The council members are coming back in already. Not a good sign for you, my dear." Ian smiled and stood.

"Sit, please." Damian and the other two members settled into their chairs. "We have discussed this case and have come to a decision." He picked up a paper. "Miss Aglaophonos, we find that you were not held captive and are not owed damages. However, you are guilty of deceptive practices and have cruelly injured Dr. MacDonald. Because of this we are awarding *him* one hundred thousand dollars in damages. If you cannot pay this amount in cash, you will have to arrange a method of payment satisfactory to Dr. MacDonald. So ordered by this council. Court is adjourned." He banged his gavel, stood and walked around the table to shake Ian's hand.

"Good luck. You are quite right. We cannot condone paranormals using their powers to entrap the vampire citizens of our town. I think this will send a message that we have zero tolerance in these matters." Damian didn't smile. "But be careful promising women to turn them vampire, even if it's just to get into their *biancheria intima*. We have zero tolerance for making new vampires too. Understand?"

"Of course. We are men of the world, you and I." Ian slapped Damian on the back and offered him a cigar. "Pillow talk is just that. I have made many promises I never intended to keep when my blood is running hot. Know what I mean?" They both laughed.

"I can't believe this. My very own brother treating Aggie like she was a *criminale*. He will so hear from me." Flo and I were waiting in the back of the room for Richard and Aggie.

The former Siren hadn't moved yet. I wondered if she had fainted. Richard was arguing with the other council members but all he got were negative head shakes. They were more interested in sharing a cigar with Ian than in Aggie's plight. Richard finally grabbed Aggie's arm and almost dragged her down the aisle.

"Let's get her out of here. This was a joke." Richard was furious.

"Aggie, are you all right?" I grabbed her other arm. She seemed barely able to walk.

"A hundred thousand dollars. Are they kidding me? Where am I going to get that kind of money?" Aggie looked dazed.

"It was a kangaroo court. Vampire all the way. You never stood a chance, Aggie." Richard hurried us down the stairs.

"Can we appeal?" She looked up at him hopefully.

"No, they're the only game in town." Richard shook his head. "You'll have to see if Ian has an idea about how you can work off this debt or if it's enough justice for him that he won. It's given him bragging rights and entrée into the power circle." Richard looked back at the men gathered around Ian, lighting up. "I think we need elections. Term limits. I don't care if Damian is my brother-in-law."

"Calm down, darling. I hate politics. Don't get involved in them." Flo patted her husband's arm as she pulled us down the stairs. "Perhaps Ian will surprise you and be satisfied with this night's outcome and forget dear Aggie."

"Satisfied? No way in hell. I want Aggie to work off every dime." Ian strutted down the stairs, his guards behind him. He was puffing on a cigar and stopped next to the former Siren. "I know just what you can do too."

"I won't sleep with you. Or give you my blood." Aggie pulled the tunic's neckline up to her chin.

"Don't want either one. Sick of both." Ian blew a perfect smoke ring up toward the ceiling. "No, I need a housekeeper. Someone to clean my toilets and scrub my floors. You'll do nicely." He looked her over. "I even have a uniform you can wear. Though I guess I'll have to send out for a bigger size now. What have you been doing lately, eating your way down Sixth Street?"

"Pig. I don't do housework." Aggie backed away from him.

"You do now." Ian nodded at Richard. "Tell her, Counselor. I just had a nice talk with Damian. He agreed that if Aggie doesn't pay off her debt to me that he'll slap her in lockup. Did you know they have one now?" He grinned. "Yep, a jail. It's really for vampires so you might have a little trouble being fed." He chuckled. "Which is one way to lose those extra pounds you've packed on. Hope you like tight spaces. It's a coffin in Damian's basement."

Aggie turned pale and looked like she was about to faint. "A coffin? Richard?"

"Housekeeping can't be that bad. I want something in writing, Ian." Richard was still in full counselor mode. "How many days does she have to do it before the debt's paid?"

"Well, let's figure the going rate for housekeeping is fifty bucks a day and *you* run the numbers. That's how long it'll take her." Chuckling, Ian headed for the door. "You're mine, bitch, for a long, long time."

"Two thousand days." Richard had pulled out his phone and used the calculator. "That's how long it will take you, Aggie."

"I'll be dead by then."

I heard a thump and looked down. Aggie had hit the floor and I didn't blame her. Payback really was a bitch.

Flo pulled on my sleeve. "Where are the kangaroos? I didn't see them."

Richard and I looked at each other and rolled our eyes. Between Flo and Aggie, we had our hands full. He took Flo, carefully explaining what a kangaroo court was. I knelt down next to Aggie and gently patted her cheeks.

Damian and the other council members stopped to watch.

"A little help here?" I glanced up at the men.

Damian handed me a bottle of water. "Flo told me you used to be a Siren. You haven't pulled any of the dirty tricks Aggie used, have you, Glory?"

I sighed and pressed the cold water bottle to Aggie's forehead. I could see she was waking up. I needed to get her out of here and without a scene.

"No. But I have some pretty awesome powers now." I smiled. "I suggest you guys clear out so you don't have to hear Aggie bitch when she comes around. You're not exactly her favorite people now."

"You get tired of Blade, call me." Damian moved closer. "I have always liked you, you know." He looked down when Aggie moaned. "We're out of here. She got what she deserved, I think. Be careful around her, Glory." He and his two council buddies strode off toward the library, trailing cigar smoke behind them.

"I can't believe this. So unfair. Judge Judy would never have run her courtroom that way." Aggie struggled to sit up. "Guess you're stuck with me, Glory. Toilets!" She checked her nails, painted in a bright red for court. "My hands will be ruined."

"Rubber gloves, Aggie." I pulled her up beside me.

"You'll have to teach me to drive. And loan me your car . . ." She kept chattering as we walked toward the parking lot.

All I heard were the sounds of my life falling to pieces. Stuck with Aggie. I had to get her some of that Siren treasure. Maybe I did need to take a trip to Olympus. I was surprised my mother didn't appear on the spot. It was almost as if she'd planted Aggie in my life as a way to get what she wanted. Oh. Surely not. Now I was just being paranoid. Or was I?

Eighteen

My cell rang just as I drove into my parking lot. It was Jerry.

"Hey, where are you?"

"I just got back from Miami. Where are you?"

"I'm about to head into the shop. Can you meet me?" I slammed the car door. Aggie had already headed inside. She'd complained that she was starving. I think there was a pint of ice cream with her name on it upstairs. I didn't need a diet book or a psychology degree to know she was stuffing her stress.

"What about your apartment? We'd have more privacy."

"No, we wouldn't. Aggie will be there. Why do we need privacy?" Not that I didn't like to be alone with him, but something in his voice made my stomach clench. What was this about?

"We need to talk. I've been thinking about the way we left things before I took off for Miami. You were right. Everything I do is your concern. I'm ready to come clean. Can you come over here, to my house? Lily's not here." He sounded really serious. What kind of secret had he been keeping? Murder? Another woman? My mind raced.

"Let me run inside and check for disasters. If everything is okay, I'll be there in thirty minutes. Lily is here, by the way. I hope you don't mind that I put her to work." Aggie had left the back door into the apartments wide open; I shut and locked it then dealt with the one into the shop's back room. I would have to get onto her about security.

"No, she needed to face reality. I don't mind setting her up in an apartment, but a job is good for her. Lets her see how ordinary people earn a living."

"Yes, that was the idea." I just hoped Lily was through stealing from those ordinary people. "Look, I'll hurry. See you soon." I hung up and headed into the store.

Lily was there, helping a customer. She wasn't like Flo about vintage clothes; she actually liked them as long as they were high quality. I still had to work on her snob factor since some of my vintage clothing, especially the sixties and seventies stuff, originally came from discount stores. But she'd gotten into dressing for the job and apparently still had some of her favorites from the last century. Tonight she wore a great sixties Goth outfit in black leather and lace that I'd meant to compliment her on earlier. Her thigh-high boots had spike heels and she'd worn her dark hair in a mass of tangled curls. She was a walking advertisement for the stuff we sold.

"How's it going, Lily?" I stopped next to her at the cash register.

"Fine. You know you should really put all of this on a computer system. It would make keeping track of inventory easier." She handed a customer her change. "Hey, Laurie, come by and show me how that works out on Halloween. I'd love to see you."

"You bet, Lily. Maybe the boss lady here will let you off early and you can come with. The party will be awesome. I can get you in." The girl glanced at me. She was a regular but I'd never caught her name before.

"Sure, we'll work something out, though Halloween is a big night for us." I glanced at the sales total. It was a sizeable cash sale. Nice. "Thanks for coming in." The girl left and I turned to Lily.

"Don't say it. I know she's mortal." Lily held up a hand. "But I can be around them and not go all bloodthirsty." She kept her voice low so none of the other customers could hear. "I am trying to be friendly. I don't have any buds here."

"I wasn't going to say anything about that. I'm glad you're making friends. And she's nice. I know she's a student at UT. As long as you don't put her on the menu, I think it's a good idea to make friends." I glanced around and saw everything was under control, the other night clerk helping another customer. "Your dad is back in town and I'm headed over to his house. Aggie's upstairs. Her hearing didn't go well. When you get off, you might want to go up and give her your sympathy."

"Oh, wow. Sure." Lily sighed. "No surprise. I didn't want to say it, but the deck was stacked against Aggie all the way."

"Right. Look around the apartment while you're there. I heard there's a vacancy on the third floor in this building. Could you stand to live so close to me?" My place was on the second.

"On Sixth Street?" She actually hugged me. "I'd freaking love it. Thanks, Glory. That's exactly what I need—a place of my own near all the action. I can use my own laptop to get your inventory online here, then transfer the files to yours. You get the apartment for me and I'll do that for you. On my own time." She glanced around. "You know retail isn't a bad career option. I've enjoyed this. I have lots of ideas for improving this place."

"Slow down, Donald Trump. I'm pretty happy with the way things are, though the inventory thing sounds great." I couldn't believe this smiling vamp was the angry girl who had acted out just days ago. You'd think after hundreds of years she'd have figured out a purpose for her life. It was too bad she'd been allowed to drift so long. "Thanks, Lily. I'd love to hear your ideas. Soon." I hugged her back. "And I love the outfit. You make the shop look good."

She glanced down. "Hey, I was just trying to fit in. I could have sold it six times already. But thanks. Now go, don't keep Dad waiting." She winked. "Work your magic and get me that place."

I shook my head. No magic here. I waved and set off. I lost my smile fast. What did Jerry have to tell me? A move and name change. Well, I'd done the same thing many times. I had to stop guessing and see him there, so I could find out the truth.

When I drove up to his house, I saw that he'd turned the porch light on for me. Before I could get out of the car, my mother materialized in the passenger seat.

"Whoa. You startled me. Thanks for not doing that while I was driving."

"Of course I waited. Wouldn't want you to have a wreck, darling." She glanced at my outfit. "I see you are wearing the dress I gave you. That pleases me. I still want us to go shopping together, my treat. It's a fantasy of mine to have a mother-daughter night in a mall."

"Mother, Jerry is waiting for me. Did you have something important to say?" I leaned back against the door. She was still in her toga. "Did you come straight from your duties with Zeus?"

"Yes. It was exhausting. Especially since I was keeping tabs on you while having to dole out pardons and listen to the endless bickering that goes on up there." She put a hand to her forehead. "It's enough to give me a migraine. Did you ever get one of those?"

"You're the only headache I have at the moment. Speed this up, please. I have a dawn time limit, you know." I sighed. "Sorry, but Jerry says he's going to clue me in about his big secret. I'm a little worried."

"Of course you are, darling." She reached out and stroked my cheek. "If he disappoints you, Mars told me he would be happy to punish him for you." She smiled. "Now as to why I'm here . . . I heard what happened with that fallen Siren. And you have her in your apartment, making messes, spending your money. Such a nuisance!"

"You got that right. Can you help me out? She owes Ian a ton of money." I leaned forward. "Do you carry cash with you?"

"Don't be silly. I'd never bail out that bitch." She brushed off her toga like the very idea had soiled her. "But I have a way that you can do it yourself." Her smile was crafty.

I didn't like this. She was definitely up to something. "Okay, what do you have in mind?"

"Well, the Siren treasure is there in Olympus for the claiming. I can talk my way into a bit of reparation for you. Aggie"—she shuddered—"such an ugly nickname, probably not. Even though you both left the program, you left involuntarily. Achelous definitely owes a debt for that. I can make sure you are paid your fair share."

"Seriously? I don't want part of anything Siren, but Aggie really needs a small fortune. To pay Ian and to support herself so she can move away from me and my place. What will it take to get her a piece of this treasure?"

"You can choose to give her your portion, of course. If you truly don't want it for yourself." There was that secret smile again. "If you are that desperate to be rid of her, it will require just a small sacrifice on your part, Gloriana. You must come to Olympus personally with me and ask for it." She sighed and touched my hand. "I know how reluctant you've been to do that very thing. You've made your views perfectly clear."

"And you can't get this treasure *for* me?" Wasn't this falling in with her wishes just a little too neatly?

"Oh, no. Only a former Siren can claim the gold. And, if you've been paying attention to the news, you know that gold is very, very valuable right now. Your portion, if you give it to Aggie, would set her up for life, whether she

remains mortal or ends up a"—exaggerated shudder—
"vampire."

"Mother, did you do this? Orchestrate this Aggie fiasco?"
I squeezed her hand.

"Darling, you're hurting me!" She jerked her hand away.
"My, vampires are strong, aren't they?" And that wasn't an
answer, was it?

"Maybe I can live with her after all." I tried not to picture
Aggie as I'd last seen her when I'd run upstairs to check.
She'd fallen asleep on my couch, the overturned carton of ice
cream making a puddle on my new coffee table. Her spoon
was stuck on the front of her robe, her snoring so loud it
drowned out Judge Judy awarding money to a sobbing
woman who'd been tossed out naked after a fight with her
boyfriend. My cat, Boogie, had braved the noise to lick up
the mess. Every light in the apartment had been left on and
the refrigerator door was ajar.

"Fine. I'm sure after a few years you'll be just like real
sisters." She pulled down the visor to check her hair, acting
like she hadn't just described my worst nightmare. "I just
wanted you to meet your grandfather at least once."

Years. Wait. Had that been a confession? "Mother . . ."

"I'm not saying I had a hand in any of this, just offering
you a way out. Be logical, Gloriana. I'm sure Zeus will be
putty in your hands if you tell him how desperate you are to
get that former Siren out of your apartment." She shut the
mirror then leaned back in the bucket seat to stare at me.
"Are you? That desperate?"

Well. No one could ever accuse my mother of missing an
opportunity to get what she wanted. I rested my head on
the steering wheel. Two thousand days of Aggie in my home
while she bitched and moaned on her way to cleaning Ian's
house. Two thousand days of Aggie eating like she needed a
drop cloth, watching reality TV endlessly and using up all
the hot water. And after that? Would she have the money to
move out? No.

"Think you're brilliant, don't you, Mother?" I sat up and grabbed my purse.

"I think I have a way to solve your problem, darling. When do we go?" She had a Cheshire cat grin.

"I'll let you know. Give me some time to work up my nerve. From what I hear, Olympus isn't exactly Club Med. I'm taking my life in my hands going up there." I opened the car door and the inside light came on. The glare didn't do my mother any favors, showing how hard her mouth got when she was disappointed. "What? Did you think I'd just grab your hand and hop on the fast track to Olympus?"

"I had hopes." She sighed. "I can protect you up there."

"Forget it. Someday soon. Maybe. Right now I have this thing with Jerry. I'll be in touch."

"So difficult. Go. I'm exhausted. I'm heading home to bed. Alone. I hope that makes you happy." She frowned and rubbed her temples.

"I'm sorry you had a rough day. I said I'll think about it. Good night." I got out and slammed the door. She must have decided to leave things there because when I looked back she was gone. I started up the walk.

Suddenly I couldn't go any farther. The air reeked of evil with a smell like burnt sugar. I knew that smell way too well and almost expected some familiar demons to pop out of the bushes. I looked around, my stomach knotting and my fists clenched. Yes, I had new skills, but usually found they were useless when I was fighting the kind of powers that crackled and surged around me now.

"Gloriana St. Clair." I heard my name whispered on the slight breeze. I shivered at the malevolence that each syllable carried with it.

"Who are you? Come out and face me!" I looked from side to side. Whipped around and stared behind me. No one. "Coward! What? Afraid a vampire can take you down? Lucifer? Back for a rematch? I know you won't hide in the bushes." I kept taunting who or what must have crept into Jerry's yard and decided to spook me. The air swirled around me, cold and menacing, as it tried to knock me off my feet. I wasn't going down but I felt like I was about to jump out of my skin.

Jump. Good idea. I concentrated and dematerialized, only to pop up on Jerry's doorstep. Immediately, I felt safe again, as if I'd somehow passed over the malicious barrier and into the land of good and plenty. I breathed a sigh of relief and pushed the doorbell. An owl hooted and I stumbled, twisting my ankle. Great. Made it past the big bad and let a bird spook me. *Nice going, Glory.*

Jerry answered almost at once. "You were sitting in the car for a while." He pulled me in for a kiss. "Something wrong? Are you hurt?"

I looked behind me. Of course the sweet and creepy air had vanished. "My mother was in the car. I'll tell you about it later." I dropped my purse on a hall table. "Took a wrong step and hurt my ankle." Which actually throbbed like a bitch. "It'll heal but I wouldn't turn down an ice pack."

"Sure, I'll get it. You want a bottle of synthetic while I'm in the kitchen?" He started to lead me to his leather couch but I shook my head. I couldn't get the picture of Lily's threesome there out of my mind.

"That would be great, but let's go upstairs to talk. In your office." I tried to shake off the heebie-jeebies.

"Whatever you say. Careful on the stairs." He walked toward the kitchen.

I limped up to the second floor. It seemed to take forever but we finally settled in his office in two leather chairs. The man did like his leather.

"How was Miami? Did you hire a new manager?" Bring back a souvenir like maybe something spooky for the front lawn?

"Yes, but it wasn't easy to leave so soon. I hired from within. That helped." He ran his hand through his hair. "Screw the business. I never should have told you my past didn't concern you, Gloriana. Not after all you did for me when I lost my memory."

"Jerry, I took care of you because I love you. You don't owe me explanations. When I was in Las Vegas for five years and you were wherever, it was understood that we were free to live as we chose." Of course Jerry had hired Valdez as my bodyguard and I'd learned that my shifter buddy had reported pretty much everything I'd done to his boss. Secrets? I just had one big one now.

"I know. When we took breaks from each other, we had lovers. I know you did and I did too." He drank from his bottle, no glass for him, though he'd made the effort to pour my synthetic into one. Jerry and lovers. Here it came.

"Mortals are the easiest, of course. Then when things go south, you can erase their memories." It was like he was talking to himself. He glanced at me. "And you know how I am. I prefer mortal blood when I can get it. So I had a mortal lover who I drank from on a regular basis."

"Is this your big confession?" I took a deep swallow to hide my feelings. Jealousy, first. Disappointment, second. Using mortals. It wasn't anything I admired, though I'd done it myself in the past.

"That's not it." He got up and started pacing. "You know I like powerful women." He stopped in front of me. "I met someone in Miami. She reminded me of you, though you look nothing alike."

"I don't need the details, Jerry." Oh, who was I kidding? I wanted to know every excruciating one. Was this payback? For how I'd hurt him with my affair with Rafe? I jumped up, wanting to run out of the room but my ankle gave way. He grabbed my shoulders to steady me.

"I'm not trying to hurt you. I have to warn you. Sit down, Gloriana." He pushed me down into the chair and carefully adjusted the ice pack on my ankle again. "Listen to me. This is important or I wouldn't bother you with it."

"Warn me?" I put two and two together. "Does she have anything to do with, um, magic or evil? I just had the weirdest experience outside. I had to dematerialize to get to your front door."

"What?" He looked like I'd dropped a house on him. Then a knife suddenly appeared in his hand. "Did she hurt you? Is that what happened to your ankle? Outside you say?" He didn't wait for answers, just ran out of the room before I could stop him.

I started to go after him. And what? Watch some mystery woman work her magic on Jerry? Was he under a spell? Could I shift the blame for their affair to her and let him off the hook? Wouldn't that be nice? Was she beautiful? Of course she was. And he was a man with needs. I knew that. While I waited I let my mind run on an endless loop of what to do or not to do. Then Jerry's front door slammed and he bounded up the stairs.

"No sign of her except that smell . . . Did you get a whiff of her magic?" He slipped his knife back into his boot. "Is that how you hurt your ankle, Gloriana? Did you two have a confrontation? I'll kill her if she hurt you."

"A confrontation. You could say that, though I never saw her." I couldn't hide my relief that he was back and obviously more concerned with me than that other woman. "She tried to keep me out of here, Jerry. I think it's pretty clear she wants you for herself. And she's evil. I know evil when I smell it. You know that."

"What did she say? Melisandra is a voodoo priestess. Yes, she's mortal but more than just that. She's dangerous, Gloriana." He knelt in front of me, seriously worried. I liked that look on him.

"Jerry, I have powers. I can handle her." I took his hands. "Not saying it was fun dealing with that shit again. It kind of knocked me for a loop so I stumbled, twisted my ankle. It'll heal. But I guess I know now how you felt when things happened between Rafe and me."

"Jealousy bites, doesn't it? I can't believe she's already here. I tried to erase her memory of our time together, like I'd do with an ordinary mortal. No dice." Jerry sat on the arm of the chair next to me. "I don't blame my infatuation with her on one of her spells. I know better. It was her blood,

Gloriana. It was almost addictive. It was as if I drew power from it." His eyes lost focus for a moment, like just remembering it got him high.

"Do I really need to hear this, Jerry?" I dropped his hand.

"Yes, you do." He was up and pacing again. "She knew I was vampire and got off to it. She was comfortable in the paranormal world. Too comfortable. It made me uneasy. I knew I had to end the relationship so I stopped drinking her blood. It was a relief to know I could give it up. I told myself that when word of your move to Texas came it was a sign. I needed to get away from Mel completely, make a clean break and get my relationship with you back on track if I could. So I put my hotel there into good hands and took off. I didn't know that she would take it so hard."

"You did say good-bye, didn't you?" I could see how this woman might feel like he owed her after giving Jerry her blood night after night and maybe imagining a future with him. Then he took off to parts unknown to be with me. No wonder she hated me.

"Of course. I told her I had a commitment somewhere else but didn't name the place. As an extra precaution I decided to change my name. Problem was, I couldn't sell my hotel then, the market wasn't right. I guess you've noticed I've had problems with the management there ever since I moved here." He glanced at his laptop. "I'm still worried about it."

"Yes, you've made quite a few trips there. To straighten things out or to see her?" I gripped the arms of the chair to keep from launching myself at him. Had he been having an affair all this time? And then put a guilt trip on me for being unfaithful?

"I didn't intend to ever go back. I'm pretty sure all my troubles at the hotel have been caused by Mel. She can use her voodoo powers to make things happen—accidents, illnesses among the staff, even an infestation of vermin. It's been a nightmare. I'd have to go back and then she would show up, smelling the way she does." He looked at me, his eyes dark with a familiar hunger. "It's the blood, Gloriana. It calls to me. I'd like to blame it on a voodoo spell but I'm afraid it's just my damned vampire nature taking over." He looked away and I took that as an admission that blood wasn't all he got from the woman.

"Well, shit. What am I supposed to do with this, Jerry?" I couldn't sit still another minute. I glanced down and saw that I had ripped lines in the chair's leather. Tough.

"Please, let me finish. This last trip she threatened you. Said my manager had told her my girlfriend had given him his orders while I was in Scotland. That really steamed her. She has some way of seeing things, like that damned sorcerer did. Said you'd been unfaithful to me and that you didn't deserve me. If I didn't come back to her, she'd make sure I had no choice to make." He reached for me.

"No, keep talking." I wasn't about to let him touch me then.

He ran his fingers through his hair. "I wasn't going to be threatened into a relationship. I told her that I was done with her even if you weren't in the picture. But she kept on, messing with my business, making her threats. I figured it was just wild talk, a woman scorned, you know. I wanted to kill her." He had a knife in his hand again and I knew he meant what he said. "But she has protection." He met my gaze. "I know, not very nice of me, wanting to kill a woman. She's evil, Gloriana. Like you said."

"She must be a servant of the dark arts." I believed him. That he wanted to be done with her.

He put the knife away. "This is serious. Now that she's here, be careful, Gloriana. She's capable of just about anything." He dropped to his knees in front of me. "I'm so sorry to have brought this to you."

I ran my hands through his hair. How could I condemn him? I'd brought pretty bad things to him. The latest had been amnesia and a spell that had almost boiled his brain.

"It's okay, Jerry. We've both made mistakes. And I've faced a lot worse than some witch who smells like a kitchen mistake." I faced where she probably still lurked, trying to listen in with her voodoo magic, and shot the finger. "Bring it on, bitch."

Jerry pulled me to my feet and slipped his arms around me. "Tough talk. You don't know her. Yes, I think you can handle just about anything. But can you handle the fact that I betrayed you?" He rested his cheek on my hair.

I just stood there for a minute. Betrayal. Oh, I so did not want to go there. I could rationalize his slip with a voodoo priestess. It had started before our reunion in Texas and of course she didn't want to let him go. If we were keeping score, I was way ahead in the infidelity department. I decided then and there that I wasn't going to tell him about my slip with Ray. We had enough hurt feelings between us. Bringing up Ray now would do nothing but damage our relationship and ease my conscience. It would be selfish of me to unload on Jerry now.

Luckily he'd assumed his lover's vision of my slip had been about the Rafe incident. I was leaving it at that. I slid my arms around his waist.

"She's brought this fight to Austin. First thing you need to do is convince her that you would never ever be with her again no matter what she tries. Is that the way you feel? Can you be around her and resist her blood now?" I touched his cheek and stared into his eyes.

"Of course. She was a bad chapter in my life that I'm ready to close the book on. You're my future, Gloriana. I'll do whatever it takes to keep us together." He didn't look away and opened his mind to me so that I could see his truth. I felt ashamed that I couldn't do the same. "I love you, Gloriana. I don't want to lose you. Just take this seriously. Melisandra is powerful. I've seen her power at work and it's scary as hell."

I smiled and leaned against him. To hell with guilt. As far as I was concerned, we were even. And if I was his future, he was mine.

"I've got news for you, Jerry. I'm scary as hell too."

"Oh, really." He picked me up, holding me close as he strode to the bedroom. "Lucky for you, I like a challenge." When he tossed me on the bed, we both were smiling.

"I'm not giving you up, Jerry. Whatever she tries, she's not running me off." I reached for him, more than ready to forget everyone but him.

"Stubborn and scary too. What more could I ask for in a woman?" He came down on top of me, his body fitting perfectly against mine, just as it always did. "Guess we were meant to be, Gloriana. Now I think we've talked enough, don't you?"

My answer was to kiss him. *Meant to be.* I heard thunder and the bed actually shuddered beneath us. Of course we were. I inhaled his scent, dear, mine. No one was going to come between us. No one.

Read on for a special preview of
Gerry Bartlett's next novel

Real Vampires Know Size Matters

Available December 2013 from Berkley Books!

We'd been invaded.

You can do this. Suck it up. Attack. Use your powers. Instead I leaped up on the sweater table, shaking and screaming along with the mortals in the shop. *No. Get down, Gloriana St. Clair, and face the enemy.*

Weapons, I needed weapons, and I sure as hell wasn't using my fangs this time. I glanced around. The two women perched on the chair next to the dressing room were no help. Their shrieks could have broken glass. Three more women crouched on the counter in front of the cash register. More mortals, totally useless, though one swung an umbrella at the horde of invaders. Impressive compared to me.

I tossed a sweater at one. Stupid. Didn't even slow it down. I was a failure. A wimp. I couldn't quit shaking and couldn't force myself to get off the table. If a god from Olympus attacked, I'd be right in his face, toe-to-toe. Or another vamp. Bring him on. But whoever had planned this invasion had found my weakness. I thought I heard one right there, on the table, and moaned, horrified.

Mice! Dozens of them. Even Achilles had his heel thing. Glory St. Clair has hers. I don't like anything that's creepy or crawly. Now my reputation and the business I'd built from nothing were in shreds along with my pride. Would you shop where you saw mice? I'd have joined the stampede for the door myself if there'd been time.

My clerk Lacy, a were-cat, was in Kitty Heaven, running around like a starving woman at an all-you-can-eat buffet. She whipped past me with a smile on her face, making sounds too gross to think about.

"Oh, God, there's another one!" The brave soul on the counter with the vintage umbrella slashed at the floor, knocking a mouse toward the door. That got the logjam there cleared with a chorus of screams.

I heard a smack near my feet. "Lacy, what the hell are you doing?" I gagged and realized I was going to have to whammy every mortal in the place.

"Glory, relax. I've got this under control." She held up a brown bag that rustled ominously. "There must be dozens of them. I wonder who sent them. An early birthday present from Mom?" She scrambled after a dark shadow that streaked across the floor. "Naw. She knows a stunt like this could get me fired." She glanced at me.

"She'd be right." I didn't want to know what had made that streak on her cheek. Lacy was a natural beauty, red hair, porcelain skin. She dressed in the vintage clothes we sold here and looked like a model in them. Tonight the seventies bell-bottoms and tie-dyed tee were taking a beating.

"Well, not Mom. These are feeders. For snakes, that sort of thing. Someone brought them in here. Planted them. There goes another one." She dove and disappeared under a dress rack.

I heard a crash and a mannequin bit the dust. The women who'd been balanced on the chair had made a run for the door but were tangled up in a dress display.

"My God! My God! Get it off of me!" Loud sobs then the sounds of my mannequin being used as a sledgehammer.

Obviously I had to suck it up or we'd have mass hysteria on our hands.

"Ladies, please, calm down." At least I wore boots as I jumped in front of them, staring into first a pair of brown eyes, then blue. I had them mesmerized in a second. "You are fine, the store is fine. There are no mice, just a little game we're playing with discount coupons." I shivered as a mouse ran by and I kicked it toward Lacy. "Here's a twenty-five-percent-off coupon for your next visit. We're closing for some minor repairs. Mugs and Muffins next door has great coffee if you want to wait. We'll reopen in about thirty minutes." I snatched coupons from behind the counter then tugged them both to the door, dodging even more mice. *Planted.* I had a feeling I knew who'd done it.

I got those two out then went back for the three hugging their knees near the register. Ignoring Lacy's crows of triumph as she claimed more victims, I got the last customers whammied and out of the shop, coupons in hand. Finally, I hopped on the counter myself and waited for Lacy to finish.

"Whew. That was amazing. I bagged at least three dozen." Lacy grinned, her mouth smudged with something I didn't want to think about. "Whoever pulled this stunt must have cleaned out a pet supply store." She stapled the wiggling bag closed then pulled out a wet wipe from the container under the counter and cleaned off her hands and face. Lacy glanced at me. "You okay?"

"Not really." I sighed. "Had your dinner break?"

"Um, yeah. Sorry about that. I got a little carried away. I need to clean up the floor too." She laughed. "Hey, I'm a predator. Think how you'd act if someone came in and offered you that negative blood type you love."

"I get it." I swallowed, not sure I wasn't going to hurl. "Thanks. You saved the shop."

"No problem. But I can sniff out a mouse a mile away." She wiggled her nose. "They weren't here yesterday. I wonder who . . ."

The phone rang before I could answer her. "Vintage Vamp's Emporium, the best store on Austin's Sixth Street."

"Really? Is it? I heard it just closed." The female voice was full of satisfaction. "Mice infestation. Disgusting."

"Who is this?" I jumped off the counter, pretty sure I already knew.

"Is this the owner? Gloriana St. Clair?"

"Yes. And is this the woman who thinks she can win Jeremiah Campbell back? Mel?"

"How did you like my little gift?" There was a throaty chuckle. "Did you scream? Of course you did."

I bit my lip, refusing to answer. Had she been in here? Seen me make a fool of myself? Damn it, if I'd known . . . What could I have done differently? Dematerialized and damn the consequences.

"Give him up, Gloriana. Or I will run you out of business. Leave town and leave him to me. It's the smart play." The line went dead.

I stared at the receiver, tempted to throw the cordless across the room. "Are you kidding me?"

"What?" Lacy had a mop in her hand. "Who was it?"

"A woman Jerry used to be with." I carefully set the phone back where it belonged. Killing it wouldn't help. It was the woman I wanted to tear into pieces. "Clean up and I'll reopen. I'm not going to let that bitch ruin my business."

"It'll take a minute." Lacy didn't move. "Tell me about this woman. Mr. Blade has an old flame? What's going on? She sent in the mice?" She dipped the mop into a bucket of sudsy water that reeked of pine cleaner.

"She wants Jerry back and thinks running me out of business and out of town will do it. This was just her latest trick. I'm surprised she didn't use magic." I quit breathing. I hated that pine smell. "She's a voodoo priestess, Lacy. Have you seen anyone in here who looks like she might be into that?"

"Voodoo? Don't know. How do they look? Would she be wearing a caftan and a turban, have a scary vibe? Carry around a bottle of Love Potion Number Nine?" Lacy shook her head and began mopping. "That would be too easy, Glo."

"You're right. All I know is that Jerry says she's beautiful"—I made a face—"with dark skin, black hair and unusual gray green eyes."

"Bet you loved that description." Lacy shook her head. "You know her name? I'll watch for her credit card."

"Good idea. Melisandra Du Monde." I sighed. "Of course she's beautiful. I need more info on her. I'm calling Jer right now. This mouse thing is just her latest in the war on Glory."

"Latest? What else has she done?"

"There have been a few accidents." I headed over to turn on the ceiling fans to air the place out and dry the floors faster. "I realize now that they were her work. Remember I told you that big shelf in the back room fell on me?"

"You think that was voodoo?" Lacy's eyes widened. "Crap. Maybe we should get out the holy water again."

I smiled. "Couldn't hurt. But that loaded shelf sure did. It weighed a ton and went over for no reason that I could see. Luckily I have good reflexes and dove under the table back there to avoid the worst of it." I had actually broken my arm but it had healed with a good night's sleep and lots of synthetic blood.

"That woman's crazy if she thinks you'll just give up your business after a few setbacks. We've gone through plenty before, even been firebombed. But we reopened, better than ever. And you and Mr. Blade have gone through a lot. Yet you two have been together for hundreds of years." Lacy finished and headed back to the storeroom. "I'd better take my to-go bag and scoot. Shift's over. Will you be okay until the night crew gets here?"

"Sure. I expect Megan in a little while. Please get that bag out of here. Are you sure all the mice are gone?" I righted the mannequin and straightened her dress.

Lacy sniffed. "All clear. Open the doors. We're good to go. And be careful. If she really wants Mr. Blade back, she'll go for you harder next time."

"I'd like to see her try. A mortal? Bring it on." I headed

for the door, surprised that most of the customers had stuck around. But we were close to Halloween and my shop had great vintage clothing and costumes. I flipped the lock.

"Come in, everyone. We're having a sale. All furs, twenty percent off." That got a reaction, especially since we were having a cold spell. The crowd surged inside. I couldn't believe I had actually laughed about the crazy woman who'd sworn to get Jeremy Blade back as her lover. A voodoo priestess? Okay, maybe I could buy that. Though I'd never actually seen her, I'd smelled the evil spirits around her.

But I could deal with evil. I'd even fought Lucifer and won. You'd think a mortal would be easy compared to him. Right? Wrong. First, Luc and I were both fairly reasonable people. Who knew? But the angel of darkness actually admired my spunk. Melisandra didn't admire anything about me. She just wanted me gone. In her warped worldview, I was an annoying speed bump on her fast track to bliss with Jerry.

Obviously she thought that once I was out of the way, he would realize she was the one for him. She'd tuned out when he'd told her to take a hike. He had even changed his address and name to get away from her. Mel wanted Jerry and would do anything to get him, even if it meant chaining him in a mausoleum somewhere until he felt the love. I shuddered just thinking about it.

Of course, picturing Jerry as a victim was ridiculous. My guy was strong, an ancient vampire. But I was more than a little aggravated that he'd hooked up with a voodoo queen in the first place. What had he been thinking? More accurately, what had he been thinking *with*? Men.

I wasn't about to quit seeing Jerry. Jeremiah Campbell, aka Jeremy Blade, and I had been through way too much lately for me to call a halt while Mel moved in on him. Instead, I was going to show her just how not scared I was after her little trick.

• • •

"Gloriana, you've got that look again. What are you thinking?" Jerry arrived less than an hour later. We were going to our favorite club for a little dancing, even meeting friends there. Did you expect us to keep a low profile? That would feel too much like giving in to the wicked witch.

"That I've got to do something about Mel." I told him about the mouse invasion.

"I'm sorry." He put his arm around me. "What can I do? I've tried to talk to her but my seeking her out makes her happy, no matter the reason for it."

"You sure you've made it clear you're done?" I could read his mind and he knew it. But I didn't even try. We had to trust each other now. I'd come to terms with the fact that this was the man I wanted to be with forever. Not an easy decision. But this complication from his past was ruining what should have been a special time for us. I knew I'd made some big mistakes with my choice of hookups in the past, but a wacko like this?

"I said, 'Go away, I don't want you.' Is that clear enough?" He held on to my shoulders, his eyes meeting mine.

"Ouch. Now you're making me feel sorry for the bitch." I sighed and leaned against him. "No wonder she's acting out."

"I made it clear that she's not to hurt you or your business." Jerry rubbed my back. "She swore she'd back off." He stared down at me. "Are you sure she's responsible—"

"Damn it, Jerry. Are you under a spell or something? She called to gloat. And then what about this gift box?" I tapped a present I'd received the day before. A voodoo doll. Cliché much? Of course it looked like me, though she'd padded the hips until I looked deformed. It was riddled with pins. Bitch. "Did I send it to myself?"

"No, of course not. She laughs at those. Calls them tourist trinkets. They don't mean a thing. She's just pulling your chain. Don't let her play mind games with you." He pulled me close again. "Come on. Let's go. Try to have some fun. And I won't meet with her again. Obviously her word means nothing. I'm not sure I can think straight when I'm around her."

I stiffened and pushed back. "That cinches it. I want a face-to-face with her."

"Glory, you and Mel in the same room? A recipe for disaster. She won't back down and you'll probably lose it." Jerry wouldn't let me go. "You aren't the kind of person who can just rip out a throat and walk away."

"She'd probably taste like raw sewage anyway." I'd had a whiff of her when she'd spied on Jerry and me, lurked in the bushes outside his house. Stalker. She'd smelled like burned sugar, evil left too long on the stove. I really didn't want to get close enough to her to touch her. Why didn't she just crawl back to Miami and pick a man who wanted her?

"Let's go. Our friends are probably already at the club. Your pal Israel Caine and Sienna Star are supposed to sing their new duet tonight." Jerry tugged me toward the back door.

"How do you know that? Are you and Ray or Rafe actually communicating?" I rested my hand on Jerry's chest. This was unlikely. Jerry was jealous of both guys because he knew I'd had a special relationship with each of them. They were still my friends, but had been more than that in the past. I'd made it clear to both of them that I was with Jerry now.

"Richard told me. He and Flo get a newsletter from the club with the coming attractions. I'm surprised you didn't get it." Jerry pulled open the back door, pausing to check out the security like he always did. "Come on. We don't have much time. Caine doesn't float my boat, but I know he does yours."

"You got that right." I laughed when I saw his face. "Oh, come on. We both enjoy good music. I'm way behind on e-mail or I'd have seen the newsletter myself and dragged you there." I grabbed his hand and we hurried down the alley toward N-V, the club my former bodyguard Rafe now owned. It wasn't far and the shifter stationed at the door waved us in ahead of the line at the door. We settled at a table with my best bud Florence da Vinci and her husband Richard Mainwaring. We ordered synthetic blood with alcohol, stocked here for us by Rafe, and settled back to watch the show.

"*Amica*, how are you doing? Any more *disastros* in your shop?" Flo leaned in to whisper.

"Nightly. That bitch won't give up." I told her about the mice and she shuddered.

"That could ruin your business. I know I would never go back to a place where I saw *topi*." Flo patted my shoulder.

"Me either." I sniffed the air. "What perfume are you wearing, Flo?"

"Nothing. Ricardo says it destroys his defense. He needs to smell the enemy coming." She stroked her husband's arm. "He takes very good care of me."

"I bet she's lurking around here right now. Following us." I glanced around. If he were a woman, Jerry would have pictures of her on his phone, but I'd never seen him snap a photo. Too bad.

"No!" Flo grabbed Richard. "Ricardo! Glory says the bitch is here."

"Where?" He leaned forward. "Blade, do you see her?"

Jerry stood and scanned the crowded balcony. "Not up here." He sniffed the air. "There's a faint whiff . . . I'm going downstairs to check it out. Richard, you stay here with the ladies."

"No, we're all going." I got up.

"Here? *Puttana!*" Flo glanced around the narrow balcony. "We will make that creature sorry she bothers our Glory."

"Don't taunt her, Flo." I squeezed Flo's hand. "She's got some mean tricks up her sleeve. I told you."

"Mice, falling shelves. Child's play." Flo's eyes gleamed. "I say we can take whatever she dishes out. *Mi credi?*"

"Sure." I smiled at her, feeling better than I had in days. The band was taking the stage, the people on the dance floor surging forward as we headed for the stairs. It was Ray's band and I knew the guys from a time when I'd pretended to be engaged to the rocker. Publicity stunt. I'd been Ray's mentor right after he'd been turned vampire. Had even been his date to the Grammys. It had been a magical night. I could use another one about now.

"I heard Ray and Sienna are a couple now." Flo studied me for a reaction as we stopped on the stairs.

"I'm glad. He needed someone." I saw Jerry and Richard waiting for us.

"No sign of her." Jerry held out his hand. "Let's just enjoy the show. I can get us closer to the stage. Follow me." He rubbed the back of my neck. "Are you okay?"

"Sure. Did you know Ray and Sienna are together and not just to sing?" I stayed close to him as we eased around the crowd and the lights dimmed.

"Glad to hear it. Keeps him away from you." Jerry kissed my cheek. "But he's stupid to pick a mortal. He'll screw it up, mark my words."

"Hush, Jer, they're getting ready to start." Very afraid he was right, I slipped my arm around his waist as we found a spot close to the stage. Ray was reckless, impulsive and a fairly new vampire. Sleeping with a mortal could have consequences and none of them were good. The house lights went dark except for spotlights on Ray at the piano and Sienna leaning against it. They started singing and you could have heard a mouse squeak in the huge club. The song was beautiful, the lyrics haunting. The way the two sang to each other, it was clear this love song had meaning for both of them.

Jerry turned me into his arms and we danced, making the song ours too. I was sure all the lovers in the audience felt the same way. He held me against him, his hands sliding down to rest on my butt as we moved slowly. I lay my cheek on his chest, my fingers delving into his hair while I breathed him in. We were together and no bitch from hell was going to pull us apart. If Mel was nearby, she could just watch and see how much we loved each other. I was sorry when the song ended.

"Wow. *Meraviglioso!* It makes me want to take you home and ravish you, Ricardo." Next to us, Flo kissed Richard on the lips. "What do you think, Glory?"

"Oh, yeah." I sighed, struggling to come back to earth. For a few moments it had been great just to dance and forget everyone but Jerry. I squeezed his hand. Ray and Sienna jumped up to sing together again. They put their arms around each other, bumping hips as they danced and sang a rock song this time. It was high-energy and fun.

"You okay?" Jerry said softly into my ear.

"Sure." I turned and ran my hand over his jaw. "Flo's right. That song put me in the mood to make love to you. What do you think?"

"I could handle that." He grinned and pulled me toward the door. "We're out of here." He nodded to Richard.

"Right behind you." Richard hauled a giggling Flo up into his arms and followed us. "Caine has a hit on his hands."

"Ricardo, put me down." She hit his shoulder. "You are embarrassing me."

"These kids think it's funny. Look at them." He grinned and nodded. Sure enough, his stunt helped clear a path for us to the front door. Once, I thought I caught a whiff of that sweet, nasty smell again but I never saw anyone fitting Mel's description. Then we were outside, the fresh October air a welcome relief after the crowd inside.

"See you later." Richard set Flo on her feet then hurried her toward his car, ignoring her protests about manners. He had a look that promised a passionate night for them both.

"Well, now what?" I grinned at Jerry. "You know I have a roommate." And she was a terror. No way was I dragging my man home to that.

"Come home with me. They don't need you in the shop again tonight, do they?" He pulled me toward his car parked down the street.

"Not unless Mel unleashes another invasion. Roaches maybe?" I shuddered then patted my pocket. "I've got my cell."

"Let's go." He glanced around. "If that woman knows what's good for her, she'll leave you alone. This isn't the way to win my heart." He helped me into his convertible, then settled in, hitting a button to let the top down before steering into traffic. The cool air felt good and I let the wind blow my worries away.

"I still don't understand how you ever got involved with a woman like Melisandra Du Monde." My comment made Jerry's hands tighten on the steering wheel. We were stopped at a red light.

"She is a strong woman and there is something about her . . ." He punched a button and the CD player came on. Trying to distract me? I punched it back off.

"Come on, Jerry, try to explain. This is important to me." I twisted under my seat belt to face him.

"Right. So can you explain why Israel Caine has your panties in a twist every time you see him?" He gave me a knowing nod, like he'd made a point, before he stepped on the gas.

"I guess so. He has musical talent and I'm a sucker for that. He's handsome, tall, has those piercing blue eyes that make a woman feel—"

"Enough. I really don't want to hear a catalog of Caine's fine qualities. Mel got to me. She has a way of looking at a man that makes him feel powerful. Like he's a sex god."

"I swear you're blushing." And I swear I was getting pissed. Well, I'd asked for it.

"You make me feel that way too, Gloriana." He reached out and snagged my hand. "I have always wanted to protect you because you make me feel like I'm invincible. It's something a man needs—to be wanted, looked up to." He kissed my knuckles. "You and Mel have more in common than you know. But you're two sides of a coin. You're the good side. I discovered too late that she's the bad one."

"Oh, gosh, Jer." I glanced around and realized we were in his neighborhood, almost to his house. "This is bizarre and yet I understand what you're saying. It's like when a man makes me feel that I'm the most desirable woman in the world." I pulled our joined hands to my lips and ran my tongue across his knuckles. "You always do that to me."

"But I don't just see you as a sex object. I hope you know that." He pulled the car up in front of the garage and hit a button on the remote. He turned to face me as we waited for the door to open. "You are much more to me than a way to get my rocks off."

"Back at you." I smiled and popped off my seat belt, leaning over to kiss him. I crawled right over the console to make sure I could reach his mouth and give it my full attention. The steering wheel cut into my back but I didn't care.

"Let's put the car away and go upstairs." He gently lifted me off of him and drove the car into the garage.

I let him pull me out of the car and then followed him to the house. The garage door came down and we stepped into the kitchen. The house was quiet and smelled faintly of the cleaning supplies his housekeeper used. It was reassuring. At least Mel hadn't managed to come here yet.

Jerry lifted me into his arms and was about to carry me upstairs to his bedroom when my cell phone buzzed in my pocket.

"Oh, no!"

"Ignore it." He leaned down to kiss me then strode toward the staircase.

The buzzing was insistent before the call went to voice mail. I gently shoved at Jerry's chest when he stopped at the bottom of the stairs. "Let me check the message. I told them not to call unless it was an emergency in the shop."

"Go ahead." He set me on my feet. "I'll be upstairs in my office checking e-mail. Come and get me when you're done."

"Count on it." I jerked my phone out of my pocket. The voice mail was from a number I didn't recognize. I hit play and pulled the phone to my ear.

"If you want our lover to live, you will meet me tonight. Be in the alley behind your shop in thirty minutes. Believe me, I would rather put a stake through his heart than see him with you forever more."

I recognized the voice instantly, smooth yet determined. So I'd finally get a face-to-face with Melisandra. Now I'd have to make up something to tell Jerry, because he'd never let me meet her alone if he knew about it. I looked up the stairs toward his office. Damn. I really wanted to forget this woman's demands and enjoy an evening in Jerry's arms. But she was just crazy enough to kill him rather than let me have him.

Did I really believe my man couldn't handle her? I leaned against the banister, suddenly weak in the knees. Maybe he could but I wasn't willing to take that chance. I'd almost lost Jerry recently and it had been the worst time of my life. No way was I going to risk that again. Who knew what kind of tricks a voodoo priestess had up her sleeve?

So I put on my game face and headed up. I hadn't told Jerry but I'd had strange pains in my body in the exact spots where those pins had been in the voodoo doll in the nights before it had arrived. Crazy? Or was this woman more powerful than we realized? Lying to Jerry was nothing new even though I hated it. Saying good-bye to him? I just hoped it wasn't a permanent thing this time.

I was on high alert when I flew into the alley behind my shop. The smell hit me immediately. It was bad enough that Mugs and Muffins was baking at this time of night, but added to the sugary muffin scent was that overpowering reek of evil. Melisandra was waiting for me.

"You must be Gloriana St. Clair." The husky voice came out of the darkness near my parked car. I heard the click of high heels as a woman strolled into the light. A breeze brought the unmistakable evidence that she was mortal. She trailed her hand over the trunk, the smile on her face making me shiver.

"I don't have to ask who you are, skulking here in the dark." I'd hoped Jerry had been exaggerating but she *was* beautiful, her dusky skin the color of milk chocolate. Her long black hair tumbled to her shoulders and her unusual gray green eyes, framed by long lashes, examined me like she could see right down to my soul. I straightened my own shoulders when all I wanted to do was shift again and head back to Jerry's arms.

"Yes, I am Melisandra Du Monde. I've been wanting to meet you for a long time, Gloriana. Gloriana. Ah, yes, the most interesting Gloriana." My name had become a chant. She gestured with her right hand, her scarlet nails gathering air around her.

I stepped back before I could stop myself when that air swirled and darkened around her. Witchcraft. I recognized it and quit breathing, sure inhaling it would sear my lungs and either muddle my senses or make me pass out. I glanced around, almost expecting some familiar demons to pop out from behind the cars to sing backup for her.

Hey, I was no ordinary vampire. I could take her. Malicious tricks or not, she could die. *I* couldn't. I smiled.

"I've seen your handiwork in my shop, Mel. Do you really think those stunts are going to help your cause with Jerry? So far you've just pissed him off on my behalf." I couldn't help noticing her voluptuous figure under a sharp black business suit that came from a well-known designer. She would have fit right in at a conference table in any Fortune 500 company. She was just Jerry's type, with full breasts and generous hips. Only her eyes betrayed the crazy beneath her professional demeanor. "He really doesn't like to see me upset."

"Ah. Were you? Upset?" She blew on her palm, and dust peppered my face, making my eyes burn. "Glad to hear it."

"Didn't you hear me?" I blinked to clear my vision, refusing to rub my eyes which stung like a son of a bitch. "Your dirty tricks are alienating Jerry."

"He'll get over it." She smiled. "When we are back together, Jeremiah will forget all about you. I have ways to ensure it. I know what he likes, you see."

"Get a grip on reality. He kicked you to the curb a long time ago. Where's your pride, woman?" Taunting her probably wasn't my best move, but I really didn't like being reminded that she'd had Jerry in her bed. I was trying not to lose my cool and jump her, rip out that beautiful hair and pound her head against the concrete. That would make me feel better but would probably give her the out-of-control reaction she was hoping for. I drew on every reserve I had and stared at her, trying for cold and disdainful.

"Did he tell you how we met, Gloriana?" She leaned against my car, drawing a line with her nail on the trunk.

"No." I wanted to hear this.

"I had rented a ballroom at his hotel in Miami. It was a sellout. People pay small fortunes to hear me speak, get motivated." She smiled, her red lipstick perfect. All of her makeup was perfect. Damn.

"I can't imagine. What do they say? A sucker is born every minute?"

"I am worth every penny. As a life coach. People hear me and they are reborn. They leave my seminars and become successful, do great things." She flicked a disdainful look at the back door to my shop. "Some people are satisfied with a little life. My clients are not. Check out my Web site. Read the testimonials."

"You know nothing about me or my life." Why didn't I just rip out her throat now? But that would make me as evil as she was. And then there was that cold, malignant wall surrounding her. I'd be stained by it, my soul tarnished, if I gave in to my urge to kill her.

"You have worked your vampire wiles on my Jeremiah. But I will put an end to that. Then he will realize that I am his soul mate. The only woman to make him truly happy." She ran a fingertip down her throat. "You should see him when he drinks my blood, Gloriana. The pleasure, the passion—"

"Shut the hell up!" I vibrated with the need to tear her apart. Her smile was so sure, triumphant. Had Jerry actually kissed that mouth? I wanted to retch, or launch myself across the alley and obliterate her face so that she'd never kiss anyone, ever again.

No.

I forced a laugh. "Seriously? Don't you realize vampires will do and say anything to get mortal blood? Jerry played you, bitch. Used you as a donor and then moved on." I took a step toward her. "You were handy when he was in Miami, but that's over. He's lusty, I can attest to that. Obviously you were easy." I gave her my own cold smile. She didn't take it well, her teeth snapping together. If she'd been a vampire, she would have been snarling, her fangs down. "Now he's got his number one lover back. Me. You are old news, Mel. He's throwing you out with the trash."

"Old news? I'm not the one with hundreds of years invested in a failed relationship, Gloriana. *Pobrecita.*" The air around her swirled and pushed at me, frigid and menacing. "You are a bad habit that Jeremiah needs to break. But once you are gone, he will be all mine."

"Get a grip. Jerry's not some trophy you can pass around, the prize in your pissing contest. He's a man who knows what he wants and it's not you. Now why don't you go back where you came from? Find some other man to terrorize." I shoved at her creepy air and met resistance. I hated that I was even arguing with her, sounding desperate. Damn it.

"You'd like that, wouldn't you? For me to just leave him to you?" She raised her arms and howling creatures appeared around her. Spirits? Ghosts? Whatever, they gave me the creeps. "As long as you are between me and happiness, Gloriana St. Clair, you will never have peace of your own. This I vow." She muttered an incantation and the restless things around her wailed louder, rising and falling as she got more agitated. They zipped past me, tearing at my hair and snatching at my clothes.

Okay, I admit it. I hit at them like they were real and got nothing but air. It was all I could do not to dematerialize, just vanish the hell out of there. I reminded myself that I was dealing with nothing more than a mortal playing with the dead. Yeah, dead. How much could they really hurt me? The ghosts I'd dealt with before had been benign, helpful. But the chilled air brushing against me when one of those howling creatures darted past made me jump in spite of myself.

"All right, you want to play hardball? It's on." I showed fang. "I don't think you know who you're messing with."

"We will see." She threw her arms wide and my ears rang as her followers screeched a final time, twirling into some kind of otherworldly dust devil before they disappeared. "He will be mine, Gloriana. It is decided."

Decided? I couldn't stand it. I threw myself at her, finally giving in to my hatred. I landed on empty concrete. She'd disappeared, just poofed. I jumped up and took a quick look around. She must have had an escape route figured out because she was really gone, nothing left of her but that stench of bad news.

I leaned against the back door into the shop, my stomach doing a pitch and roll as I hit the code for security and practically fell into the storeroom. I needed a bottle of synthetic blood. The first gulp helped; the second felt even better. A voodoo priestess. What next? I should know better than to ask that question.